THE GUARDIANS OF TIME BOOK IV

# The Shadow



MARIANNE CURLEY

COPYRIGHT

The Guardians of Time, Book Four, The Shadow



Visit the author's website at https://mariannecurley7.com/

Printed in the United States of America

First Printing: April 2018
MTC Services Pty Limited

ISBN-13 978-0-6482636-0-9
ISBN-10 0-6482636-0-6

This book is for the fans

To all who have read The Guardians of Time
The Named, The Dark, The Key
Welcome to The Shadow
Where it all begins again

*"Trust is what the Guard is all about.*
*Faith in what doesn't always make sense."*
*Rochelle Thallimar, RIP*

There once was a Prophecy...

*Before the world can be free*
*A bloom of murdered innocence shall be seen ~ Sera*
*In the woods above the ancient city of Veridian*
*Where nine identities shall be revealed*
*It will come to pass that a king shall rule ~ Richard*
*But not before a leader pure of heart awakens ~ Matthew*
*And an ageless warrior with an ancient soul*
*Shall guide with grace and providence ~ Arkarian*
*Beware, nine shall see a traitor come and go ~ Marduke*
*From whence a long and bitter war will follow*
*And the Named shall join in unity*
*Yet suspicion will cause disharmony ~ Marcus*
*A jester shall protect ~ Jimmy; a doubter cast a shadow ~ Dillon*
*And a brave young warrior will lose his heart to death ~ Ethan*
*Yet none shall be victorious until a lost warrior returns ~ Shaun*
*And the fearless one emerges from a journey led by light and strength ~ Isabel*
*Take heed, two last warriors shall cause grief as much as good*
*From the midst of suspicion one shall come forth ~ Rochelle*
*The other seeded of evil ~ Neriah*
*Yet one shall be victorious while the other victorious in death*

**The Guardians of Time**

Lorian – Immortal, first-born of triplets, formerly Lord of the Guard, deceased
Dartemis – Immortal, Magician, last-born of triplets, Lord of the Guard
Arkarian – Eternal, Named, son of Lorian
Matt – Immortal, Named, son of Dartemis
Jimmy – Protector, Eternal, Named, charged by Lord Dartemis to keep his son safe on Earth
Shaun – Named, married to Laura
Ethan – Named, son of Shaun and Laura
Isabel – Eternal, Named, Healer, half-sister of Matt
Rochelle – Named, daughter of a King and an Eternal, slain by Marduke, deceased
Neriah – Immortal, Named, daughter of Marduke and Aneliese
Dillon – Was to be Named but claimed by Lathenia first, *aka* Bastian
Sera – Was to be Named, daughter of Shaun and Laura, slain by Marduke, deceased

**The Royals - Tribunal Members**

Lady Devine – Eternal, House of Divinity, Sector China and the Middle East
Lord Meridian – Eternal, House of Kavanah, Sector Europe
Queen Brystianne – Eternal, House of Averil, Sector India and Indonesia
Sir Syford – Eternal, House of Syford, Sector North America
Lady Elenna – Eternal, House of Isle, Sector South America
Lord Alexandon – Eternal, House of Criers, Sector Russia, deceased
Lady Arabella – Eternal, House of Sky and Water, Sector Australia
Lord Penbarin – Eternal, House of Samartyne, Sector Africa
King Richard – Eternal, House of Veridian, Sector Angel Falls
King Andrej – Eternal, formerly King of the House of Criers, deceased

**The Order of Chaos**

Lathenia – Immortal, second-born of triplets, formerly Goddess of the Order of Chaos, deceased

Keziah – Eternal, Magician, Healer, Chief Advisor to the Goddess

Jesilla – Immortal, daughter of a King and Goddess, leader of the Order by right of birth

Marduke – Eternal, First Traitor, elder half-brother to Marcus Carter, deceased

Marcus – Named, Second Traitor, younger half-brother to Marduke

Bastian – Claimed by Goddess *aka* Dillon Sinclair

Zander –Soldier, bodyguard, married to Pearl

Pearl – Soldier, bodyguard, married to Zander

Peter – Father of Dillon, rescued by Lathenia, Adviser and Engineer for the Order

# Contents

# Chapter One

## Ethan

No one can see it. No one can feel this other than me. It's as if someone carved my heart out with a sword dipped in poison, leaving a hole in my chest the size of a fist. The poison continues to corrode the edges, enlarging the hole, while the weight of its emptiness grows heavier every day.

I miss Rochelle, and I don't know what to do.

Knowing she's gone and never coming back is so final, I ache trying to understand that she doesn't *exist* anymore. How is it even possible? One second she's talking to me, smiling at me, kissing me, and the next she's falling limp into my arms.

I think about her all the time. About what we almost had. Now, without Rochelle, there's nothing.

I roll onto my back, kicking my sweaty, tangled sheets to the floor. So much thinking locks up the space my lungs have to expand. It's as if there's a steel cage around my chest. Rubbing my palms over my ribs I feel the cage tightening again. If this continues, soon I won't be breathing at all.

How am I supposed to stop thinking about her? How do I do that?

*God*... how do I live knowing she doesn't?

I drag my gaze from the ceiling and force my legs over the side of my bed. I could fall back, curl my legs up to my chest and sleep all day. Only in sleep does it not hurt as much. Until I dream. My mouth trembles and I let my head fall back and stare at the ceiling some more.

*Noooo*...

Today I have to push hard because I have something to do, somewhere I need to be. Today will be the second worst day of my life.

I have to shower, so I get up and head to the bathroom. It's been days so it will make my parents happy. But I have no energy. My legs are heavy, as if weighted down with bricks. I lift my hand to collect the soap, only the soap weighs as much as a bar of concrete. After a few minutes I slide down the tiles until I'm sitting with my knees up, head down, and the hot spray stinging the back of my neck.

For Rochelle, I find the energy to get up.

I dress in my best pair of black pants, white shirt and blazer. Sitting on the edge of my bed I slip on the new pair of black socks Mum must have left here while I was showering. Shoes next. I stare at the tie. What am I supposed to do with that? I don't wear ties and I doubt it would matter to Rochelle. I leave it untouched on my bed.

A knock at the door has Mum poking her head in. 'Honey, are you ready?'

'Yeah, I'm ready, Mum.' My words are mechanical. How is anyone ever ready for this?

'Isabel phoned. She'll meet us there, and she said someone named Ar-kar-ian will be there too.'

'Arkarian is coming?'

She nods. 'Dad had the same surprised reaction as you. Who is this Ar-kar-ian?'

My bottom lip trembles again. I bite on it. 'Arkarian is Isabel's boyfriend. He has blue hair.'

'What? Blue hair?'

I walk out and she hooks her arm through mine. She can tell I don't want to talk about Arkarian's hair. It's just better she knows.

'Honey, it may not seem like it now, but everything will turn out all right.'

She's wrong. Nothing will be all right again. I try to take a deep breath but the cage is too tight.

Dad is waiting by the car. He sees me and opens the front door.

Instead of moving forward I step back. Then again. And with each step my lungs open a little more.

Mum and Dad share a worried glance. Dad says, 'Ethan, where are you going?'

Mum steps towards me but stops, worried that if she comes closer I'll run. I *am* going to run, but not because of what she might do.

'I won't be long,' I tell them, and before either try to stop me, I take off jogging into the forest and don't stop until I break free of the trees. There's not a lot of warning before I reach the cliff. I stand with my toes at the edge and take my first real breath since Marduke avenged his heart and slayed mine.

Far below is the valley of Angel Falls. In the distance I can just make out the ocean beneath a winter morning mist. To my right the upper falls cascade down the adjoining ridge over rocks and boulders, pooling in the valley floor.

Once I thought they were spectacular. Coming to this place would keep me sane, and calm.

Now they mean nothing.

Except a memory.

It was here that Rochelle ran to that day. It was here I peeled off her gloves and tossed them over the cliff, my heart beating hard as she held my hands. And it was here I looked into her emerald eyes and kissed her. Her mouth melted against mine, and our two hearts merged. We were finally together, and I had no intention of ever letting her go.

And today I'm supposed to say... *good bye.*

Her life shouldn't have ended the way it did.

I have loved her since the day we met. I didn't know it then, but my heart did. And now my heart is gone. In its place there is nothing. Who knew that nothing could weigh so much, and give out so much pain?

The valley blurs before my eyes and I drop to my knees, rage and reason churning my insides into rocks that give me no answers for why this happened. Now I have to live without her. I tip my head back, stretch my arms to the sky and shout at the heavens, and the world, and anyone who will listen, 'IT'S. NOT. FAIR!'

# Chapter Two

## Jesilla

I pull myself into a sitting position inside a small dark cave. My hair, skin and clothes are stiff with dried blood. I crawl out a small opening between boulders to see the sun is high, the helicopters gone, and when I check my head there's no wound, not even a bump.

I need to get home fast. Keziah and Bastian will be waiting for me. Together we'll count our losses, see who is left of the team after the last tumultuous twenty-four hours. I can't imagine what will happen to us now. My mother was everything.

The creek is not far. Although the air is cold, I tug my blood-soaked jeans off, leave my black tee-shirt on, and immerse myself in the even colder waters of the creek. The water turns murky pink with the blood that washes off my skin and hair and out of my jeans. But it does the job and after a few minutes I stand at the edge wringing out my jeans and peering into my forest surrounds to ensure no one is watching.

The Guard appears to have done a good job of cleaning up. It's quiet now, the forest is calm, the sky blue, no helicopters in sight, and no indication of the wind that left the air tinged with darkness.

Grabbing my long red curls, I squeeze the excess water out and twirl it into a bun on top of my head. I then pull my jeans on, which proves no easy job with my long, skinny wet legs.

There's a hill above me. I climb up hoping to find a road. I've been hearing the occasional car passing since I came to. As soon as I get my bearings I'll use my power to shift.

The opportunity arrives after walking along an unsealed road for about twenty minutes. I spot a sign to Angel Falls High School. Now that I know where I am, I can focus on where I need to go, and shift. It's a power my mother activated, the ability to move from one place to another almost instantly. Closing my eyes, I visualize the way. When I open them a moment later, I'm outside the black gates of my home, a large estate high up on Angel Falls' tallest habitable mountain.

I would shift *in*side the perimeter but I'm not sure how hard the battle has hit us yet, whether or not the invisible sensors are still functioning. I glance up at the big white house at the end of the sweeping driveway. Three stories high, it's made of concrete, steel, and triple-glazed unbreakable glass in a design that makes the most of the sloping rear landscape. You would never suspect there's a six-level command center below ground where two hundred soldiers live at any one time.

I wonder how many remain.

The last time I came through these gates the battle had turned against my mother and she'd ordered my security guards, partners Zander and Pearl, to take the Volvo Wagon and get me to a safe house off the mountain.

But that plan didn't go well either.

On the way the wagon took a hit from one of our own beasts. Injured by a grenade the size of a pebble it slammed into our vehicle, rolling onto the bonnet, where it exploded, taking the engine out with it.

With our vehicle totaled, we slipped into the forest unseen and continued on foot. Half-way down the mountain, hidden in the backyard of our caretaker's house, is the entrance to the secret tunnel to our underground complex.

But somewhere in the midst of the forest we found ourselves under attack.

Pearl had thrust a pistol into my hand. 'Use only if necessary. You got that, Jesilla?'

'Got it.'

'We can't reach the safe house on foot,' she'd said. 'Find the tunnel and head back to the complex while Zander and I keep the Guard's soldiers off your trail. See you at home.'

I'd fled to the sound of gunfire, the sizzle of electricity and the stench of burning flesh. On the way my mother checked on me. I showed her the crash through my thoughts. She told me to find a safe place to hide, letting me know she was in a duel with her brother Lorian. Though I wasn't supposed to use my powers, I raced to the site faster than any human could move.

They were on top of a ridge, each with a sword and a dagger in their hands. I didn't want to miss a second of my mother slaughtering my uncle, so I climbed up a tree near the forest edge that had views all the way to the cliffs. I sat on a sturdy branch about two-thirds up, bringing my knees to my chest. I watched as my mother and uncle bantered verbally back and forth while lunging with their swords.

And then Lorian disarmed my mother. Not expecting this, I gasped as her sword flew in my direction. She watched it too, spotting me in the tree. Lorian noticed her momentary distraction and he thrust his sword into her chest.

Shocked, my mother's eyes had bulged. Understanding he'd given her a lethal stab wound my mother closed her eyes, and Lorian walked away. It was then she lifted her hand holding the dagger, and knowing he'd still hear her, she whispered her brother's name. As he turned she launched that dagger with great force into his throat.

I don't know how long I stayed in that tree. Shock kept me immobile and dazed. My mother was dead. And it was my fault.

I slept in that tree until a persistent buzzing noise woke me. I flapped my hand at the air around my head to scoot away what I assumed were bugs. With stiff limbs I'd shifted around for a more comfortable position. My eyes adjusted to the darkness and I peered through a thin canopy finding pale stars blinking back an eerie dawn light.

The buzzing grew stronger. It wasn't bugs making the sound. From my perch I glanced around looking for the lights. Helicopters were zooming in on Angel Falls, no doubt bringing the world's press to our doorstep.

I climbed down like a chimp, swinging on the last branch before jumping to the ground. I needed to hurry home before someone spotted me. The choppers were closing in. One in particular made an unnatural sputtering sound. I looked up through the trees and groaned. It was spinning and dropping fast. With a deafening roar it clipped a tree, breaking branches, and tearing apart so close I could have counted the pieces that plummeted around me.

Despite the dangerous falling debris, I ran, zigzagging around the trees to avoid them. The chopper's main body hit the ground and shattered into smaller pieces, some as lethal as bullets. I smelled petrol an instant before the broken chopper's fuel tank exploded, lighting up the trees around it. The explosion pushed a wave of hot air over me, and for a moment I thought I was on fire too. But I wasn't, and so I kept running.

A whirling, whistling sound grew louder behind me. I started to turn, making it only partway when a rotor blade sliced open the back of my head. I went down with my face in the dirt, blood pooling around me. There was pain like I'd never felt before, but knowing the area would soon be swarming with rescue crews, I staved off collapse to crawl away from the fumes, the flames, and whatever wrecked parts were still moving.

Blood drained from my head-wound faster than my self-healing powers could replace. It dripped into my eyes and while not seeing clearly my foot caught a tree root. I rolled down an embankment, clawing at undergrowth so I didn't fall into the creek I knew was at the bottom. I stopped with my face half buried in damp foliage and close to passing out. Needing somewhere to rest while my body healed itself, I lifted my head for a last look. But I'd lost so much blood by then that darkness, and not the light of early morning, danced around my peripheral vision. I spotted an opening between two boulders that might have been a cave. At that point I would have shared a snake's den for somewhere to lie down. Using my elbows, I dragged my body inside and gave in to the darkness.

Shaking off the memory of the last twenty-four hours, I step up to my front door, high enough for a giant to pass through. You see; my mother was seven feet tall. I'm glad I took after my human father in that regard, whoever he was. I might be taller than most eighteen-year-old girls are, but at least I'm not a giant. It's enough that I have Lathenia's red hair and rare silver eyes, one of the reasons my mother wouldn't send me to a normal school. She used to tell me that if anyone knew of my existence, lives would be in jeopardy, and not just mine.

So where is my security? Slaughtered by the Guard's soldiers? No doubt if Zander and Pearl had survived, they would have come for me when I didn't return home last night. A thought suddenly occurs. Do they know? Did they see Lathenia glance at me in that moment she needed her concentration more than any other time in her life?

Bastian opens the door before my fingers close around the handle. 'Jesilla!' He drops back as if he's seeing a ghost, his eyes wide, and as always, since the day he moved in with us when he was twelve, those bright green eyes reach into my soul. 'Holy hell, kiddo, you scared ten years off my life.' He charges forward, pulls me into his arms, squeezes me tighter and longer than, well, anyone's held me before. Even my mother. Especially my mother. Lathenia wasn't the hugging kind. 'We've been looking everywhere for you.'

*Really?*

His hand slides up through my still-damp hair, inadvertently releasing it. He cups the back of my head as he draws in a deep sighing breath. 'Jes, I thought you were...'

A chill ripples through me and the urge to breathe becomes urgent. I tug his hand out of my tangled hair. 'Dead? You thought I was dead? Like my mother? Like Marduke?'

'When we couldn't find you -'

'What?' I rub my nose and sniff.

He pulls me in close again, cradling my skull, murmuring over the top of my head in a soothing voice, 'Shh now, it's going to be okay. Don't cry.'

Carefully, I extricate myself from his arms. 'I'm not crying. Really. I'm... What am I supposed to say, Bastian? My mother is gone. I'm alone now and it's all my -'

He smacks his chest with an open palm. 'Hey! What am I, a brick wall?'

As if his words are an invitation my eyes roam over him. But really, it's not as if I don't already know every inch of his body. We've trained together for six years. I'm more than familiar with the firmness of his chest, the strength in his long legs, the reach of his arms, the next move he'll make an instant before he makes it. But there's more to Bastian than fighting skills, there's the caring tone of his voice when he's thrown me too hard, the way he'll rush to my side if I'm hurt. And as always when I think of Bastian's softer side, the blood in my veins hums to a faster beat of my heart. My eyes lower as I contemplate sensations gathering inside me with just his simple look, as if he has the ability to speak straight to my heart.

Lifting my face with a finger under my chin, he arches one of his dark-blond eyebrows and grins through one side of his mouth. 'Jesilla, are you checking out my butt?'

I roll my eyes. 'What's to check? I see you every day. It's not like anything's changed.' I give him my profile. When did it get so warm in here? It's never warm in here. My mother insisted on a cold house, but sweat is beading on my brow and my jeans are sticking to my legs. To catch my breath I step back and focus on the white alabaster walls. My mother surrounded herself with objects that don't burn easily, like the glass panels to the ceiling and steel doors.

'Jes, are you OK? What happened to you?'

'You know, Bastian, this is your chance.' I swallow to work moisture into my mouth. 'With my mother gone, you're free to leave. Free to embrace your Guard persona. Be "Dillon Sinclair" for real and leave this behind.' *Leave me behind.* 'Your loyalty passed their test. Lorian initiated you before he died. There's nothing to hold you here now.'

He's in front of me before I can blink. His hands on my arms lift me to his height, leaving my feet dangling above the shiny white floor. His strength pulses under his skin, even as he holds it in check. It's one of his powers, his superior strength, enhanced by one Immortal and magnified by another. When his eyes blaze with a green glow as they are now, he could crush my arms into dust. He could toss me at a wall and send me crashing through it.

'Maybe I don't want to be some squeaky clean Guardian.' His eyes at my level, his lips so close to mine, catch me off guard and my breath shortens. I cross my fingers he's too wound up to notice. What would he think?

'Bastian, put me down.' He lowers me and before he notices my hurried breathing, I ask, 'How do I know you aren't playing *me* like you played *them* when you created chaos pretending to be infatuated with Marduke's daughter? Did it stop them from looking too deeply into who you really are? How do I know you're not doing that with me by wearing your clothes two sizes too small?'

'Lathenia orchestrated my moves and I gave her everything I got from them. And for your information, what I fed the Guard worked exactly how your clever mother planned. The Guard trusted me. They still do. And so should you because I've never given you reason not to, and right now we don't have a lot of choice but to trust each other.'

I could tell him he's right and that I do trust him, but the words don't make it out of my mouth. Instead I ask, 'Why don't you want to be a Guard?'

'They overlooked me from the beginning and I don't like being second best. And maybe I've got everything I need right here.'

I swallow at the intensity of those glowing eyes staring down into mine. I have to put space between us so I can breathe evenly. This... whatever it is... grows stronger every day. I have to be careful it doesn't consume me. We live in the same house with bedrooms across the hall from each other. He inches closer, lowers his head, when suddenly he tilts it sideways, his mouth forming a lopsided smirk, a glint of mischief stealing the burning glow from his eyes. 'You think my clothes are two sizes too small? Really?'

*Did I say that aloud?*

Trying to hide my grin I shove him playfully backwards. 'Where's Keziah? I need to talk to him.'

He glances away, swearing viciously.

I search his thoughts. No. It can't be true. Keziah raised me. He taught me just about everything I know.

But Bastian still won't meet my eyes.

'Tell me.'

'We should have known the battle would be too much for his old ticker. Jes, I'm afraid -'

'Don't speak. Stop thinking.' I point to my head where the thoughts of others never stop. 'Keziah is not going to die on me too.'

Bastian closes his eyes in a blink that lasts too long and tells me too much. 'I'm sorry, Jes, but Keziah doesn't have much time left. He's holding out to see you.'

I shake my head. 'Why hasn't he healed himself?'

'The battle drained him, and now he, well, maybe he just can't. Maybe he's too weak to heal himself. His heart held on these last few days, but he's failing fast now.'

*No. Please, no.*

Once we'd moved from Mount Olympus to Angel Falls, our soldiers lived and trained underground. Lathenia didn't want anyone dropping by and accidentally seeing them. But she kept Keziah close even though he looked and sounded more different than any staff she had working in our underground facility. She called him her Magician and she trusted no one as much as she trusted him.

'Wait,' I lift my hand. 'Did you say, last *few* days?'

He nods.

'H-how long has it been since the battle?'

His eyes narrow. His brows pinch together. 'Jesilla, you've been missing for seven days.'

'*What*? Seven days?'

Why didn't they find me? Where did they search? Why did they stop? Who told them to stop? But my questions will have to wait until I've seen Keziah. 'Is he in the Clinic?'

He nods. 'Come on, Jes, let's shift together.'

He takes my hand, and in my mind I'm moving through the formal living space, through the spotless white marble kitchen, into a corridor with ice blue walls lined with priceless artworks my mother collected from her trips to the past. At the end is a wall panel that conceals the lift to the underground complex. Next is the swirling white staircase to our bedrooms, Bastian's, mine, and Keziah's, with my mother and Marduke's suite on the next level up. And finally I'm moving through the informal living area where Bastian and I chill out after training.

An instant after closing my eyes and visualizing the way, I'm standing at the Clinic door. But before I go in, I have to ask, 'Did Marcus Carter return?'

He shrugs. 'No word. We presume he's dead.'

So much to take in.

I punch the code and the lock clicks, but as I'm about to turn the handle into the network of sterile rooms, Bastian stops me with his hand on mine.

'I have to go,' he says.

'What do you mean?'

'I was on my way out when you got home.'

'But Keziah is so sick.'

'I know. I've been by his side all week. He's hardly said a word other than calling for you, so don't expect too much.' He runs his hand through his hair and starts backing away. 'If you need me, use one of the untraceable phones from *Resources*, and don't forget to throw it away when you're done.'

'I'm not an idiot,' I snap back.

'Of course not. I just...' but he doesn't finish. He has something to tell me, but he can't bring himself to say the words. With regret stamped across his face, he says instead, 'Take care of yourself, Jesilla.'

It sounds too much like good bye.

# Chapter Three

## Ethan

A week ago we won the battle. We saved the Earth from a Goddess hell bent on destroying the barriers that keep the worlds of the living and the dead apart. She tore rifts between them, destroyed the white bridge, and brought through beasts that had once been human; their changed forms unrecognizable even to themselves. But they knew to follow orders, specifically Marduke's. At least no one has to worry about *him* anymore. The curse meant to 'protect' Rochelle finished him off for good. But she died anyway, falling into my arms with my own arrow lodged in her chest.

But we won. Right?

Yep. We won. We should be celebrating.

But how do you celebrate when you've lost so much?

Seven days and I still can't wrap my head around what happened. The Prophecy warned that I would lose my heart to death. Well, screw the Prophecy. It should have told us how to intervene to prevent the tragedy in the first place.

On that same day Arkarian lost his father. I don't know how he's holding up because I can't absorb anything outside my own impenetrable bubble. I don't like it. I hate myself for it. But I can't help it. I close my eyes and Rochelle's face is always there. At the moment of impact. At the moment she put herself between Marduke striking the arrow and it hitting me. I watched the light drain from her eyes. She had no regrets. She'd do it again a thousand times to save me. It eats at me that I didn't get a chance to tell her that I would do the same for her, a million times, if that were what it took to save her. She will never know that now. She will never hear my voice again. And I'll never hear hers.

I open my eyes to Neriah's tear-streaked face staring at me.

Damn it, I can't even grieve in private with Truthseers around.

Arkarian called a meeting in his chambers. It's why I'm sitting at the conference table with Neriah, Jimmy, Dad, Isabel and Dillon, who's just walking in, nodding and mumbling apologies under his breath. He sits on my right while Isabel is on my left. As for the others, Arkarian and Matt are late, and Mr Carter... well, even if he had survived, he would know better than show his face here.

No one is talking to me because they think I'm at flashpoint. I don't want to be here and it shows. I don't want to be anywhere and that shows too. I don't like company right now, not even my own. Especially my own. But I won't ignore a direct command from my superior. Arkarian has been there for me since I was four. Now I need him more than ever. But he left in a hurry after I came to him a few days ago, telling me we'll talk on his return.

Across the table Dad searches my face, compelling me to look at him so he can read how I'm going today. What does he think he's going to find? Anyway, I'm not ready to have a father-son chat. Sitting next to him, Jimmy has the good sense to whisper stuff to distract him from bugging me.

The delay is irritating. Isabel hears my low growl. She puts her hand on my knee and gives me a small smile. 'He should arrive soon.'

'Yeah, well, I hope he has a good reason for making us wait.'

She presses her lips together, biting back a remark, something she's doing heaps of lately.

'So where did he go?' I ask.

She shrugs.

'Didn't he tell you?'

'No, Ethan, he didn't.'

'But you're his girlfriend. Do you know where he goes when he's not in Angel Falls? If he were leading a double life, could you tell?'

She looks straight into my eyes. 'Thanks for putting those thoughts in my head.' She flicks a glance at the others as color creeps up from her neck to her forehead.

I should feel bad about what I just did. This is Isabel. My best friend. There'll never be another like her. But that hole in my chest would fit a tree trunk today. It aches. And what's worse, deep down, I can't accept that Rochelle's gone. I'm still feeling something I can't explain, like when she'd walk into my classroom and I wouldn't have to look up to know it was her.

Watching me, Isabel says, 'I don't know.'

'You don't know what? Where your boyfriend has gone? Where he really lives, because you know he doesn't live here, right?' I lift my hand to indicate his secret mountain chambers.

Her big brown eyes serve me a warning not to go further. 'He hasn't shown me that part of his life yet.'

Jimmy catches her eye. 'Doesn't he live in the Citadel, darlin'?'

'*Used* to live in the Citadel,' Dillon drawls. 'Mate, I thought he lived *here*.' He shrugs. 'Does anyone know?'

Neriah is holding the brush King Richard presented to her at her Initiation, staring at it as if its handle is solid gold and not sandalwood, its bristles diamonds, and not the hair off a pig's back. She tweaks we're all staring at her. With carefully considered movements she lays the brush on the table and looks directly at Isabel. 'Arkarian has a suite in the palace in Athens, but you know about that, don't you?'

Isabel nods. 'Yeah, I've seen it. He only uses those rooms when he's working at the palace. It's not his home. He hasn't mentioned where he lives when he's not in Athens or Angel Falls.'

Jimmy, who is more Isabel's father than step-father, gives her a consoling smile. 'He's a private fellow, been alone for a long time.'

I stare across the table at Jimmy. 'That's lame and missing the point.'

Dad says, 'What point would that be, Ethan?'

He tries to hold my gaze steady, but I look away first. 'This is about secrets and keeping them after a whole year together.' I give Isabel a sidelong glance. 'What's with that?'

She shoots me *that* look, the one with her head tilted towards her shoulder, her lips pressed together, her brown eyes darkened by sadness, moist with tears. I've hit on a sore spot, not thinking of anyone's pain but my own. But I've gone far enough and I mouth the word, 'Sorry.'

Dillon leans forward, sliding his elbows across the table like he's so exhausted he has to hold his head up with his hands. 'So the dude has secrets,' he mumbles, 'he's still a good dude.'

He gets a few chuckles. But he makes Isabel smile. How bitter I must be to make her doubt Arkarian of all people.

'I hear the Citadel's reconstruction is coming along well,' Neriah chimes in, changing the subject.

Dad joins in, 'But not as fast as the Royals would like. Lord Penbarin and Sir Syford won't rest until they have the Command Center fully functioning again. Resident's rooms are not the priority. The emphasis is on rebuilding the master transporter.'

'Maybe that's what Arkarian is doing now.' Dillon shrugs his shoulders. 'You know, looking for a place to live, a place to stay between missions, somewhere to shower and change.'

'So we stew in this underground meeting room waiting for him to take a bath?' I question, my impatience returning in a flash.

'Whoa, buddy, you need to blow off some steam. Do some rounds in the ring.'

'Are you volunteering, Dillon?' I ask.

I catch Dad's eyebrows rising as he glances at Dillon with a flicker of amusement in his eyes.

'Uh, not today, mate. I think there's been enough death around here this last week, don't you?'

Dillon realizes his mistake before I'm even out of the chair. But by then I already have his shirt bunched in my fists, his back against a wall. In a grinding voice I hardly recognize as mine, I ask, 'Any death in particular you want to discuss?'

He backs down. To give him his due, he looks mortified. His hands out to the sides, fingers splayed. 'No offence meant. I just forgot for a sec.'

'You *forgot*?'

Isabel tugs my arm and keeps tugging until I look at her. Dad and Jimmy are standing behind her ready to pull me off Dillon. She shakes her head and they return to their seats. She doesn't say a word but the compassion in her eyes makes the anger fall right out of me. She wraps her arms around me tightly. Lifting up on her toes, she whispers in my ear, 'It's OK, Ethan. It's OK to be angry.' A little more loudly, she adds, 'We all know Dillon is full of crap.'

Isabel is the only person I can tolerate right now. She knows what I need from Arkarian, and while she's not supporting my idea, she's not going to let me do it alone.

Thinking about my plan helps to ease some of the surliness inside. Of their own accord, my arms come around Isabel's back and I hold myself in check to stop from collapsing over her.

We sit again, but she doesn't let go of my hand.

The silence that follows magnifies every sound in the room. Dillon yawning, Jimmy making small talk, Dad clearing his throat. Especially annoying is Neriah's deep frustrated breaths as if her world is ending. With the King's brush in her hand, she closes her eyes, slows her breathing and paints a large square on the table before her. Dad leans over for a look. Jimmy gets up and stands quietly behind her. Meanwhile Dillon stretches out in his chair and promptly starts snoring, bringing out a few smiles.

'Wow,' Isabel remarks while looking at Neriah's creation, 'did you just create a portal with your brush?'

I try to see whatever Isabel is seeing. Nothing but shades of blue mist swirls in the square's framework.

Meeting Isabel's excited look with a disappointed scowl, Neriah raps on the mist area with her knuckles, making the sound of knocking on timber. The mist disperses and the table-top reappears without a scratch. 'Not yet.' She lifts the brush, running her fingers reverently over the handle and bristles. 'Can you believe what this brush is capable of doing?'

Isabel smiles at her. Clearly, she finds Neriah's attitude endearing. But it's just a brush. One that doesn't even work.

'You'll get there,' Isabel encourages. 'Just keep trying.'

'I work on it every day. Arkarian says I'm getting closer, and I feel like I am. I'm just not there yet.'

'Is that what's been bothering you? Not being able to figure out how to use the king's brush to make a portal?'

She tosses her black hair over one side of her head and pierces me with her dark doe eyes. 'Matt is missing. That's what I'm worried about.'

Dillon opens one eye and laughs. It begins softly but as it starts to build Dad gives him a scolding look. He clears his throat and pretends he's coughing.

Evidently Neriah's not joking.

'How can you be so sure something's happened, luv?' Jimmy asks.

'I can't feel him,' she says simply. 'And that's never happened to us before. He's been a mess since the battle. He blames himself for what happened to...' She flicks me a pity look.

'*Rochelle?* Is that what you're trying to say?'

'I'm sorry, Ethan. I don't want to add to your pain.'

'You don't? Then just say it, Neriah. Say her name. Don't pretend she never existed.'

She gasps. 'I wouldn't do that.' A tear trickles down her face, but she still doesn't say her name. It's as if none of them can.

'Funny how you all didn't mind saying her name when you thought she was a traitor, and now that she's proved herself by giving her life, you can't say it. It's like you want her memory to disappear so you can stop being embarrassed, and ashamed.'

'Ethan,' Dad says, voice slightly scolding.

'What, Dad? We should be shouting Rochelle's name from the top of Angel Falls. We should be screaming it out of cars from here to Melbourne. Rochelle Thallimar is a hero, a freaking hero.'

Nobody knows where to look and the silence isn't just deafening, it's defining.

Until Jimmy gets to his feet. 'You're right, lad. Rochelle is a hero and we should honor her. Give us a little time to regroup and we will. You'll see. We'll make you proud.' He winks.

I nod my gratitude. 'Thanks, Jimmy.'

When he sits down, Dad gets up. 'Rochelle would have been a welcome member to our family, son. Giving up her own life so that you would live,' he shakes his head, 'makes her more than a hero in my eyes.'

My vision of Dad grows hazy. Isabel wipes my cheek. 'I wish I'd been a better friend to Rochelle,' she says, hanging her head and wiping her own eyes.

'I always liked Rochelle,' Neriah says, lifting her brush from the table and tapping it on the palm of her free hand. 'I didn't know Rochelle when she worked for the Order of Chaos, so I never had cause to doubt her. I will miss her, Ethan. We were friends.'

Dropping a fist on the table and making it jump, Dillon says, 'Rochelle was *hot*!'

I can't help but crack a smile as everyone laughs.

Dillon rests a hand on my shoulder and leans in close. 'I will always remember her as a hero, without a doubt, buddy.'

I nod and thank everyone. The air between us clears, though I thought it would help more. My chest is still dark and empty and hurts like Hell.

'Why are you so worried about Matt?' Isabel asks Neriah.

'Because he's taking Rochelle's loss really hard.'

'Why?' I ask.

'He was supposed to protect her but on that last day he seemed to only make things harder for her.'

Isabel watches me from the corners of her eyes.

'He's never been away from me for so long without making contact,' Neriah says. 'What we share is so binding it's difficult for anyone who hasn't experienced this level of connection to understand.'

I push back from the table, too wound up to listen to more of this. 'Connection or not, Matt will be back when he's ready to return. He's perfectly fine, Neriah. Your concern is unfounded.'

She follows me to the door, and reaching for my arm, she grips my wrist. 'How do you know it's unfounded?'

'Because he loves you. He's not going anywhere.'

She regards me with her dark eyes. 'Thank you, Ethan, but you know more than you're telling me. You know where he is.'

Damn Truthseers. I catch Dillon's amused smirk. Trying not to let that throw me, I make sure not to even blink. 'Where Matt's gone and what he's doing is clearly important to him.'

'But where is he, Ethan? Why can't I feel him?'

'I'm sorry, Neriah, but I can't breathe in here.' I look back at Isabel. 'Tell Arkarian I'll return later. I have to go... and...' *stare at the damn ceiling some more.*

Neriah tightens her fingers around my wrist. 'Don't go, Ethan. Please... I'm sorry.'

The tears in her eyes undo my anger, leaving it in shreds on the floor. I nod and offer her a small smile. On the way back to my seat Arkarian's blue light appears beside Isabel. Another bright shimmering light alongside him reveals he's bringing a guest, and by his height I'd say it's our King, Richard.

King Richard wears a modern and stylish dark grey suit, clothes he seems more drawn to than the regal robes the other royals wear. He acknowledges each of us with a nod but stops at me and holds my gaze. 'I offer you my deepest condolences, Ethan.'

'Thank you, sire.'

'Rochelle's passion and sense of righteousness will be missed by us all.'

After a moment of solemn silence King Richard summarizes how the battle played out, and afterwards in Athens, how Dartemis has taken the place of Lorian as Tribunal Head.

'I'm sorry to inform you,' he says, his words putting us on edge, 'we also lost Lord Alexandon, House of Criers, Sector Russia.' Shaking his head slowly, he tells us the story of a curse put on the House of Criers by the preceding king. 'It's a sorry story we don't need to hear all the details today, only that the king before Alexandon, believing he was removed from his titles, lands and all his holdings unfairly, cursed all succeeding Tribunal Heads of the House of Criers with a life far shorter than an eternal can normally expect.'

Isabel asks, 'How long did Lord Alexandon rule over the House of Criers?'

He says, 'Just eighteen years.'

Dillon lifts the glass of water in front of him as if he's going to make a toast. 'Cheers to Lord Alexandon's replacement.'

Gasping, Neriah turns angry eyes on him. 'You have no tact, Dillon.'

Dillon lifts his glass higher. 'And proud of it, kiddo.'

Neriah huffs, slapping her paintbrush across her open palm with a look that says she'd like to slap Dillon with it.

Jimmy says, 'Don't be too hard on Dillon. No harm done; and it was kind of funny.'

Neriah looks straight across at Isabel. 'Did you find Dillon's remark amusing?'

Isabel doesn't hesitate. 'Not a chance.' She's never had a high opinion of Dillon anyway. 'It was deeply insensitive.'

King Richard clears his throat. 'Yes, well, I have other news.' He waits a moment to glance over us. 'Lady Arabella has taken a leave of absence from her duties.'

Isabel's says, 'Is she all right?'

'Can we see her?' Neriah asks.

'Arabella has already departed and asks to be left alone in her grief.'

Neriah says, 'I hope she's not away for long.'

Neriah's words echo our thoughts. Heads around the table nod. Lady Arabella had a difficult time leading up to the battle, but she was always the first to help us when we needed it.

Arkarian sits and asks if we have any questions.

I don't get a chance to speak before Neriah's hand shoots up. With my mouth half open, Arkarian sends me a pleading look to be patient. His grief-stricken eyes connect with the dark spaces inside me. Instinct tells me where he's been these last few days, attending to needs so personal he hasn't even shared them with Isabel. How much he's hurting is anyone's guess. My gut churns for the guy. How hard would it be to learn that the man who was your mentor for two hundred years is really your father, and a short time later have him taken away from you forever? He hears my thoughts and turns his head, his eyes holding mine. 'I'm sorry,' I mouth the words soundlessly.

He nods. Returning his focus to Neriah, he tells her to go ahead.

'Matt is missing and I'm concerned for his welfare,' she says. 'Ethan tells me he's fine and that he'll return when he's ready, but what if something happened to him. I've looked in all our usual places, everywhere I can think he might go. Can you help me find him, Arkarian? I don't know where else to search.'

Wow, so much for my assurance. Arkarian can't spend his time on a pointless search when I need his help with something far more important.

'Please, Arkarian, if you know anything...'

She'll have to take a ticket and wait in line.

'Ethan knows where he is but he won't tell me.'

Damn Matt, he should have warned me that his usually gentle girlfriend is really an alley cat underneath. But I get it. She's just worried.

'Please, Arkarian,' she pleads, 'tell me if you know anything.'

I don't like to break a promise to a mate, but I can't stand by and watch Neriah torture herself, or have Arkarian be the one to break a promise. 'Damn it, Neriah, I told you Matt is all right. He'll be back soon. Can't you leave it at that?'

She turns and faces me. 'What are you not telling me?'

Arkarian says, 'I agree with Ethan. Matt can take care of himself. Why don't you and Isa –'

'With or without your sanction, Arkarian,' Neriah interrupts, flicking a glance at me, 'or your help, Ethan, I will continue to search for Matt myself because I can't reach him and that means something is wrong.' She peers at me with her dark brown eyes glowing like burning embers. It's a crazy wild look for her. She has an exotic look anyway, but this takes her to another level. 'Ethan, you know what it's like to have a gut feeling that everyone ignores.'

Sitting beside me with his long legs stretched out under the table, hands locked behind his head, Dillon sniggers. 'First, Neriah, I just have to say, that's a good look on you. You should get angry more often.' He glances at Jimmy and Dad. 'Are you seeing her eyes?'

She frowns at Dillon. 'What are you talking about?'

He shrugs. 'Never mind. Secondly, Ethan's instinct is a gift. It's one of his powers, and therefore less likely initiated by emotions. And lastly, whatever harm comes Matt's way, it's not going to kill him. If he's injured, his body will heal itself. The more severe the wound the faster his body heals, that's the way it goes, isn't it?'

She shoots Dillon a dark look. He raises his hands, and she shifts her piercing gaze to me. 'Ethan, please... will you tell me what you know?'

Isabel touches my arm, her voice rising with concern. 'We're talking about my brother here. If something has happened to him...'

There's a time to support your mates, and there's a time to ease your loved ones' concerns. 'He came to see me a few days ago.'

Around the table most look surprised, but not Arkarian and King Richard, whom I suspect know as much as I do, and maybe more.

'What did he want?' Neriah asks.

Isabel encourages me to tell her with eyes rolling in Neriah's direction.

'To apologize for something that was not his fault. But you know Matt, he takes his responsibilities more seriously than most.' Dad and Jimmy nod. 'He had a theory he wanted to explore and he asked me to go with him.'

'Clearly, you didn't,' Neriah accuses. 'You let him go alone.'

'There's something I have to do first. But he didn't want to help me with that, and he wouldn't wait, so... yeah, I let him go on his own.'

'Where, Ethan?'

Arkarian nods at me and I explain, 'You can't feel Matt because he's underground. He has a theory that the Prophecy has changed. He went down into Veridian to see what he could find.'

# Chapter Four

## Jesilla

I open the clinic door, swearing on my mother's recently departed soul that if there is any way to keep Keziah from dying today I will find it and make it happen.

The clinic has four private healing rooms. He's in the first. I peer into the glass panel a moment before entering, bracing for the worst while hoping for the best.

*Seven days? I was out for seven days?*

His choking cough lasts longer than usual. When it finally ends he gasps and sucks in as much air as he can, his breaths sounding like pebbles scraping the ocean floor.

Keziah has been a prevailing force in my life, helping to bring my powers out and teaching me how to use them. He taught me how to protect myself, to kick ass, and most importantly how to control my mind, to block the thoughts of others and bring about an inner state of calm.

His color is grey, his breathing shallow. A trickle of blood seeps from the corner of his mouth. I grip the alabaster slab that serves as a healing procurer beneath the thin mattress so he doesn't see my hands shaking. 'Hey, Kez, I'm home.'

He opens his eyes, looks straight up at me, lifting his hand to my face slowly because he's so weak. 'I knew you would make it home, child.' He attempts to rise. 'I need to...' Coughing stops him from continuing.

'It's all right.' I ease his head back onto the pillow. 'I'm not going anywhere.'

'When you didn't return with...' He coughs again, bringing up blood.

'Sh-sh-sh, save your strength, I was...' I raise my hand to the back of my head but as before there's no wound, no scar, not even missing hair. 'I had to hide out,' I explain. Wiping the blood from his mouth, I help him sip water from the cup on his bedside cabinet, holding the straw to his lips. 'Do you know what happened to Zander and Pearl?'

'They came in at dawn... looking all night.' He has another sip, swallows, and takes his time to gather his breath between sentences. 'They formed teams, searching. Bastian went out on his own, said he could cover more ground that way. That boy searched so hard he didn't sleep for days. And Pearl is still running searches.'

'Where's Zander?'

'He's meeting with our two remaining captains, taking stock of our losses. They're on Level Two. You... you should let them know you're here.' He closes his glazed eyes to rest.

'They know. I had my eye scanned at the gate.'

'Of course.'

Gently, I lower my ear to Keziah's chest, just as I used to do when I was a little girl, and listen to his constricted lungs. The wheezing vibrations are the worst I've heard. Back then they used to make me giggle. Keziah hasn't been well for a long time but this last year has been his worst. If only my mother hadn't been so enamored with her absurdly ugly lover, she might have noticed his deterioration and healed him.

I sit in the steel chair beside his bed. 'You seemed to manage OK at the battle. I saw you working awesome magic on the enemy before Zander and Pearl attempted to drive me to a safe location.'

His chest rumbles with soft laughter followed by another bout of coughing. I help him sip water. He says, 'Jesilla...' His long fingers shake uncontrollably as he lays his hand over mine. 'There is so much I must tell you. Here. Take this.'

He puts something hard and metallic in my hand, and then he chokes. Gasping for air I help him sit forward and watch helplessly as dark blood pools inside his mouth. Finding a disposable sick bag in his bedside drawer I shake it out and hold it around his mouth. He fills a third of it with glossy, dark-red blood clots.

He really is dying. Just as Bastian tried to tell me; only I didn't want to hear it.

But there has to be something I can do.

I have powers inherited from my Goddess mother, and skills I learned from Keziah, the best magician on earth, surely I can utilize something to save him. At least give him more time.

Exhausted from the effort to expel the clots, I help lay his weary body back on the slab. 'I'm going to fix you, Keziah.'

One white eyebrow rises higher than his other. 'But you are not a Healer, my dear, and there is something vital I need you to know before I take my -'

'Whatever you have to tell me can wait until I make you well again.'

'No, Jesilla, listen... I've done something. Good or bad, right or wrong, I've done it now and... and... with or without me, you have to deal with it.' As another fit of coughing grips him, he holds my hand against his chest until the cough blessedly subsides. 'Please, child. Look in your hand.'

It's a key. 'What does this open?'

'There's a gold chest in your mother's secret room.'

I cringe at the thought of having to go into my mother's bedroom to access her secret room. The key's on a gold chain so I pull it over my head and make myself busy preparing a syringe. I show him the syringe. 'Morphine. For your pain.'

He nods, but holds up his hand and says softly, 'Your mother is... gone.'

Syringe in hand, I pause. He'd been with Lathenia for at least a thousand years. He wouldn't have stayed with her for so long if he hadn't cared for her. 'I saw what happened to her, Kez. And I know Marduke turned to stone.' *Damn curse.*

He nods. 'It's your time now, child.'

'My time for what?'

'To lead the Order. Fulfil your mother's dream. Take the Earth to her destiny, and... and... not her destruction.'

If he weren't so sick I would laugh. 'Has someone else given you morphine because this sounds like you're hallucinating, Kez.'

'Not hallucinating.'

'But you can't be serious.'

'With every breath, I am.'

I shake my head. 'What is there for me to lead? Where is our army now? All the beasts are dead.'

'But our soldiers are not. Your mother's army was much more than beasts and creatures of suspect origin.' He coughs and frightens the hell out of me when blood pools in his eyes. 'That was only the first wave,' he says. 'But our Goddess didn't get the chance to give the command for her soldiers to attack, and since she... she died so abruptly, and you... you were on your way to a safe-house but never arrived.' He struggles with the words, but I understand well enough. 'I... I decided that we needed to regather.'

I find it hard to locate a vein. They're shutting down fast. My hands start shaking and are no help at all. I end up injecting the morphine into his calf muscle, which unfortunately will take a few minutes before it starts to ease his pain.

'So, *you* gave the order to withdraw?'

He holds my gaze, then nods, his eyes remaining on me as if searching for my judgement.

'You did the right thing, Keziah.'

'There are some below who do not agree.'

I lift my brows; they would be feeling cheated out of the battle for which they'd trained so hard. 'I'll speak with them.'

His breathing eases a little. 'Soldiers need a leader. A General. A Queen. An Immortal.' He gathers some energy, enough to say what he needs. 'Your mother spent much of her life formulating a plan where governments of all the countries of Earth would bow to her will. And her army would hold them to the truth, that she and she alone would rule Earth.'

'Dartemis has come down from his perch,' I remind him.

Keziah dismisses Dartemis with a flick of his fingers and a puff of air pushed out through pouted and shriveled lips. 'Your uncle is weak. It's why Lorian protected him by keeping him outside the universe and feigning his death. He was only to emerge as a last resort. He is not an immortal of any worth.'

'Are you sure you're not underestimating him? Hidden as he was, how would you know his strengths?'

'You're right. It would be foolish to underestimate him. But the Order needs a leader in the same way that the Earth needs someone to protect her. That is *you*, Jesilla.' He blocks my denial with a sharp look. 'You must finish your mother's work. Inside the chest in her secret room she has left you a letter with instructions should the worst happen. You will be Queen of Earth. And Bastian will be your right hand. I have taught him all he needs. He will help you transition.'

'Transition?'

'From school girl to world leader.' I scratch my head and he adds, 'This day was always going to come, Jesilla. It happened sooner than we had hoped. You must continue to unlock your powers and become stronger than any single being on this planet.'

'Kez, you're not thinking straight. That's just crazy. So please, and I say this respectfully, shut up and let me work on you so you can wake up and realise what foolish things you've been telling me.'

He grabs my wrist with a hold that's far from foolish. 'You must let Bastian be your right hand. Promise me you will –'

'Bastian just left and I don't even know if he's going to return. He doesn't have to, you know. He has another world he can slip into where they already accept him.' I peel Keziah's fingers off, careful not to snap a bone.

'Bastian *will* return,' he splutters and blood sprays across my face. He tries to apologize but I shake my head and tug out an antiseptic wipe. 'She raised him,' he says. 'She was more a mother to him than his own was. That pathetic creature would have drowned him in a scalding bath when he was four. More than once, if not for your mother's timely interruption, Bastian would not be alive today.'

I shrug. 'So he owed her his life. But she's gone. He doesn't owe her anymore, and he certainly doesn't owe me anything. There's nothing to hold him here now.'

Suddenly Keziah's body jerks, his eyes roll back into his head and blood oozes from their corners. He's worn himself out talking. He tries to cough but the fight in him is slowing. The morphine is taking effect, making him drowsy but also easing the seizure. I lay his head carefully onto the pillow, spreading his thin white hair behind him.

'Keziah, can you hear me?'

His eyes roll down. The whites are swimming in blood. It scares the heck out of me, but I need him to hang on a little longer.

'Kez, I want to ask you something. It's important. Are you with me?'

He nods. More blood trickles out that I swiftly wipe. 'Keziah, is it only your physical body that's failing you?'

'Do you mean, is my brain too far gone to save, and my mutterings those of a deluded old man?'

I smile, unsurprised to find my eyes filling with tears. 'Yeah, that's about it.'

'Why?' he asks.

'Me first.'

He huffs in protest but answers anyway, 'My brain is that of an eighteen-year-old, with the wisdom and experience of a thousand lifetimes. Why?'

'Think about my gifts, Kez. Not the *special* one I'm only to use once.'

'For Bastian.'

'That remains to be seen.'

'My dear, you have more talent than most. A clue might help.'

I smile despite the dread in my gut. Keziah knows me more than anyone, more than my own mother did. He knows what I'm capable of achieving.

'You want to rejuvenate my body?'

'Yes. Yes, I do.'

'Hmm... I would like that.'

His words, his twitching lips, make me chuckle.

'But this procedure is not without tremendous risk,' he adds. 'Even your mother never used it.'

'That might be because she couldn't. She couldn't do everything, Keziah.'

I would hate to think she could rejuvenate him but chose not to.

'Kez, if it is possible, at this point,' I touch my fingertip to the blood seeping from his eyes, 'I think even an elevated level of risk is worth taking.'

He nods, blinking out small streams of blood. 'But wait.' Using more of his meagre energy than I would like, he grabs my wrist and peers into my eyes. 'If this doesn't work there's something...'

My patience is running out. He doesn't have much time before no powers of the universe will work on him. 'What is so important that you risk dying that I might know?'

He tries to tell me, but his breathing fails, his meagre coughing becomes horribly more ear piercing than husky. 'There is... y-you need to know.' He points at my chest where the key he gave me hangs.

'Kez, we're running out of time. I need you to live. There's less risk if you still have brain function when I attempt this'.

'If I don't make it... open the chest ... read, and ... and... avenge her.'

'I was always going to avenge her.' I give him a tolerant smile. He doesn't even know that it was because of me that her life ended. Even if I didn't want to avenge Lathenia, didn't want to fulfil her plan, my decision on this is already decided.

'Then... then, child, you must take your place...'

His blood pressure drops. I hear his heart beat slowing down. He's on the cusp of death, about to slip into unconsciousness, and then I won't hear his voice again. No one will. 'No, don't you leave me. Damn it, Kez, if you want me to be this... this... queen or world leader you talk about, I'll do it with you alongside me. *You*, Keziah, as my Chief Advisor. So work with me here.'

I squeeze his hand and he opens his eyes and whispers something.

I move my head down to his lips. He says, 'I stopped...'

'What? What did you stop?'

'Death.'

*Huh?* 'Death? Who's death?' Marduke's would be impossible. You can't turn stone into flesh. Hope flares in my chest. 'Kez, do you mean my mother? Is Lathenia alive? Am I going to get a second chance with her?'

Pity darkens his eyes. It's not her. 'Sorry, child, but I could not alter what the immortals did to each other.'

I can't think of anyone else whose death he would want to meddle with... except... maybe... of all the deaths that day one gut-wrenching, heart-stopping death comes to mind. 'Do you mean...' I mouth a name that I don't dare utter aloud.

He nods.

'But she had no heartbeat. I was there. I saw how hard they tried to stop the blood pouring out of her, and how hard they tried to resuscitate her.'

A familiar mischievous glint flickers to life in his eyes, and, as if he's given himself a shot of adrenaline he finds the energy to explain, 'She had no heartbeat, but she did have a trickle of brain activity. I... I masked the sound of lingering life in her as I slowly mended and re-started her heart.'

'Oh my God, Keziah, where did you put her? And whose body lies in her tomb?'

He lifts a trembling finger and points through the glass panel. I look. Door 3.

He says, 'There was another girl who died that day. I... I applied a glamour of the familiar.'

'So anyone who looked at her saw...'

He nods. 'My dear, with your skills...'

'But why would I want this girl to live?'

He squeezes my fingers with the pressure of a bird. 'The Guard destroyed us at our heart and... *he* is *their* heart.'

I peer at him, still not sold on his motives but starting to see where he's coming from. He's not alone in holding Ethan Roberts the one most responsible for our failures. I point to Door 3. 'You're telling me that she's lying in that room, and now you want me to ease his – *their* - suffering? But how does this help to complete my mother's plan or avenge her?'

He stops me with trembling fingers closing over mine, a smile twitching at the corners of his withered lips. 'My precious girl, who says you have to give her back?'

# Chapter Five

## Ethan

'But it's flooded. What will happen to Matt down there?' Neriah's gaze goes straight to Jimmy. Since he designed the complex paths, traps and locks, he's the one to allay her fears.

'Most of the floodwaters that destroyed the ancient city have receded over the last week,' he says, 'but there are still pockets lying around, walls collapsing and debris everywhere.'

'That's why Matt didn't tell you where he was going,' Arkarian explains. 'He didn't want you to worry, Neriah, and he didn't want to disrupt your training.'

She glances at the brush and her cheeks darken. But she has no reason to think she's not trained enough. Since the Citadel fell she's hardly had the brush out of her hand. She practices everywhere, and not just in Arkarian's training rooms, but at Isabel and Matt's place where she's living now, and especially in the forest. I see her on my walks, her brush glowing as she attempts to open portals in the empty spaces between trees, shrubs and even spider webs.

'Matt made it clear that not telling you was an order,' Arkarian says, and looking directly at me, he raises his eyebrows. I nod, and Neriah huffs.

Yep, she's still pissed at me.

'Well then,' she says. 'Jimmy, will you show me where Matt entered the city?'

'I'm not sure that's a good idea. The city is unstable.'

But Neriah is too worked up to take no for an answer from anyone. 'Did he command you to silence too?'

Jimmy opens his mouth, but closes it again without saying anything. Beside me, Dillon smirks, copping a harsh glare.

'I'm going into the city whether Jimmy helps me or not,' she announces, 'so why not make it easier, quicker, or at least safer for me?'

'Jimmy,' Arkarian says, 'unlock the city for Neriah to enter.'

'Do you want me to escort her until she locates Matt?'

'Your presence is required elsewhere. Neriah will find Matt through her senses.'

'But, Arkarian, you know I can be quick.'

Isabel chimes in, 'Neriah isn't going by herself, Jimmy. I'm going with her.'

Arkarian swings his head around. 'Isabel –'

But she cuts him off, 'You can't stop me, so please don't pull rank. That's my brother down there.'

'I wasn't going to stop you,' he says. 'I would never pull rank in order to keep you safe, Isabel, no matter how much I might want to sometimes.' His smile is only for her.

She bites down on her lower lip, guilty as sin for even thinking he would. She knows Arkarian better than that. We all do. And now no one knows where to look.

'I was going to say, at the first sign of trouble, call me before putting yourselves in danger and I will arrange backup.'

She holds his gaze level. 'I'm sorry, Arkarian, but if waiting for backup adds to the danger my brother might be in, I can't promise I'll wait.'

His eyes burn vibrant purple with his need to protect her, but you can't stop Isabel when her mind is set on saving someone she loves.

'You would do the same,' she offers, her head tilting, her voice lowering to a whisper, 'if it were me in trouble.'

With a knowing smile he nods.

'OK then,' Jimmy says, stacking ropes, torches, energy bars, water and a few other items into the girls' backpacks, 'since there could be any number of unforeseen dangers, you might need a few things.'

'Like what dangers?' Isabel asks as he hands the girls a knife each, indicating they should tuck it inside their boots.

'Some walls are still giving way from the waterlogged foundations. Ceilings are still collapsing, paths upending and breaking apart. There's the occasional torrent of trapped flood waters causing landslides, and I've seen a few animals that wandered in and couldn't find their way out. Now they're starving.'

The girls exchange a wary look. Neriah says, 'Isabel, I can go by myself. I could fly down to Matt and be back in no time.'

'I'm coming with you so hang on to those shape-shifting powers for when you go flying with my brother. It'll be too dark down there without a torch unless you plan to hold it in your beak?'

They laugh. 'All right,' Neriah says. 'But we should go now.'

Isabel turns to leave, when Arkarian stops her. He tugs some of her loose blonde strands behind her ear and looks into her eyes. 'Take care.'

'We'll be -'

She doesn't finish because Arkarian closes the space between them and kisses her like... well, like I would have kissed Rochelle had I known it would be the last time I'd see her alive.

I glance away, fighting a flood of emotions. Dad's hand comes from nowhere to rest on my shoulder. I shrug it off. The way he handled his grief when we lost Sera is no comfort to me. He set no example to follow. Rather, what happened to Dad scares the hell out of me.

King Richard announces that he has to leave immediately. 'Athens is calling,' he says. The meeting closes and everyone leaves.

Finally there's just Arkarian left. He gets up and motions with his hand for me to follow. 'Let's have that talk now.'

He takes me to his octagonal chamber where the sphere hovers in darkness in the center of the room, machines and screens around the walls remain silent and unmoving. Closing the door behind me with his mind, Arkarian produces two chairs facing each other. He sits in one and points to other.

'I'd rather stand.'

'As you wish,' he says with a sigh. 'It's been a hell of a week, hasn't it?'

His father's death and Lord Alexandon's are two who were close to him. There were others as well he would have known; soldiers in the field. One in particular comes to mind. 'Any word on Mr Carter? Any signs of his remains?'

'No, but it's not unusual for those beasts to... leave no trace. Still, something to confirm his death would end speculation and bring closure to many.'

'I'm sorry.'

He looks up at me. 'What for, Ethan?'

'Mr Carter was your friend. It must hurt to know that for many of those years he was deceiving you.'

He nods. 'It would have hurt more if the traitor had proved to be Arabella.'

I sit opposite, elbows on my knees, bringing me closer to him. 'How are you really holding up, Arkarian?'

'I'm adjusting to the changes like everyone else.'

'I mean on a personal level.'

'Oh. I'm coping. Thank you for asking. It was... difficult to watch so many of our loved ones die, and hard to understand the reasons behind the deaths.'

'Will we ever learn the answers?'

I'm not expecting a reply and he can read that in my thoughts. We study each other for a minute before Arkarian says, 'Explain your plan, Ethan.'

I close my eyes and see her face again, always at that moment before the arrow strikes, her small startled cry of pain and loss rolled into one before she shapes her beautiful mouth into a small smile of acceptance. 'Arkarian, I have to go back in time. I have to save her.'

He blinks slowly and says nothing. Inside my chest, the hole that was my heart burns as if I'm on fire.

Finally, he asks, 'How far back?'

'Eight days.'

'The day before the battle.'

I nod, waiting.

'Let us say I somehow organized this, what would you do? How would you accomplish saving Rochelle?'

Animated by a spark of hope, I lift my hands to help explain, 'I'll warn her. Tell her what's about to happen. Considering what we do, it's a safe bet she'll believe me.'

'You might run into yourself, Ethan. That would cause an anomaly.'

'I'll to talk to Rochelle when I'm sure the other me is nowhere nearby.'

'Ethan, no matter how many times you go back to warn Rochelle, she will still choose to save you from Marduke's arrow.'

'Then I'll find Marduke first and kill him before he shoots the arrow.'

'And what if Rochelle doesn't believe you? How far will you go to ensure she's not with you on that day? Remember, she had a strong mind. Will you be willing to lock her in a cell? Or take her place?'

'I'll do whatever I have to, as long as I save her.'

'So if you die and Rochelle doesn't, what then, Ethan? That's a plan I cannot agree with.'

'What if I go back ten days, destroy Marduke ahead of the battle. I call your name and I'm out of there.'

'Ethan, what if you fail? What if something else changes? What if Marduke kills both of you?'

'What are you doing, Arkarian? You know I won't hurt anyone intentionally. My mission would be to kill Marduke. Nothing else will change.'

'Ethan, when have I or anyone of your elders sanctioned a kill?'

'You're doing my head in, Arkarian.'

'Are you willing to put everyone through that battle again?'

*What?* I think about this for a moment. It's still so raw; watching so many people get hurt or die. The civilian losses, though not many, were hard on everyone. There was even a child who lost his life. Should I save that little boy too while I'm there?

Arkarian asks again, 'Well, Ethan, are you willing?'

'If I have to.' But I can't meet his eyes.

From inside his trouser pocket he tugs out a black ribbon, and gathering his blue hair at the base of his neck, he ties the cord around it. With his hair pulled back his eyes appear even hollower, the dark circles around them more pronounced.

Arkarian looks like Hell.

He leans towards me, sliding his elbows down to his knees, his violet eyes probing. I don't have the energy to block him. 'Ethan, if you managed to lure Marduke out and kill him, it would change things like the first slab of shifting ice that causes an avalanche, and we don't know what those changes will mean. We can't foresee those things.'

'We'll deal with whatever transpires.'

He gets up and paces the chamber. 'After all these years, it's grief that blocks you from grasping how the present, and likely the future too, will change from the alteration of one important past event.'

'This one event needs to be changed. It's all I can think of.'

He comes up behind where I'm sitting and settles his open palms on my shoulders. Surges of calmness shoot into my body. I soak them in. I'm not so stubborn to refuse something I could really use. But it has no effect on my mind. Or my drive to make this happen. 'Arkarian, I can't do this without your help.'

His hands stop and he sits opposite me again. 'Ethan, we still have no means to travel through time yet.'

'But we will soon, right?'

His nod is slow. 'Sir Syford has brought a new team together, but it's not as straightforward as you're thinking.'

'I only want to jump back a little over a week.'

'Let's say Sir Syford has the machinery running again in a few days, and you do jump back a week or so, if you are successful in killing Marduke, Lathenia will lash out in a fully-fledged rage. She will kill innocent citizens, people you know, more of the Guard's soldiers, maybe others who are Named like Isabel, Dillon, Jimmy -'

I slice the air with my hands. 'Don't say those things. We don't know what Lathenia will do. She might go into mourning so deep she forgets to release her beasts, or kills herself to join her soul to Marduke's in that crazy grey world.'

'Or she becomes so enraged she finds a deeper source of energy to fuel her powers. What would happen then, Ethan? Tell me what happens then?'

'Lorian dies, but Lathenia lives?'

He nods, and looks as defeated as I'm feeling inside.

'You've been going over this scenario too.'

'I've been anticipating this conversation since Rochelle's entombment.'

'Arkarian, I just want Rochelle back.' I lean forward, folding my arms around my gut to stem the scream that wants to rip from my lungs. 'I'm nothing without her. Nobody knows what this feels like.'

He shifts closer, locks his hands around my forearms, his eyes overflowing with so much compassion that tears run down his face. 'It's because you lost your soul-mate.'

'What?'

'Grief is harder when you lose your perfect life partner.'

King Richard appears beside the door before I get to ask Arkarian more about his theory, but... I shake my head as it makes sense now.

'Good, you're both still here,' King Richard says. 'Ethan, I...' He stops, his eyes swinging from one of us to the other. 'I've interrupted something. Is there anything I can do to help?'

Arkarian releases my arms and quietly shakes his head.

King Richard clears his throat. 'Right. Let's get to it then, shall we?' He places his hand on my shoulder. 'Ethan, even if it were possible, you are not time-shifting to save Rochelle. It's fraught with too many dangers.' He pats my shoulder a few times, and with a deepening voice he adds, 'That is a direct order.'

I want to rip his fingers from my shoulder. My hands tremble with the urge. I clasp them together in my lap. 'They thought she was a traitor. Why did she have to prove herself with her life?'

Arkarian produces a chair for King Richard, but he waves it away. 'Thank you, but I don't have time,' he says. 'Ethan, I don't have the answers you seek, but you will get the chance to ask the one who might.'

'What's happening?' Arkarian asks.

'Lord Dartemis has called a meeting of Tribunal heads, the Named, all Sector Leaders and their soldiers from the fields.'

'*Everyone*?'

'Gather the Named and bring them to Athens.' King Richard pats my shoulder again, 'And my lord Dartemis wants you, Ethan, to return with me now. He requests a few minutes with you before the meeting.'

There is so much sincere compassion in both of their eyes, but what use is their pity if they don't at least try to help me get Rochelle back?

Arkarian leans forward, grips the back of my neck with his hand, bringing his forehead down to mine. 'Ethan, it has to be this way.'

I pull out of his grip and swing my eyes up to my king. 'I rescued you from that god-awful rat infested tower, why won't you help me?'

'Rochelle's death was foretold in the prophecy,' Richard reminds me as if I haven't gone over that damn prophecy a thousand times already.

I stand and point at him. 'Don't mention that prophecy to me again.' I get to the door and swing it open, taking a deep breath before speaking again. 'My Lord... Arkarian... I need some air.'

King Richard stops me with a heavy hand on my shoulder. It feels like a chain around my throat. 'Ethan, you will come to Athens as ordered by Lord Dartemis now, or your leaving will be considered a refusal of a direct order.'

*Refuse a direct order?* The thought is chilling. If I don't go to Athens I'm risking ex-communication. If I walk away they could take my memories. And those memories are all I have left of Rochelle.

'Ethan?' Arkarian nudges gently. 'Your king is waiting.'

I meet King Richard's gaze. 'I'll come with you now.'

# Chapter Six

## Isabel

Every time I look at Ethan my heart aches. He's so broken up, it's killing him. And I foresaw Rochelle's death in a vision. I knew how it was going to happen, just not when. I should have stayed closer to her. I would have recognized signs. She'd still be alive today if I'd done my job right. I can't let it go. The guilt is eating at me.

Then there's Arkarian keeping things from me. Where did he go these last few days? Why doesn't he let me into his personal life? Doesn't he trust me anymore? Love and trust go together. Without one, the other doesn't exist.

Jimmy waits until we have our backpacks on and hard hats fastened before he starts the lift. With the door shut, a mildew smell makes me want to hold my breath. The lift drops only a few meters before it jerks to a sudden stop, knocking us against each other. Dust fills the cabin space and hangs in the air. As Jimmy gets the lift going again Neriah's hand reaches for mine.

A sudden bright light that has nothing to do with being in a bumpy, fast-dropping lift flashes before my eyes, making my head throb. I groan, alarming both Neriah and Jimmy. I lift my hands to indicate that I'm all right, but the light rapidly becomes too bright to bear and the ache so fierce I tug at my hard-hat needing to get it off, but my fingers struggle with the fastener.

'Whoa there, girl. Let me do that.' Jimmy gets it off fast.

'What's happening, Jimmy?' Neriah asks, worried.

I don't hear his reply as my legs suddenly give out from under me. But he knows. I'm getting a vision. And as the white light surrounding me dims, my eyes roll up and I get a sense of falling backwards into another place, far, far away.

*I'm in a hotel room behind a glass wall high off the ground. On the outside is a balcony with open sliding doors. I walk in slow motion towards a vista of tall buildings both north and south. I'm in a city. It's night; the buildings have their lights on with people everywhere appearing to be partying. Sounds kick in of excited chatter, a burst of cheering from another floor, laughter and music I don't recognize from a neighboring high-rise. I smell the ocean, and in a momentary lull I hear the swell and splash of waves.*

*The balcony is crowded with people, some with the familiar faces of my friends but many others I can't identify, yet sense that one day I will. Arkarian is there. His blue hair, longer and brighter than usual, flows back from his face with the force of a breeze. Neriah and my brother are beside him. Matt leans over the balcony rail pointing something out to a tall man on his other side. Well-dressed in dark grey pants and a white sweater, I recognize King Richard.*

*Arkarian waves me over to where he's standing at the railing but at the opening I can't move past an invisible barrier. I shrug and Arkarian points to the thousands of people packed around the shoreline, waving flags from their yachts, or on balconies and rooftops, in the streets around our building holding up that same flag I don't recognize but again sense that I should.*

*'Is it New Year's Eve?' I call above the party ruckus.*

*He tilts his head to the side with a bemused expression on his face, and I gasp at his ethereal look, his luminous skin, lips full and ruby colored, purple eyes brighter than ever emitting a penetrating glow.*

*My God, he's never looked more beautiful. He's so radiant it's as if he swallowed the sun and it's beaming out from his heart. As I observe him more intently an aura appears, a shimmering gold light around his head and shoulders. I haven't seen auras before and it seems appropriate that my first would be Arkarian's.*

*'It's the protest,' he says. 'Every major city around the world is holding one at this very moment, no matter the time difference.'*

*'What are we protesting?'*

*He frowns and peers at me as if I've lost my senses, like I'm the only person in the world who doesn't know.*

*The hairs at the back of my neck suddenly stand on end. It's a warning, a premonition that something bad is about to go down. Here. Now. 'Arkarian, bring everyone inside.'*

*He frowns, and I scream, 'Hurry!'*

*He turns first to King Richard, then Matt. They spin around and look straight at me, but by their confused expressions and wandering eyes neither can see me.*

*Sudden darkness shrouds the city skyline. As I try to figure out what's making the night sky intensely darker, the vision jerks my focus. It pulls my head back as if someone is dragging on my ponytail so that I have nowhere to look but at the sky. The stars have disappeared. I call out, 'Arkarian, look at the sky!'*

*It takes him less than a heartbeat to figure it out. 'God help us,' he says, and wasting no time he, Matt and King Richard begin shepherding everyone off the balcony.*

*Last in, Arkarian just makes it when explosions from above set the sky on fire. He comes straight for me, but his arms pass through me, and he drops backwards in shock.*

*'It's all right,' I tell him. 'I'm not really here. It's a vision.'*

*His frown deepens. Matt calls him from the front door to hurry, but Arkarian won't leave me.*

*Screams charge the air, fueling fears and deepening panic. Flags drop from balconies. Yachts explode on the water. Buildings burn. Everywhere, people run for their lives as a shower of fire rains down on the city. The night sky shudders with sonic blasts and illuminating apocalyptic explosions.*

*Amongst the chaos, Matt comes back for Arkarian. 'Go,' I tell him when he still refuses to leave me. 'If you don't leave now, this is where it ends for you. Please, Arkarian, go.'*

*This time Matt is able to drag Arkarian out the door. Unable to break free from my vision's hold, I lose sight of them both.*

*A flash of blinding light together with a wave of exploding energy sends me reeling over lounge chairs and other furnishings until a wall stops me. I stagger to my feet as the building shudders, walls tremble, the ceiling cracks and white dust fills the suite like a fog.*

*This building is coming down fast with people rushing to stairwells or still in their rooms.*

*King Richard, in a voice so God-like that no one would argue with it, orders all residents down to the bunkers, his voice reverberating through every suite in the building.*

*The screech of ripping metal and a great gust of wind makes me glance over my shoulder. Shock has me stumbling blindly. I hit a wall and sink to the floor with my eyes glued to the balcony as something – some* thing *- rips it from the building and hurls it into the wind. Other buildings to the north and south suffer the same fate, torn apart or burned to the ground. Even the landmarks, massive, solid structures sink broken into the sea.*

*I'm the only one left in the room when the building collapses around me. Floors, walls, ceilings, drop with an almighty force like curtains of debris. I'm standing in the center, watching floor after floor hit the ground, kicking up a mountain of crushed cement. When the building is dust beneath my feet, I'm standing in darkness, quietly becoming aware that I'm not alone. With my gift of seeing through all forms of light, I only need a speck, and that's how I see what's really happening here. What's really going down. I scramble to my feet and run as fast as I can.*

'She's coming around,' Jimmy says, his hands supporting my head, helping me into a sitting position.

'Thank *God*.' Neriah raises a bottle of water to my mouth. I guzzle some and thank her.

Jimmy's eyes don't leave my face. 'I suspect you had quite a vision.'

I nod and reach for the water again. I'm starting to feel better, but it takes a minute to recall where I am and what I'm doing.

'Don't rush it,' Jimmy says, but seeing me getting up he makes sure I'm steady on my feet before releasing me.

'What did you see?' Neriah asks.

'A city under attack.'

'What city? When? Who? Was Matt in your vision?'

'Neriah, leave her be. Isabel will explain at the debriefing,' Jimmy says, and pats my shoulder. 'You need rest. I'm taking you back.'

'No, I'm fine. Really.'

'Isabel.'

'I'm OK, Jimmy. I'm going to find my brother.'

'I can come back down or send someone else to help Neriah.'

'Thanks for the offer, Jimmy, but I'm staying.'

He stares into my eyes, his voice now serious, 'Isabel, you need de-briefing, and immediately after the vision is your best recall.'

'True, but, trust me, I won't have a problem recalling this vision. It's not the kind I'll easily forget.'

'Since you insist, I can't see I have much choice.' He rubs his jaw.

To reassure him, I pull out a smile and try hard not to let it tremble.

Jimmy takes his role as Matt's Protector seriously. Even though Lord Dartemis isn't my father, Jimmy protects me with the same enthusiasm as if I were the Immortal's child too.

'You can leave us now, Jimmy.'

'I can, can I?' he jokes, but his smile quickly turns serious. 'You take care down here, Isabel.'

'I will, Jimmy. I promise.' Catching up to Neriah, she turns, looking distraught. 'What is it?'

'I still can't sense him.'

'Oh. OK. Listen, Neriah, my brother is alive. He's immortal, just like you.'

'But immortals can die too,' she says. 'We saw it happen before our own eyes.'

'This is not going to get better for you until we find him, is it?'

She shrugs, the fear of losing Matt brimming in her eyes.

Back at the lift, Jimmy suddenly calls out, 'Wait up, girls.' He darts over. 'Lord Dartemis has called a meeting in Athens today and wants everyone to attend.'

We both groan and Neriah asks, 'How long do we have to find Matt?'

'Just do your best and come as soon as you can.'

Leaving him, we return to the path, finding it broken up and missing in places, making us wary of each step.

'There's so much destruction,' Neriah remarks as we tread carefully over fragments of a shattered wall.

We find a boulder as big as an overturned bus in our way. Neriah scuttles to the top where she stands and closes her eyes. As I come up beside her, she shakes her head. 'I'm forging a mind-link. It's not like him not to answer.'

With the light from our helmet torches activating my gift of sight, I can see far into the city's belly where there are mostly fragmented walls tossed on their sides like toy building blocks. Skeletons of machinery lie in mounds atop each other, some like anthills, others stacked up against a rock wall, though the majority is smashed to pieces. Where once there was a deep chasm, a river has sprung up that dips under a cave-like overhang, disappearing from sight. The secrets these walls once hid are nothing now but exposed and shattered debris.

'How far does your gift allow you to see?' Neriah asks.

'Wherever the light reaches.'

'So not through walls.'

'No.'

'Any sign of Matt in those areas?'

'Not yet.'

'Then we'll keep moving.'

She reaches for my hand and we jump off together. Looking ahead there's a path leading into a structure resembling a tunnel. This structure slices through some of the flood's worst wreckage. We go down to inspect it. As we stand at the entrance looking in I gnaw on my fingernail.

Neriah says. 'This could save us time.'

'If it's stable and there are no surprises in there.'

Neriah grips the ceiling and tries to shake it. Only a timber shard breaks off in her hand.

I recognize it. 'It's a bridge. The flood waters must have inverted it.'

'Lucky for us,' Neriah says, stepping inside. 'Are you coming?'

Inside is even darker. Neriah won't be seeing much from her light. She reaches for my hand. In here it's difficult to identify where a noise comes from or when it could be a danger to us. A wall collapses somewhere in the city. The metallic screeching means the wall had machinery hidden inside it. The reverberations echo and shake the inverted-bridge walls. We hold our breath until it's silent again.

'We'll be out soon,' Neriah says, trying to sound positive, but unable to hide the anxious note in her voice.

Something heavy drops on the roof and a spray of fine rock debris hits our hard hats. We both jump and scream, but it proves to be nothing serious and we laugh in relief.

The further into the inverted-bridge the sharper the downwards slope. When we reach the end and climb out, we're far lower than when we started. Considering we need to reach Matt quickly, this is a relief.

The path leads to a staircase of descending brick steps so narrow they're like a ladder. At the bottom is a flat area walled on all four sides. Three of those sides are roughly double our height, the fourth just high enough for Neriah to peer over. 'I don't like this.'

'Do you think the flood formed this?'

I shrug. It doesn't matter. We climb up some smashed machinery near the center, careful not to cut ourselves on sharp corners. The view across the lower wall is well worth our effort. I smile and bump Neriah's elbow with mine. On a flat area not far away Matt is sitting on the Ancient City's floor with his knees to his chest, his head buried in his hands.

Watching him, I get an uneasy feeling inside. Is his sadness the reason he's not responding to Neriah? How much has Rochelle's death affected him?

'Any sign of Matt yet?' she asks, unable to see as far as I can. 'He's still not responding even though –'

The wall on our left suddenly quivers. We glance at each other when without warning something heavy slams into it from the other side. Cracks appear and the quivering intensifies.

'What was that?' Neriah shouts.

'Nothing good,' I say, grabbing her hand and jumping off the machinery. 'We need to climb over that ledge.'

But it happens too quickly and we don't make it before a large portion of the wall shatters, spraying rocks like shotgun pellets. We drop for cover, our legs splashing in water that's filling up fast and forming a whirlpool in the centre. Crushed machinery with sharp edges begins shifting as the whirlpool grows. Neriah reaches the ledge and grips it with her free hand. Holding on to me with her other, my weight combined with the rising water stops her from leaping out.

Our eyes meet. She reads my thoughts and shakes her head, tightening her grip on my hand. 'No. Isabel, I'm not letting you go.'

An eerie noise like metal moaning has us looking back at the wall where the last remaining section shakes with the pressure behind it. This is not a good sign. Without taking my eyes off the tilting wall, I say, 'Neriah, let me go.'

'No.'

'But you can't –'

'I'm immortal, remember?'

I turn to look into her face. 'Not fully until you're eighteen. Let go and find Matt. I saw him. He's not far.' With water lapping under my chin, I jerk my head to point in his direction.

She holds on, closing her eyes. I know that look. She's calling to him in her thoughts again. And suddenly he materializes on the ledge. He reaches for Neriah, pulling her up with one arm.

By the time he swings back for me, I'm on the top edge of the whirlpool that's become so strong it's an effort to keep my face above water with the drag on my arms and legs.

Then Matt is beside me in the water, unaffected by its pull. He catches the rope Neriah yanks from her backpack and ties it around my waist, but it's his arms that make me feel safest. 'I got you, squirt,' he says.

'What took you?'

He shrugs.

'Thanks, bro.'

Lifting me out, Neriah helps me to my feet while Matt jumps up after me. 'Come on, I have a dry area not far.'

When we get to Matt's area we're soaking wet and shivering. Matt pulls a towel out of his backpack and puts it around me.

I shrug it off. 'Give it to Neriah, she's been standing in the cold longer.'

He insists. 'No, Isabel, you need it more.' Winking at me he pulls off his shirt. I roll my eyes as he wraps his arms around Neriah, moving his shirtless upper body in close.

I look away as Neriah bites down on her lower lip, smiling up as Matt nuzzles her neck. I spot Matt's electronic notebook on a rock. 'What have you found?' I ask, touching the screen and scrolling through Matt's notes.

He indicates the remaining parts of the silver wall behind them with a flick of his head. There, in an intricate and finely written calligraphy that looks more like hieroglyphics, are parts of the original prophecy. I read what's left, line after line to the tragic end, but it's still the same.

Turning her face up to Matt, Neriah asks, 'You thought it had changed?'

'I had a compulsion to come here that I can't explain. I even dreamed about it. There's nothing else down here worth anything to us so I assumed it was the prophecy. I thought that maybe it had changed since... you know, the way it had played out with her death and everything.'

Like most of us carrying guilty consciences, Matt is also having trouble saying Rochelle's name. What's wrong with us? Ethan is right; we should be shouting *Rochelle is a hero* from the top of every damn building in Angel Falls. 'Matt, I was Rochelle's bodyguard. My failure to protect her is on me.'

He scoffs, pushing his hair back with his long fingers, determined to carry my guilt too. 'I ordered you to stick close to her, but I was in charge. It stops with me, Isabel. It all stops with me.' He throws up his hands, looking more vulnerable than ever. 'I hoped there was something written down here that could explain why we had to lose her, or something that could give us hope for the future, something I could take back to the team. To Ethan.'

Neriah takes his face in her hands. 'We need to stick together, Matt, not run off on our own. And as hard as it is for Ethan, with all of us supporting him, even when he pushes us away, he'll come through this.'

'I hope you're right. I'm sorry. I should have told you. At first I didn't want you to worry, and when I found the prophecy unchanged, I needed to be alone for a while.' He pulls her into his arms. 'I did find something down here, though.' He links his fingers with Neriah's, then catches my eye. 'Come on, I'll show you both.'

But now we've found him, we're under orders to go to Athens. He reads my thoughts and stops. 'We have to go now?'

Neriah says, 'Show us another time.'

'Sure. So what's going on up there?'

'Your father called a meeting. He wants everyone to attend.'

'Did he say why?'

'No. He sent King Richard to inform us.'

He nods and busily rushes around collecting his tools and whatever else he brought with him, shoving them into his pack and lifting it over his shoulder so quickly his movements from beginning to end are little more than a blur. 'I'm ready. Let's go.'

But Neriah and I are gawking at him.

'What? What is it?'

'Nifty new power, bro. How long have you been able to move like that?'

His jaw shifts left then right and he shrugs.

# Chapter Seven

## Ethan

Lady Devine meets me at the front gates. Black and made of solid iron they're three times my height. No one has dropped me outside the gates before; it's usually in the courtyard. Maybe this is a new rule or, I hate to think, a mistake. I shield my eyes from a baking sun and glance over my shoulders. Behind me the historic hills of Greece fall away to azure waters.

She ushers me in, the gates locking automatically. Lady Devine's blood-red hair is like silk, piled high atop her head, making her appear taller than I remember. Her black dress flows over her slender body to her ankles where today she's wearing shoes.

'Only inside,' she says.

'Sorry, my lady?'

She lifts the front of her dress enough to show her petite black ankle boots. 'No matter the distressed state of your heart, Ethan, you must still block your thoughts. You never know who is listening. These are uncertain times. One battle does not necessarily end a war, but it could galvanize the beginning of another.'

Inside, as always, the palace is refreshingly cool. On our way through a maze of corridors, I ask what happened to King Richard. 'We left Angel Falls together. He didn't get displaced in the shift, I hope.'

She laughs with a tinkling bell-like quality, 'Don't worry, your king is safe. He had another errand to run so we diverted him. That is all.' She glances at me. 'Do you believe that, Ethan?'

'Of course, my lady.'

'Why?'

'Well, you've never given me reason not to believe what you tell me, and...'

'And?'

'It feels right.'

She smiles. 'Believing in what you cannot see is not easy, and your gifts ask this of you all the time. Your gifts have the power to instill faith in others. Always remember that.'

I nod, and as we turn a corner the once golden courtyard comes into view through a series of glass doors. The flowering shrubs and leafy trees that provided shade from the hot summers are gone. All that's left are a few shriveled plants, smashed benches and broken golden bricks. A crew of six workers dressed in all-white busily make repairs.

'Has anyone heard from Lady Arabella?' I ask, unable to take my mind off the courtyard and the memories contained there as we move into the palace's north wing.

'You, of all people, Ethan, should understand that her healing will take time.'

'Has she forgiven Matt for accusing her of being the traitor?'

'That, I'm afraid, will take longer.' She sees my frown. 'Matthew needed to prove to himself that he could be a capable leader.' She casts me a sidelong glance. 'He has a long way to go before he can be the leader we need for the harder times ahead.'

*Harder times ahead?*

A sinking feeling settles uncomfortably in my gut. I want to ask her about these times ahead, but she answers my thoughts with a grave look. 'Careful, Ethan, you need to watch your thoughts when you're in mixed company.'

'I'll work on it, but these harder times you speak of –'

'Until you become expert at keeping your thoughts hidden, they will not concern you.'

'Fair enough.'

She lifts her chin and walks on, her steely profile letting me know she's done talking. We remain silent until she stops before a pair of white doors with gold trim and two palace guards standing at attention.

The guards turn sideways as a man in a baggy white suit with long brown hair opens the doors. 'My lady.'

'Janah.' Lady Devine gives me a cursory glance and leaves quietly.

'Come in, Ethan,' Janah says. 'My Lord Dartemis is eager to see you.'

I walk into a spacious open-style living area where high ceilings, walls of clear glass, and white furnishings give a sense of serenity and space. Glass doors open to a shaded garden with views across the northern hills. Paintings depicting warfare throughout the ages hang or sit on stands around the room including the Battle of Kadesh, War of the Roses, a number of different Crusades, and one particularly realistic painting that catches my eye of Vietnam. The helicopters look as if they're bearing down on me, drawing me deeper into the immortal's space.

I pick up an eerie sense that someone is watching me and glance up a marble staircase to a balcony that sweeps back around to the entrance. About halfway along I spot a pair of white lions sniffing me through the rails.

*Whoa.*

It's unnerving, and it takes an effort not to plot my escape.

The lions get fed up with waiting and romp downstairs, leaping over furniture in what looks like a race where I'm the prize and the winner takes all.

'*Prohibere!*' the immortal calls out in Latin. The lions slam to a halt right in front of me.

As Lord Dartemis casually makes his way downstairs the lions, one male with a magnificent golden mane, the other female, sniff my hands hanging by my sides. They rub their faces against them, their bodies against my legs, emitting deep purring sounds like kittens.

I drop to my haunches and run my hands over their coats. They smell fresh, as if straight from a bath of perfumed water. I breathe it in and sigh as my head fills with a sense of peace I haven't felt in a long time.

With his eerie luminous skin, unusual, oval-shaped eyes of gold, Dartemis stands in front of me staring. He holds out his hand. I take it and his light touch catapults me to my feet.

He tilts his head as his lions rub against my legs and try to climb up. 'They have taken to you as if they have known you all their lives. Do you have a special affinity with animals, Ethan?'

'Not that I'm aware of, my lord. I like animals. They don't judge. They love unconditionally, and I'm fairly sure they can see through everyone's crap.'

His eyebrows shoot up, but he doesn't say anything about my choice of words.

'You wanted to see me, my lord?'

'Yes, come and sit a moment.' He looks at Janah waiting quietly in the background. 'Could you bring us some tea?'

Janah nods and heads downstairs. Dartemis gives the lions another single-word command and they follow Janah, who pats their heads like children.

'Ethan, until the day Rochelle passed away she led quite a tortured life, first by her mother abandoning her in infancy -'

'Abandoning her? But I thought her father murdered her mother. He's still serving time for it.'

He frowns. Deeply. He's probing my thoughts. I don't bother blocking him. I doubt there'd be a point. 'The woman you speak of was not her biological mother. Rochelle's birth mother is still alive.'

'For freaking real? Did Rochelle know?'

'The two had met, but Rochelle's mother could not bring herself to tell Rochelle the truth at the time.'

*I can't believe this. Rochelle will never know she had a mother, a mother that was in her life the whole time.*

I shake my head. My mind spins. My gut churns. My entire body aches for the girl and all that she missed. I glance up at Dartemis' powerful eyes. 'Who is it? Tell me her name.'

'Ethan, I cannot do that without her permission. This woman confided in me. It might ease your pain to know she is sorry for her mistakes and has sought forgiveness, but she cannot yet forgive herself.'

'I hope you didn't forgive her too easily. The woman doesn't deserve peace.'

'You are angry, and it was not my intention to bring you here to upset you.'

'Why did you want to see me?'

'Rochelle was a remarkable girl.'

'I know that.' I hit my chest with a closed fist. 'She's in here every day.' *Every minute.*

His lips press together with sympathy.

'It sucks, my lord. I don't want Rochelle forgotten.'

'You will not forget her, Ethan.'

'I will *never* forget her, my lord. But it wouldn't be right that I be the only one to remember her after everything.'

'That's what I wanted to talk to you about.'

Janah returns with a tea set on a silver tray that he lowers to a small table.

While we sip herbal tea, Dartemis says, 'Today, I intend to posthumously award Rochelle the Guard's highest honor so no one will forget the sacrifices she made.' He leans towards me, his oval eyes penetrating deep into mine. It's hard to hold his gaze but looking away proves impossible. 'Ethan, will you accept this award on Rochelle's behalf?'

My mouth dries up and no words come out. I lick my lips and nod. 'I would be honored, my lord.'

'Good. Then let us get started. Everyone is waiting in the Arena for my inaugural formal address, but to keep the identity of the Named safe, I will present Rochelle's award in the Tribunal Meeting Room first. When the time is right, Rochelle's story will be written up on the Honor Wall for all to see.'

'I understand.'

'Excellent. You had best get along for you have yet to change, and I have other things to discuss at the meeting with the Named and my Tribunal that I do not want you to miss.'

Arkarian is waiting outside Dartemis' chambers, dressed in a silver robe. 'This way, Ethan.'

I follow him to a guest room where a deep purple tunic lays across the bed. I recall the colors of Rochelle's initiation as I slip the garment on, wrapping the gold rope around my waist. Now I'm wearing them to honor her death. The irony is not lost on me, and as I stare at my reflection in a full-length mirror, my breath catches before it escapes in a long shudder.

Arkarian's hands come down on my shoulders releasing calming energy into me. I soak it in. By the time he lifts them I'm feeling a little steadier. 'Thanks for that.'

He smiles. 'Are you ready?'

I remember the room from our Initiations, though today those functions seem such a long time ago. The Tribunal members are here already, all but Lady Arabella and recently departed Lord Alexandon. Everyone else sits as they always do in the form of a clock-face, with our King Richard at the first point on the right.

Today, the Named sit on the inside in a semi-circle facing Lord Dartemis at the head. Everyone is dressed in formal tunics and robes.

Arkarian and I walk to the two vacant seats in the center. Isabel, Matt and Neriah are on the left, Dillon, Jimmy and Dad on the right. Naturally Arkarian sits beside Isabel, leaving me the seat next to Dillon, who mumbles something under his breath that sounds like a string of impatient dribble.

'You got somewhere else you'd rather be?' I ask.

'Nah. Why?'

I stare at his bouncing knee.

He laughs.

Whether he admits it or not, he's suffering from nerves being in here. Rochelle always did, though she wasn't fidgety and thought no one noticed. I did. But I noticed everything about her.

Matt leans forwards and gives me a nod while Neriah and Isabel give me small smiles. Isabel stretches her hand out and gives my arm a quick squeeze. Arkarian catches her hand on the way back, keeping it locked on his lap. The sight of their joined hands makes my gut churn.

Isabel notices and gently tugs her hand from Arkarian's. I shake my head at her, but it has no effect. Once she makes up her mind, well... that's Isabel. A more caring soul would be hard to find. Maybe it's part of her healing gift, looking out for others. Arkarian hears my thoughts and smiling sadly, he nods.

Lord Dartemis walks in, and in a black suit and long coat, his light brown hair hanging to his shoulders, his yellow-gold eyes shifting over each of us, he carries a more commanding presence than when I saw him in his chambers earlier wearing white. Everyone stands and applauds. This is his first appearance in his new position as the Head of the Tribunal. He lifts his hands and all goes quiet. In a short speech he welcomes us and introduces the award he's giving Rochelle, relating the story of the time she rescued Matt when he was unreachable. Matt keeps his eyes lowered. He reaches for Neriah's hand, squeezing her fingers so tightly that her knuckles turn white. Isabel elbows him in the ribs, whispers something I don't hear but color slowly returns to Neriah's fingers.

I shake my head. What's up with him? At least he still has the warm hand of his soul-mate to grip.

'Ethan, come and stand before me.'

As I walk towards Lord Dartemis, he announces, 'Today I am awarding Rochelle Thallimar the Guard's Golden Heart Medallion, an honor bestowed on only the best of us for courage, self-sacrifice and martyrdom. Throughout our long history, there has only been one other award of this caliber given.'

He indicates with his hands for everyone to stand, and as they do I take the gold box in my hand.

'Open it, Ethan.'

I lift the lid and I'm struck speechless. My eyes flutter to the immortal's and down again. It's a pyramid-shaped crystal of a size that would fit in my hand with an impressive stone set into the top. I lift it to catch more of the light, not sure at first what I'm looking at, but this gem has the cut and shimmer of a rare purple diamond. I glance up at the immortal and smiling, he nods.

Leaving the lid open on the priceless medallion, I turn to a room that has erupted in applause. First one royal, then another calls out Rochelle's name. Queen Brystianne puts a tune to it. Arkarian and the others join in, and the room fills with the sounds of a choir singing her name.

If only she could hear this.

Damn.

Choked with emotion I close my eyes for a moment. Gradually it quietens and I head back to my seat.

'Due to the recent death of my brother,' the immortal announces, 'I will preside over this Tribunal, officially filling the position of Head of the Guard.' After a round of applause, he motions to Matt and Neriah to stand. 'In my capacity as Head of the Guard, it is my belief that neither of you are ready to take your places in Athens. You will earn that right with time and experience.'

Disgruntled murmurs erupt on their behalf, but soon quieten as Matt and Neriah's relief becomes evident. They hug each other and can't stop smiling.

'You will both complete your education while living in Angel Falls. In the interim you will continue to train and build on your knowledge and experiences in preparation for the time when this Tribunal will need you. When that time comes you will have no choice but to take up your positions here in Athens.'

They thank him and the immortal motions for them to sit, 'Lastly,' he says, 'there is still no trace found of the traitor

Marcus Carter. A man who resided amongst you, who kept his blood relationship to Marduke secret from all, remains elusive and therefore must be considered a deadly threat.'

Sir Syford stands up. 'Just like his brother, my lord, the traitor is gone, for no one can survive that length of time locked up with a beast.'

'Perhaps that is the case, Sir Syford,' Dartemis agrees, 'but human beings will be safer and I will sleep better with evidence of his annihilation. Our forensic teams have found many traces of him in those tunnels, but not enough to substantiate his death.'

Hushed whispers grow into questions. Dartemis quietens everyone with a dark look from suddenly glowing eyes. 'It is possible that Marcus Carter escaped. If you suspect he is in your Sector, inform me immediately, and remember he is extremely dangerous. Do not approach him on your own.'

Dartemis walks past each of us. 'To my Named ones, you will continue as you have always done, for there will be missions beginning again soon.'

Whispers start up.

He lifts his hands. 'I have recently learned that the Order of Chaos has a new leader.'

Now questions come from everywhere. Dartemis waits until the noise settles. 'My people, it appears our enemy is back in business. Arkarian is tracking their movements as they prepare for another mission.'

'My lord, how is this possible?' Sir Syford calls out. 'The engine room is incomplete. Transportation would be a risk. Inaccurate at best.'

'Then you had better hurry and make it accurate for the Order's facility is only days away from being fully functional. They sustained low casualties due to their use of other-world creatures.'

'My team will do its best to be ready, my lord.'

I hope Sir Syford can be prepared in time.

'As for the rest of you, *doubt* is unnecessary. That's not what we do here.'

'Is he looking at me?' Jimmy wonders.

'No, I believe he's looking at me,' Dad says.

'Nah, you guys are both wrong,' Dillon says. 'That's me he's looking at.'

'No way, it's me,' Isabel argues.

A few of us snigger then, but Dartemis' gaze is hard to take, especially when he's probing our thoughts and finding more of us with doubts.

'Remember, at the Citadel's heart is technology of unsurpassable intellect.'

He gets my attention with this, taking my mind off the possibility that Carter is out there somewhere plotting revenge. I lower the lid on Rochelle's diamond medallion.

'This technology has the capability to see the future.'

Lord Meridian shoots up out of his seat, 'How is that possible, my lord?'

Dartemis nods at the smallest Tribunal member, and turning, he returns to his seat. 'The intelligence I speak of was created by my ancestral Gods many millennia past, when Earth came into being and had begun the long process of cooling down. Those Gods watched Earth and human development carefully. They passed on all that they had learned into humankind's evolving DNA structure. Then, when the time came, humans would possess the capability to advance in the most favorable direction for survival.'

A tremor runs through my spine from top to bottom. How many knew this ancient superior technology lay at the heart of our time-shifts? And who knew of its origins?

'The more this advanced technology learned about humankind, the closer it came to making accurate future assessments.'

'That's why it was imperative the past not change,' I murmur under my breath, now understanding the importance of our missions. We needed to stop interference.

Dartemis nods. 'Yes, Ethan, and much of this manipulation of the past was my sister's attempts to carve out a future to suit her.'

'We've made mistakes in the past, Father,' Matt says.

'Yes, my son, but those mistakes were made by human operators, by those who believed they were smarter than immortal minds and superior technology, and by those who thought to manipulate the future.'

It's as if I've had the wind knocked out of me. When I look up, the immortal is studying me, waiting for me to word my question. 'Are you sure, my lord, that the Order is working without their Goddess, without Marduke, without Mr Carter and probably without their magician as well?'

Besides me, Dillon's nervous jumping has settled down. If anything, he's gone quiet, and still.

Lord Dartemis notices too and while watching him, closes his eyes. What can he be doing? Assessing Dillon? Testing his loyalty or something? But then Lord Dartemis's focus shifts back to me. 'Yes, I am sure, Ethan.'

Dillon squirms and leans forward over his knees as if he's about to throw up.

I shoulder him lightly. 'Are you okay, buddy?'

'Yeah, yeah,' he whispers, and as the immortal moves back to his position he whispers, 'I'm, ah, just surprised he knows so much for someone who's been in hiding for a few thousand years.'

'Whoever leads the Order today,' Lord Dartemis announces in a serious voice that carries to the edges of the large room, 'they will have plans to seek revenge on us all for eliminating their Queen and their General. The Order will do anything to succeed. They will crush the people of Earth. It's up to us to stop them. Lathenia was willing to kill her own brothers to achieve her goals. I survived because my brother kept me from her reach. Now an unknown leads the Order. You must all work on identifying and eliminating this new leader. It is imperative to the survival of humankind.'

# Chapter Eight

## Jesilla

It's Sunday morning. The days are passing quickly. The school break is almost over. Lucky for me building repairs keep the school closed for an extra twelve days. It re-opens on Thursday for second semester. Today is my last session with Keziah and I'm excited. I'm so excited I could do cartwheels.

Reigning in my enthusiasm with a deep breath I approach Keziah's bed with cautious steps. As with the girl in Room 3, I have to work in increments between sleeps for their bodies and minds to accept the changes. Sleep has the restorative and healing qualities needed for those with supernatural powers in their DNA.

I fold the bedsheet down to Keziah's hips, exposing his bare chest, and then stand back and admire my handiwork.

*Damn*, I'm good.

I've restored Keziah's physical body back to the man he was in his early forties. He now has a well-shaped muscular physique, and even though he's still lying down, I can see he's become taller. Maybe not as tall as Bastian, who's six feet three, but Keziah will be able to stand without stooping; resuming the height he once was before age shrank his bones. Of all the changes, he will love this one most.

*Whoa, look at that hair.*

Keziah's thin white hair is now thick, dark brown and shoulder length, but with a little white creeping through the sides. I can't help smiling. This is like the most amazing thing

I've done in my life so far. It's huge. It's mega. The scientists on Level Four would go crazy if I could share this with them.

If only my mother could see Keziah now. She wouldn't think so poorly of my powers today. It's why she kept me under strict protection with bodyguards everywhere I went. Her lack of faith in my powers made it hard to strike out, to even attempt something different to training and retraining the skills I knew.

'What are you looking so smug about?'

I jump at Bastian's voice from the door. So caught up in my handiwork, I didn't hear him enter the clinic. I wave him over. 'Come see for yourself.'

He stares down at Keziah for so long I get fidgety, while inside I'm still buzzing and trying not to show it.

Finally his eyes lift. 'You did this?' He looks around as if he's going to find the old Keziah hiding in a corner. 'Is he alive?'

Rolling my eyes I toss him a stethoscope from a stack of medical implements hanging on the wall. He catches them and listens to Keziah's heart, then looks at me with his wide mouth hanging open, his eyes staring with a mixture of shock and admiration. 'Jes, this is blowing my mind.'

His praise makes me want to smile again. So I do.

He stares at me, then shaking his head he flicks his fringe off his forehead with a puff of air aimed upwards. 'So this really is Keziah?'

'Who else would it be?'

'He was so near death, it's like you resurrected the man.'

'I didn't do anything except reverse the effects of aging,' I explain. 'He wasn't dead, and if you'd stuck around that first night when I got back you wouldn't be in such shock today.' Which reminds me of something, and I ask before I think how it sounds, 'You've been taking off a lot lately, where have you been going?'

He ignores my question by asking one of his own, 'Will he stay young, or will this...' He shrugs. 'I don't know, wash off?'

'It's not a fake tan, Bastian. It's not a facelift or makeup.'

He cracks up, his laughter rippling with sarcasm and I want to slap him.

Then kiss him.

Oops. I hope I kept that thought concealed. 'I don't know why I have this power. Maybe I can only use it once to save Keziah so he can continue where my mother left off, or keep mentoring us.'

'How did you do it? Tell me everything.'

'Well, when Lathenia realized I had power to shrink inanimate objects, she enhanced it to include living things.'

'That's still a far cry from this.' He rolls his hand, palm upwards, over Keziah's body.

'You know how my mother was always getting me to practice?' He nods. 'One day I finally did it. I shrank a mouse, remember?'

His mouth twitches upwards at the corners, one side higher than the other.

*It's an adorable look and I can't take my eyes off the corner of his mouth that's highest, wondering how it would feel to kiss him there.* My heart accelerates. It's a wonder he doesn't hear it bouncing like a tennis ball gone bananas.

'I remember,' he says. 'That was an awesome day. You shrank everything. Flies, frogs, even a crocodile.'

I laugh at the memory from last year. 'When we got home that afternoon I went out on my deck, and while I watched some birds feeding I shrank a Blue-Winged Parrot. You know, those bright colored birds that pick out the flower buds.'

'What happened?'

I swallow so I can moisten my lips. It's not a memory I like to recall. I still have one of its feathers tucked away in the middle of a thick book. 'I shrank it so far back it became, well... an egg.'

He gasps and laughs at the same time.

'Don't laugh. It was awful. The egg rolled off the deck. It cracked. I couldn't save it.'

But he just laughs louder, and our voices make Keziah's eyes flicker as if entering a dream state, or waking up.

'So you realized you weren't shrinking these creatures, you were restoring their youth, like turning their body clock back in time.'

'Yeah, but I don't think my power will work on anyone other than Keziah.'

'Why not? I'm counting on you doing that to me when I'm fifty.'

I laugh. For some reason I can't imagine Bastian growing old. 'Keziah's brain stopped aging when he turned eighteen.'

'Like the eternals and immortals,' he says.

'Yeah, like those people.'

'So while his body grew old his mind remained young with a brain that was never going to age anyway.'

'That's why his thoughts were always as quick as lightning.'

'Yet he looked like an old man.'

'I heard that.' Keziah's eyes flutter open. He lifts his hands and studies them. A long moment later he shifts his stare to me. 'Praise the Goddess, my girl, you did it. Bring me a mirror, will you, dear. Bastian, help me sit up.'

I bring him the mirror. He holds it up to see a much younger face looking back. I wonder if he remembers it. He touches his skin, feels the smoothness of youth and sighs. 'You left creases around my eyes,' he says, still smiling.

'I have a plan.'

'I did not think it would take you long.'

'What plan?' Bastian asks. 'It had better include me.'

'Of course it does.' I then lay my hand on Keziah's arm. 'You, sir, are Kevin Quinn, who has returned to Angel Falls after losing his wife in a tragic car accident. You want to reunite your daughters with their homeland and spend time with your sister,' I point to Bastian, meaning his mother, 'before she, well... dies of liver – '

'I know what my mother is dying of, thanks,' Bastian snaps, looking away. He never talks about his mother. An alcoholic, she would go on benders that lasted months and when he didn't hear from her, he assumed she abandoned him. The truth is she was scared to be with him, afraid she might harm her only child. She left when he was four and then again when he was eight, and at twelve she never planned to return but she got sick.

'Sorry, Bastian. You're OK with this right? It's a good plan.'

They both stare at me as if I've lost my mind. 'What's wrong?' I turn to Keziah and clarify his role, 'You want to see your children finish their education here in Angel Falls. It's vital in your opinion, considering that you're a teacher and looking for work.'

He rubs his chin. 'Well, then, *daughter*, you had better fill me in on the details so I can adequately impress the school Principal. I believe there is currently a vacancy at Angel Falls High School for a history teacher.'

Bastian is still staring, his mouth open, eyes sharp and fixed on me, his adorable smile nowhere in sight. His rudeness is starting to annoy me. 'What's up with you?'

'You want me to play your cousin?'

'Yeah, it gives you cause to "watch out" for us, you know, like an older brother.'

Keziah puts the mirror down and watches us.

'Why didn't you run this plan past me first? What about working together?'

'I don't work well with people.'

'I'm not people,' he spits out. 'How long have I lived here?'

'So you're staying now and not running off to join the Guard? Maybe if you'd told me I would have included you in the decision process.'

'I was always staying. This house is my home.'

'Whatever.'

He strides over and stands in my space. 'Don't say *whatever* to me.'

I inhale a deep breath. 'Lathenia is dead. I make the decisions now.' I lift a hand to my hip. 'And if you want to stay in this team, you have to be willing to do as I say.'

He shakes his head, disgust darkening his eyes. Disgust for *me*. 'You freak me out when you sound like your mother.'

'You always followed my mother's orders, so what's wrong with following mine?'

'I thought things might run a little differently now that the Goddess is gone. Apparently I'm mistaken.'

'Yes, you are.'

He stands his ground, towering over me. I look up, and up and hold his gaze. From the corner of my eye I notice Keziah sitting up in his bed looking amused.

'Do you want to be in charge?' I ask. 'Is that it?'

He huffs, blows his sun-lightened fringe to smithereens. 'I'm fine with being your right hand. For God's sake, Jesilla, I'll even be your driver if that's what you want. I'll do anything except play the role of your brother.'

'Cousin. Not brother.'

'Close enough.'

'Give me one good reason why you can't play my cousin and I'll seriously think about changing it.'

'It's... it's family.'

He flicks his glance to Keziah, who gives him a commiserating grimace. He looks back at me, his eyes so intense they're probing my soul. 'I thought it was obvious, but apparently you only see your own needs.'

'That's not true,' I yell. 'That's not even fair.'

'Isn't it? Then give us the details of your plan.' He folds his arms across his chest and murmurs in Keziah's direction, 'This should be interesting.'

I hesitate because there's nothing like sarcasm to screw with your confidence. I want Bastian's support. We're a team. A good team. I can't stand the thought of fulfilling my mother's dream to unite the world under one ruler without Bastian's support.

So maybe I should have brought him in on this particular plan earlier. *Damn it. I'm a fool.*

But... there have been times when I didn't want this, when I craved to be a normal girl with no powers and no concept of other lifeforms. Right now, with Bastian peering down at me with his bottom lip curled up, cold judgment in his eyes, I would swap everything to be that normal girl.

To lead an ordinary life.

But I can't be like other people. The powers that make me who I am require strength to control. It's not as if I can ignore them. I have to be amongst my own kind to enjoy anything that resembles normal, and that's Bastian. I'd honestly be lost without him.

Both of them are still looking at me, waiting. 'I want to keep my mother's dream alive. I want to finish it for her.'

'Which is what, exactly?' Bastian asks. 'She wasn't always forthcoming with me.'

'My mother always said that humans understood chaos better than any other race or realm in the universe. Brutality came into their living rooms through entertainment consoles, feeding them terror on a daily basis. The human child knows no other way. Most of the games they play are violent. They grow up with it. They can't get away from it. By the time they're adults they're so numb that nothing shocks them. My mother used their own violent ways to carve out a future where she could become their one true leader so she could unite the races and fix the Earth's problems. Her plan is – *was* – to turn the Earth into a better functioning, safer environment for us all to live in.' I glance at Keziah. 'Wasn't it?'

Bastian shifts his gaze to Keziah too, who suddenly gets busy searching in his empty bedside drawer.

'How was the Goddess going to achieve all that?' Bastian asks, still looking at Keziah.

'It's why we made those missions into the past,' I explain when Keziah stays quiet. 'To change integral parts of history to make sure the future took the direction she knew would be best for Earth.'

'For Lathenia to take control over the Earth, don't you mean?'

I shrug. 'Same thing.'

He opens his mouth as if to argue the point but closes it again.

'Okay,' I throw my hands up, 'I admit that some things my mother did were harsh.' I tug Keziah's hand out of his empty drawer with a look I imagine a parent would give a recalcitrant child. 'Is Bastian right, Keziah? Did my mother want to take over the world for her own pleasure, or to fix the Earth?'

His eyes are round and large when he looks first at me, then Bastian. 'Our Goddess believed she had to have complete control to augment the changes she knew would save the Earth,' he says. 'She needed to be in charge of the world to implement what some might say are harsh decisions. They would not give their consent otherwise. But if anyone could fix the problems of this world, it was your mother, my dear,' he says, his voice strong with conviction.

I sit in the visitor's chair not sure what to think except, whatever my mother planned, she can't do it now and that it's my fault. I get up and look Bastian straight in his eyes. 'Are you going to be stubborn about this or fall in line?'

'Jesilla, I don't want to play the role of your cousin.'

'But why not?'

He moves closer. Now there's nothing between us and his warm breath tickles my forehead. I don't move a muscle but watch as the gold leafy flecks in his eyes start to glow. He says, 'Because... because I –'

'Ugh-umm.' Keziah makes the sound of clearing his throat. 'If I might interrupt a moment,' he says. 'I'm still the eldest here, and have more experience than both of you put together.'

This brings a grin to our faces and I move up close while Bastian makes himself comfortable sitting near his feet.

'So how about for today I have the final word on who takes what position. It seems to me the most important role is with the girl lying in Room 3, and who will be with her the most.' He looks at me. 'How is your work with her progressing?'

'You rejuvenated someone else?' Bastian makes it sound dirty.

'Not exactly, my boy,' Keziah answers with a raised eyebrow at me. 'You haven't told him?'

When I don't answer, Bastian asks me directly, 'What's going on, Jesilla? Who's the girl in Room 3?'

'Someone Keziah brought back from the brink of death.' I shrug as if it's no big deal, even though what Keziah did was a very big deal. 'I'm in the process of giving her the memories she needs for her new identity. I'm containing her powers so she can fulfil her role as my sister and your cousin.'

'Jesilla, what have you done?'

# Chapter Nine

## Jesilla

Keziah is doing so well in his rejuvenated body, leaving me more time to spend with the girl in Room 3. She's awake throughout the day now, passing the time reading, writing reviews and posting them on the blog created for her by Bastian's father, Peter, our resident computer engineer. On my instructions, Peter made her blog sound and look like something a smart nerdy teenage girl would do.

And now that I'm sure I've contained all of Rochelle's powers and established her identity, tonight I will give her the last of her new memories. Since we're sisters born only a year apart, it's reasonable that she and I share the same ones, like home, holidays, our past school, those sorts of things. Those I select are the only ones she will be able to recall.

As she falls into a deep sleep, I gingerly pull the cover down to her hips. One more session and she'll be ready to join her new family with no memory of her past life. Last night Keziah finished healing her chest wound. I switch on the overhead lamp to examine his work. He's a good healer, but this is something else. He had to re-build bone, blood vessels and muscle – heart muscle. He healed what he could on that first day but he was so weak himself he couldn't ensure that he'd left no scarring.

Any marks could give the game away.

Satisfied, I switch off the overhead light with a smile. There's no sign of where an arrowhead pierced her rib cage. No one will pick it out, but it's more important that *she* doesn't suspect that almost four weeks ago she sustained a lethal injury to her chest.

I pull the cover back up, pour some lavender oil in the infuser and ignite it. Dimming the overhead light, I take a deep breath and place my hand gently on her forehead. I draw on the source of my energy and wait for it to flow into my hands. The rush expands throughout my body and I give a silent gasp. It's always this way when I draw on energy so pure. My hands feel like gloves filled with too much water. The skin is tight, fingers swollen and glowing with red light. When working with the mind, one wrong move can incapacitate it in a variety of ways, none for the better. Keziah taught me most everything I know but it was my mother who taught me this. Even though she had little faith in me, she was a good teacher. She showed me precisely what part of the brain holds our memories and their links to all the other areas, depending on what the memory is. She taught me how to examine them, and well, not so much remove them, as that could cause damage, but to disassociate them from reality. You could say, putting them to sleep, ensuring the real memories remain out of reach. And most importantly, Lathenia taught me how to insert memories – in this case mine, with some imaginative twists for Rochelle. After all, we're not twins. Rochelle will need her own identity, and I'm making it as far from her old self as I can.

She will of course need a new name. I've chosen *Crystal.* I embed it into her memory with every session.

I work through to dawn, exhausted and sleep deprived, but aware of how close I am to finishing helps me to push on. School starts back in a couple of days, nearly two weeks longer than other schools due to building repairs, and I need everything to be perfect. Rochelle – *Crystal* - and I are going to be the two new girls, sisters in Years Eleven and Twelve.

Before I finish the session, making sure to keep my hand still on her forehead, I increase the intensity of my will. When the red glow spreads from my hands to encompass her whole head, I close my eyes and speak directly into her vulnerable mind, '*Sister, when you open your eyes the first thing you will remember is your name, Crystal – C-R-Y-S-T-A-L - Crystal Quinn.*'

# Chapter Ten

## Jesilla

Straight after the long session with Rochelle, I head up to my room. I'm so tired I don't bother sliding between the sheets but crawl over the top until my head hits my pillow. When I open my eyes again it's dark. The stirring of a sense of accomplishment in the pit of my stomach generates a lazy smile. Waking more fully, I feel the weight of a key on my neck. It's Keziah's. He put it in my hand when he thought he was dying. I've been carrying it on a chain around my neck ever since. Sitting up, I listen for a sound, but the house is sleeping. And of course it's silent up on the third floor where my mother shared her suite of rooms with Marduke.

It's the last place I want to be, but I have to do it some time.

Standing at my mother's bedroom door, I shudder with the effort not to turn and run.

But hey, what am I thinking? Nothing is going to happen. Memories can't hurt me. It's not as if her brute of a lover will be sneaking weird looks at me anymore. Or stepping out of the shower and dropping his towel in front of me. I shudder. It's lucky for Rochelle I haven't given her any of my memories of *him*.

It's dark inside. Someone has been here. Made up the room. Drawn the drapes. But it still has that wet-dog smell. How did my mother stand it? *Ugh!* I tug my top up over my nose and hurry across the living area to Marduke's private rooms, closing the open door with a loud bang.

Now I smell *her*. I close my eyes and pick up the scent of my mother's perfume. I wonder how long the fragrance will linger here before this last reminder of her completely disappears.

Pain sears through me. It feels as though I've crashed into a brick wall and brought the whole thing down on my chest. Lathenia is not in my life anymore. This powerful woman is gone. I will never see her again. For all that my mother was, a Goddess who could deal cruel punishment without a blink, who kept her distance from everyone except Marduke, she was the only mother I had. And while she only ever touched me to enhance my powers, this woman, this *Goddess*, was an enigma, and, come to think of it, good at keeping secrets. Her own brothers didn't know she had a daughter. But then, she didn't know that her brothers each had a son.

Using Keziah's instructions, I open Lathenia's bedroom door and make a right turn for her walk-in wardrobe. A full-size room on its own, clothes hang on racks along three white walls, interlaced with shelves, cabinets, drawers and a dressing table in cool white marble. White leather lounge chairs positioned in front of floor-to-ceiling mirrors back on to a bathroom, complete with white vanities, and a claw bath with a glass ceiling for a clear view of the sky. There's a sense of peace in here with no lingering scent of Marduke. This was my mother's private space - away from the brute. Away from everyone.

Running my hand along the wall behind a rack of hanging coats, I locate a small door knob and turn it anti-clockwise. It clicks. The coats roll to my right and the wall disappears to form an opening into a secret room.

Overhead lights come on revealing walls fitted with steel shelves, glass-facing cabinets and racks of weapons of all descriptions. Some are ancient such as daggers, swords, medieval bows and arrows, then muskets and pistols and different gun types up to modern-day machine guns and army-issue assault rifles. Deeper inside are more gun-racks holding hundreds more weapons of a type I haven't seen before. These guns are mostly black but with silver stocks, pistol grips and handguards, where the silver parts disappear, depending on which angle I view them.

What are these weapons doing here? Where did they come from? Spoils of war from our missions? I doubt that. There are too many. Besides, we're not supposed to take anything from the past, though my mother bent that rule a few times, and well, I did too once or twice.

I look around. 'What were you planning, Mother?'

I rub the back of my neck with my right hand. The only logical explanation is that these guns were in preparation for something big. My mind whirls with questions and the room seems to shrink around me. It gets harder to breathe. I need air and turn to go when I notice the domed glass cabinet standing on its own, a gold chest the only item inside. Leaving with more questions than I had coming in here, I lift the gold chest and make my way back to Lathenia's suite without disturbing the weaponry.

Keziah will have answers.

I'm so grateful he's still alive.

The gold chest smells like my mother. Whiffs of it float up and I catch myself looking for her. My eyes take in the contemporary furnishings, glass-top desks, lamps, low tables, and if the drapes were open, a breathtaking view of the upper falls. No one would think that an immortal and a monster lived here and shared this comfortable space.

Except now it has an empty feel.

Empty in the way that no one is coming back to live here.

It hits me that my mother is not away on a mission or downstairs in the strategy room with her chief advisors, or off plotting with Marduke. No, she's gone. She's out of my life and she's never coming back. Not to this room. Not to me.

*She really is gone.*

I sink to the floor, knees to my chest and inhale a deep shuddering breath. 'Mother, I'm so sorry. You were always thinking of me and I couldn't see it until now. On the day of the battle I should have known better than to climb a tree just so I could watch. I thought you'd win. I didn't think you would... that you could... If only I'd gone in a different direction that day. And when the battle was in full swing, I should not have caught your eye when you needed your concentration most. It's my fault that you died. But I won't let your dream crumble. No matter what it costs me, Mother, I promise, I will finish this for you.'

Tears fall and I let them. I'm tired now. Tired of everything. My chest shudders with sobs until I'm out of breath and exhausted. I drift off to sleep where I am against a wall, the gold chest clutched in my arms.

Sometime later strong arms pick me up from the floor and carry me to my room, where they lower me to my bed with a tenderness I've not felt from anyone before. The arms linger around me as if reluctant to leave. I want to see who's being so kind to me but my eyes are too weary to open.

The strong hands tug the gold chest from my arms and set it down on my bedside table.

Peace spreads its soft arms around me as it sometimes does when I'm in that moment between being awake and asleep. A sigh escapes as I slip further into slumber.

'Give yourself a break, beautiful girl. This world is not yours alone to fix.'

I'm dreaming. No one calls me *beautiful*, and the reason is simple... I'm not. My mother was beautiful. In her presence, I was her shadow. I am everything like her but in cloudier detail – like her red silky hair, mine is dull, dark-red and a mass of curls. Her perfect features, her flawless, translucent skin, and her oval-shaped silver eyes. Lathenia looked like a Goddess, where I'm human looking and ordinary with grey eyes, blotchy skin and I'm so shapeless I could wear boy jeans backwards.

Someone is staring down at me, so close his warm breath caresses my forehead. I sense his scrutiny as his thoughts probe inside my head. He tugs strands of hair from across my face, pulling my quilt up over my shoulders.

I want him to stay, but all too quickly his footsteps are at the door, and I haven't opened my eyes yet. I have to see his face before he leaves. See if that genuineness in his voice and gentle touch is also in his eyes.

The door opens.

With slow thoughts and a heavy slurring voice I call out, 'Thank you, Bastian.'

He freezes in the door way. Oh no, I've made a mistake, it's not him. But then he says, 'I didn't realize... I mean, I thought you were asleep.' After a heavy pause he adds, 'You know, Jesilla, when I-I said those things...'

His voice is regretful. He's stumbling over his words as he tries to find a kind way to take back what he said.

I roll over, not bothering to open my eyes. 'That's all right,' I murmur. 'I knew you didn't mean it.'

'Mean what?'

'When you called me... you know... when you said I should give myself a break.'

'Ah. Yeah. About that. Jesilla... I think you might have the...'

I try to keep awake. I try to listen to what he's saying, but my mind drifts into a dream and for the life of me I can't find the energy to stop sleep taking over.

It's late in the day when I finally wake. It's the sound of my grumbling stomach that rouses me. But someone has brought me water and left a sandwich sitting beside the gold chest on my bedside table.

Picking up my sandwich, the water and gold chest, I head outside to my deck, sit on the cushioned chair over-looking the valley, and fold my legs beneath me. With the town of Angel Falls in the distance, the forests and mountain ridges on either side of this vast estate, I inhale a deep breath and open the chest.

Inside is a gold envelope with the Goddess's wax seal on the back, my name on the front. I recognize my mother's sweeping calligraphy. Everything she did was elegant, even her handwriting. I pull out the letter and read her first word, *Daughter*. My hand stills. I'm not ready for this. I put the letter back and find three test tubes in the chest. Two are empty. One has a hair in it.

I hold the tube with the hair up in front of me. 'What on earth?'

A knock at the door is a welcome reprieve. I'm not sure I want to know why my mother left me with someone's DNA.

It's Keziah, Mr Kevin Quinn, or, at least for me, Dad. He looks smart in a navy shirt, purple tie with a dark grey suit, and shoes so shiny it's like looking into a mirror. He runs his hands over his hair, thick dark brown and still on the longish side even after a haircut. He walks in with sure steady steps, not at all like the old man he was so recently and for so long.

'Do you like your new look?' I ask.

He leans down and kisses both of my cheeks. 'My dear girl, in case you haven't noticed, I love the new me.' He twirls. 'I should make a good father and a great teacher, don't you think?'

'Yeah, but you'd better ditch the *Armani* outfit when you front your classes. Angel Falls is hardly the Eastern Suburbs of Sydney... *Dad*.'

His smile deepens.

'Come join me on the deck?'

He follows, sitting in the chair beside me. His eyes fall to the open gold chest and all remnants of his smile fades. 'Your mother knew you wouldn't simply accept her word, so she left you something you could prove for yourself.'

'And what would that be?'

He frowns, glancing at the chest again and lifts a pronounced dark eyebrow.

I hold up the envelope, unbroken seal facing.

'Ah. Then I should leave you to get on with it.'

'I don't think I'm ready to read it,' I admit, looking across at him. 'What does the letter say?'

He studies me for so long my face grows hot and I don't think he's going to answer. He clears his throat. 'The letter says many things that you need to hear in her words.'

'Like what?'

He gets up and walks over to the railing where he looks out over the township far below for a minute before he turns and thrusts his hands deep into his pockets. 'Your mother never told you. But Rochelle – sorry, *Crystal* – is your sister.'

'*What?* But how?' I walk over and grip the railing beside him with trembling fingers.

'You have the same father. But you are still Lathenia's only child.'

'But... but...' the denial dies on my lips as questions swirl through my mind. 'Why did she wait until after she'd gone? Why couldn't she tell me face-to-face?'

With his hand under my elbow he walks me back to the deckchairs. 'Sit down, Jesilla.'

His younger features are a picture of genuine concern, *like a real father.* 'Are you sure there's no chance you could be my – *our* – father? I wouldn't mind, you know. I'd be happy about it.'

He shushes me gently. 'I would be proud to be your biological father, but it's not me.'

I nod, unable to keep disappointment from showing. 'So who is it?'

'Before I explain any more you should know that your mother wanted a child. If she could have created you without the assistance of a man, she would have, but the truth is she loved your father.'

'Name. Please. Now.'

'He was a king.' He raises his hand. 'If you want to know more, read the letter your mother left you.'

'Kez!'

The hard set of his jaw, his lips pressed together, tell me that's all he's going to say. And that sucks because I can't deal with this yet. 'And Rochelle?'

'I believe the king was seeing another woman.'

'Sounds like a gem.'

He laughs, but it has no humor in it. 'In case you're wondering, he never knew about you.'

I recall what I'd learned about Rochelle's father through her memories - incarcerated for beating his first wife to death, and assaulting his second. Or was it the other way around?

*Mother, what were you thinking*?

'Keziah, why didn't Lathenia want me to know that Rochelle was my half-sister?'

He tries to smile but it's more of a grimace with his lips pressed together. 'I don't know. But once Rochelle defected to the Guard, Lathenia's anger knew no bounds. From that moment on everything accelerated.'

'So why now? Why tell me when there's no chance I can question her?'

'Dear girl, I can't speak for your mother now,' he says. 'Perhaps she had meant to tell you soon but death got in the way.' He shrugs. 'Knowing this truth will work for you.'

'Care to explain what that means?'

'When *their* Truthseers hear you introduce Crystal as your sister at school, they will believe you.'

I nod slowly. He's right.

'You can't have doubts in your head with Truthseers around. It's the one area we could come unstuck.'

I nod again.

'Run the test for paternal DNA.'

I show him the test tube with the hair already in it.

'Ah, yes, that would be your father's.'

I take an empty test tube, unscrew the end, pluck a hair from my head, check it carries DNA material and close it inside the tube. I then lift the other empty tube. 'Well, there's no time like the present.'

'Would you like me to come with you?'

'No need. I can handle this.'

I go straight to the clinic, open the door to Room 3 and walk over to Rochelle sleeping soundly, though not for much longer. Carefully, so I don't have to do this more than once, I tug a single strand of hair from her head. Holding it to the light, I check there's enough root for DNA testing and slip it into the remaining test tube to take down to our lab.

A soft sound draws my attention back to Rochelle. Her eyes flicker. She's waking up, but this time she gets to leave the clinic and move upstairs into a real bedroom. Today she assumes her new life with memories locked and loaded and ready to test.

I glance down at the sister I never knew I had. How different would my life have been if I had known?

She opens her eyes and recognition shows straight away. I've done my job. She smiles groggily, stretches her arms above her head and moves to sit up. 'Hey,' she says, feeling around the top of her bedside drawers.

I lift the black-rimmed glasses she now wears and believes she can't do without. 'Looking for these?'

Smiling with eyes that remember nothing of her former life, her heart-shaped face and emerald eyes beam with enthusiasm. 'That's better. Thanks, Jes. Do we start school today?'

'No, that's tomorrow. Today, Crystal, you're finally well enough to move in to your new room upstairs.'

She jumps up to her knees and drags me into her arms for a hug.

# Chapter Eleven

## Jesilla

Now that Crystal has joined the family, we can't slip up with our names. Mine doesn't change. Since I've been home schooled all my life, my identity remains uncompromised. Bastian is different. Inside the complex we all know him as Bastian, the name my mother gave him. But in the house from now on he's Dillon. We can't risk confusing my sweet little sister.

For Keziah, I chose a name starting with the same first letter. Should we begin to say his real name, it will give us a chance to correct ourselves before anyone notices. Anyway, I get to call him 'Dad'. The thought makes me smile.

My biological father was a king, but since he's not a royal anymore, I suspect my mother stripped him of more than just his title. I would have liked a chance to know the real man, the one who loved women, not the abusive thug he became after losing his identity.

Crystal's room is across the hall from mine, next door to Bastian's. After she settles in, 'Dad' spends a few hours driving us around the valley.

We return home in time for our evening meal. And since it's Crystal's first time with the family, we sit in the formal dining room. It's one of my favorite spaces. With its dome glass ceiling and bay windows, it's more like a conservatory with natural light beaming in from the falls to the valley. The chairs are white high backs, the table white marble with grey swirls. The room's feature is the crystal chandelier that hangs down from the dome's center. With the sun setting early these days, the light is on already, leaving the candles to make their delicate lacelike pattern over the table and across the walls.

As earlier arranged we're testing Rochelle's memory for flaws. Tonight is the last chance we'll have before school tomorrow.

Sitting beside Rochelle, Bastian leans away from her, and when she speaks, he's not maintaining eye contact. He's having trouble glancing at her face. He's the only one of us who knew this girl before. When it was time for her new memories to go in, I took everything he told me about Rochelle and instilled in her not just memories of being a seventeen-years-old girl from South Australia, but desires and tastes and personality traits as far removed from her true identity as I could.

So Rochelle Thallimar is now Crystal Quinn, whose favorite color is pink, who loves to wear short skirts with white t-shirts, short socks with white canvas shoes. She listens to pop music, singing along at the most inappropriate times, and laughing at anything that's remotely funny.

At the first lull in conversation, Rochelle glances into the adjoining living room and further to the entrance foyer, her brow creasing. When I ask her what's wrong, her frown deepens behind her dark-rimmed spectacles. 'Are you sure I haven't been here before?'

Bastian pauses while buttering a bread roll. 'What makes you say that?'

'It feels familiar.'

'Like how?' he asks.

She shrugs.

Keziah suggests, 'You may have come here once when you were a little girl.'

'Well, that must be it,' she says, smiling, though not convincingly.

Keziah and Bastian give me troubled looks. The only way Rochelle would feel familiar in this house is if Marduke brought her here without any of us knowing.

She looks at Keziah. 'Did I like it when I was here, Dad?'

'Why do you ask, sweetie?'

A shiver runs through her. The three of us see it and glance at each other. But as hard as she tries to grasp the memory associated with the sight or smell of this place, she can't. It's not there. I locked her Marduke memories away in an inaccessible area of her brain.

'Your mother brought you girls here to visit your aunt once or twice, so you would have been here with your sister.'

She glances across at me. 'Did I like it here, Jesilla?'

Keziah shares the thought, *You can't have her asking you for her memory.*

I acknowledge this with a barely perceptible nod as I take her glass and mine to him. 'We girls could use a little heavier refreshment tonight, Dad. First days can be daunting.'

I tap Rochelle's glass with a finger twice, making sure he doesn't tip the sedative in my glass by mistake. *Strong enough to last until morning.*

When I take our drinks back and hand Rochelle hers, Dad lifts his glass. 'Let's toast to your beautiful mother. May all the good times we shared together remain in our hearts for ever.'

'How long ago did Mum pass away?' Rochelle searches her memories but comes up foggy again.

Bastian studies the food on his dish, stabbing the fish with his fork, each stab fiercer than the last. 'Three months.' He doesn't look up. 'Your mother - my aunty - died three months ago.'

'Do you remember going to the hospital?' I ask. 'We arrived just in time to say goodbye after that awful accident.'

'Yes, of course. Our Mum was T-boned by a speeding truck, but my memory of the hospital is sketchy.'

I mumble under my breath, 'It won't be tomorrow.'

# Chapter Twelve

## Ethan

Dillon is waiting for me when I get off the bus. 'Hey, bro, I gotta talk to you before the others get here.'

I point over his shoulder to Isabel, Neriah and Matt, sitting at our usual winter table, which is just our summer table moved out from under the trees into sunlight. 'Too late, and once Isabel sees me –'

He runs his hand through his hair, muttering incoherently. 'What is it with you two these days? Mate, it's like she's attached to your hip. Better watch out before Arkarian notices.'

'Don't be ridiculous. He wouldn't doubt Isabel.' An image of Arkarian frowning when Isabel tugged her hand from his to hold mine at Athens comes to mind and I shake my head. No way. Not those two. 'What don't you want the other guys to hear?'

He looks around, his eyes following a bus pulling out as if the motion might help him think clearer.

'Dillon, are you OK? You seem unsettled.'

His focus instantly sharpens. His green eyes glow with a lustrous iridescence. 'Nah, I'm good.' It's weird seeing him so... *powerful*, comes to mind. It's weirder still how intense he is today. But we're all weird and intense these days. Matt's eyes glow like liquid gold, Arkarian's the deepest of all violets.

He glances at the office administration building, then the school car park, but there are kids everywhere and he shrugs. 'Let's just walk.'

While we walk between blocks of classrooms, I remind him not to say Arkarian's name in general conversation. 'Don't even think it. Anyone could be listening.'

'I got it. Sorry, I forgot for a sec.'

'Yeah, well, it pays to be doubly careful these days.'

He shoots me a sideways look, his eyes doing their glowing thing again for a second, 'Mate, I said I got it.'

I whack his shoulder with the back of my knuckles. 'Hey, chill out, what's eating you today?'

Finding a vacant bench at the rear of L Block, we sit and watch a group of Year Eight boys playing hand-ball.

'I don't know where to begin,' he says, leaning forward to support his head with his hands.

'Try the beginning. It's usually helpful.'

He laughs a little and sweeps me a calmer look. 'Okay. About three months ago my aunty living in South Australia passed away. She was driving home from work, turning into a main road when some idiot driving twice the speed limit T-boned her.'

'Oh my God.'

'They got her to the hospital but she didn't make it through the night.'

'Dillon, I'm so sorry.'

'Thanks, bro, but, um... it's just that my uncle and cousins have moved in with Dad and me.'

'Is that good or bad?'

He shrugs. 'I guess I'll find out soon. They want to help with Mum, but there's more to it.'

'You and your Dad could probably do with some help. The company would be good too, unless your cousins are little brats and you have to share a bathroom.'

'Nah, they're not brats and the house is big enough for all of us.'

'So what's the problem, then?'

He sighs. 'It's complicated. You see, my grandfather left this really big house to both my mother and my aunty, and now there's some legal stuff going on with the wills.'

'That sucks. You got a lawyer handling this?'

'Yeah, but that's not what I want to talk to you about.' He takes his eyes off the handball game to catch my eye. 'Ethan, one of my cousins –'

'There you are!'

Dillon is so intense that when Isabel comes round the corner her voice makes him jump and swear under his breath but so viciously everyone around us stares.

She sits beside me and says to Dillon, 'Is this a private party, or can I join in?'

Before I get a word out Dillon says, 'Private, if you don't mind, Isabel. Leave.'

'What?' She's not expecting this.

'Just like I said, Isabel. Private. Now get lost. *Please*.'

She shoots him a death stare and they start arguing.

'Don't talk to me like that.'

'Like what? At least I don't follow Ethan around like a lost dog,' Dillon says.

Isabel gasps. 'Did you just call me a dog?'

Dillon rolls his eyes. 'You know what I mean. Besides, your boyfriend might get the wrong idea.'

'My boyfriend would never get the wrong idea.'

'Maybe if you showed him a bit more attention instead of giving it all to Ethan your boyfriend might stick around more on his days – '

Isabel attempts to swing her fist at him, but his hand and eye coordination is superior. He catches her wrist without even blinking.

Around us, kids start chanting, 'Fight. Fight.'

I step between them and shove them both back with open palms. 'What's wrong with you two? Are you trying to get detention?'

They lower their fiery glares to the ground. 'Well, whatever it is, keep it to yourselves. I'm going to class.'

They catch up, Isabel apologizing from my left, 'I don't know what got into me.'

On my right side, Dillon tells her to stop talking, 'If that's even possible.'

Isabel gasps. 'You got a hide saying that to me.'

Ignoring her, Dillon lays a hand on my shoulder. 'Buddy, I was just about to tell you something important. Something you *really* need to hear. I may not get another chance.'

I swing round to face him. 'I've heard enough today with that stupid argument you two got into.'

'Ethan -'

'I don't care, Dillon. See you in Math's class.'

'Homeroom,' he yells as I take off in a light jog.

I realize I left them together. Nothing I can do about that now. But Isabel finds me at my locker before classes start. I lift my two Ancient History textbooks out. Everyone's rushing now to get to their homerooms.

'I wonder what Dillon was on about? Have you ever seen him so intense? Or rude?' she tags on as an afterthought.

Her question gives me pause and I turn and look into her face. Her eyes are glistening and rimmed with dark circles. Damn. I close my eyes. If only I could find a way to stop from seeing my friend's pain.

'Ethan? Are you OK?'

I open my eyes. 'You're right, I haven't. But Dillon's home life is messed up again. Now he has family from South Australia moving in and he doesn't sound too keen to have them.'

'I didn't know.'

We head off to our homerooms. I want to tell her something. It's probably going to make her think I'm losing my mind. But there's really only one way to say it, 'Isabel, remember in Arkarian's chambers, the first meeting after the battle when Neriah was worried about Matt because she couldn't *feel* his life force?'

I wait for her to say something. 'Uh-huh.'

'The thing is... since I got to school this morning, I'm *feeling* Rochelle.'

# Chapter Thirteen

## Jesilla

No matter how many hours a week I observed Angel Falls High School from the sphere, thanks to my mother's obsession with the Named, making me learn all I could about them, nothing could prepare me for the real thing.

Keziah drives the black Land Cruiser into the teachers' parking area, which, conveniently, he is now. A secret smile threatens to bust out at the thought that I could do something amazing that my mother couldn't, but the guilt that's ever-festering inside me slaps that little bubble of joy back into obscurity.

I sink deeper into the luxurious front passenger seat, usually Bastian's spot if he isn't behind the wheel, but he drove himself in early this morning, said he had some catching up to do. He was lying, but I can't be worrying about Bastian, no matter how my mind drifts to him more than it should. Angel Falls High School is like a second skin to him. He doesn't have to memorize rosters, classrooms, teachers' names, or where the senior restrooms are.

It's the noise that's doing my head in. How do they bear it? How can anyone concentrate in this racket? Especially Truthseers like Rochelle was.

Keziah watches me for a moment. *First days can be daunting, my dear.*

*Kez, I'm not five years old.*

*True, but it is your first time with hundreds of teenage voices in your range.*

*How do I stop them?*

*You will find a way.*

*I wouldn't mind a hint.*

He chuckles in my thoughts. *Single out one voice. Focus on it. Block it. Then try a group.*

While I practice, he swings round and gives Rochelle his focus, 'Since you and your sister were home-schooled back in Adelaide, you might feel out of place for a while, but once you make friends that will wear off.'

He waits for a response. I reach for Rochelle's hand to draw her attention away from staring out the window. She tugs her hair behind her ears, which is now a shoulder-length layered cut, thanks to Roslyn, our chef and caretaker. She also gave her temporary brown highlights. It suits her more than I imagined, especially with her oversized black-framed glasses, which draws your focus away from her emerald green eyes.

She pushes the glasses higher up the bridge of her nose before she glances at me with a raised eyebrow.

'There you are,' I joke, forcing a smile. 'Ready for this?'

She laughs, her smile huge, her perfect white teeth gleaming, eyes sparkling. 'Am I ever,' she practically sings. 'Aren't you excited, Jes?' She pulls her backpack onto her lap, her hands busy inside until she extracts her electronic tablet, and without taking a breath her fingers fly across the keys.

'Hey...' I know exactly what she's doing, but I still query her as a good sister would. 'You're not writing a book there, are you? I'm not sure we have time this morning.'

Her fingers keep moving as she flicks me another mega smile. 'No, not a book.'

Keziah asks, 'What are you up to, darling?'

He indicates her tablet with a downward look.

'I'm writing my next blog. I'm calling it, "*Impressions*". It will be about our first experiences of attending a mainstream school, meeting new people, making new friends.'

I probe her thoughts. Her big smile is genuine. She leans forward and gives Keziah an airy kiss on the cheek. 'See you in Ancient History, Dad.'

'Yes, it's a combined class, so I'll see you both there. Don't gang up on me.' He stares at me as Rochelle exits, pulling her backpack onto her shoulder.

With her tablet in hand like an ever-ready notebook, she taps on my window and peers in. 'You coming, Jes? We have people to meet and places to see for the first time. Aren't you even a little excited?'

I glance at Keziah who's still staring at me. *Congratulations, Jesilla, you've done an extraordinary job with this girl. You might just pull this off.*

*Don't doubt me, Kez. You started this but I'm finishing it. This plan will work.*

*From what I can see, it's working already.*

# Chapter Fourteen

## Ethan

Isabel stops at the door to her homeroom, stepping aside to let a few classmates in. She smiles and nods as they make some comment about the new teacher. As they walk past and see it's me she's talking to, they glance at each other. They don't know what to say to me. I'd tell them it doesn't matter, don't bother trying, nothing will heal the pain residing in the place where my heart once was, but I've found people are funny. They talk when there's nothing to say, but develop verbal diarrhea when there's nothing they should say.

Devan Salter pats my shoulder. 'Sorry to hear about Rochelle. I didn't know her that well. She kept to herself a lot, but, man, she was a *babe*.'

Isabel reaches for my hand and threading her fingers through mine she squeezes it.

Leonie Hill gives me a hug. 'I'm glad to see you're moving on, Ethan.'

'What?'

She glances at where my hand and Isabel's are together. I shake it free. Her face turns bright red. 'I thought... well... it's been a couple of months, right?'

Isabel says, 'Not quite four weeks.'

'There you go, almost a month. Anyway...' Leonie is hurrying now. 'We should go in. See you around.'

Isabel moves to follow, but I tug her back a few steps from the door.

'I should go in too, Ethan. I don't want to land a detention on my first day back. Mum would not be impressed and as for Jimmy -'

'Isabel, stop.' I wait until she takes a breath and looks at me. 'About what I said.'

Her eyes swell with tears. She opens her mouth to say something but I put her out of her misery, 'I'm not turning into my Dad.'

'Of course you're not. That wasn't what I was thinking.'

'Everyone's thinking it.'

'I don't know about everyone, but I'm not. I know how strong you are.'

'I don't feel strong.'

She puts her arms around me but I can't lift mine to hug her back. I'm still as dead inside as the day I lost my heart to death.

'Ethan, this sense of physical presence you're feeling could be easy to misread, especially here at school where you saw her every day.'

I glance at the floor, counting the cracks. My shoulders drop with the weary load they carry. If I'm lucky I'll melt into the cracks and disappear. 'You're right. I suppose I just needed to hear you say it.'

'It would be impossible,' she says softly.

'It felt real. I wanted it to be real. I miss her, Isabel. I miss her *so* much.'

As she moves in to give me another hug, I step back and shake my head. 'You should go in.'

She hesitates. 'I'll see you in the break, near the fig tree?'

'I got nowhere else to be.'

'Wait.' She pulls out her diary, checking our timetable. 'We have combined Ancient History in Period Three.'

'OK, then I'll see you in Period Three.'

As I walk towards my own homeroom a few doors past Isabel's, on the opposite side, two girls enter the corridor from the top end and make their way towards Isabel's homeroom. I haven't seen these girls before, and in no mood for conversation, I keep my head averted as we pass each other.

It happens again, this time stronger than earlier. I get a sense of Rochelle being close. A fragrant breeze from seemingly nowhere swirls around my head, ruffling my hair. But most confusing is the sensation at the back of my neck like a butterfly flapping its wings against my skin.

I spin around but there's only a few straggling senior students rushing into their homerooms, and those two new girls slipping into Isabel's class. I catch a glimpse of the taller one's long red hair tied up in a ponytail, and the other's shoulder-length dark hair. It lifts suddenly, fluttering on one side as if also caught in a breeze. The dark-haired girl stops and flattens it with her hand. My heart, which I have not felt from the day Rochelle died, suddenly beats, slow and heavy and loud like thunder between my ears.

I stand still, frozen in place.

What just happened?

Unconsciously my feet move towards Isabel's homeroom. I have to see that girl.

A few steps from the door Dillon calls out, 'Hey, wait up.' He's running up the hall towards me. He hooks my elbow and turns me around. 'We're in the same homeroom, buddy.' He points back the way I came. 'It's up that way, remember. Come on, we're already late.'

I stand still and breathe deeply. He notices something. 'What's up? You look like you've seen a ghost.' He raises his eyes straight up and smacks his forehead. '*Damn*. Sorry, Ethan. I can say the stupidest things sometimes. Man, am I glad Isabel isn't here. She'd have me roasting over hot coals with a dagger pointed at my throat.'

He laughs and the sound penetrates my haze and I crack a smile. Because I'm exhausted from weeks of fitful sleepless nights, I let him lead me to our homeroom.

# Chapter Fifteen

## Ethan

The class is rowdy when I walk into Ancient History. Our new teacher hasn't arrived yet. I spot Isabel in the last row, but as I move through the second aisle my eyes automatically shift to the desk, second row from the back.

No one is sitting there today.

'Hey, you made it,' Isabel says, suddenly at my side. 'I have our usual seats saved.'

I nod without moving my eyes from the vacant seat. Rochelle's seat. Memories flood in of her looking at me, hating me, loving me, and I can't move. The class goes quiet but I don't care. I forget to breathe and the urge builds inside my lungs. I want to run and never come back. But I've never run from anything in my life and I'm not starting now. She wouldn't want that.

Eventually, because I have to, I draw in a deep breath and it shudders all the way down to my toes.

Isabel slips her hand in mine. 'Please come and sit with me.'

Overpowered by sadness and Isabel's concerned voice, I follow her to the back wall. As she pulls a few items from my bag, she whispers, 'It'll get easier. I promise.'

She's wrong. But she can't understand and I hope she never does. No one can fathom this darkness, this corrosive emptiness, not without losing one's soul-mate.

She glances around. 'Dillon not coming?'

'He had to drop a subject.'

'So he dropped History?' She shakes her head. 'I will never understand that boy.'

A male teacher walks in which has the girls whispering and sitting up straighter. Maybe it's his slick dark hair, tied behind his head, or his grey suit and white shirt that he didn't get on his teacher's salary. When he tugs off a red silk scarf, some girls swoon. I glance at Isabel and she rolls her eyes.

The new teacher gets everyone's attention by standing beside his desk and waiting until every last person is looking at him. When it's completely silent he writes his name on the board and with a tap of his marker he turns. 'Welcome to a new semester of Ancient History.' His voice has authority, his words modulated without being preachy. He moves his eyes around the room, making eye contact. 'My name is Kevin Quinn. I'll be taking this class indefinitely. I have some big shoes to fill in the absence of your last teacher. Mr Carter has been at this school for a long time, and while I didn't know him personally, I was sorry to hear of his tragic disappearance.'

His sincerity sounds real and keeps our attention, but suddenly the feeling of being near Rochelle occurs again. It's the third time today. What is this? What's happening? Isabel thinks it's the sense of being in a place where Rochelle spent so much time. But what does that mean? That part of Rochelle's energy lingers in these classrooms like a ghost?

More likely, I'm imagining it. Or hallucinating.

After fielding a few more questions from the class, Mr Quinn waves over two girls standing at the door, the same two girls I glimpsed this morning entering Isabel's homeroom. I sit forward, elbows on my desk, conscious of a strange fluttering in my chest, like butterfly wings, or moths. Hundreds of them, trapped in the steel cage.

'Come in girls,' Mr Quinn says, introducing them as they walk across the floor. 'Some of you may already have met my daughters in an earlier class today, but in case you haven't, here are Jesilla and Crystal, born a year apart. Jesilla,' he points to the red-head, 'is in Year 12 while Crystal, my youngest at seventeen is in Year 11. She's my baby.'

'*Dad*, enough information,' the brunette scolds to an outbreak of laughter. She pushes a pair of black-rimmed glasses further up the bridge of her nose, keeping her hand over her brow, casting half of her face in shadow.

Between some murmured 'hellos', Mr Quinn indicates the girls can sit wherever they want. They fold themselves into two seats directly in front of their father's desk. He then makes a joke about our grades and that being *nice* to his daughters might earn extra credit from him. His grin says he's kidding, but the girls groan and slink deeper into their seats.

Their embarrassment endears them to the class, who erupt in laughter again, warm and friendly.

With a wink at his daughters, Mr Quinn begins the lesson, explaining how this class is going to run, what options we have, texts we'll be working from, assignments, that sort of thing. While I hear what he's saying, I'm not taking any of it in. I'm waiting for Crystal to lift her head. I'm not sure why but my gut is compelling me to check her out. Only she keeps her head lowered as she watches a screen she's typing on, making her hair fall forward around her face. She tugs it behind her ear but more drops from higher up.

Mr Quinn gets on with the lesson, Ancient Egyptian culture. Half an hour passes and I still haven't seen Crystal's face. I formulate a plan. I shouldn't use my powers in public, I've been in trouble for that before, but if Crystal doesn't lift her head soon, turn sideways, or glance over her shoulder when students respond to Mr Quinn's questions, I might have to do something I shouldn't.

The Guard has a strict code of secrecy. Revealing our powers in public risks expulsion, our memories wiped, and our powers contained. I can't risk that. My instinct, though, doesn't seem to care.

Then Crystal laughs. It's spontaneous and catches me off-guard, a sweet, joyful rippling sound, with a clear, melodic quality and husky undertone that is so like Rochelle's voice that my head spins.

I turn to Isabel. 'Did you hear that?'

'What?'

'That girl. Her laugh. She sounds like Rochelle.'

Isabel grabs my arm, squeezing it to make me look at her. 'Ethan, no. Think about what you just said.'

'But what if... somehow...?'

She frowns, her eyes filling with tears. 'Let's get out of here. I'll fake being sick and –'

'No, I can't leave yet.' I get half out of my chair with Isabel dragging on my arm. I give it a shake. 'Let me go.'

We attract the attention of those around us. They turn, frowning and flicking brief concerned looks at us both. But I can't worry what people think. I have to figure out what will make the dark-haired girl with Rochelle's voice turn around. I can't wait until class is over. What if she disappears as quickly as she turned up?

I could create an illusion but that would be using my powers. If I can avoid that, I will.

I try again to leave my desk, but Isabel digs her nails into my arm. She cares, so I'm not going to get mad at her or make a scene, which might actually serve the purpose of Crystal turning around, but not at Isabel's expense.

'Ethan, stop. I'll ask Matt to probe her mind and you'll have your answer right away.'

'Your fingernails are putting holes in my arm.'

'I'll heal you later.'

'Isabel, I won't break any important rules.'

She raises her blonde eyebrows. '*Important?*'

'I mean *any*.' She still doesn't believe me. 'I promise.'

'You won't do anything stupid?'

'I just want to talk to her.'

'Is there a problem down the back?' Mr Quinn asks, approaching us. 'Anything you'd like to share with the class?'

'No, Sir,' Isabel jumps to answer first, finally releasing my arm.

The redhead, Jesilla, turns around. Half the class does, but Crystal continues tapping away at her keypad.

*Damn it.*

I sit. 'What is she doing?'

'Who? Crystal?'

'Yeah.'

'She's writing a blog about her first impressions of her new school.'

'She has a blog?'

'Uh-huh. She posted her first book review at twelve years of age. She reads a hundred books a year. Does that sound like Rochelle?'

'Rochelle liked to read.'

'A hundred a year?'

I shrug. 'How do you know this stuff?'

'Crystal is in my homeroom class. Her sister dropped her off this morning on her way to her own homeroom. It's a wonder you didn't see them. Anyway, she told us a little bit about herself. Her family moved from Adelaide after her mother died in a horrific car accident last year. They came to live with family.'

I stare at Isabel, scratching my head.

'Ethan, these girls are Dillon's cousins. Mr Quinn is his uncle.'

Walking through the aisles, Mr Quinn hands out homework sheets. The class is finishing already. Isabel smiles at me sadly and when I stand this time she doesn't stop me.

The Quinn sisters are packing up. Jesilla is first to notice me. She nudges her sister. Crystal turns and looks up at me. Our eyes connect and my world spins off its axis. She's wearing black framed glasses that are too heavy for her heart-shaped face. Despite this impediment, no one has eyes like this girl. No one but Rochelle.

Tears I can't stop spring into my eyes. I close them and squeeze, but it makes no difference and my tears spill out.

Glancing at the ceiling, I pull myself together and start over, this time getting down on my haunches so we're even. It makes my suspicions stronger. By God, I could swear this *is* Rochelle. And the sight of her is bringing me undone. Gasps erupt all around, but I ignore them. My hands tremble with the need to pull this girl into my arms and... and... at least pretend I'm holding Rochelle.

Her lips part in a small sad smile. The last time I saw Rochelle smile was at the moment she passed from this world to the next. I will never forget it. This girl's smile is identical. How can that be possible? I study the shape of her lips, their fullness, the curves, the dips. These lips are Rochelle's too.

I need to touch them.

She tilts her head to the side. Confusion takes over, beginning in her eyes, quickly spreading across her face. She blinks and gasps softly, though not loud enough to attract attention. Her eyes shift to her sister, then to where her father is moving around, and she frowns. Returning to me she stares with a searching, probing intensity. Her mouth opens and her lips silently form the shape of my name, *Ethan?*

Oh my God. Did she just recognize me? Did she just mouth my name? Or did I imagine her mouthing my name? No. No. I didn't imagine... I... Could this girl *really* be Rochelle?

Her frown deepens. 'You... I... Have we ever...?'

Her voice... It's Rochelle's. This *is* Rochelle.

My pulse leaps. Blood rushes between my ears. My mouth goes dry.

Her electronic notebook slides from her hands to the floor, attracting the attention of her sister who swoops down and picks it up. 'Crystal, you klutz, what are you doing?'

'Sorry, Jes,' she replies, her eyes still holding mine, still searching, until... as if pulling herself out of a dream, her demeanor changes, her eyes fill with pity. 'Are you talking to me?'

'Uh, yep, I sure am.'

Withdrawing further into herself, she blinks hard as if trying to see me through a fog. A tug from her sister and her expression turns even vaguer. 'I believe you have mistaken me for someone else.'

'What? Is that what I've done?'

'Sorry, but I don't know you.'

'Are you absolutely sure about that, Ro –'

'My name is Crystal,' she interrupts. 'C-R-Y-S-T-A-L. Crystal Quinn. And I *am* sure about that.'

The bell goes and everyone rushes out. I stand in the aisle watching her leave.

Isabel hands me my bag. 'That went well.'

Ignoring her sarcasm, I take the backpack and toss it over my shoulder. 'Thanks for packing up my stuff.' Out in the corridor I ask, 'Did you see which way the sisters went?'

'Nope.'

'Don't be mad, Isabel, I had to see for myself.'

She sighs. She's worried.

'Did you notice how fast her sister shoved her out the door?'

'I did.'

'There has to be a reason for that.'

'Yeah, keeping her sister away from you.'

Mr Quinn walks out, and without catching anyone's eye he strides off in the opposite direction.

'Isabel, when I looked into that girl's eyes, for a second or two I swear she recognized me.'

'Ethan, that girl is not Rochelle. That's your heart missing her, seeing her wherever you can, in any way you can.'

I glance away from Isabel's knowing eyes pleading with me to listen to her logical explanation. 'Isabel, tell me you saw how she reacted to me.'

'Ethan, the whole class reacted. You just couldn't see anyone else.'

'But...'

'You singled her out. You were staring at her with tears in your eyes. God, you had all the girls and more than half the boys crying. What else could she do?'

*Damn*, Isabel's so logical, but... 'How do you know for sure that girl is *not* Rochelle?'

From behind, a heavy hand lands on my shoulder. 'Other than the fact that Rochelle is dead?' Dillon says. 'Sorry, mate, but as harsh as that is, it's fact and you have to face it. This is exactly what I was worried about, why I tried to warn you before you saw her, but was regrettably interrupted.' He stares pointedly at Isabel.

The three of us step outside to a chilling wind blowing. I hardly notice. 'She's so like her.'

'She has shorter hair and a darker complexion,' Isabel volunteers.

'I didn't notice, but those things are easily changed with a pair of scissors and a solar lamp.'

'Sure, but try explaining how she *doesn't* know you. If that were Rochelle, she wouldn't be Mr Quinn's daughter who recently moved from the other side of Australia, or Dillon's cousin, or have a sister. Do you seriously believe Rochelle would sit in a chair beside you pretending she doesn't know you? Come on, Ethan, think about that.'

Isabel is right. It's just... this thing in my gut is my instinct. It's one of my powers. It's the one part of me that I can normally trust.

# Chapter Sixteen

## Ethan

No one is at our table when Isabel and I put our bags down, but then the older Quinn girl comes over. 'Hey, I'm Jesilla, Dillon's cousin,' she says. 'Apparently my sister resembles a friend you recently lost. I hope that having us at your school doesn't prove too hard for everyone.'

She says *everyone* but she's looking straight at me. I search for resemblances to Rochelle but this girl doesn't have any, not even to her own sister, though her light silvery eyes give me a sense of familiarity.

Isabel says, 'Thanks, Jesilla, I'm sure we'll be fine. Would you like to sit with us? The others will be here soon. I'll introduce -'

'Is your sister coming?' I interrupt, to Isabel's withering look. She'd rather I left that girl alone. But I can't. Not yet.

'I asked her to hang back for a minute so I could talk to you guys about what happened in class –'

'About that,' I jump in. 'I'd like to apologize to you and your sister. It was rude to draw attention to you, especially on your first day at a new school. I'm sorry if I embarrassed you.'

'You didn't embarrass me, but maybe you could give Crystal some space for a few days.'

Dillon walks up, throws his bag on the table and pulls out a sandwich. While Jesilla watches him demolish the sandwich, I study her inconspicuously. She's tall and thin with pale skin, and those eyes have a hint of arrogance in them. I think this is what sparks my memory, but I still can't pin it down.

'Have we met before, Jesilla?'

'*Dude*, what were you thinking?' Dillon says around the last mouthful of his sandwich. 'Did you seriously hit on Crystal in class?'

'It wasn't like *that*,' Isabel jumps to my defense.

But I've tuned out. Crystal is close. I search the groups of students sitting on benches in corners protected from the cold wind and soaking up what little warmth the sun has to offer. Then I see her walking this way and I can't take my eyes off her. Maybe this girl isn't Rochelle. She has her walk, her voice and her eyes, and as I watch she curls her hands into fists and thrusts them into her skirt pockets. A frisson of energy darts up my spine. That's what Rochelle used to do to hide her electrically charged hands from public view. After a while it became a habit.

Crystal comes up to me, and I swear she even breathes like Rochelle, softly, through slightly-parted, full rosy lips.

'Hi, guys,' she says, lowering her backpack to the table and glancing around briefly before zeroing back to me. She extends her hand. 'Nice to meet you officially, Ethan. I'm Crystal, and I have a blog.'

Her mention of a blog is something I hadn't expected and I crack a smile as I reach forward to shake her hand. Only, her sister steps between us before our hands meet, turning Crystal around by the shoulders. 'Sorry, Ethan, I don't mean to be rude,' Jesilla says, over her shoulder, 'but Dad wanted us to check in with him before our next class.'

She tugs on her sister's elbow. 'Come on, Crystal, let's go. We'll come back later.'

'At lunch?' she asks sweetly.

'Yeah, at lunch.'

But they don't go more than a few steps when Neriah and Matt arrive. Dillon jumps up and introduces them. Things get awkward when Matt sees Crystal and goes still except for a swallowing movement in his throat. Finally, he lifts his head to me, his eyes bursting with questions.

Neriah maintains her smile through the introductions, though her eyes remain wider than usual. Yep, she's stunned too. No doubt about it. It's comforting to know that I'm not the only one who sees the striking resemblance.

The way their eyes swing to each other's tells me Matt and Neriah are using their Truthseeing powers to communicate. Even though I can't do that, they can hear me if I purposefully throw my thoughts at them, so I warn them to be careful who might be listening in.

Neriah nods as she discreetly watches the new girls walk away, supposedly to check in with their father. Meanwhile Matt pulls Dillon over to an area behind the tree line. 'What the hell, Dillon, who's that girl? She looks so much like Rochelle for a second there I thought it *was* her. What's going on?'

'Nothing's going on,' Dillon snarls. 'Let go of me, Matt, or I'll put you in the ground.'

'Really? That's what you want to do? Well how about a heads-up next time? That might have helped. Don't you think he's suffering enough already?'

I get between them just as vice-principal Mr Trevale comes out. 'Knock it off you two, you're drawing the wrong kind of attention.'

'Well?' Matt says over my head. 'What's your involvement with these girls?'

Dillon gives Matt the same story he gave me, virtually word for word. As rehearsed as Crystal spelling out her name in class earlier. My instinct kicks in again. Something is off. But what exactly? This is Dillon. Our friend since we were kids. He wouldn't hold anything back from us.

But wait a minute.

Before he defected from the Order of Chaos, Dillon worked for Lathenia. She was his boss. Probably his mentor, his trainer, and who knows what else. She trusted him enough to give Dillon his wings. She would have nurtured his powers – strength, and...?

Wait, I don't know what Dillon's other power is. And if I don't know that fundamental thing about him, what else don't I know? What else hasn't he told us?

# Chapter Seventeen

## Ethan

I have to talk to Crystal alone. I think about it all week, all weekend, hardly leaving my room. On Monday morning I'm ready to put my plan into action. They say the simplest are the best, and well, this plan is as simple as it gets.

*Wait.*

*Watch.*

*Find Crystal alone.*

*Ask her questions that only Rochelle would know the answers to.*

So now I'm in a hurry to get to school, to watch for those rare moments when Jesilla isn't by Crystal's side. I'll wait all day, or another week if I have to. The more I watch them the more I learn their routines. This family sticks close together. But the empty hole inside my chest has a companion now. A glimmer of light that shines through the darkness I've been living in these last five weeks. The quest for truth has given me a purpose, a reason to get out of bed.

I take the stairs down from my bedroom two at a time. Mum and Dad are rummaging around the kitchen, probably fixing another breakfast I can't eat. At the front door I call out goodbye.

Dad calls back, 'Keys are hanging.'

I look up at the hooks. He's letting me take the car?

'Drive safely, honey,' Mum calls out.

I'm not stupid enough to question why. I take the keys and thank them both as I walk out the door.

When I arrive at school it's still early enough that the seniors' parking area has only a few cars yet. Directly opposite is the designated teachers' area. As I step out and pull my bag over my shoulder, another teacher arrives. It's not unusual for teachers to get in early, set up their classes, and prepare for their lessons. Maybe Mr Quinn is one of those, and since he drives down from one of Angel Falls' highest peaks, some twenty Ks from a bus stop, his daughters would probably ride in with him.

I head to the senior's rec room first in B-Block, but there are only a few Year Twelve boys making themselves breakfast and a Year Eleven girl curled up on one of the cushioned chairs reading from her Kindle. Seeing her reading makes me think of another place seniors might hang out before classes start.

Walking out of B-block I head over to the admin building in A-Block, where I pass a few of the office staff setting up for the day.

'We don't usually see you in so early, Mr Roberts,' Mrs Carson says, friendly as always. Her voice lowers as she asks, 'How's your mother these days, Ethan?'

'She's great, thanks, Mrs C. Hey, do you know if the Library is open yet?'

She smiles. 'Sure is, luv. Go on through.'

The first door past the front desk is the Principal's office. Opposite is a parent-teacher meeting room and waiting area. The Library takes up the rest of A Block. I push through one of the Library's glass doors and stop at the front desk. My chest flutters as if butterfly wings are beating against it. My mouth twitches into a smile. My sense that Rochelle is close just kicked in.

The head librarian Ms Fenwick sits at her desk. Watching me as I gather my bearings she nods. 'Good morning, Ethan.'

'Morning, Ms Fenwick.'

'Can I help you with anything?'

'Ah... I'll be right, thanks.'

The library has four divisions – lounge area with low-height book racks, comfortable chairs, digital desks and a semi-circular amphitheater that seats two classes at a time. Behind this is the fiction section with rows of high shelves all the way to the wall. To my right is the reference area for silent study, with a dedicated digital space for about sixty students at one time. Beyond the computer desks are six glass-front private study rooms, two of which are sound proof.

Dillon and Jesilla are in one of those.

They're sitting at right angles with laptops open that neither is looking at because they're staring into each other's... *No.* Dillon leans towards Jesilla and, whoa... *whoa,* they almost... *No way.* Really?

There's an intimacy between those two that doesn't sit right for cousins.

It makes my skin crawl.

I shift my gaze before they notice me. Who knows what other power Dillon has, and I suspect Jesilla is more than she seems. What connection she has to the Order is something else to investigate.

That leaves Fiction. Six long rows of back-to-back shelves.

That's where I'll find Crystal.

Ms Fenwick heads off to her tea room with an empty mug in her hand. While she prepares herself coffee, I make the most of the opportunity. With no one in sight but a couple of Year 7 girls giggling over a magazine in the lounge area, I risk it and use my wings, shifting from the front desk to the last row.

Crystal is half-way down, her finger on the spine of a hardback. Before I move or even breathe she gasps and slowly turns in my direction. Seeing me, her eyes widen.

I lift a finger to my lips and walk towards her, my heart beating faster with every step that delivers me closer.

She waits, her eyes moving over every centimeter of my body. I try to ignore my reactions to her scrutiny. It's as if she's drinking me in, locking me into a secret section of her memory.

Returning to my eyes, she blinks several times quickly. My breath catches at the sight of a tear trickling down one side of her face. I keep moving until I'm deep in her personal space, noticing with a spark of hope that she doesn't move away.

Doesn't even try.

We're so close that my exhaled breath stirs the loose strands of hair on top of her head. Her breath warms my chin and makes me tremble all the way into the marrow of my spine. I reach up to the book she was looking at, a book I enjoyed reading myself last year. 'That's a great story,' I tell her.

She says softly, 'I'll keep that in mind. Hello, Ethan.'

I drop my hand by my side to focus on her face. My scrutiny has pink color filling her cheeks and spreading all the way down to the V of her crisp white school shirt. She nibbles on her lower lip, trapping her tongue inside her mouth as if she needs to say more but is stopping herself from forming the words. I want to tell her that somehow I will find out what's going on and everything will work out. But I have to play this right. Only... it's hard because those lips are Rochelle's. I'm certain of it. If I kiss her I'll know for sure.

*Kiss*?

My God, just the thought sends me to the brink of being able to think straight.

Being this close to this girl is harder than I thought it would be. I close my eyes to bring my body and mind under control.

'Ethan,' she says, and with my eyes still closed I'm convinced that somehow the Order has done the impossible and brought my girl back to life. Right now. In this moment, I have no doubt at all.

Opening my eyes, I clear my throat, giving myself a second to recall my plan. 'I'm glad I found you here. The only class we have together is Ancient History and your sister and father are in that class too. Can we meet somewhere to talk, just the two of us?'

'I'm afraid that might prove impossible.'

'Why? Your sister?'

She nods.

'Is she always this protective of you?'

'*Always*? What do you mean?'

'Well, was she like this at your last school?'

She frowns. When she looks at me again, her eyes are troubled as if she can't remember her last school. 'Um... I...' She scratches her head, growing more distressed with each moment she can't recall.

'Hey, don't worry about it. It's not important.'

She breathes, smiling, her eyes lighting up with relief.

'I'm sorry about that. I didn't mean to upset you,' I say.

'There's no need to apologize. I understand,' she says.

'Do you?'

She nods. 'You lost someone you loved very much.'

'*Love*.'

'Sorry?'

'I still *love* her. I will love Rochelle until the end of human life on this planet.'

She inhales a sharp breath. 'But... that doesn't leave room for you to find love again with... someone else.'

I glance away as moisture stings the backs of my eyes. *I don't want anyone else*, I say to myself, because it's true. *I just want Rochelle.*

'You don't mean that,' she whispers.

My eyes pivot back to hers and we stare at each other. She blinks rapidly again and a spark of recognition occurs.

'I didn't say that aloud.'

'But I heard you,' she says.

'You always could.'

Her eyes skitter up and down the aisle.

'They're in a sound-proof room on the other side of the library.'

She sighs, and I bring up my first question, 'Do you mind if I ask you something that might sound strange?'

Her eyes lock on mine. 'Go on.'

'Do you have a scar down the center of your chest?'

She tilts her head to the side, eyes narrowing as she stares at nothing above my shoulder. It's a real reaction. Either she doesn't have a scar, which mean's she's not... or she doesn't know she has one.

But how could something as harsh as that arrow in her heart – and me ripping it out of her ribcage – not be visible weeks later? How could she have no memory of that?

'I don't know what you mean, Ethan. What sort of scar?'

I ask another question, 'Do you remember a day when strange creatures flew across the sky and beasts walked over the landscape looking for prey, and we fought them? You and I?'

She frowns deeply, her eyes narrow. She's trying hard, but in the end she shrugs.

*What in God's name did they do to you?*

'You remind me of someone,' she says, 'but I... can't seem to remember who.'

'That's OK. Maybe you could work on trying to remember.'

She smiles. Pushes her over-sized glasses up her nose. 'Sure, I can do that.'

She slips away, starts walking up the aisle. I don't want her to leave yet. The rest of the questions can wait, but I can't let her walk away without trying one more thing. So I call out to her, '*Rochelle.*'

She stops. Turns, and walks back. 'I'm Crystal. Crystal Quinn.'

Disappointment tries to stab out my hopeful light. But I'm not ready to give up. There are too many similarities to discard just yet.

I take her hand between both of mine. Her skin is soft and warm and holding her feels so right. And then it happens – a spark shimmies from her palm into mine, shoots up my fingers and into my arm. She gasps, yanking her hand back. Glancing at it for only a second she quickly shoves it inside her skirt pocket and looks at me with her eyes wide, her mouth open.

'Are you OK?' I ask.

'I think so. Did I hurt you?'

'Not at all. Has that happened to you before?'

'No, never.'

I bite my tongue to stop from saying too much. I have to be careful not to take her too far too quickly. They've done something to her memories and powers. Getting them back all at once would be a bad idea.

'You have a lot of holes in your memory. Does that bother you?'

She laughs. It stuns me. The rich timbre of joyfulness, I'm not sure I ever heard Rochelle laugh with such abandon. Is it wrong to coax out her real memories if she would be happier without them?

'Sometimes,' she says. 'I try not to let it.'

Not exactly the proof I can take to Arkarian or Matt, or King Richard, but I'm getting there, unravelling the truth like a puzzle, piece by piece.

She steps backwards; her head hits a shelf, knocking a book onto its side. She turns to right it at the same time as I do, and now I'm behind her and so close. 'I have to go now,' she whispers, turning to face me. 'My sister warned me about you.'

My eyebrow rises. 'What did she say?'

'That you're grieving for a lost love and because I resemble that girl, you could find you have mistaken feelings for me.'

I roll my eyes and mutter under my breath, 'She's thought of everything.'

Her eyes dart up the aisle, but quickly return.

She's about to leave me. I don't know when I'll have another chance to be this close. The pull is so strong. I lean down so our foreheads touch. She doesn't move. I'm not even sure she's breathing. I'm not sure *I'm* breathing. Our noses brush. She looks into my eyes, and slowly, watching for a sign of recognition – anything - I lower my mouth over hers.

Only... just as our lips are about to make contact, she's wrenched from my arms by a sister trying hard to conceal the fact that she's seething.

'Well, hello, Ethan,' she says once she has Crystal standing behind her with enough distance to put a bus between us. She tries to smile but it's not going anywhere near her eyes. 'Fancy seeing you here.'

'It's the school library. I come here all the time.'

'I'll remember that.'

*I bet you will*, I say internally, quickly scrambling the thought.

Jesilla takes her sister by the arm and drags her out past Dillon, who is now standing at the end of the aisle with his arms folded over his chest. 'Bro, what happened?' he asks, as if he hasn't the foggiest idea what I'm doing here.

'I was just talking to your cousin.'

'You know, mate, it wouldn't be fair to lead Crystal on. You'll crush her spirit when it sinks into your grief-stricken skull that she's not Rochelle. She lost her mother a few months ago. She's vulnerable. OK?'

I step up to Dillon and look him in the eye. 'I wouldn't do anything to hurt that girl. You have my promise.' I poke my finger into his chest. 'But can you say the same?'

# Chapter Eighteen

## Jesilla

He almost kissed her. He almost *kissed* her.

I force myself to smile for as long as Ethan Roberts is watching. Grasping Crystal's arm between her wrist and elbow, I drag her past Bastian, waiting to distract Ethan from following us.

Ms Fenwick scrutinizes us as we approach the front desk. 'Do you have anything to declare, girls?'

'Not today, miss.'

Walking out the doors, I pinch Crystal's wrist, giving her a jolt of raw energy that travels up her arm and straight to her heart. She shudders, giving me a startled doe-eyed stare from behind those ridiculous glasses.

'Don't call out or you'll be in bigger trouble.'

'Why? Because I like a boy? Because he might like me? Or because he likes me and not you?'

I twist her arm. She can't say things like that to me. 'Call out and I'll snap it in two.'

She makes a few tight-lipped moans while I twist further and pinch her wrist again. She'll have bruises if I'm not careful. I don't want that. I don't really want to hurt her. Somehow I have to shake off this anger.

I start by explaining, 'I'm not interested in Ethan the way you think.'

'But you stare at him when no one's looking. You're obsessed with him.'

I stifle a laugh. She's right but she's wrong too. Not that I can tell her, but I'm obsessed with making Ethan suffer. He has to pay for all the harm he and his people have caused my family.

We reach the front office. There are so many students here now they're standing in rows back from the counter. Two female and one male staff member answer their questions. There are teachers too; one has his head bent down to hear what a softly-spoken boy from a younger grade is trying to tell him. Another is listening to a couple of students in trouble for fighting on school grounds. He threatens them with detention and a trip to the principal's office if they do it again.

I've only been here a week but I hate school already. Too many idiots think they're in charge.

'If it's not jealousy, then what is it?'

Sliding my hand up to her elbow I appear as if I'm simply supporting my sister as we walk towards the exit doors. An office lady notices. 'Are you girls all right?'

I keep walking, forcing Crystal forward but at the same time sparing a smile over my shoulder at the cheerful office lady. 'It's my sister. She needs some fresh air.'

'Oh, poor dear. You girls are Mr Quinn's daughters.'

I nod. *Smile. Keep moving.*

'Are you sure I can't help? The school nurse is in. I could call her for you.'

'Thanks, but there's no need.'

The woman refreshes her smile. 'You're a good sister.'

'Aw, thank you.' I give her my sweetest smile; even scrunch my nose up a little, and by the time I swing my head back round we're walking out the front doors.

The first bell rings, a warning that classes begin in five minutes. In a hurry now, I half drag Crystal to our land cruiser in the teachers' car park. Unlocking it with my mind, I pretend I have a key in my pocket in case someone is looking. Over her protests, I shove her into the rear seat, and follow her in.

'All right, Crystal, start talking.'

She rubs her arm, giving me a confused look. 'That hurt, Jesilla.'

*Whoa.* What was I thinking? I sweeten my voice, 'My God, sweetheart, I'm so sorry. There's no privacy in there. I had to get you out quickly and I panicked. I'm so, so sorry.''

She shakes her head. Mad at me, and rightly confused, she stays silent.

'Crystal, I don't want to hurt you, it's just important that you tell me what happened in the Library with Ethan.'

'Why?'

I glance down at her balled fists and take one in mine, smoothing out her fingers with gentle massage. 'When Mum was clinging to life on that cold hospital bed, I promised her I'd look out for you.' I lift my eyes, pinning them to hers. 'I'm new at this. I'm raw at the edges. But I'm trying. Trust me?'

She shrugs, lifts her eyes to the ceiling while trying to decide. 'I guess. What do you want to know?'

'The words you and Ethan exchanged.'

'All of them?'

'Yes.' She looks confused, so I give her a prompt, 'He walked into the same aisle you were in. You saw each other. Who approached who first?'

'He approached me and we talked... about... the book I was looking at.'

'What book? Who was the author?'

Her eyes widen. 'I-I don't remember... His eyes... they distracted me.'

'How so?'

'Looking into them felt like I was coming home.'

I bite the inside of my cheek to stop the sarcastic retort from coming out. 'Crystal, I think you don't know the name and author of that book because there was no book. Tell me the truth. You met Ethan there on purpose. This was planned, wasn't it?'

'Khaled Hosseini.'

'What?'

'The book I was looking at. *A Thousand Splendid Suns* by Khaled Hosseini. Ethan had read it and recommended it to me.'

Is she making this up?

I peer into her eyes and check her thoughts for signs of deception. It's something I can do as part of my Truthseeing powers with more accuracy than a lie detector.

So Ethan approached *her*. Does this mean he suspects already, or does he just need to be close to the girl who reminds him of his dead girlfriend? Either way doesn't matter since it shows he's suspicious and suffering already. My plan is working, though I will have to find a way to slow him down. There are many forms of torture; this being just one. But torture isn't torture if it's over too quickly. The pain must be long-suffering. So after Ethan proves that my sister Crystal is indeed his love Rochelle, I'll set part two into motion – where he begs me to give Rochelle back her memories of him, and when they're finally a loving happy couple, he gets to watch her die, all over again.

And this time no one will bring her back.

'Honey, Ethan is drawn to you.'

'Because of the way I look.'

'Right. And if you let him get close, he'll break your heart. After all we've been through, watching Mum take her last breath, well, I want us to be closer. That boy will drive a wedge between us. You don't want that, do you?' And with a heavy dose of sisterly concern, I add, 'I care about you, Crystal. We're sisters, and sisters are forever.'

She feels the love I'm pouring into her, and when I open my arms she moves in for a hug. 'I'm so lucky to have you, Jes.'

I release the doors and we go to our first class as if nothing happened.

But I'm still angry inside because she didn't tell me everything. One thing in particular she didn't mention at all. It drains my patience to have to wait until school is over to find out just how close those two came in that library, so at lunchtime I go and see Keziah in his office.

Bastian catches up with me on the way. 'Hey, you still upset?'

I lie and tell him no. He wouldn't understand. What drives me and what drives Bastian are poles apart. Bastian is loyal, and in his own way he loved Lathenia, but I know my mother, and though she's gone now she would be relying on me to avenge her death and follow her plan through to the end. I can't be soft if I'm going to make that happen. I have to toughen up. Like my feelings for Bastian. Whatever they are, I have to keep them under control. I glance at him sideways. He meets my glance with a cheeky wink that has blood rushing to my head.

Yeah, that shouldn't be too difficult.

He takes off to keep an eye on Crystal, while I knock on Keziah's door.

It's a small office with only three desks and fortunately the other two teachers are out. Keziah's not expecting me, but as soon as he sees me, he meets me halfway. 'Come, sit down. What's happened?'

'She met Ethan in the Library this morning where they held a secret conversation.'

He sits on top of his desk and folds his arms over his chest. 'I see.'

'When I came into the aisle, Ethan's head was bent down over hers.'

'He kissed her?'

'I separated them just in time, but their hands were together and from the heightened energy surrounding the pair I think something happened between them.'

'You're not thinking Ethan released her memories?'

'I doubt he could do that. I'm more worried about her powers, and if there's still a connection between them,' I explain. 'To sever it I might have to eradicate every last memory of her other life.'

'Jesilla, it's a fine line when you go that deep into the mind. If you eradicate memories attached to performing basic functions, like movement and speech, or even breathing, you could destroy her ability to function.'

'There are risks with everything. I want to be further along in our plan before Ethan learns her true identity. I'm good at what I do and I'll be careful.'

He turns to the window. I glance over his shoulder. No one is playing their usual games, the day is too cold, the wind icy. Students sit where they can find a sunny spot that's also sheltered.

'Is there any way you can make her *not* like Ethan? That would add to his suffering.'

'Do you think I haven't tried? I would have enjoyed seeing that.'

He chuckles, and the tightness in my chest eases. 'I'll keep my eye on Crystal at school when you can't be nearby.'

'Thanks.'

'Where is Ethan now? Is Bastian watching our girl?'

'Don't worry, Ethan was gone by eleven. He jumped over the back fence.'

'Ah, he'll be visiting his mentor.'

'Now I better work out how far and how deep to take the refresher.'

Let's think on this, Jesilla,' Keziah says. 'Tonight, just give her a general refresher, not deep enough to risk causing damage.'

'Fine.'

'And when you're finished with Crystal, you and Bastian will need to report downstairs.'

I spin around to face him, my heart kicking up a notch as it always does before a mission. 'You had no problem bringing the mission forward?'

'Everything is in perfect working order.' He smiles.

'And the Guard?'

'There's no chance they'll be ready in time.'

# Chapter Nineteen

## Ethan

At Recess, under the cover of trees, I jump the back fence, rocking up Arkarian's mountain without letting anyone know. Not even Isabel. She would have tried to stop me.

As soon as I arrive, an opening the size of a door appears in the rock wall. Arkarian is at his work station, studying the sphere that today is glowing like the sun and spinning at a pace slow enough to catch glimpses of a dry sandy landscape. And while it's fascinating to know what time period is beginning to show, I resist the pull to move towards it.

The sphere is not why I'm here.

Arkarian watches me. Producing two stools, he points to the one nearest me and sits on the other. 'Your thoughts are jumbled. I can't make them out today. It's progress. But now you're going to have to tell me what's on your mind.'

'Did you know Dillon had an uncle and cousins living in Adelaide?'

'I learned recently.'

'Don't you think it's odd that we only just find this out?'

'There's a lot going on in Dillon's life at present with his mother so ill.'

'Sure. Of course.'

In my silence, Arkarian frowns. 'What's this about, Ethan? What's bothering you?'

'Dillon's cousin named Crystal resembles Rochelle.'

He leans forward. 'Isabel mentioned it. She also said there were substantial differences.'

'Slight.'

He says, 'Slight or not, you're going to have to focus on those differences to remind yourself that Crystal cannot be Rochelle.'

'But, Arkarian, this girl is the same height, same build, has the same voice, same smile, same walk.'

'Eyes?'

'Exactly the same.'

His frown deepens. 'Ethan, it's a coincidence that Crystal resembles Rochelle. Maybe it's true that everyone has a double somewhere in the world. Perhaps this girl is Rochelle's –'

'She's not.' The words I need to explain how I know this don't form. Instead I choke up. A golf-ball-sized nugget lodges in my throat while tears blur the room. I need Arkarian to believe me, to be on my side.

'Arkarian, I'm not arguing the fact that Rochelle died, but, inexplicably, I'm still *feeling* her.' I sit forward, my elbows on my knees, my fingers like a steeple under my chin. 'It only happens when I'm near Dillon's cousin Crystal.' I peer at him with my eyes narrowed. 'What's happening to me, Arkarian? Have I slipped into a crazy world of denial? Is my heart fooling my brain? Am I simply seeing things because I want to? Am I going crazy? I feel like I'm going crazy. Or is it possible this sense of Rochelle could somehow be real?'

'Ethan, instinct is one of your powers, but only you can tell the difference.' He pauses. Looks away a moment. 'I don't want to give you false hope. Grief is a painful process that I would not wish on anyone twice.'

'Don't worry, Arkarian, it can't get darker than this.'

'Tell me, Ethan, do I need to investigate?'

'Yes.'

'I will take what you have told me to someone who also loves Rochelle, and mourns her still. No one will explore this possibility more thoroughly.'

I don't have to think long about who this person is. 'Lady Arabella.'

'Yes.'

'That's why she had to go away. She misses her too.'

Arkarian gets up. 'Leave this with me, Ethan.'

'You'll give me updates?' I follow him to his workstation.

'Of course,' he says. 'Now... you have a mission for which you will need to remain alert and completely focused.'

'What's going on?'

He lifts his troubled eyes from the sphere. 'Sir Syford has informed me that while his team is close to completing the necessary reconstruction and repairs, he can't guarantee the high level of accuracy we usually command.'

'Great. So how will this impact our mission?'

'The Order has opened a portal. As long as it remains open, we can get you into the same place and time. With part of the Citadel functioning, it's not that different to how we've always done the leaps.'

'So what's the problem?'

'We're not able to decipher the portal's precise time, so we can't give you and Isabel the information you need to work out what the Order is doing there, who their victim is going to be and how best to protect that person after you jump.'

'Damn.'

'They have a team ready to go.'

'They beat us to it. But didn't they sustain the same losses as we did when the Citadel came down?'

With a sympathetic look, he says, 'They must have been maintaining a secondary system in a secret location we couldn't detect, and once the new Citadel became functional, they were ready.'

'Meanwhile we're way behind them.'

'This is what Lord Dartemis is worried about. The Order has had an over-arching plan in motion for some time, and the deaths of Lathenia, Marduke and no doubt others have not ended those plans.'

'This is not good for us.'

'Not good for anyone. This could be the beginning of a new era for the Order.'

I shudder at the prospect of fighting the Order of Chaos when they're so far ahead of us. 'This mission is important, isn't it?'

'We don't know what this new Order is capable of yet, what their agenda is for the future, how they want to alter the past to shape the future to favor them.'

'We won't fail, Arkarian.'

'I selected you for this mission, Ethan, because your grasp of historical knowledge is incomparable among the Named. But if you want to sit this out, I'll see what I can do.'

'I'll go. When do we leave?'

He hesitates, as if he's re-thinking his selection of me.

'It has to be tonight,' he says. 'On the bright side, Neriah is working hard on strengthening her powers with the brush. It won't be long before she will be opening a time portal with just a few brush strokes.'

'Good for her.'

'Ethan...'

'Neriah has King Richard's brush in her hand all day, every day, practicing those brush strokes in the air, on tables, on trees, but unless she can create a time portal before tonight or link us to the Order's portal, she's no help. We still won't know the year we're going to leap into.'

I force my voice to soften. There's no point in taking my frustrations out on the hard-working innocent members of the Named. They can't feel the emptiness inside me, the sense of hopelessness, the anger and frustration that's become such an integral part of me now that I fear I've become the kind of person I would normally hate.

'Do you have any advice that might help us, Arkarian?'

'Protect your identities. Do not become side-tracked in this place as it will be easy to do so. Isabel will be particularly fascinated with this era. And remember, as soon as you two are ready to return, call out my name.'

'Does Isabel know where we're going yet?'

'No. But she'll be here soon.' He glances from the sphere to me. 'Ethan, you're the leader on this mission. Your decisions are final. Remember your instinct is your strength. Let it guide you.'

I nod.

He turns and grips my shoulders. 'You can do this. And you will have Isabel to help figure it all out.' His hands fall away as he detects a signal that I don't hear. 'Ah, your partner has arrived.'

'Ethan!' Isabel calls out, running down the main corridor, trying doors here and there.

'I will never tire of hearing her voice,' Arkarian says, smiling in a boyish way that makes him appear even younger than, well, eighteen going on six hundred and something. He moves to the door. 'We're down here, sweetheart.'

Isabel rushes straight past him to me, throwing her arms around me, her head on my chest before looking up into my eyes. 'Are you OK? Oh my God, Ethan, you disappeared before a double Math's class without telling anyone where you were going. You could have at least told *me* you were ditching the rest of the day.'

As he watches his girlfriend fret over me, Arkarian lowers his hands awkwardly. His disappointment at Isabel being more concerned with me than greeting him shows in the dulling of his purple irises.

*Damn it.*

'I don't report to you, Isabel. My life isn't the center of your world.' I say these words harsher than I would normally speak to Isabel. I hate doing it, but I can't have Arkarian getting the wrong idea. There is no 'us' and so I set her back from my personal space.

She drops into one of the chairs Arkarian provided earlier. It's then she notices Arkarian watching her from the door, his head tilted, and a crushed look in his eyes. She gasps, her hand swinging up to her mouth. 'Hey,' she says, her voice little more than a whimper. 'H-how goes the sphere? Do you know where we're going yet?'

I glance at Arkarian, scrambling my thoughts on purpose. He has to be noticing the attention Isabel is giving me since the day of the battle. Since I lost Rochelle. And that's the point. He has to know that.

'You two are the Guard's best team,' he says. 'I need you to be the best you can on this mission. Do you understand?'

I nod, and he turns his attention to Isabel. 'Do you think you can do this without taking your emotions with you, Isabel? I don't want to switch you, but if it's better that I do, speak up now.'

'Switch me? Send someone else?'

The tears in her eyes make me feel like a rat. But her tears make Arkarian melt. He rushes over, hunkering down in front of her, linking her fingers through his. 'What is it, sweetheart? What's causing you such heartache?'

She sniffs, rubs her nose with the back of her hand and straightens her shoulders. 'It's nothing. You don't have to concern yourself with me. You have enough to deal with.'

He leans in and kisses her forehead tenderly, his lips lingering. Closing his eyes he whispers words I don't hear properly but sound like, *He will be all right, love*. She reaches up and pushes his blue hair back with her hands on either side of his face. He turns his face into her hands and kisses her palms, first one, and then the other.

I can't watch anymore so I walk over to the sphere. It's slowing down again, moving at a snail's crawl, revealing more details of where our mission will take place.

After a few minutes they join me.

'Have you figured out where we're going yet, Ethan?' Isabel asks.

'Somewhere hot and sandy.'

'A beach?'

I huff. 'Think more along the lines of a desert.'

She glances at Arkarian.

Arkarian manipulates the sphere's angle with the touch of his hand, shifting the view while simultaneously zooming in so people become visible. A few hundred appear, dressed in only white pants that look more like skirts. Their skin is dark gold, reminding me of a mango left to ripen too long on a tree.

Wide slabs of flat sandstone cover the ground, while in the distance a series of stone structures blow my mind with how enormous they are. In front of these are even bigger upright statues with stairs between them leading to multiple rows of decorated pillars.

Words vanish. I'm freaking speechless. Other than our mission to Atlantis, this would be the furthest in time any of us has travelled. As interesting and amazing as it is to be visiting Ancient Egypt, I don't want to be stuck there, and there's always that niggle of doubt in the pit of my stomach, the what if something goes wrong with bringing us back over such a long stretch of time.

Arkarian moves the image to a river that's too wide to see the other side from this angle. Whoa. I spot the nostrils of a hippopotamus swimming in it. No guesses which river I'm looking at. The longest in the world. Hundreds of men are busy hauling huge slabs of oblong-shaped boulders off a boat. It takes a heap of the men to co-ordinate and yet there's a rhythm that speaks of them having done this many times before. Workers yell instructions to each other. But one man standing to the side, with black hair, wearing a white tunic to his knees, a staff in one hand, a whip in his other, shouts orders over all of them. And they listen. Some, I notice, cower, or spit, or give his co-workers a dark stare when he's not looking.

This era spans more than four thousand years, and died out two thousand years ago. I shake my head. Could we go any further back in time? 'You're kidding me, Arkarian.'

Isabel inhales sharply at the ancient sights, the river flowing past the metropolis of pebbled roads and stone buildings, women washing clothes on the green edges under palm trees, cows grazing beside them, and naked children running around squealing like cheeky monkeys.

She turns to Arkarian with wide round eyes sparkling with excitement. 'Oh my God, we're going to Egypt. *Ancient* Egypt.'

Arkarian smiles at her enthusiasm, but over her head he sends me a warning look. I nod to let him know I'll have her back.

'What year is it?' Isabel asks.

'We know that it's the Twentieth Dynasty, somewhere around 1155 BC.'

'So how many years is that from today?' But she figures it out herself and gulps. 'Oh wow, that's a long time ago.'

Arkarian bundles her into his arms and rests his chin on her head. 'That it is, my love. A very long time ago.'

# Chapter Twenty

## Ethan

Neriah arrives for her training session, King Richard's paintbrush as always in her hand. She sees the sphere and calls out, 'Good luck, guys.' She catches my eye. 'You'll be great, Ethan. You're a natural.'

Arkarian shows Neriah to the room they'll be working in this afternoon, telling us he'll just get her started. Back in no time, Arkarian rolls over his workstation chair for Isabel. When we're all sitting around the sphere, he explains how I'll be going into the past as a priest. While I digest this information and try to picture the responsibilities of an Ancient Egyptian priest, Isabel gets the giggles.

Amused, Arkarian says, 'And you will be a physician.'

She points at me, trying to control her giggling. 'Oh my God, this just gets better and better.'

'Ha ha,' I say. 'Priests have more power than doctors in Ancient Egyptian times.'

'Really?' She looks at Arkarian, who nods. She rolls her eyes. 'What about medical tools? Will I get a bag?'

'It depends on what you need. The knowledge, language, clothes and skills you require will be given to you in the new Citadel's wardrobe rooms.'

'Doesn't sound as if much has changed,' she says, clapping her hands really fast like a child who just heard Santa coming down the chimney. 'I can't wait.'

Arkarian shares a grin with me. 'We can see that, my love.'

'But it's *Ancient Egypt*.'

A smile of pure love escapes from Arkarian's eyes as he reaches out and caresses her face.

I glance away before I ruin this tender moment for them.

But he quickly returns to briefing us. 'The king in power will be one of the early Ramses. The New Kingdom is the height of Egyptian civilization.'

'But?' I ask.

'As you pointed out, Ethan, the priests of this time have immense power. They're growing wealthier while the Pharaohs and the Egyptian people become poorer. There was a priest called Amun who fused with the sun god Ra and became the deity Amun-Ra.'

'That's one of the gods we studied in Ancient History today,' Isabel says. 'Amun-Ra, or Amun-Re.'

'You studied that Pharaoh today?' Arkarian sounds surprised. He rubs his jaw, gazing at Isabel as if he's looking through her. But he quickly regathers his thoughts. 'The era you're going to enter comes after the heretic's rule.'

'The heretic?' Isabel asks.

'He dismissed the multiple gods,' I explain. 'He brought in a monotheistic religion of one god, Aten, the sun disk.'

'I knew that.'

Arkarian smiles at her before continuing with the history lesson, 'After Akhenaten's death, Tutankhamun reinstated the gods. He was only a child and his reign was short, as we all know. General Horemheb followed, strengthening the young king's decision. After Horemheb the dynasty came to an end and Ramses One was appointed, beginning the new dynasty we know as the nineteenth. After him came Seti One and then Ramses Two.'

'Also known as Ramses the Great,' I add.

Arkarian nods. 'These two pharaohs left indelible marks on Egypt through their military successes and the buildings they had constructed. You saw glimpses of those in the sphere.'

'Is this the era we'll be jumping into?' Isabel asks.'

'We're getting closer,' Arkarian says. 'The kings that follow are not as successful and Egypt has fallen into a time of unrest. The Trojan War has caused a large volume of human displacement.'

'Refugees?' Isabel asks. 'Even then?'

'Where there is war, there is always going to be destruction.'

'Yep, houses, schools, roads, entire cities demolished.' I should have more empathy for these people, especially the children, the innocent ones from any war, pulled from their homes into a life of begging on the streets and slavery, but the hollow space inside me is still too dark and doesn't allow it.

'The Mycenaean culture has collapsed,' Arkarian says, 'causing more problems with people movement from the Mediterranean areas. Poor harvests are causing widespread famines and now,' he locks eyes with each of us, 'there are plagues and poverty.'

I look directly at Isabel. 'Still can't wait to get there?'

I wait for Isabel outside Arkarian's rock wall so they can have a few minutes together before tonight's mission. When she emerges it's virtually dark. There's just enough light to see her mouth all puffed up. I glance away with a small smile and start walking, hoping this means Arkarian was able to sort out whatever was bothering her.

'What's up, Ethan?' She catches up. 'Why can't you look at me?' She dabs gently at the corner of her mouth with her fingertip as if it hurts.

I roll my eyes.

She grabs my sleeve. 'Stop.'

I wait.

'Tell me what's wrong.'

'It's nothing. Nothing I want to discuss with you.'

'I don't accept that.'

My eyebrows rise.

'I mean... we're partners. You can tell me anything.'

At my silence, she doesn't question me again and we continue walking. A couple of times she glances back at Arkarian's secret chambers, longing in her eyes. I take this to mean their problems haven't gone away with a few steamy kisses.

It's not really my business, but we're about to go on a mission to one of the most distant places in time we've been so far. 'What's going on with you and Arkarian?'

She shrugs and attempts to straighten her messed-up hair with her hands. 'I miss him when he's not around.'

'And he's not around like a "normal" boyfriend.'

She purses her lips.

'He's been busy lately with all that's happened.'

She says, 'It's not that.' Turning around, she starts walking backwards. 'He can't live in my world and he won't show me his.'

'If he's keeping something from you, he has his reasons.'

'It doesn't mean I have to accept them.'

'Fair enough.'

'Arkarian knows everything about me. And all I know about him is that he has a place somewhere that he goes to unwind.'

'You mean his home.'

'That's exactly what I mean. But it's as if he doesn't want me to be part of that life. I feel like I'm a casual girlfriend. Ethan, I don't like secrets between us.'

Yep, that would suck. Still walking backwards, I reach for her hand. 'Come here.' She spins around and walks by my side again, and I throw my arm over her shoulder.

She says, 'Arkarian has lived for so long there are people he's met I've never heard of. Over that time there had to be... *others*, but he doesn't tell me personal stuff. I asked him directly about his home, and he avoided answering.' She glances up at me. The stars catch her tears. 'I don't want it to ever be awkward between us.'

'Do you want me to find out for you?'

'Find out what?'

'Where his home is, and why he doesn't include you in it.'

'You mean you'd follow him like a stalker?'

'I was thinking more like a private detective, but if you prefer stalker that will do. Isabel, you don't think he's cheating on you?'

She doesn't answer immediately and I throw my head back and laugh. The best laugh I've had in months. 'He's not cheating on you, Isabel. The dude *worships* you.'

Her voice barely above a whisper, she says, 'Arkarian has lived a long time already, maybe he even ...'

'Got married? You think he has a wife? Kids stashed away he goes home to every night?'

Swiping at some runaway tears is answer enough, but she adds, 'Arkarian has six hundred years of living before meeting me and I don't know how he's spent even one day of them.'

We reach her house. I walk her to the door. It's dark enough now for sensor lights to switch on as we step onto her front veranda. She needs to resolve this problem, but not tonight, not when we're going on an important mission with potential for errors. 'When we return from our mission tomorrow, you sit down with Arkarian and tell him what you told me. Tell him that his secrecy, whatever his reasons are for keeping you in the dark, is putting a wedge in your relationship. But now you have to put it out of your head.'

It's what I have to do with Rochelle.

She smiles, nodding.

I grip her shoulders. She waits, looking up at me. I want to say, *Give your Mum a big hug and tell her that you love her*, but it's against the rules to arouse suspicion in someone who doesn't know about us. It could be dangerous should someone check on us while we're not really there. Instead, I lean in and kiss her chastely on the cheek. 'See you in a little while.'

I can't sleep, and if I don't sleep soon, Isabel might be going on this mission by herself. Dad must hear me wrestling with my sheets. He raps his knuckles on my bedroom door. 'Ethan, can I come in?'

I pull myself into a sitting position, straightening my twisted T-shirt and switch on my bedside lamp. 'What is it, Dad? I'm trying to sleep.'

He sets a glass of water down on my bedside table and hands me a bottle of pills from his dressing gown pocket. I roll it around to read the label. They're prescription sleeping pills in Dad's name.

Is this the sedative that turned Dad into an unfeeling zombie after Marduke killed my sister?

I hand them back. 'No thanks.'

Ignoring me, he sets the bottle down on my bedside table. 'Arkarian called. He's not going to pull Isabel into the Citadel until he knows you will be asleep soon.'

I shake my head. 'I just need a few more minutes.'

'Ethan.'

'No, Dad. I'm not having pills.'

He gives me a look that says he knows how I haven't been sleeping... since the day my life changed forever.

Uninvited, he sits on the edge of my bed. 'How long has it been since you had a good night's sleep?'

'How long do you think, Dad?'

He wraps his strong arms around me, cradling my head to his chest as if I was a kid again, and for a minute I don't mind and I rest it there, listening to his steady heartbeat. But when I close my eyes I see Rochelle, her eyes on mine, the light of her life slipping away.

'I want to tell you it will get better, but you probably won't believe me. When your sister died...'

I push him away. 'Don't, Dad. Not now. Tell Arkarian I need five more minutes, tops.'

I straighten up and search my bedside table for my phone, but I left it on my desk under the window, making sure that while drowsy I don't accidentally pop it in my pocket before the shift.

'What are you looking for?' he asks.

'What time is it?'

'Two in the morning.'

*Hell.* I stare at the bottle Dad left at my bedside. It would be easy to take a pill, but... I don't want to get used to doing things easy. What if I'm still under the influence of the sedative when my soul shifts to Ancient Egypt in my new borrowed body? How will that help Isabel to fulfil the mission?

'Dad!' He turns at the door. I throw him the bottle of pills. 'Don't do that again.' He frowns. And even though I know it's going to hurt him, I still say it, 'I'm not you, Dad. I will never be you.'

I switch my bedside lamp off to the sound of my bedroom door clicking shut.

I close my eyes and as always, Rochelle is laying in my arms peering up at me with an arrow in her heart, but this time her eyes flutter and its Crystal looking at me, her black-rimmed glasses slipping down her nose. She pulls them off, tossing them aside without a care, and smiling she tugs me down to kiss her.

I wake with a sense of falling, my body covered in perspiration, my pulse racing. I get just enough time to control the drop and not land on my head, or my butt. I don't recognize where I am. The room has dark walls but is well-lit with a fire crackling in a brick fireplace. There are a couple of couches and a rug on the floor. It's cozy and comfortable. I plonk down in one of the chairs and wait for Isabel. She drops squarely on her feet an instant later, her eyes automatically taking in the space around us.

'Nice room,' she says. 'It has a homely feel. I hope that's a good sign.'

'I never was one for superstitions.'

'And you're going to be a priest in Ancient Egypt,' she says, smiling.

'Hmm, well, that should be interesting.' I get up and hold out my hand. 'Shall we go?'

She links her fingers with mine and a door opens with a staircase hovering in front of it. We jump on, and gripping the railing with our free hands, we climb up a few stairs. The staircase moves, taking us up three levels at a gradual pace.

This gives us a chance to take our first look at the re-built labyrinth. It's similar to the original one, only smaller and brighter with a scent of fresh paint in the air.

Isabel shivers suddenly.

'What is it?' I ask.

'I was just remembering the last time I was here and it blew up around me.'

'Rochelle was with you.'

'Yeah. She'd just seen her father. He'd pulled off his belt and glared at her threateningly, though he wasn't really there. She defeated him by calling him what he was - a memory that had no power over her.' She squeezes my hand. 'She was always so brave. I wish I could tell her how sorry I am. I was under orders to protect her and I -'

'What did you say? Protect her from what?'

'Because of the curse and... damn it, Ethan, I forgot you didn't know. I'd had a vision -'

'You *knew* she was going to die? You *saw* it, and you didn't tell me?'

'She was already nervous about having the curse hanging over her head; we didn't want to make it worse.'

'We?'

She groans. 'Matt.'

I wait for her to continue.

'When Rochelle ran off after Dillon's callous remarks that horrible day, you made it clear you didn't want anyone to follow, but I still should have. You didn't know. I did. It was my job to stick close to her because I might have recognised something from the vision. So you see? Rochelle's death is my fault.'

A door opens to a room on the top level. We're staring at each other so intensely that the staircase begins to move away from the landing. I squeeze Isabel's hand. 'Come on. Jump. *Now.*'

We land in a wardrobe room. Racks of Ancient Egyptian clothing line the walls with several more rows in between. As I walk past them my thoughts swing to Rochelle and the different ways that horrible day could have played out. But I remember Arkarian's warning to give all my attention to this mission, and with a deep breath I set aside my thoughts of Rochelle's death for now.

I end up dressed in finely woven, premium quality, white linen kilt to my knees with a matching shirt, secured at the waist with a belt made of glass beads. Like many men at the time, especially priests, I have no hair on my head. I run my hand over my baldness. It will take some getting used to. Glancing down, I wiggle my toes. Having bare feet is not much of a surprise since most Ancient Egyptians only wore sandals when they needed them.

I hear Isabel groan and glance over. She's staring into a mirror and looking miserable.

'What's wrong?' I ask, making my way to her side of the room.

Folding her arms across her chest, she turns.

I'm still a few meters away, but see her problem instantly and stop. I try to think of something good to say but it takes a while to get my thoughts together. 'Ah...'

'I know! Look at this dress.'

'I see it... perfectly... clearly.'

She grabs a hat from a stand and hurls it at me. 'What am I going to do? This is the third one and I don't know how many times I can choose.'

'Three.' I give her the bad news quickly while I gaze over the dress.

Vertical pleats drop from thin shoulder straps that cross over her chest to form a belt around her waist. It's a long gown that fits Isabel's frame perfectly, only the linen is so fine it's see-through, outlining Isabel's tiny waist, rounded hips and, whoa, for a small girl she has some nice curves happening, only... 'They don't wear underwear?'

She scowls, 'Apparently not the women.'

I walk towards her again, making sure to keep my eyes at neck height. 'You know, your look's not that bad.'

'Really?' She glances at the door as if she might run.

I stand beside her in front of the mirror, pointing to the black kohl around our eyes, makeup that makes us appear uniquely Ancient Egyptian. 'It's not as if anyone is going to identify your eyes. And seriously, Isabel, you look hot.'

Her face turns bright pink. 'How am I supposed to heal someone dressed like a... a... prostitute?'

'You don't look anything like a prostitute, more like a high priestess.'

She fingers her necklaces, all of them gold with glistening jewels. An amulet of the God Horus circles her upper arm. She pushes it up a little higher while I adjust a sparkling trinket in her hair. Not sure what I'm looking for, I turn to the racks of accessories, selecting a long scarf in thicker linen and offer it to her. 'Why don't you try...' I twirl my finger, pointing at her chest.

She snatches the scarf and wraps it around her chest twice, tying it into a knot at the front so that the ends drop to about thigh height.

She glances at her image in the mirror. 'Thanks. It helps.'

While still standing at the mirror, sparkling colored dust drops down from above us. A burst of heat rushes through me as we receive the knowledge we need for our mission.

'That was intense,' Isabel says in flawless Egyptian.

'I'll say.' Born and raised in Thebes, my name is Amenshef and Isabel is the physician Henttimehu.

A door opens. This is it. Our last chance to hightail it out of here, only, that's not really an option. If not Isabel and me it would be some other team and Arkarian says we're the team with the best chance of succeeding.

We step into a long corridor with no windows but wide enough to walk side-by-side. Sunlight streams in from the open end, along with the sounds of many people, like a gathering at a temple courtyard, or a marketplace.

Even before we reach the open doorway, hot air wafts up to us, so thick with humidity it's like nothing I've felt living in the high altitudes of Angel Falls. I take Isabel's hand and hold it with a strong grip. 'Are you ready to check this out?'

Her eyes are wide, her mouth open. She nods and we glance down together. Looking north first, massive structures still under construction have us gawking in awe. But the river is closer, with a wide bank of irrigated green fields. Several families till the fertile soil with children playing around them. Isabel points to the palace, an unmissable gold tower on a hill surrounded by white buildings with paved streets. People are everywhere, hundreds, maybe even thousands spread across the entire city. The marketplace is where the loudest chatter comes from with people haggling for the best deal.

Isabel licks her lips and swallows, making a gulping sound as she stretches out one of her long black curls with a finger. She turns her face up to me, her color paler than when she first got her identity. 'Are we really doing this?'

I hold her eyes steady. 'Not until we're ready.'

She takes another peek at the streets below when suddenly she sways towards the opening.

'Whoa!' I pull her back with my arm around her waist. 'You OK?'

'Yeah, um... remind me will you, this part is all about trust, right?'

'Arkarian knows what he's doing.'

'But we don't know what year it is, or what we have to do yet, or who the Order has marked to execute, or –'

'Hey, hey, Isabel, we'll figure it out.'

Nodding, she closes her eyes and inhales a deep breath. When she opens them she has some of her color back. 'I'm ready.'

'Sure?'

'Yeah.'

'OK. Let's do this.'

# Chapter Twenty-one

## Ethan

I drop into water. Deep water. And my gut is feeling the dread that this might not end well. Maybe a rush of adrenaline is escalating my anxiety. I'm underwater with no control over the situation, and I don't like it.

Isabel crashes through the surface a beat after me and we go down like bullets.

*How could this happen, Arkarian? What were you thinking?*

Finally my feet hit the bottom, shaking up a pile of sand and dark silt. I use the firm surface to push upwards. Unprepared for a river drop, I didn't take a deep breath, and now my lungs are straining. I'm damn sure Isabel didn't either. The last I saw her face she was screaming.

She hits the riverbed a second after me, landing directly into my kicked-up debris, making the water murkier and more difficult to see through. Two fish at least a meter long swim past me, their swishing tails brushing my legs. My gut says this is not going to go well for Isabel. They swim straight into her and she loses it. Frantic splashing, arms flailing, bubbles spilling out, dirt and debris going everywhere.

Down here, she could drown losing her cool.

I glimpse her through the confusion. *Oh no.*

Reaching her as fast as I can, I pull her hands away from the fish and put them on my shoulders. Taking her face between my hands I hold her still and motion upwards with my eyes.

With bubbles coming out of her nose, her eyes open too wide, she nods.

She's clearly running out of oxygen fast now. Without letting go, I get behind her, wrap one arm diagonally over her chest, and put all I can into kicking us to the surface.

We break through gasping for air, but it takes Isabel longer to level out. She collapses on me, her arms hanging limply over my shoulders, her head on my neck. I rub her back while she coughs up a bucket-load of water.

We stay locked like this, treading water and just breathing until she's feeling all right.

'Thank you so much,' she says. 'I lost it down there when those eels swam into me.'

Continuing to tread water, I jerk my head at the nearest shore where irrigated crops line the banks in both north and south directions. 'That way.'

She glances and nods. 'OK.'

'Think you can manage it?'

'Yeah, I'm good.'

Something in the water about halfway between us and the opposite riverbank puts a shiver up my spine.

Isabel sees where I'm staring. 'Oh my God, are they...?'

'A herd of hippos? Yep.'

'We have to get out of this river.'

'No argument there.'

We set out with steady strokes. Intermittently, I check on the hippos. They continue swimming along the river's centre without paying us any attention.

'Oh-oh, what are those bumps sitting on top of the water over there?' Isabel asks.

'Where?'

She points to the bank ahead of us without breaking her rhythm. 'Ethan, do they look like eyes to you?'

My gut sinks. They say ignorance is bliss. In this case, they would be right. Since she hasn't figured it out yet, Isabel is better off not knowing. I swim up beside her. 'Keep splashing to a minimum and follow my lead.'

Even though I change direction, Isabel keeps peering over at the 'eyes'.

'No point in looking. Just keep pace.' I take in some river water and spit repeatedly to expel it. Who knows what bacteria could be thriving in this ancient river? Hippo waste comes to mind.

'Tell me what they are.'

I pretend not to hear her.

'Ethan.'

God, she can be stubborn. 'Focus on swimming fast and quietly.'

'I'm not going to swoon. Just tell me.'

'You don't need to know.'

'*Ethan*!'

'All right. They're crocodiles. About a dozen are sunning themselves on the bank and in the water nearby.'

Water splashes over her as she loses her rhythm for a second. 'You really didn't have to tell me that.'

'What?'

'Just saying, you're the leader. I don't have to know everything.'

She grins at me. I don't want to swallow any more water so I keep my mouth shut.

The urge to swim the shortest distance to the shore is hard to resist, but I'd rather be safe and give those crocs a wide berth. While watching them, one lifts its head. It seems to inhale the air, and suddenly it's gone, slipping beneath the surface with millennia of practice. It reappears close enough to be lining us up for its next snack. *Damn it.*

'Uh... Isabel, I don't want to alarm you but -'

'This is my fastest already.'

'Not today it isn't.'

'Have those crocodiles finished sunning themselves?'

I look for that sneaky croc, spotting it only a body-length behind us with the others all turning to follow. '*No way.* Move, Isabel. Go, go, go, go, *go!*'

'What's happening?'

'Don't talk. Focus. *Faster!*'

With the pressure on, Isabel does a great job of keeping up. She's feeling the pressure and swimming her heart out, faster than I've seen her move before. If only she had her wings as I do, together we could disappear out of this croc infested river and onto the shore in front of us.

'How many are there, Ethan?'

'A few. I don't know.'

'How close are those few?'

'On our heels, I think.'

'You think?'

'Yeah, they're sneaky.' Moving into position beside her I set an even faster pace and she matches me stroke for stroke.

One goes under and I lose sight of it.

'What's wrong?' Isabel asks.

I spot it deep under water. When it comes up it's going to take one of us in its jaws and put us in a devastating death roll. It could take minutes or even an hour, but it's how crocodiles kill their prey. Once taken, it's almost impossible to break open its jaws to make it let go.

'Use your wings,' she says.

'Not a chance.'

'Ethan, please. One of us has to finish this mission.'

I refuse to answer. I'm not going to abandon her, and the next time she breathes in my direction, I give her a look that says just that.

We make it to the riverbank with a crocodile lunging at our feet and ibis scattering into the air.

We scramble up a grassy hill like two old drunks, tugging on grass roots, dragging each other over a retaining wall made from reed mesh urns filled with stones. An earlier flood has seen some of the wall falling away, which ironically gives us helpful footholds.

I have no idea how far crocodiles can move away from water and don't want to find out the hard way, so with legs that feel boneless, I grip Isabel's hand and together we cross the green leafy crops before collapsing face down in an irrigation drain.

It takes time to recover, but knowing how much we lost by having to swim for our lives, we get to our feet and look around.

Streets stretch back for as far as we can see, both sides lined with flat-roofed houses made from mud-bricks that stand so close together they each share a wall with their neighbor. The cloudless sky is a brighter blue than I've seen it before. And it's hot here, with the type of heat that could dehydrate us in minutes.

'Wow,' Isabel says, staring at the sight of an Ancient Egyptian city teaming with life.

We select the first street we come to, but it doesn't take long to figure out which streets lead to the palace. My instinct kicks in and draws me towards a hill that would have a commanding view over the city. I stand still and tilt my head back. There are other buildings within its walls, one that towers above the rest. Made of rectangular stone blocks, rows of columns rise to a commanding height. Giant statues stand out the front with wide stairs between them leading up from the street. It's the palace we saw from the Citadel, and it's so damn big it's intimidating.

The knowledge dust is working and I recognize the temple alongside. It's here I attend every day to look after the Gods inside. It's my job as priest to clean and polish the statues and leave food for the Gods.

Information streams into my consciousness, making me aware that this is not the only job I do here. I'm also a General of the Pharaoh's armies, and his advisor on the running of not only this city, but also all of Upper and Lower Egypt. The influx of refugees is straining the city, while Egypt's borders are under threat from another race, that of the '*Sea People*', who first conquered our usual enemy, the Hittites.

Information continues flowing in. I try to keep it on a need-to-know basis to concentrate on the temple, but an attached building demands my attention. This mansion sits on the hill overlooking the city. It's the current reigning Pharaoh's palace, also mine, along with my mother, Queen Ta-Opet, the harem she's in charge of, and my many siblings.

*After a shaky start, Arkarian, you've outdone yourself.*

'This is amazing,' Isabel says as we begin walking again, turning into another street, though she's not Isabel now and I have to remember not to call her by her real name for as long as we're here, whether that's an hour, a day or even a month.

Thebes is a thriving capital city with people dashing in and out of houses, meeting up with others, going about their daily duties. There's a cheerful vibe in their voices coming from all directions along the streets or from inside their houses. A young couple walks past us carrying washing with their two naked kids running around them squealing as they chase each other to the river. There are older children too, and teens wearing white kilts with the traditional hairstyle of one long piece of hair hanging down one side of an otherwise bald head. I run my hand over the top of my own bald head. Oddly, it doesn't feel strange anymore.

We walk into a market where stalls, shaded from the hot sun with overhead awnings, display food, pottery, dishes, clothing, jewelry and even animals. A man exchanges two fish for a gold anklet with colored stones embedded in the chains. 'A gift for a special girl,' he says. 'My daughter.' No money changes hands.

As pleasant as it is to stroll through the streets of Thebes, with our clothes still wet, in whatever year this is, it worries me that I'm not getting that vital information yet, but the palace is drawing me to it. A sense of needing to be there grows stronger.

The roads become busier the nearer we draw to the palace. Finally, we're not far away and beginning to dry out. After that swim with the crocodiles and this uphill walk I wouldn't say no to a change of clothes, a meal and a good sleep. I bump my shoulder to Isabel's. 'Remember when Mr Carter dropped us in the middle of a battlefield between the French and English.'

'The Hundred Years War. We were going to save Arkarian before he was born.'

'I'd prefer that to being dropped into a river infested with hippos and crocodiles.' She laughs, and I add, 'I'm going to smash your boyfriend for that drop. Worst one I've ever had.'

She flicks me a sideways glance. 'Take a ticket and get in line.'

Turning a corner, the temple and palace buildings appear ahead, gleaming under the hot African sun. Two young men, teenagers by the look of their white kilts and shirts, cause a ruckus on the temple steps. They see us and begin waving their arms in the air. The taller one cups his hands around his mouth and yells out to me. Realizing the distance is too far to hear; he glances back at the palace, slaps the shorter one's shoulder and motions to run with him.

I recognize them as my brothers, the next closest to my age. Only, I can't remember the shorter one's name.

'Brother!'

Takairnayu, the taller of the two arrives first, punching my upper arm with a force just short of being hard enough to hurt. 'Where have you been?'

Shorter-bro has a lighter voice. 'We have been looking for you everywhere. When you weren't in the Sanctuary, the temple or the kitchens, we put word out on the streets and suddenly a farmer comes running into the palace.'

'Mud everywhere!' Takairnayu exclaims, moving his arms out wide. 'You should have seen Meresankh.' Laughing for a second, he quickly turns serious again. 'The farmer said, "The prince is in the river!" And I said, "What is he doing there, dancing with hippos?" And he laughed and said, "No, not hippos. A girl."'

It's at that moment the two of them look at Isabel, and stop breathing. Their eyes go wide and round as a disc, which is hard to do with the black kohl meant to make them into oval shapes. Short-bro sucks in a deep breath, and then the brothers exchange sly smirks that say *now* they get it.

Isabel returns their stares with a suspicious frown.

But then I notice her dress. She's lost the scarf, probably when swimming for her life. *Thanks Arkarian.* At least it's dry now, but it's also shrunk a few sizes and is hugging her curves like a second skin, a see-through second skin. '*Whoa.*'

She peers at me sideways. 'What did you say?'

I whip my shirt off and toss it to her. 'Put this on.'

'Oh my God.' Turning around to slip it over her head, she gives the boys another view altogether that brings cheeky grins to their faces. 'Is that why your brothers are staring at me like a pair of bug-eyed puppies?'

Shaking his head, Takairnayu brings his eyes back to mine, his humor gone. 'You have to come with us, Amenshef.' He leans in and whispers, 'The king is sick. Our father is dying. He's calling for you from his bed.'

I indicate Isabel with a nod. 'I brought a doctor who can help.'

'Then she must come too. He has a doctor with him now, only...'

'What is it, Akumosh?' Shorty's name finally comes to me.

'The doctor brought a guard with her. He's huge. He stands at our father's bedchamber door and won't let anyone in.'

Isabel and I exchange a knowing glance. This new guard has to be from the Order, or why else would he bar the door to the Pharaoh's bedroom while his partner goes inside?

'And the Queen?'

'We sent a messenger but she is still a day away.'

'Good work, brothers. Let's go.'

As we run to the palace I ask what the guard looks like. 'He is big,' Akumosh says, lifting one arm up towards the sky. 'He carries a spear, a sword and a shield, and his armor is bronze with leather straps over his chest. He wears a helmet that comes down low over his face. It's hard to see his eyes, but when he's angry his eyes catch on fire.'

'On fire?' I repeat, trying to work out what he means.

'Do they glow?' Isabel asks.

'Glow? I do not know this word. They are like... flames.'

Akumosh says, 'But he will let *you* in, brother.'

'Why are you so sure?'

'He's one of your soldiers.'

Without thinking, I say, 'But I'm only a Priest.'

They both laugh, and Akumosh says, 'Yeah, yeah, stop showing off.' He ticks off his fingers, 'Priest. General. Chief Advisor.'

'First-born,' Takairnayu adds.

At the foot of the palace steps, Isabel touches my arm. 'I need to clean up. Find another dress.'

'We don't have time.'

'All right, but, well, can I keep your shirt?'

'You do that.'

'Hurry, hurry!' Akumosh motions us to follow him up the front steps into an entry hall of gleaming mosaic floors. Isabel's eyes dart all over the place as we move through the main hall with brightly painted walls and decorated pillars that hold up a ceiling too high to see in detail.

'Quicker this way. Come on.'

We follow Akumosh through a covered arcade with palms and ferns and other greenery. It's a refreshing drop in temperature from the heat outside. He takes us past three bedrooms in a row before running upstairs and into a dark corridor lit by a candle at each end. We hurry after the brothers, passing soldiers standing guard who straighten up when they see me, and servants scurrying around on silent bare feet.

Finally, as we round a corner into a long room void of all furniture except a few low, hand-carved chairs, but with the same story-telling painted walls and high pillars, the boys stop and Takairnayu whispers, 'That's him.'

At the opposite end a tall soldier with broad shoulders stands in front of the Pharaoh's private chamber door. His size makes him a daunting figure. Just like his bizarre helmet, this soldier doesn't belong here. Of more concern is what his partner, the 'doctor' is doing alone with the Pharaoh behind the closed door.

I point to two palace guards whose faces are familiar, though frustratingly I'm not getting their names. 'Soldiers, you, and you, come with me.' Falling in behind me without question, the three of us march between the center pillars to stand before the intruder. I try to engage eye contact, but he keeps his eyes lowered beneath the visor. 'Soldier, stand aside.'

His guarded eyes lift to study mine, suddenly they widen as if he's recognized me. I doubt that very much. I've never looked so different from my real self before.

The soldier regains his composure quickly and blinks. 'Apologies, Highness, I am under the Pharaoh's strict orders to let no one into his chambers until the doctor finishes her examination.'

As Isabel comes up beside me, the intruder stares at her too, only this time he shakes his head and mutters a savage string of incoherent words under his breath.

Whatever his problem I don't have time to figure it out, I have to get him away from this door even if it means drawing him out in combat so Isabel can slip inside. 'I don't know what game you're playing, soldier, but the doctor who needs to treat my father is standing beside me. Step aside before I have you arrested.' I move closer so that my face is in his face. My lips brush the fine hairs at the base of his ear. 'I *will* arrest you, soldier, and lock you away in an *inescapable* cell that will block any attempt you make to *call* for help. Do we understand each other?'

He shifts his eyes to mine and speaks with a fierce warning, 'You do not want to send your doctor in there, my prince.'

'Explain.'

He clears his throat, expelling an irritated breath through tight lips. 'There is no need, Highness. The doctor presently treating your father has everything under control.'

Takairnayu brings another two soldiers with him. Behind me, he whispers, 'Brother, there is something strange about the doctor with our father.'

'What do you mean?'

'She's wearing an unusual mask.'

'A mask?' My gut drops. What the freaking hell is going on in that room? I need him to describe the doctor's mask, but not in front of this guard.

'I have never seen anything like it,' Takairnayu says as we move out of hearing distance. 'I'm no priest, brother, but I swear the Gods haven't either.'

I pat my brother's shoulder. 'Good work, Takairnayu. Take the soldiers and stand back. I'll come and see you soon.'

All four soldiers snap their heels and return to the room's entrance to await my orders. Beside me, Isabel's eyebrows rise, but I can't stop to tell her my suspicions. Not while an Order's member is inside with the Pharaoh, Ramses Four, or one of the many other Ramses that lived around this time. I search through the knowledge dust downloaded earlier, but this particular Pharaoh's details are still missing. If it's important, it should be in my head by now. That's how it works, unless this is one of those errors that had Sir Syford worried.

Maybe it doesn't matter who this king is, when he lived, or what he's going to do, my objective remains the same as always, stop the 'doctor' from completing her mission.

It's clear the Order's guard isn't moving without force. I need to regroup to figure out a way into the Pharaoh's room.

I get an idea to work an illusion that will appear as if the doctor has completed her mission. Working an illusion that creates a living breathing person and not just an object is a leap for me and I'm not sure how long I'll be able to keep the illusion going. But at this point I have nothing else but force, which could result in more deaths of soldiers and princes than we came here to prevent. So I have to try.

I lead Isabel away from the Pharaoh's door, but not too far that she can't see it. The Order's guard doesn't take his eyes off us, so I turn my back to him, giving Isabel cover.

'He's not from this time, is he?' Isabel whispers.

I shake my head.

'How am I going to get in there?' she whispers.

'This is how,' I whisper. 'When the Pharaoh's bedchamber door opens and the doctor walks over to her guard...' But what I can't say is, *the Order's doctor will appear as if she's completed her mission and is leaving but she won't have left at all. She'll still be inside oblivious to my subterfuge.*

'I won't be able to fool the guard for long,' I explain, 'so we have to act fast. As soon as the door opens – '

'I'll slip straight in.'

'No. *I'm* going in first,' I tell her.

'You don't have to check it out for me,' she snaps.

'My instinct is telling me.'

'Your instinct is also telling you that Rochelle is back from the dead.'

She gasps. 'Oh my God, I can't believe I said that. I'm so sorry.'

I fight to control the tidal wave of emotions that suddenly crashes into me, that threatens to take me under. My lips tremble. My breath shudders. But I get myself under control.

'Once I give you the signal, come inside and go directly to the Pharaoh. While you heal him, I'll distract the Order's doctor. That's an order. Do you understand?'

She hangs her head. Tears hit the floor. *Damn.* Arkarian warned us to keep our focus. Now I understand his reasons. Isabel is taking Rochelle's death personally. Guilt has her gripped in a tunnel of swirling emotions. But I can't deal with them while I work this illusion. She will have to wait. I shut my eyes. But this is Isabel, the last person I want to see hurting. I lift her face with my thumb under her chin. 'Are you OK?'

She shrugs.

I give her a sympathetic look. 'We'll talk tonight.'

'Forgive me?'

'There's nothing to forgive.'

She stares at me, her mouth open. I give her a small smile. 'Now, please keep your eyes on the Pharaoh's door.'

'I will.'

I turn to my Ancient Egyptian brothers and ask for a description of the 'doctor'. Without knowing what she looks like, especially the unusual mask, the appearance of my imagined doctor won't fool the guard. I drill them for details. With an image in my mind that I hope is accurate enough, I close my eyes and visualize the doctor coming to life at the Pharaoh's bedchamber door, and then opening it.

The guard sees my fake doctor exiting. His hard expression softens in relief. He nods at her as she moves quickly past him. As expected, now that he believes their job is finished, he takes off after her, eager to leave. He catches up and I overhear the soldier quizzing the fake doctor, 'Are we done? Did you get the two vials? We have to leave right now.'

My illusion is working. This is my chance. I hurry to the now unguarded door. At any moment, when the 'doctor' doesn't respond, the guard will realize she's not real.

I slip inside the Pharaoh's room, ready to face the Order's 'doctor', and stop her from completing her task, whatever that proves to be. In the process of closing the door and walking in, I glimpse the guard glance over his shoulder. He sees me and gets a frantic look on his face. He rushes towards me but Isabel intercepts him. She tries to come in after me but he stops her, his voice so desperate it's as if he's stopping her for *her* sake.

A chill runs down my spine as I slam the door shut, spin around, and come face-to-face with a nightmare none of us saw coming.

# Chapter Twenty-two

## Jesilla

This is taking so long I could scream. This Pharaoh has to give me what I need so Bastian and I can go home. It's because the king is so sick that it's proving hard to find a vein. One after another they collapse before I get enough. I have to work my butt off for every drop I manage to drag out of his nauseating skin. The thought crosses my mind that maybe I should cut a finger off, let the lab extract the blood we need from that. But there's so little blood left in the king's body I'd probably have to amputate a whole hand. I don't think he'd appreciate that without anesthetic. I don't care what the lab would think, but history might change in a way that doesn't suit my plans, so I persevere.

He moans again. I push the needle in deeper each time to get another drop out of him.

Eventually I have enough. The truth is one test tube is sufficient for what we need, but Paul Withers, the Order's chief scientist, insists I bring him a backup vial just in case.

I loosen the tourniquet on the king's right leg and carefully remove the syringe from his calf. After all, I wouldn't want to prick my finger accidentally. Not that anything can penetrate these gloves. The lab has done a good job protecting me.

This king is close to death, an hour or two tops, but at least on this mission he's not going to die from my actions. No one will, and that's a nice change. This king was dying before I got here, and nothing I do can save him from his fate.

But his death is not an event I need to see. His family will arrange the long process of preparing his body and soul for his passage through the Underworld.

And then Ramses the Fifth will still go down in history as the first human to die of this disease.

I pack up quickly, mindful of how I handle the implements and the king's blood. A mistake now would jeopardize everything. At the same time, now that I'm done, I'm in a hurry to leave. It's gone smoothly, as I thought it would. Why Bastian was so worried the Guard would show up, I have no idea. Habit, probably. But their quantum super-computer wasn't ready, and the way their Elders, Councilors, Royals, whatever they call their sector heads in Athens, take care of that special group they call the Named, they wouldn't risk sending them back in time without perfectly-working machinery.

Tucking the modern pathology tools into my nylon zip bag, I pick up the first test tube full of the Pharaoh's diseased blood, check the lid, drop the tube into the sterile plastic bag and seal it. I then carefully slip this sealed bag into the steel cylindrical canister I brought for this purpose, and start the process over again with the second test tube.

As I pick up the second test tube full of the Pharaoh's diseased blood a sound at the door interrupts me. Shivers race across my arms because this is not Bastian. Someone else has entered the room.

I turn slowly, keeping my right hand closed around the second test tube that I still need to secure. It's the Prince. Those younger boys must have found him. Damn them. But how did he get Bastian away from his post? What did he do to him?

The Prince frowns, runs a hand across his bald head and peers at me with narrowed distrustful eyes. 'What's this?'

'Majesty, there was a guard outside my door?'

'He is fine.'

'Majesty, do not approach. It's not in your best interests. If it pleases Your Majesty to allow me a moment to explain before I leave.'

Completely ignoring me he strides over, his eyes falling to the test tube gripped in my hand. 'Why have you drawn blood from my father? What are you testing him for?'

*How would he know the purpose of a test tube?*

'Your father is gravely ill. He called for me.'

He catches a whiff of the Pharaoh's rotting flesh and jerks his head. 'What's wrong with him?'

'Your father is dying of a debilitating illness. No one can stop its progression. It will destroy many of your people, but not all. Enough will survive to continue the species.'

He swallows deep in his throat. I watch him study the Pharaoh, his mind putting pieces together – the dark red skin, the rash, weeping blisters. Just what he's come up with is anybody's guess. I probe his thoughts but strangely get nothing. How is that possible? It's not as if he would know to block me. And while I think about that, he turns his anxious face to me and his penetrating blue eyes hold me captive.

'That's one hell of a deadly illness,' he says, running his hand over his baldness again. '*Sweet Jesus*, what are you people up to?'

His mention of *Jesus* snaps me out of whatever mesmerizing shock I slipped into, because *Jesus* hasn't been born yet. 'I don't know who you are, but for your own good, step back and let me through that door.'

His lips twitch into a smirk. 'Put the test tube down along with the other one in the steel canister and I'll let you go home.'

*Oh no.* 'You're not supposed to be here.'

'Well I am. So how about telling me what the Order wants with the Pharaoh's diseased blood? You could kill millions if that disease got out. No one's been vaccinated for it since 1979, but you know that already,' he says.

The door opens and a girl in a man's shirt bursts in. Lucky for her, Bastian is right behind her. He wraps his arm around her waist and yanks her back out. 'You can't go in there,' Bastian hisses, and catching my eye with his own eyes raging with fury he slams the door shut.

'Smart girl, your partner,' I say, glad we're alone again. 'Listen to me, you need to turn around and join her out there before...'

'Before what?'

'Look, you can't win this one.'

'Maybe not, but I can't afford to lose either.'

'You don't understand. Dammit, I'm warning you. Stay back. Where you're standing now is risky enough without a mask. You'll need to be isolated and tested regularly until you're cleared.'

He's in front of me before I figure out what he's going to do next. But I'm quick too and I shift to the door. I get my fingers on the handle when his hand closes over mine. His other hand tries to grab the bag with the canister and tool kit. We fight for it, wrestling across the floor to the other side of the room. Breathless, I end up with my back against the wall with the Guard straightening up in front of me. I shift back to the door, but find him there before me. He's a fast shifter. And now we're standing close with a glass test tube between us.

'You're not getting out of this room with that Pharaoh's blood,' he tells me.

'I *will* be leaving with the Pharaoh's blood because it's my mission, and I will do whatever it takes to finish it.' *Whatever it takes.*

He reaches for the test tube.

I scream, 'Don't, it's glass and you're not wearing gloves!' Twisting to protect the test tube, I curve my back over it and cradle both the sealed and unsealed vials against my chest. Elbowing the Guard, I warn him, 'Step back! Let me go! You don't understand how dangerous it is to get near this stuff.'

'That's where you're wrong. I see what it is. And I assume you're going to use it to slaughter masses of people, or control the world's governments with threats to get what you want. And that's why I can't let you take it from this room.'

Damn him. Bracing to protect the vials, I bring my heel up into his groin - hard. It must hurt. Glancing over my shoulder I watch his face turn red and moisture spark in his eyes. Every muscle in his body stiffens around me. But he doesn't allow himself to go slack. He doesn't double over, shriek in agony or get off me. He holds still, absorbing the kick and staring at me with pain-wracked blue eyes.

Into the quiet I ask, 'You would sacrifice your life?'

'It's what I'm prepared to do every time I set foot in the past.'

'How honorable of you.' *Oh my God but it is.* 'I'm sure your fellow Guardians will ensure an inscription of the sort appears on your headstone.'

'Hand over the blood.'

'That's not going to happen. So, whoever you are, this is your last chance to step out of my way.'

'Or what? Are you going to threaten me? I just admitted I'm willing to die here to save the millions your Order is going to kill with this disease. And if I have to, I'll keep you here with me until the portal closes.'

'That's not going to happen. Believe me; I will hurt you to get out of here.'

His eyes narrow as he peers at me, and I hope he can see that I make good on my threats. Still, he doesn't move, so I force the issue. Tucking the glass test tube deeper into my shirtfront, I shove my back into his chest with extreme force. Most people would drop with that, their ribs fractured, piercing their lungs, but not this Guard. I spin around, shoving him over, and leap for the door.

But I don't get to open it before he drags me away and we shift around the room, hurting one another with my high kicks and his punches that remind me of the time I fought one of the Guards in Atlantis as it was sinking into the sea. It was a rare occasion when my mother chose me to be her partner.

The Guard kicks hard. He gets one into my kidneys, something he wouldn't be able to do if I didn't have the test tubes to protect. Not being able to use my hands and the energy I can bring to them if I didn't have to wear these gloves, puts me at a disadvantage. With no time to catch my breath, I spin around, and find his fist flying straight for my face. With an instant to react, I lay myself out horizontally - head, shoulders and back in a flat line. His fist misses by a whisker and I follow through with a spinning kick to the side of his head.

He doesn't see it coming.

Even though speed is one of my skills, my mother still made me work hard at it in training, and today when I have to keep my hands crossed over my chest, I'm grateful to her. It's keeping me a step ahead in this duel.

The Guard sways. My kicks are wearing him down. He blinks, shaking his head. Taking the advantage, but still keeping the vials secure, especially the test tube I didn't get time to put in its protective canister, I throw another spinning high kick to the side of his head. It slows him enough that I finally get to the door with time to yank it open, only to see Bastian in a scuffle with that same girl, the prince's brothers and three soldiers all on the floor in various states of consciousness.

*I'm coming!* I send him my thought. *This will be over soon.*

But the girl suddenly breaks away. Maybe fed by a burst of adrenaline at seeing the door open. She elbows Bastian in his ribs, shoves the butt of her palm into his nose without looking, and runs straight at the open door.

I groan. Loudly. I can't believe I'm doing this, but I slam the door shut in her face, locking me back in the Pharaoh's bedchamber with the Guard with the death wish. The stupid girl yanks the door open. Looks like she has a death wish too. I slam it shut again and we have a tug-of-war that sees my medical toolkit drop to the floor.

That's it. Game over.

I close my eyes and call up some extra power of my own. With my eyes burning, and probably glowing as well, I spin around and push my back up against the door. She has no chance of opening it now until I decide to move.

'*Whoa,*' I cry out, finding the 'prince' right up in my face again. 'Do you mind?'

'Well I do, actually. I'll just get this.' He shoves his hand down my shirtfront and takes the test tube from me. 'Now I'll be on my way.'

'No, don't,' I warn, reaching for it. 'It's glass. Be careful not to...'

But he turns away and it shatters in his strong hand. Blood spatter goes all over his bare chest, his neck, and even his face.

'Oh my God! Oh my God!' To my horror there's blood on his eye lashes and bottom lip. 'Don't blink. It will go in your eyes. I'll get something to flush it away. And don't – '

'But I can't *not* blink,' he says before I can warn him not to talk either.

With only one option left – to ensure he doesn't return this disease to our time, I draw power into my arms and shove him deep into the room, muttering, 'I'm sorry. I didn't want it to be like this.'

And just my luck, I run out the door and straight into his partner. I grab her arms and stop her from going further. Standing on her toes she peers over my shoulders and sees her partner on the floor far across the room, staring at his hands. Suddenly everything feels like it's moving in slow motion. Bastian pulls the girl off me. I rip off my mask and gloves and thrust them into her hands. 'I can't stop you from going to him. But you have to put these on first. Tell your people that your Guard was exposed to *smallpox variole major.*'

Unworried, she says, 'I'm a Healer. I'll fix this.'

'Have you been vaccinated against this disease?'

'No.'

'Then you can't heal him. You can't go near him without protection because you can't bring this disease into our time. It will serve no purpose yet. Many thousands will die needlessly.' *And I have to be in control to carry through the rest of my mother's plan. I have a lot to do before this disease plays its part.*

But I don't tell her that. She's still staring at me as if she's in shock. 'Hey! Do you understand?'

She blinks and nods. 'What can I do for him? Do you have a vaccine with you?'

I bite down on my lip and shake my head.

'What is it? What aren't you telling me?'

I fasten my eyes to hers to make sure she understands. 'Time travel will accelerate the virus.'

'How fast?'

'I don't know.' But I can't maintain eye contact and she can tell I'm lying. I'll be damned if I'm going to tell her that the most time her partner has left is a few days.

'Tell me, how long does he have?'

I swallow. 'I. Don't. Know. Listen, it's too late for your partner. You have to leave him here.'

She shakes her head, her eyes going wild. 'I won't leave him.'

'You can't take him.'

'This is not your business now. Step out of my way.'

She tries to pass me. I don't let her and she screams, 'Let me through!'

'Not until you put the mask and gloves on.'

When she doesn't move, I yell, 'Put them on now!'

As she begins to put the gloves on she mutters, 'Why do you care anyway if I catch this disease?'

Seeing that she's past the initial shock and finally putting her protection on, I release her, and walk away mumbling under my breath, *I have no idea.*

# Chapter Twenty-three

## Jesilla

Outside the Pharaoh's bedchamber Bastian looks at me as if I were a poisonous snake he wanted to kill yesterday. Through a jaw clenched tight and lips trembling with his rage he spits out a question at odds with the venom in his eyes, 'Are you hurt?'

'What? No.'

His anger is a tangible entity brewing like a storm in my bones. 'Bastian.'

He slices the air in front of my face with an open palm. 'Not now.'

Gripping my elbow, he drags me into a vacant room. I only let him because his anger has caught me by surprise. I am speechless.

He looks up at the ceiling. 'Bring us home, Keziah. *Now*.'

I wake in my bed. It's still dark outside, but the stars I glimpse through my windows are not shining with their usual brilliance. I sit up and swing my legs to the floor. I'm so out of it. How long have I been sleeping? What is the last thing I remember?

My stomach churns as memories flood in. Why did *they* have to be there? Their equipment wasn't ready yet. I checked the data myself. I had Peter explain anything I didn't understand. He assured me they needed seventy-two hours. It was why I insisted we bring the mission forward two days and Keziah organized it.

In a flash of panic I run my hand around my torso, but nothing's there. I rummage through the sheets, but again nothing. I sit still and focus, picturing our return to the control room. Keziah unhooks the canister, asks for the toolkit. I mumble that I must have left it behind. He raises his hand to my forehead to send me back into my sleeping body. I try to stop him. 'I need to explain.'

He says, 'I know. I saw.'

'No, wait. Kez, we have to alter this disease in case the Guard get their hands on it and create vaccines.'

He nods. 'I will notify the lab immediately.' He lifts his hand to my forehead once more. 'We will talk more after you rest.'

*They shouldn't have been there. In the least, had they known what king it was, they could have come prepared.*

'They mustn't have known that either,' I mutter into my silent room.

An image of the blue-eyed Guard bravely accepting his fate steals my breath away. Such was his loyalty that he was without anger at what went wrong. There was no blame, no judgement, only an honorable adherence to his cause. An inner strength I could only admire. In a split second he assessed the situation, deciding his best option was to stop me - no matter the consequences for himself. No matter it meant he would die a horrible death in the distant past.

Though my enemy, I applaud what he did last night. The Guard will definitely feel his loss.

A tear drops onto my hand. I touch my cheeks, knowing already that my face is wet.

*Tears for my enemy?*

What in all the universes would my mother think?

Shock? Outrage? Disgust?

My tears turn to laughter as I imagine my mother's reaction. But seriously, what's happening to me? And not knowing the answer, I laugh even harder. I laugh until I'm breathless, my fingertips tingling, the tip of my nose numb.

Am I losing my grip on reality? I sit on the edge of my bed. I don't think so. After all that I've been through, I can allow myself this one moment to *feel.*

Suddenly the door flings open. I'm still catching my breath from laughing so much that I'm not ready to see anyone. But I have no choice when Bastian switches the overhead light on, disappears from the door and reappears in front of me. I get only a moment to take in the spread of his legs, muscles coiled so tight they strain against his denim jeans, his hands balled into fists. I look up with my mouth hanging open, completely unprepared for his anger. But when he grips my upper arms and hurls me across the room I'm utterly speechless.

I look up from the wall just in time to see him coming for me. He grips my upper arms again, his hold even more punishing. He sneers down at me, and his glowing eyes reek with self-hatred. 'You said they wouldn't be there.' His lowered voice holds more menace than if he were shouting. 'You said their machines weren't ready, that they had to be perfect before any of the Named would be sent that far back in time.'

'Maybe they weren't *Named*.'

'News flash. They both were.' He inhales a deep breath through flaring nostrils, keeping his fingers wrapped around my upper arms. 'I have to know, Jesilla. I have to ask. Did you do it on purpose?'

His stance and flaming eyes should intimidate me. They don't, because I'm not afraid of Bastian. I know him. I know what sets him off, what makes him smile, what makes his blood run cold. And recently, what makes his blood turn to fire. And one thing above all else, Bastian knows how much I can take, how far he can go. He would never hurt me beyond my abilities to self-heal. I return his disgusted look with a cold one of my own. 'Do you really believe I would do that?'

'You were laughing when I knocked on the door.'

'You knocked?'

'You didn't hear me, you were laughing so hard.'

I open my mouth and close it again. 'That wasn't laughter. Well, not in the way you think.'

'Just answer the question, Jesilla. Did you set a trap for them?'

His insinuation hurts, but I would rather die than let him see how much. His lack of faith in me is another thing that cuts deep. But while I can hide my hurt feelings, I can't do the same with my anger. I punch out the words, '*Release me now.*'

He studies his hands and a look of surprise and self-repulsion comes over him. He releases my arms from his bruising grip, but he doesn't step back. He's angry and he's not ready to let go of it yet. 'Well, did you do it on purpose?'

'I made a mistake,' I admit. 'I assumed the Guard would not take certain risks with their teams. They must be so worried about what we can still do if they're willing to risk two lives to stop us. Apparently, losing our Goddess and our General in one blow hasn't decreased our capabilities in their eyes.'

'Hmm.'

'What are you thinking?'

He shrugs his shoulders. 'That you're right. They don't think our losses have shaken us.'

'Is that a guess, or do you know for sure?'

'They're worried. They know we still have our army, they assume we're going ahead with the Order's plans to control all the governments of the world but they don't know what our plans are, and they think we're going to retaliate against them in an act of revenge for losing Lathenia and Marduke.'

'How long have you known this intel? And why are you only telling me now?'

He doesn't answer, doesn't even look at me.

'Want to tell me why you're so upset? Bastian, sometimes I wonder where your true alliances lie.'

He turns, his eyes blazing again. 'After all we've been through, you can still question my alliance?'

'They are *your* friends,' I remind him with a sneer.

All this time, how hard has it been for Bastian to play two sides? Has he ever mixed the boundaries?

'Don't blame me just because you're feeling guilty, Jesilla.'

'Think about it, Bastian. What did I have to gain by luring the Guard into a mission they weren't prepared for? I'm not responsible for what our enemy does. I don't know what they're thinking. Do you?' I accuse. 'Because you certainly sound as if you do, and that might have helped.'

'I told you everything,' he hisses through his tight jaw. 'But you're in charge, Jesilla. It's your job to know everything.'

'I couldn't foresee this, Bastian, so stop blaming me.' *Isn't it enough that for the rest of my life I will see the calm acceptance in the blue eyes of that noble Guard?*

'That was Ethan with the Pharaoh's diseased blood all over his face.'

I gasp, 'Ethan?' Those blue eyes did seem familiar, but in that prince's body, looking older with the elongated bald head, Kohl blackened eyes, I'm not surprised I didn't recognize him. But... *Oh my God.*

Bastian nods, his mouth still tight with anger, hatred in his eyes.

Is that hatred for me? Wow. That didn't take him long. I mean, I can hate myself for not being more thorough, for not checking again at the last moment. But Bastian's anger is suffocating, as if he's holding my head underwater. No one should see their leader this vulnerable, or feel they have the right to throw her across a room because they're angry at her actions.

I have to face the fact that my mother's plan is my responsibility. No one has the desire or the will or reason to finish it except me.

'You have to get off my case, Bastian. Sometimes in war things happen that we can't change. It doesn't mean we have to like it. There's just nothing we can do about it.'

'Is that right? So Ethan's death is collateral damage, and you're all right with that?'

*No, I'm not all right with that!*

But I would rather be damned to Hell than admit to my mistakes more than once. I would have no dignity left. I can't rule a force this complex, with a plan this important, if I'm forever apologizing, because it will make me appear weak, and no one will take my decisions seriously.

I get to my feet and without thinking, as if I have no control over my own limbs, I raise my hand and slap Bastian across the face.

The smack is loud in the silent room. He lifts a hand to his cheek that's already turning red.

*Oh, shoot.* I'm surprised and instantly sorry because after all this is Bastian and I... and I... and I never want to hurt him.

He leans down so that his forehead presses against mine. 'I'm angry at you, Jesilla,' he says. 'I needed to know if you secretly set this up.' His hands lift to the sides of my face where he gently brushes his thumbs over my moist cheeks. I'm not expecting his tenderness. 'But I understand the position you were in when Ethan went for the canister. By then you were left with no choice.'

I slip my hands between us and shove him away from me with open palms. They tremble, so I ball them into fists. 'Do you think I threw the Pharaoh's diseased blood over Ethan to defend myself?'

'Well... yeah,' he says. 'Isn't that what happened?'

'I protected that test tube even while we fought, but Ethan still managed to get to it. He crushed the glass when he wrenched it from my shirt.

'It was an *accident*?' He pulls me into his arms. I resist, hurt by his assumptions, but only for a moment.

'I'm sorry, Jesilla. I had it wrong.'

'I tried to warn him.'

He pulls back to see my face clearly. 'You tried to *warn* him?'

I nod, and he pulls me against his chest even tighter, cradling the back of my head with his hand. It's such a comforting hold. A safe hold. As if there is nothing in the world that Bastian wouldn't do for me. A part of me wants to stay locked in his arms, forget who I am, the powers I have, the things I have to do.

But of course I can't. There is too much ahead. I haven't even read the letter my mother left me, or checked the DNA results. She may have left me instructions to follow. I wouldn't know.

Bastian's hand moves from my head to the back of my neck where his fingertips work magic on tense muscles there; and his thoughtfulness, his tender touch, is undoing all the hard edges inside me. A sob climbs up my throat, a sob for all that I've lost and all the harm I've caused and must yet generate to finish this.

His hand sweeps down my spine to the small of my back, while his other hand cups my chin and tips my head back so that I'm looking into his eyes. He whispers, '*Jesilla, Jesilla.*' Lowering his lips, he caresses my neck and his kisses light my body on fire. He brings his mouth to hover over my eyelids, again whispering, '*Jesilla, Jesilla, Jesilla.*' The sound of his voice saying my name over and over is like a poem. Like a prayer. Then he brushes his cheek with mine, and chaos reigns amid my senses.

Tugging a stray curl behind my ear, Bastian lets his fingers explore my throat. Peering into his eyes I find something that's not been there before. It's dizzying to know that being this close affects him too. Thinking that we're about to kiss is playing tricks with my brain. Synapses are firing in all directions inside my skull.

He leans down so that his lips hover over mine. I think he's going to kiss me.

And I'm pretty sure I'm going to let him.

A loud thump has us lift our heads and turn them to the open door. I ask, 'What was that?'

'I don't know, but it has such lousy timing I might just kill it when I find out.'

A little laugh escapes. 'Where do you think it came from?'

'The back yard.'

'But nothing can get through our sensors.'

'No, and yet something just did.'

# Chapter Twenty-four

## Jesilla

We take off downstairs, when halfway down a high-pitched pinging alarm goes off and, *wham*, the titanium shutters close over every window, door and glass wall in the house. It's the ultimate security system, effectively shutting us inside and everything else outside, turning the complex into an impenetrable fortress.

Keziah rushes out of the downstairs lift, stopping at the foot of our stairs with an armful of guns.

Bastian jumps down on silent feet, taking the gun Keziah hands him in his left hand, a pistol in his right. 'Where's the breach?'

'There is something dark and misshapen crawling up the stairs of our rear deck.'

I'm one step behind and hear this description. What kind of creature can get through our fences? He hands me my guns. As I check them over I mind-link, *When did you check on Rochelle last?*

*She's out cold. Nothing will wake her until morning.*

With that confirmed, I hurry to the living room, which accesses the back deck and rear yard.

My security team of Zander and Pearl, along with two of our best soldiers from below, Ian Banner and Jacob Guiro, both dressed in official black uniforms, are already in positions spread out across the rear living room wall. I nod at each of them. Ian, the more senior soldier nods back while Jacob touches his cap. I look for Peter, finding him behind a workbench that doubles as a bar. He jumps on a stool and begins working the cameras while slipping his arm into his remaining shirt sleeve.

'Do we have a visual yet?' Bastian asks, positioning himself to the right of the door. 'What's taking so long?'

'Coming up now,' Peter says.

There are four screens in this open living area, the nearest is left of the door, where a split screen appears with two different camera angles. Peter switches cameras, giving us clearer images.

I throw my hand over my mouth to contain a gasp.

Sprawled across the back deck is a human. At a guess I would say male with both legs broken and a displaced shoulder. Covered in blood, some dark red, but some black like the beasts. His face is also a mess, with deep gashes around the jaw where part of his chin appears to be missing, and one eye dropped down to his cheek due to a broken socket. These disfigurements make it hard to identify him, but who could be this desperate to reach us? Who knows enough about the complex to get through all the sensors and invisible electric fences, especially in that condition?

The man moves, dragging himself over a few more timber slats with one shoulder higher than the other, his head barely off the deck as if he has no strength to raise it. Lifting up on one forearm with great effort he lunges forward, emitting a guttural scream when his torso slams into the timber deck.

'*Holy cow,*' Zander exclaims. 'Are you people watching this?'

No one volunteers a credible explanation or can identify him.

The man seems to gather himself for another forward surge, this time it seems he's more interested in raising his upper half as high as he can. Lifting his head, he looks straight into the security camera above the door.

'God, that's hideous.' Pearl remarks. 'Who wants to put it out of its misery?'

'Peter, take us off lockdown.'

'Wait, Pete,' Zander says, turning to me. 'Jesilla, are you sure that's the right move? I could slip out and put a bullet in his head before he even knows I'm there.'

'He's not an animal to be put out of his misery.' I glance at the others. 'Am I the only one who can see who this is? Someone put the spotlight on the man. And, Zander,' I wait for him to look at me. 'Don't question me again. If you have something to say, come and see me privately. Do you understand?'

I get a few glances for that. They're not used to me being assertive. Well, they had better get used to it.

Zander answers, 'You have my word.'

As Peter hits a few keys on his laptop, and lights beam directly down on the man, there is silence for a whole two seconds before everyone spins into action. House lights go on, the shutters roll up, locks click open, and lastly, we train our guns on the door.

Keziah arches a brow.

I shrug. 'Can't be too careful.' I turn to Jacob. 'Captain Guire, you get the door.'

The last thing I expect to see is *this* man sprawled across my back deck, let alone in such a mangled state. He must have quite a story to tell.

'Marcus? *Marcus?*' Keziah leaves his gun on a side table and rushes to Marcus Carter's side.

'Gentle, Kez.' I blink hard at the sight of Carter slumped on the deck and covered in dried blood. His jaw is hanging open on one side, with purple bruises from his shoulder down both arms, his legs mangled, clothes shredded and stained with urine and vomit.

He moves, desperate to come inside, but the movement sends the smell of rotting flesh wafting over us. Jacob groans, 'Oh, man, that's putrid. How long have his wounds been festering?'

The question is, how long has Carter been living like this? Hiding out from the Guard? Travelling mostly by night? I don't know how he could have survived these past few weeks alone in his condition.

'Zander, Ian, bring us a stretcher from the Clinic.'

It takes all of us working together to lift him onto the stretcher. His screams give us shivers. Bastian and Zander carry the stretcher inside while Keziah walks beside Carter making encouraging, soothing comments.

Lying on his back, Carter peers up at Keziah with wariness. He doesn't recognize him. But of course he wouldn't.

'I'll explain later,' Keziah tells him. 'Let's get you into the clinic first.'

'Did a beast do this to you?' Bastian asks.

Carter nods, his lips cracked.

We get him onto a bed in Room Two where I set up a fluid drip and an IV for antibiotics and morphine. I'm not a Healer like Keziah, but with Kez's frailty these last few years, I found the combination of traditional medicine and his healing touch worked well together.

Bastian gets Carter a cup of ice chips, giving him one piece at a time. While Carter moistens his mouth, we fill him in on our losses, remembering to go easy with the news of Marduke's activation of the curse.

'My brother is dead?' he asks, gulping with difficulty. '*She* killed him,' he spits, saliva oozing from the corner of his mouth. 'Rochelle Thallimar killed Marduke as good as if she turned him to stone with her own hands.'

Bastian opens his mouth to argue but I catch his eye and shake my head. 'So what happened to you?' he asks instead.

Carter tells us a little of his struggle to get here. As I thought, he moved mostly at night while hiding by day in the forests. But he doesn't tell us yet how he escaped the pit, how he got away from the beast, the one my mother left in there because the creature was pregnant.

Taking another ice chip into his mouth, he looks at me while I shine a slim torch into his eyes that are now as black as ebony. They were always dark, but never so black that there's nothing to distinguish his pupils from his irises. He's had it rough, but how were we to know? I had my own problems getting home after the battle. Should I have sent a team to search for Carter after so long? He was in another world, for pity's sake.

It doesn't take long to fill him in on our current position, and how I've become leader of the Order.

He lifts his hand and points a shaky finger at me. '*You* are not fit to rule this Order. Your mother and my brother will be turning in their graves if they could see how you abandoned me, leaving me to die in that underground pit.'

Keziah tries to soothe him. 'Now, Marcus, you need to be briefed before making random accusations.'

Marcus turns on him. 'And who the devil are you?'

Bastian laughs, then explains my rejuvenation power.

Carter stares at me with surprise. 'You can do that?'

'So it seems.'

He squints. 'Did your mother know about this talent, Jesilla?'

'I never hid anything from my mother, if that's what you're insinuating,' I answer with enough conviction to let him know that talk of my mother is off limits. There was always something about his secret visits that irritated me. So while Keziah and Bastian fill Marcus in on what he's missed, I run upstairs and check on Rochelle. I gave her enough sedation last night to keep her in dreamland until seven this morning. It's nearly six and she's still sound asleep. Looking at her now in bed, her hands folded over each other, her mouth relaxed in a gentle smile, she resembles an angel.

Having only selected memories must be good for people.

Feeling grubby I shower and dress for school, then bump into Bastian in the clinic as he's exiting Room 2. He shakes his head at me. That steely look in his eyes is a warning, and I stealthily back out.

But Marcus's power is in his senses of hearing, sight and smell. 'Hey, girly, get in here. I need to talk to you.'

*Girly?* He's not getting away with that again.

Bastian sees my anger flare and lifts a finger to his lips.

'I know you're there, Jesilla. Don't run off when I'm speaking to you, young lady.'

Bastian leans in and whispers, 'He knows everything.'

He means Rochelle. *Great.* 'Couldn't keep that for later?'

He shrugs. 'He had to know or it could get complicated here quickly.'

Keziah steps out, shaking his head. 'I've healed only half his broken bones and he insists on getting out of bed.' He sighs, looking at me. 'He wants to see you.'

I straighten my back and walk into Room 2. Carter is on his feet, one arm hanging limply at his side, the other gripping the IV stand. I glare at Keziah. 'You started with his legs?'

Carter walks up to my face. Instinct compels me to step back but I keep still, my shoulders stiff. Besides his smell, his spittle flies everywhere when he talks from his damaged mouth. 'I can't believe what you have done! How could you, Jesilla?'

'I assume you're referring to Rochelle's return from the dead?'

'Damn straight I am! Keziah filled me in on the how, but why? Why did you do it?'

'Marcus, this conversation is not going to happen until you're stitched and cleaned and properly re-hydrated. And that's an order.'

'An order?' he scoffs with disbelief. 'Whose?'

'Mine.' It's the calm tone of my voice that sends him into a rage.

But before he explodes, Bastian steps between us. 'You heard Jesilla. I'll help you get back into bed.'

Determined, Marcus shrugs out of Bastian's hold. 'Do you actually believe you've contained that girl's powers?' When I don't say anything, he yells in my face, 'Well, do you?'

'Whoa, man, you need to back off.' Bastian slips between us again, only this time flattens his palms on Carter's chest and shoves him backwards. 'Everyone knows you hate Rochelle with all your guts. It's not news. But you have to calm down. Right now she's upstairs in her room sleeping. This conversation will go nowhere if you wake her.'

He sneers. 'She's a *Truthseer.*'

'So am I,' I remind him. 'So is Bastian and Keziah. And I've been inside that girl's head. I concealed her memories, contained her powers, and then I gave her memories she shares only with me.'

'You naive girl,' he says. 'You think you can fill in for your mother? You don't have one tenth of her power. I watched you grow and you don't have the confidence or the guts to make the hard calls.'

This time Bastian lifts him off the ground, and uncaring of any of Carter's remaining wounds, straps him to the bed by his wrists.

Keziah reattaches the IV stand, and as the two settle him in, Carter pleads with them not to tie him to the bed. 'How can you do this to me? I'm the most senior member here. I command you to release my straps.'

Bastian leans over him, his hands tight on the rails. 'They stay until I can trust you won't do anything stupid that could ruin our plans.'

Carter points to the ceiling with his eyes. '*That* girl can hear through bricks, through stone and cement walls. You three have no idea what you've done bringing her back to life and keeping her under your roof. You're better off with her dead.'

Standing at the foot of his bed, I say, 'She fits perfectly into my plans to avenge both my mother and your brother's deaths.'

He studies me, maintaining eye contact, but when he speaks his voice is subdued. 'Jesilla, you're making a mistake with this girl. Electricity runs through her body. She's like Ground Zero inside a black hole. You can't contain that power. You can't control it. She'll play you, if she's not already doing it. And I'm guessing that's going to hurt your plans more than anything else.'

Bastian runs his hand around the back of his neck. 'We all know you hate Rochelle, but if you're not careful, she'll become your blind spot, your Achilles's heel. Before you know it, Marcus, she'll be bringing *you* down.'

Carter nods. 'You could be right there, Bastian. But I can resolve this if you let me.'

I don't like where this is going already. I exchange a wary glance with Bastian and Keziah.

Keziah shrugs a shoulder. 'How?'

'Let me test her. If we find out she's playing you, I get to do the honors.'

'So what, precisely, does that mean?' I ask, even though the sinking feeling in my gut is already telling me.

He shrugs. 'She should be dead anyway.'

Bastian sneers, 'So should you.'

Keziah lifts an eyebrow as if to say the man has a point.

'In just a few short minutes,' Carter explains, 'we'll know if she's playing you and everyone can rest easy if I'm wrong.'

Keziah shares a look with Bastian and me. 'What do you think? It's not a bad idea.'

Bastian glances at his watch. 'You need time to recover and get rid of that stink. It'll throw her off.'

Carter touches his swollen jaw, running his fingers over the raw, exposed wounds, and winces. 'I suppose I could do with a little more stitching up.' He glances at me and raises his eyebrows. 'You did a good job on *him*.' He inclines his head towards Keziah. 'Can you shake a few years off me too?'

'Not on your life.' I turn and walk away. I don't want to be late for school, and I still have to wake Crystal, but when I reach the door I glance back. 'Keziah will finish healing you. And by the way, Marcus, you have to lay low. No one can see you yet. You will remain in the clinic until you're ready to move underground with the rest of our people. You will eat in the dining room with the soldiers and security. I will arrange a room for you on the third floor, lower level, and I will find you a suitable position to make use of your skills.'

'I was your mother's Chief Advisor.'

'Not anymore. Do we understand each other?'

'You're making a mistake.'

'Only those I trust will advise me. Right now, you're not one of them.'

'You can't dismiss my experience and knowledge of the inner workings of the Guard.'

I don't answer.

'Jesilla?'

'What?'

He clears his throat with a gurgling sound that makes my stomach roll over. 'These memories you've given Rochelle, do any include me?'

I run a mental check as this could be important. 'No.'

His eyes gleam. He's an eagle, salivating over a field mouse he already has roasting over hot coals.

Bastian told me how Mr Carter hates Rochelle, though no one knows why. 'We'll gauge her reaction when she sees you,' I tell him. 'But it won't be for a few days. Keziah is the best healer that ever lived, but even he will need time to make you resemble your old self.'

'Till then,' he says. 'But any sign of recognition, and that girl is mine.'

# Chapter Twenty-five

## Ethan

Isabel struggles to put the gloves on because of her shaking hands. I push up off the floor and wait. I want to go to her, wrap my arms around her, assure her I'm OK and that we'll be going home to Arkarian very soon, but it's not going to happen that way, so I stay where I am inside the Pharaoh's bedchamber, waiting.

But the door opens and others fold in around her - servants, soldiers, my 'brothers'. I step out from the shadows. 'Stop. Everyone. The king does not have much time left, and as his eldest son, as his vizier and priest, he needs to discuss important issues with me alone.' I blink to clear a pink tinge from my eyes. 'The doctor will stay to assist. My father's business will not take long,' I assure them, pointing my arm at the door. 'Everyone leave now.'

They back out, mindful of the doctor. A servant bumps her. The mask topples from the crook of her elbow. She catches it before it hits the floor. The servant apologizes profusely, but Isabel remains oblivious while she works on the mask. In frustration she closes her eyes. She would be visualizing it on her face. It won't take her long now.

Opening her eyes she tugs the futuristic-looking mask over her head and ears, settling the clear window of a Perspex-type panel in front of her eyes, feeling with her hands how the purifying ventilation units sit like cups on each cheek.

It's a perfect fit. And now with the mask and gloves protecting her, I walk over, wiping blood off my hands with the underside of my kilt. She moves towards me too, her intention to hug me, clear in her dewy eyes. I shake my head and we stop with a meter between us. Close enough to see a vein in her throat throbbing wildly. She says, 'Tell me what to do.'

I turn to the Pharaoh. She jerks back, gasping at the sight he makes, propped up on white linen cushions spotted red with blood, his skin entirely covered in raised scabs, thick gunky fluid still oozing out of some. Bracing herself by blowing out a deep breath, she checks him out. I don't have to warn her not to touch him; her own sense of self-preservation stops her.

He's a not a pretty sight.

She frowns.

'What is it, Isabel?'

'I've never seen anything like this.' Her voice sounds different through the mask, deeper, machinelike. 'I'm not talking about his skin. Inside, the disease has destroyed his organs. It's crazy how his heart's still beating. It's weak and slow.' She looks at me. 'It's about to give up.'

'I thought so. He hasn't moved since I've been in here.'

'I'm not surprised.'

'Well, I'm glad he's still breathing.' I need the Pharaoh alive. Arkarian should know precisely what disease the Order is planning to unleash on the world. 'Isabel, I need you to do something.'

'Call Arkarian? I'll do that now before someone walks in.'

'No, don't call Arkarian yet, and don't worry about someone walking in, I bought us some time when you were putting your gloves on.'

'What do you want me to do?'

'I need you to take something back to our time.'

'Sure. What?'

She doesn't hesitate even though it's against the rules. She has no idea what I'm about to ask of her, or she wouldn't be looking at me so eager to help. 'A sample of the Pharaoh's skin with diseased tissue, fluid, blood and a scab attached.'

Without taking her eyes off me she points to the bed. 'From that Pharaoh?'

Without taking my eyes off her, I say, 'Yep, unless there's another Pharaoh infected with the same small pox virus in here.'

Her eyes dart around the furniture – the fancy bed with carved lions' legs, plush mattress and papyrus side rails, a chest of drawers, a low-legged table and two low-height carved timber seats, all exquisite handmade pieces fit for a king.

I pick up the tool kit the previous 'doctor' dropped in our scuffle and offer it to Isabel with my arm stretched out to capacity.

She takes it, nodding, 'Lucky for us, eh?'

I walk round the Pharaoh's other side, ready to hold him still when she makes her first incision. She's calm, her hands steady, even though this has to be hard for her. Hard for her not to vomit. It helps that the Pharaoh only gives a couple of moans while she cuts into him.

When she finishes removing a section of skin from the Pharaoh's side she drops it in a baggy she finds in the toolkit, then puts the sample inside the kit and holds it out to me.

Our eyes meet. 'You take it,' I say. 'Give it to Arkarian. He'll know what –'

'Stop talking,' she says. 'This is starting to sound like good bye.'

'Isabel... I can't take this disease back to our time.'

'Ethan, if you don't return with me I will remove this mask and kiss that Pharaoh's mouth right here, right now, right in front of you. And if you think I don't mean it...'

To my horror she starts tugging the mask off. Before she gets any further, I take the toolkit and shove it into the waistband of my kilt.

Her smile wobbles. 'The royals will know what to do.' And without waiting any longer, she calls out, '*Arkarian*.'

# Chapter Twenty-six

## Ethan

We shift, but when I open my eyes something is different. I'm in a room I don't recognize, windowless with white walls. I'm still in my Ancient Egyptian body, lying on my back on a steel hospital bed with twenty more stretching out to my right. The beds are empty except for the last one that has Isabel in it, also still in her Ancient Egyptian body.

She opens her eyes, sees me at the opposite end and bolts upright.

'Don't.' I hold my hand out, fingers splayed. 'Stay where you are.'

Defiant and determined, she slips off the bed and heads straight for me.

'Isabel, *stop*.'

I'm freezing and can hardly move with the chill inside my body, but where would I go to get away from her? I don't even know where we are. Somewhere in the shifting process she lost her protective mask and gloves. 'Don't risk your life, Isabel, it's not worth it.'

She says, 'Wrong. You are so worth it, Ethan.'

'You blackmailed me here –'

'Yeah, and now I'll heal you.'

A door opens halfway between us and Arkarian, Lord Penbarin and Lady Devine run in. Arkarian grabs Isabel, and lifting her off the ground, he carries her back to her bed where he gathers her into his arms and mutters soothing words while she sobs on his shoulder.

'But he's burning up!' she cries out. 'Let me go to him. Maybe I can fix this before it takes hold.'

'Listen,' Arkarian says. 'You must remain on this side of the room until Matt and Jimmy bring your sleeping form so I can return you to your body and remove you from here.'

'I'm not leaving until I've healed Ethan.'

'My love, you can't help Ethan this time.'

'I don't understand. I'm a Healer. I heal everything.'

'Not this.'

'Why not this?'

'You're not vaccinated against small pox. No one is under the age of thirty.'

Lady Devine and Lord Penbarin pull their gazes away from Isabel and Arkarian to help me sit up. Lady Devine's long red hair, today in a single plait down her back, whips past my face as she swivels her head round to tell Isabel, 'Have patience, my dear, for you will be vaccinated as soon as our stocks arrive from Athens in a few hours. All of the Named not yet vaccinated will be before the close of this day, as well, your friends, family and all the students, teachers and staff at your school.'

Lord Penbarin rests his palm on my forehead and frowns. 'She's right, Devine, our boy is running a temperature.'

'Already?'

Their eyes meet. His eyebrows lift. Her lips press together.

'What is it?' I ask.

Instead of answering they get busy fussing over me, deciding lying down is a better option. I don't argue because my head is beginning to throb. A worried-looking Arkarian passes Lady Devine a pillow and blanket, his normally violet eyes as dark as midnight. He lays his hand on my shoulder. 'We will fix this.'

Towering over us, Lord Penbarin covers me with the blanket, finding the toolkit tucked into my kilt's waistband. 'You brought something back with you?'

'It's a tissue sample from the Pharaoh.'

Arkarian reaches for it, arching a brow. 'Your idea?' I nod and fight the urge to close my eyes. 'Good thinking, Ethan.' His eyes lighten with hope. 'This might just save your life.'

Isabel calls out, 'They told me that travelling through time would accelerate the virus.'

Arkarian and the royals appear to know this already since no one wants to catch my eye.

'How long do I have?'

The door bursts open as another tribunal member rushes in. 'Where is he?' Her voice, strained and oddly high pitched, I would know anywhere. 'Arkarian, how bad is it, your message was -'

Arkarian and Lord Penbarin step aside for Lady Arabella to see me. She stops mid-sentence and rushes to my bedside, her black silk cape rustling. 'My dear boy, what have they done to you?' With a trembling smile she loses her battle to hold back tears. She strokes the side of my face and, frowning, she flattens her palm over my forehead, runs her hand round the back of my neck, over my bald elongated Ancient Egyptian head, and turns, snapping at the others, 'What have you given him for this fever? For the sake of all the dead immortals, why is he still in this... this borrowed body? It won't be as strong as *his* body, and do you have any idea how much time is passing in this place?'

Lady Devine says, 'We're waiting for his sleeping form to arrive.'

'Well, where is it?'

'Shaun is on the way,' Arkarian explains. 'Please, Arabella...' He tips his head towards me.

She sucks in a deep breath, and nods. When she looks at me next her eyes are red but the tears have abated. She spots Isabel at the other end with all the beds between us. 'She's not infected?'

'No,' Arkarian says.

'Make sure she stays that way.'

'I intend to.'

A brief knock at the door and King Richard pokes his royal head in. 'How is he doing?' Finding me, he smiles, though it's clearly an effort.

Arkarian hands him the sample. 'He will have a better chance when we know exactly what we're dealing with. I don't need to tell you how quickly we need these results, sire.'

'I will take them myself.' He comes and grips my hand. 'Stay strong, lad.' He winks, nods at the royals and rushes out.

Lady Devine leans over me. 'Open your mouth, Ethan.'

I do as she says to an assortment of gasps. Arkarian comes to see what the fuss is. After checking my mouth, he feels the glands in my throat and stands back. Deep in thought, he doesn't say a word but he's joined the royals in a conversation that only Truthseers are privy to hearing.

'What is it? How long do I have?'

Lord Penbarin chuckles softly. 'You're not going to die just yet, young man. As soon as your father arrives with your sleeping form, Arkarian will return you to your body and we will shift you to a healing room in Athens. Preparations are under way.'

'When will Dad get here?'

'He's not far,' Arkarian says and starts moving backwards. 'I need to check on Isabel.'

'Lady Arabella?'

'I'm right here.' She grips my hand.

'I need to talk to you before I... I maybe can't -'

She squeezes my hand, leans down and whispers, 'No need to explain. Arkarian has done that already, and I have begun investigating the situation... *carefully*,' she adds.

Her words reassure me that should I not recover from this disease, someone else will continue seeking the truth of whether Rochelle is somehow – *inexplicably* – still alive.

I lay back to give my head a break from the strain of holding it up. My headache is worsening. My limbs are aching too now as if I'm coming down with a heavy flu. Lady Arabella smiles, giving me hope, only her trembling bottom lip tells me she's lying.

'He's shivering again,' she announces.

Lord Penbarin unties his red cloak and throws it over my blanket. *I don't like this*; his frown says as I roll on my side and bring my knees to my chest.

Lady Arabella tugs the cloak up over my shoulders, tucking it in around my neck.

'Your fingers are freezing, my lady.'

'It's actually your overheated body that's making –' she stops, and like everyone else, looks up at the sound of pounding footsteps coming down the hallway. My first thought is Dad's arrived, but then the door flies off its hinges, lodging in the wall across the room.

'Matthew Beckett, do not enter this room,' Arkarian warns, flinching at the hard set of Matt's face and narrowed eyes, holding Isabel's sleeping body in his arms. 'Is Shaun with you?'

'No,' Matt says without elaborating.

Sitting on her bed looking groggy, Ancient Egyptian Isabel lowers her legs over the side. 'Jeez, Matt, what's with you? Have you seen Ethan yet? Have you heard what happened?'

Matt continues to glare at Arkarian. 'Ethan's predicament is precisely why I have an issue with your six-hundred-year-old boyfriend.'

'What?' Egyptian-Isabel moves to Arkarian's side. 'What are you talking about?'

Arkarian swings an arm around her shoulders. 'Stay still, sweetheart, let me return you to your body.'

She draws in a steadying breath.

'Close your eyes.'

As she does, Arkarian lowers his glowing hand to her forehead. Before our eyes Isabel's Ancient Egyptian body breaks into an infinite number of shimmering microscopic bubbles that hold her body shape for a moment as if resisting to give it up before dissipating and floating away.

At the same time in the corridor Isabel takes a breath in her brother's arms. She wakes and orients herself quickly.

'Put me down thanks, Matt,' she says. 'Now, what's your problem with Arkarian?'

But Dad arrives. 'I have Ethan! Come on, everyone. Move. Quickly!'

Isabel and Matt step out of Dad's way.

Arkarian directs Dad to lay my sleeping body beside me. The three royals stand back as I inch over to make room. A surreal, uncomfortable sense of being somewhere I shouldn't triggers a sudden out-of-body experience. 'Whoa.'

Arkarian's hand comes down over my forehead. 'Close your eyes, it will feel less disconcerting.'

In a heartbeat I'm back in my eighteen-year-old body while my borrowed body dissipates in a maze of blue bubbles.

And now I'm shivering more than ever, and the ache inside my joints, my muscles and bones, kicks in as if this disease knows I'm in a body it can claim.

Dad comes to give me a hug but Lord Penbarin stops him with a hand on Dad's chest. Dad gives me a heavy-hearted look. 'I was inoculated many years ago, but they want to ensure I'm vaccinated from whatever strain this is. I'll come as soon as they clear me.'

'I'd like that, Dad.'

'We're taking him now, Shaun,' Lord Penbarin announces.

Dad gives me a lingering glance. 'Your mother doesn't know anything, of course, but if she did she would want you to know that she *loves* you.'

'I know, Dad. I love Mum too.'

'You're not going to die, son.' Tears fill his eyes and his voice breaks as he adds, 'Ethan, I... I'm sorry for all those years I wasn't there for you. I could have been a better father.'

I nod because I'm choked up inside.

Lord Penbarin moves round and Dad goes to step back, but I grab his jacket and lock his eyes to mine. 'Dad. I forgive you.'

He gulps, tears fall, and he nods.

Aching all over now, I watch my father leave as I pull myself up on unsteady feet, but the three royals are beside me and help me to remain upright.

Outside Matt is yelling, 'Are you finished in there, Arkarian? I want to know why you risked Ethan and my sister's lives. I'm holding you accountable for this mission's failure.'

Isabel gasps. 'Don't even think about putting this on Arkarian. We all knew the equipment wasn't a hundred percent ready yet.'

'It doesn't matter whether the equipment was ready or not, Arkarian made the decision to go ahead anyway. He decided who went and who didn't. The fact that the mission failed is all on him.'

'Shut up, Matt. It would have been *you* making those tough decisions if you weren't such a coward and pulled back from your duties to lead us.'

'That was my father's decision.'

'Whatever. Failing this mission had nothing to do with Arkarian.'

'Are you telling me it was yours and Ethan's fault the mission failed?'

'Maybe. I don't know. I need time to assess what happened. You'll get a copy of my report as soon as I'm finished writing it up.'

'Tell me what you can remember.'

'There were mistakes.'

'Like what?'

'Well, we arrived late and couldn't change what had already transpired inside the pharaoh's bedchamber.'

'And if Arkarian had managed to steer you into the time period a few hours earlier, or found a better location to drop you, would it have made a difference to your outcome?'

She hesitates. She's thinking of the time we spent in the river swimming for our lives.

Arkarian says, 'It's all right, Isabel. I will answer Matt's questions after Ethan's transportation to Athens.'

But Isabel doesn't wait. 'Outside the palace steps,' she says. 'It couldn't have been a better delivery. We were still too late because the machine wasn't accurate.'

Hearing them argue churns me up inside. But I'm not the only one affected. No one knows where to look or what to say. Quietly Lord Penbarin raises his arm to my shoulder. 'Lean on me, Ethan.' Lady Arabella comes round my other side and we slowly make our way to the door.

'Everyone move back!' Lady Devine calls out, clearing a path, while Arkarian spreads his arms wide in front of Isabel, Matt, and Dad, forcing them to keep a safe distance as the royals shuffle me into the corridor.

How fast is this disease progressing? The time shift has done a number on me. If it continues to accelerate at this pace, will I even make it to Athens?

Lady Devine looks over her shoulder at me. She's hearing my thoughts. Of course she is. 'We're working on shifting us all in one move so the three of us,' she points to Lord Penbarin and Lady Arabella with the flick of a hand, 'can shelter your body through the shifting process, making it as painless for you as possible while slowing the rapidity of this disease which appears to accelerate during shifts.'

I nod and she adds, 'Hang on, dear boy. A few more steps and we'll have you in the healing room.'

'Before you take Ethan away,' Matt says, 'I have a question for him.'

Lady Devine's nostrils flare. She spins around and gives Matt a look that has him cringing. 'Only one question, my lady,' he assures her. 'I promise it won't take long.'

The royals consider Matt's request without speaking aloud. They don't want to delay the shift further, but this is Matt, our revered leader according to the Prophecy. Only, except for the battle, Matt's done little to earn their admiration. And now every second counts.

But they don't have the lab results yet anyway. 'I'll answer Matt's question.'

Lady Arabella gives Matt a dark look. 'You have thirty seconds.'

He nods. 'Ethan, in your mission to Ancient Egypt, to the best of your recollection, where did Arkarian drop you and Isabel?'

I blink to stop from swaying as the corridor fades from my view for a moment. When I open my eyes I'm looking into Matt's troubled ones. We grew up best friends, and then the Order got between us. But we're good again now, except that he ranks above me. So do I lie to him? *Can* I lie to him? From the beginning he's had a problem with Arkarian being with his sister. How much of his anger now is personal? I shift my focus to Isabel, whose eyes implore me to back her up. I glance at Arkarian. His deep purple eyes overflow with compassion for the position I'm in.

'Just tell Matt the truth, Ethan,' he says.

And that's all I need to hear.

'Arkarian dropped the two of us in front of King Ramses the Fifth's palace. Isabel is right in saying it was a good drop. Unfortunately the guard at the Pharaoh's bedchamber door was from the Order. I created an illusion which allowed us to get inside, however by this time the Order had two vials of the Pharaoh's blood. The first she'd secured in a canister. They have that one. The second was a glass test tube. I tried to retrieve both, but the test tube fractured in my hands and...'

Among a chorus of gasps, Lady Arabella huffs, and not bothering to hide her resentment, she glares at Matt. 'There's your answer, Matthew. I believe you have nothing to substantiate your claim against Arkarian. You, Sir, are now wasting valuable healing time.' She turns to Lord Penbarin. 'Are they ready for us?'

He's nodding when Isabel calls out, 'Hey, you can't go without me. You have to take me with you.'

'Isabel...' Arkarian gives her a sympathetic look.

Matt reaches for her hand but she pulls it away. 'You're not going, kiddo,' he says. 'You can't.'

She brushes him off with an exasperated look. 'Shut up, Matt. I'm going to Athens even if I have to swim there with hippos and crocodiles for company.'

I crack a smile at the jolt to my memory. She smiles through her tears. 'No one knows Ethan's body like I do.'

Arkarian's eyebrows rise and his mouth opens but he doesn't say anything and closes it again. He's not stupid. He knows not to take that the wrong way.

'I've healed Ethan so many times I'm aware of what he can and what he can't take.'

Arkarian grips Isabel's arms and makes her face him. 'You can't help Ethan without being vaccinated *and* that vaccine has to make sufficient progress in your body to protect you.'

'But that will take days.'

'They're ready for us now,' Lord Penbarin says, 'and we're not waiting any longer.'

'Please understand, Arkarian, I have to be with him,' Isabel says. 'As soon as I'm cleared I'll start healing him.' She pleads to the royals, 'I reconstructed parts of Ethan when that bomb on the Endeavour blew his chest to smithereens. You remember, Lady Arabella, you were there.'

Suddenly Isabel breaks free and runs toward us. Both Arkarian and Matt come after her, but her determination makes her move faster than they expect. Arkarian swears a four-letter word I never thought to hear him use. It catches Isabel's attention and when she looks over her shoulder at him, he uses his wings to shift in front of her. She runs into arms already folding around her. She fights to break free, but Arkarian's grip is like steel and eventually she calms and stops struggling.

'Let me go, Arkarian. *Please.*'

The pull on my limbs lets me know the shifting has begun. The royals close in tighter around me. But suddenly King Richard materializes beside Arkarian. He glances at us and says, 'Lab results are in. Healers are waiting. Go.' And as we blink in and out a couple of times, I hear him tell Arkarian, 'We cannot risk losing another of the Named because of this silly thing called *Love.*'

*Love?* Is that what people are thinking? But Isabel doesn't love me, not in the way King Richard insinuates. What

Rochelle did by sacrificing her life for me is love. I would have done the same for her. Damn it, I'd do it for Isabel too, and she would for me. But that doesn't mean Isabel and I share *that* kind of love.

Arkarian gets it. He knows everything. He knows Isabel loves *him* one way and me another altogether. But he looks confused. And hurt.

No. No way. He can't believe King Richard's connotation. Unless... unless he harbors doubts of his own. Since I lost Rochelle, Isabel's been by my side, maybe fearing that I would do what my father did when we lost Sera. Or maybe because she's my best friend.

*She's worried.* I shoot my thoughts at Arkarian, hoping he hears them. *She's anxious, that's all. Not in love. Isabel is not in love with me.*

'Take her somewhere that she can't easily find her way back,' King Richard commands Arkarian.

As the royals finally shift me, Arkarian's reply lingers in the air we leave behind. 'Yes, sire,' he says, 'I have just the place.'

# Chapter Twenty-seven

## Isabel

They won't let me go with Ethan. I watch them disappear, and the very real fear that I may never see Ethan again fires my anger into a rage I can't control. Needing to vent before my heart explodes, I see Arkarian talking to Matt, saying goodbye to Shaun, and I run at him while his back is turned. But he hears me and spins around in the last second. His remarkable eyes register surprise, and his mouth, that beautiful, perfect mouth that makes me insane with longing, parts in a soundless gasp.

It's his shock that gives me the slight advantage. Keeping momentum going, I leap, stretching upwards, and kick with my right leg. My boot connects with his temple. He falters and sways to the side.

'Isabel!' Matt grabs my arms from behind and yells in my ear, 'Have you lost your mind?'

Shaun wisely excuses himself and uses his wings.

'Let her go, Matt,' Arkarian says.

'You're not my favorite person, Arkarian, but my sister has lost her marbles in attacking you.'

'She needs to release her anger.'

'And you're content to let her take it out on you?'

'Any way that helps her,' he says, his eyes holding mine.

My anger falls away.

Matt feels the fight leave me and releases my arms. 'I may have my problems with your boyfriend, but he's a good man, Isabel. You should appreciate him more and not go chasing childhood crushes.'

I look up into my brother's eyes, more gold than brown these days, and I'm stunned. 'You're an idiot if you think I love Ethan and not Arkarian. Do I care for Ethan? Absolutely. But understand where I'm coming from, brother. Ethan is my partner and my best friend and there's a real possibility I might never see him again. And don't forget that I'm a Healer. A *Healer*, for God's sake. Do you have any idea what it feels like to have someone stop you from going to the one person your heart says you could heal blindfolded?

My eyes sting with unshed tears. 'I failed Rochelle and she died. You ordered me to keep her safe. I didn't. And if I couldn't keep Rochelle alive for Ethan, the least I can do is ensure Ethan lives for the two of them. But I'm failing that too and I don't know what to do.'

Matt pulls me into his arms. 'I failed Rochelle too. You're not alone in that, kiddo.'

Arkarian walks over. 'We all failed Rochelle.' He tugs me from Matt's arms and I fall against his chest, resting my head on his shoulder. 'I want to take you somewhere, Isabel. A place I should have shown you some time ago. But I won't do anything against your will no matter what orders I'm given.'

'If it's true that I can't help Ethan, then I'm better off far away. Is this place quiet?'

'As quiet as you need it to be.'

'Will you stay there with me?'

'I won't leave you for a second.'

I nod. 'Then, I'll go.' I smile but it's weak. 'I'm sorry I kicked you.'

He rubs his temple, catching Matt's eye. 'Your sister packs quite a hit.'

The two laugh. It's a sound I haven't heard for weeks. I miss it.

Matt points at Arkarian. 'We still need to talk, you and I. But I suppose it can wait until you return from... Say, where are you taking my sister?'

Arkarian remains silent and Matt says, 'At least tell me that it's safe.'

'I would not take Isabel any place that's not safe. You have my word on that.'

'What if I need to find either of you?'

'Call out my name and I'll get back to you.'

Accepting this on good faith, Matt kisses the top of my head, then leans down to whisper in my ear, 'Are you sure you're OK with this?'

'I trust Arkarian more than anyone else in this world.'

'Even me?'

'Yeah, even you, brother.'

He nods, looking thoughtful. 'As it should be.'

'You can leave now, Matt.'

He smiles and wings out.

Now it's just the two of us and the silence helps to keep me outwardly calm, though inside is churning.

'Before we leave there's something I have to check on.' Bringing his arms up around me, Arkarian says, 'Hold on now.'

I get a sense of moving fast, as if I were on a train with my head out the window. But it's over in a blink and then we're standing inside Arkarian's mountain chambers.

Tall and slender, his bright blue hair loose around his shoulders, Arkarian couldn't be more beautiful as he whips from one room to another. I marvel at how he moves, as if he's made of air and feathers, and also of steel.

'One more room,' he says, but stops suddenly. 'On second thoughts...' Taking my hand, Arkarian tugs me behind him and we run together into his octagonal work station where the sphere remains motionless and dark. It has him sighing with relief. 'Finally,' he smiles, 'something going our way.' He keys in a message on one of the monitors, explaining as he does, 'Jimmy will be here soon to take over the watch.'

He then leaves a note for Neriah with instructions on how to continue her work with the brush that will one day open a portal without the help of a sphere.

And finally he's folding his arms around me in a hold so tight even air would have a hard time squeezing between us. 'For the next few seconds I need you to stay close, Isabel.'

'Where are we going?'

He lowers his forehead to mine. 'You've been unhappy for a while now, and I suspect it's because I've been neglectful of your needs.'

'You're never neglectful of me, Arkarian.'

'In this I have been.'

'What are you talking about?'

'You'll see.'

'But, how long will we be gone? Ethan...?'

'We'll go directly to Athens once your vaccine has time to protect you. It will be delivered to us as soon as stocks arrive.'

I nod and he smiles. 'I'm going to use my wings to shift you with me, OK?'

'Like the royals did with Ethan because he was too weak to use his own?'

'That's right.'

'And because I don't have my wings.'

'Yet,' he says with a teasing wink.

'Are you taking me to where you live, Arkarian?'

His warm breath moves the loose strands of hair at the top of my head. 'I'm taking you home.'

My heart swells at the way he says this.

'I'm sorry that I haven't told you about this place before today.'

'I shouldn't have been jumping to silly conclusions.'

He rests his chin on top of my head. 'It's natural to be inquisitive and, well... I've been living there on and off for hundreds of years, I take the place for granted sometimes, but there are rules to keep those who live there safe.'

'Did Lathenia or Marduke know about this place?'

'We're careful who we let in, and Lathenia and Marduke were never welcome. Lathenia thought I lived in the Citadel. It was best for others to think that too so she didn't suspect there was somewhere else.'

I push his hair back behind his ears to see all his face, especially his impassioned eyes. 'Can I ask you something?'

'What is it, sweetheart?'

'Do you have a family there? I mean, am I going to find a wife, or a dozen children?'

His laugh is rich and reaches into my sad sorry soul, lifting it a little out of the darkness. 'I have no children, Isabel. Not yet,' he adds, peering into my eyes with a cheeky glint that makes my tummy tingle. 'I have no wife either, but... I did love a girl once. We stayed together even when she wanted to leave so I didn't have to go through the pain of watching her grow old and die while I... remained the same.'

'I'm sorry. What was her name?'

'Rosalee. She was twenty-one when we first met, while I was near two hundred. My hair was changing rapidly, my eyes no longer blue. My father told me about a place the locals called *The Valley.* It's where I'm going to take you. We were happy there until some years passed.'

'Rosalee grew old.'

'But no one else did.'

'It must have been heart-breaking for you both.'

'It was harder for her.' He turns his face into my palm. 'But that was a long time ago. And now I have you, and once you turn eighteen you too will stop aging. But we don't have to live in The Valley until there are signs that make you stand out. It's then our enemies find it easier to pick us out of a crowd. In the valley we can relax and be ourselves.'

'I understand now.' And for the first time since Lorian gave me the gift of agelessness I find myself appreciating it. I get to live with Arkarian for many lifetimes. And it's not as if I'll miss my brother, or have to watch him and Neriah grow old. Images of Ethan growing old sweep into my thoughts. I will find that hard to bear. I will miss him most.

Arkarian kisses me, and all other thoughts slip away. It's not like any kiss we've shared before. He's putting his soul into this, and his love flows inside me, spreading through my veins. My need to get closer to him rushes up from my toes to my fingertips. His hands glide over my back and I drown in the sensations his touch triggers on my skin. My heart beats a crazy rhythm and I moan against him. Slowly, and with a reluctance to match mine, he pulls back. 'Baby, I... uh...' he mutters, breathless, and thrusting his hands into my hair he whispers, 'You drive me crazy. Do you know that?'

'You don't make it easy for me either.'

He chuckles, his forehead resting on mine. 'I hate to say this, but we should go before Jimmy gets here.' He tightens his arms around me but we don't move yet. 'Before I shift us there, Isabel, there is something you need to know.'

My stomach drops. OK, here it comes, the part where he tells me... but wait, he already confirmed that he has no wives or children. That doesn't exclude a girlfriend on the side. Or... is he trying to tell me he's... what? My face feels hot suddenly. The walls are closing in.

'Where has your mind just gone?' he asks, his eyes dancing with amusement.

I shake my head. 'Sometimes, Arkarian, I wish I could read *your* thoughts.'

He laughs. 'Where we're going is a well-kept secret. It would be dangerous should our enemies locate this place. You cannot speak of anything you see there, or name anyone who lives there.'

'I understand.'

'Even when speaking to Ethan.'

'Uh... sure, but you can trust Ethan.'

'It's a rule we have to live by for the safety of all who live there. It's not personal.'

'Of course.'

'When my father made you an eternal, he altered your DNA by embedding an immortality gene in your chromosomes. A child of two eternal parents has a high probability of inheriting that gene.'

'Oh wow. So there are children there?'

'There are some.'

'How many live in this valley?'

'A few.'

I pull my head back enough to see into his eyes. His voice tells me he's being cagey, his shadowed eyes confirm it. 'How many live in the Valley, Arkarian? Tens? Hundreds?'

When he doesn't say anything I blink and ask, 'Thousands?'

'Perhaps a thousand, but it's a big valley and since most work for the Guard, they come and go. Sometimes there are only a dozen, other times hundreds.'

'Right.' Holy moly, it's a village. Hmm, he can't tell me there's not at least one girl – or boy – out of those hundreds that doesn't have eyes on him. But I'll know.

'Are you ready, Isabel?'

'Bring it on.'

'What did you say?'

I inject calmness into my voice. 'I'm ready, Arkarian.'

*Oh, yeah, I am so ready.*

# Chapter Twenty-eight

## Jesilla

After Crystal goes up to her room to do homework, I visit Marcus Carter in the clinic. Keziah worked on him for two days, and though the healing has exhausted him, he plans another session for tomorrow. Carter has come a long way already in recovering from his horrific injuries so hopefully Keziah won't have much left to do after tomorrow's session.

I don't know how Carter lived through his time in the pit with the beast. He's arrogant enough to simply refuse to die, but according to the story he's relating to me now, he had some luck on his side.

'The beast was in late stage pregnancy and incapacitated by her bulk,' he says, sitting in a lounge chair opposite me, his bed on my right, a mug of steaming coffee in his hands from which he is yet to sip.

Marcus is in a hurry to test Rochelle. I've come to see if his plan is viable, and if he's recovered enough not to scare the hell out of her. There were some problems with his scalp, where the beast had gored chunks of skin, leaving patches where hair would not regrow no matter how ingeniously Keziah tried. So Marcus is now sporting a shaved head.

It's the most significant of his physical changes, but nothing a cap or a wig won't fix for testing purposes. Inside his head, though, in his mind, the memories, will take their own time to heal.

'This beast couldn't move with the same agility as the others,' he says, staring over my shoulder at the white wall. He lifts the coffee to his mouth without his eyes moving. 'It was the reason your mother left her behind that day. She was in early stage labor.'

I sip my coffee, finally understanding. 'Lucky you.'

He stabs me with condemning eyes. 'You think?'

'I was being sarcastic, Marcus.'

After a scrutinizing pause, he nods. 'So after two days of chasing, catching me and goring at my flesh and bones, the beast had exhausted herself and didn't have the strength to deliver her infant.'

I'm not keen to hear what he says next, but I'm also riveted. I lean forward in my chair. 'What happened?'

'I had to help her.'

*What?* 'But... how could you do anything in your condition?'

He shrugs. 'My condition worsened later, after the infections took hold.' He shoots me that piercing ebony glare again, the one that blames me for not sending a rescue team.

I refuse to apologize.

'Anyway,' he says, giving up, 'I managed to pull the little tyke out of her.' He shudders at the memory, but it's his wide-eyed empty stare that reveals the true dreadfulness of his involvement. 'He was born hoofs first, horns last. Afterwards she was too enamored with her newborn to worry about me. I coaxed her into sitting under the exit for some fresh underworld air.' He rolls his eyes. 'I brought her food and water, and when she went to sleep I crawled up her back and climbed out.'

'She didn't wake?'

'She stirred, made eye contact, but we'd formed a unique connection by then.'

I stare; picturing him climbing over a beast's back for a leg-up.

Is it feasible?

Is it even possible?

His presence – his condition – should be proof enough. If I trusted him I would accept his story on face value.

'So once you climbed out of the pit, how did you escape the underworld?'

'Lucky for me, the rift was still open.'

'What?' My gut lurches with this news. An open rift between worlds allows creatures, animal, human, dead or otherwise to pass from one realm to the other. My mother opened the rift to bring the beasts to Earth. The underground cavern system proved to be the perfect space to house them. The Guard would have swept the otherworldly creatures back out through the rift in the first days after the battle. They must have closed the rift, knowing that both Lathenia and Marduke could not. Ever the resourceful one, Marcus must have disguised himself and hitched a ride.

He leans towards me, his eyes narrowed and fixed. 'Why didn't *you* close the rift, Jesilla? You've taken on your mother's leadership position without even so much as a vote, you should have cleaned up after her too, not leave it for the enemy. That makes you look weak.'

I sit back in my seat. What's he talking about? 'Besides the fact that I was unconscious in a cave for the first seven days after the battle, I can't close a rift between worlds. As you well know, Marcus, it takes an immortal.'

He pulls a disbelieving face. 'She didn't tell you?' At my blank stare he mumbles, 'I'll be damned. She didn't have much faith in you, did she?'

Now he's pissing me off. 'Marcus, what is it you think my mother didn't tell me?'

He pats my hand. 'Jesilla, you're immortal.'

'What?' I brush his comment off as ridiculous.

'Can you remember an injury where you didn't heal?'

'I've grown up under the protection of my personal body guards. If I even looked as if I was going to fall over, one of them would catch me.'

'Sweetheart, your mother was the Goddess of the Dark and the Underworld. And as I recall you turned eighteen recently, so by now you're fully immortal.'

I jump to my feet, restless suddenly. 'My father was human, the same man who... who...' I shut my mouth. There are some things this man is better off not knowing.

'Actually,' he says, 'at the time of your conception your father was anything but human.'

I cross my arms over my chest. 'Care to explain that.'

'Perhaps you'd better sit down.' He waits. 'Your father was a royal who sat on the Tribunal overseeing the vast sector of Earth called Russia, also known as the House of Criers.'

I hold out my splayed hand. 'Wait. My father was a Guard?'

'He was, but unlike the rest of the royals, he wasn't an eternal. He was the last king from a very old family of immortals that had all but become extinct. And your mother fell for him.' He shakes his head. 'But he was... well, let's just say, as the fairest of them all the boy was a player. And when Lathenia discovered he cheated on her with another of his fellow Tribunal members, nothing could calm her rage.'

*Mother, what did you do?*

'When Lathenia discovered he'd fathered another child at the same time he'd fathered her child, she went after him hard.'

'You need to be more specific.'

He sighs and looks up. 'All right. Your mother killed him.' Before I get a chance to react, he puts his hand up to stop me. 'Then brought him back to life, but as a human.'

'Oh my God, that's so cruel.'

'Without his powers, and with vague memories of an amazing immortal life just out of his reach, he lost his identity. He became a man who didn't know how to be a human. All he had left were his good looks, and even those faded with time. He turned to drinking, and in his blind-drunken rages he took his frustrations out on the women in his life, without knowing why he hated them so much.'

*Rochelle! That confused bitter man raised Rochelle from an infant. From a little girl.*

Her father was an immortal while her mother was an eternal, both royal Tribunal Members. No wonder Rochelle's powers were so hard to contain. And maybe that's why Keziah found her brain still functioning even after that fatal arrow struck her chest and stopped her heart.

Marcus looks at me with something akin to pity in his eyes. But he's telling me the truth. It's one of my Truthseer powers. He would have to be a very good liar to get one past me.

I'm itching to leave, see if I can find something to validate this information. Keziah would know. I could ask him. I could demand he tell me. But he's supposed to be helping Rochelle with her homework so she doesn't come looking for me, and there is another source.

'Before you go, there are two things I want you to promise me,' Carter says.

I raise my left eyebrow. 'I'm listening.'

'I want the ability to shift.'

'Twenty years with the Guard and my uncle didn't release this ability in you?'

'The Guard do not question their superiors.' He rolls his eyes. 'Come on, Jesilla, you owe me. Can you do this or not?'

'We need to get something straight. Firstly, I do not owe you anything. And yes, I can do it. When you're healed enough and your body can handle it.'

He gives a curt nod.

'And the second thing?'

'We still need to discuss my role in the Order. You don't have many choices left with my knowledge and experience. So let's confirm it now that I will remain Chief Advisor.'

I square off my shoulders. 'Don't count on it, Carter. I'm reassessing all positions and I'll let you know.'

'I could help you.'

'I'll think about it.' To sever any further conversation, I get up. But now he's looking worried and asks about testing Rochelle.

'You're not ready. We'll give it a few more days.'

He nods, and in a voice that's not unkind he says, 'Your mother must have left you something, some proof of your immortality.'

I remember the letter I haven't wanted to read. Though weeks have passed since her death, seeing her eloquent handwriting will hammer home the fact that she's gone forever.

'It's why Rochelle is a threat,' he says.

'What?'

'I'm telling you, Jesilla, that girl is playing you. She's the other Tribunal member's child. Your half-sister. Am I right?' He waits for me to nod. 'Her father and yours are the same.'

Did my mother tell Carter *everything*?

'Do you know Rochelle's mother? There can't be that many female Tribunal members.'

He huffs. 'There are four. It could be any one of them.'

I start walking away and he calls, 'There's one more thing.'

'What is it, Carter?'

'If I'm right about Rochelle, my hands won't be the ones that can finish her.'

I stare at him. What is he saying exactly?

'You, Jesilla, will have that honor.'

*Me? Kill Rochelle? But she's my sister.*

'I'll be there,' he says. 'Just promise me that I can watch.'

# Chapter Twenty-nine

## Isabel

The shift to the Valley takes longer than the last time I travelled with Arkarian using his wings. We're in a whirlpool of darkness and swirling winds. No wonder Arkarian needs to hold me close. When we stop, he doesn't release me, just relaxes his arms a little.

The air here is different. It's crisp and cool and clean. There's a subtle scent of flowers, a stronger scent of pine, spruce and fir trees, and a breeze that's so pure I feel it in my marrow.

Stepping out of Arkarian's arms I get an overwhelming sense that if I breathed this air into my lungs every day I would live forever. 'We're on a mountain.'

'We are,' he confirms, looking impressed. 'Several, in fact.' He points in three directions. I spin around and see green grass, wildflowers, hills covered in trees. 'But we're also in a valley that lies between these mountains with rivers and lakes and fertile soil.'

'Electricity?'

'We utilize the elements of wind, sunlight, water and other products nature provides to power our farms, houses, school and stores.'

'I'm impressed.'

He smiles. 'I hoped you would be.'

Taking my hand, we walk over an area of undulating hills covered in soft knee-high seed-grass. I spot something glistening on my far right. 'Is that a river?'

Squeezing my hand, he tugs and we run across fields of wildflowers like carefree children, scrambling down a riverbank to walk on pebbles and dip our feet in cold clear water. We follow the river into woodlands, and when we emerge we're in a clearing with snow-capped mountain peaks for a backdrop, the sounds of hissing and thrashing water not far away.

We approach the falls from the top. I stare, speechless at the majestic vista spread out before us. In the shape of a vast semi-circle with staggered shelves of jutting rocks, water splashes down three levels into a gorge hundreds of meters deep on both sides. The spray hits my face with a stinging freshness and I stand still and soak in the invigorating atmosphere.

'Wow,' I exclaim, 'I would be able to breathe here.'

Keeping his eyes on me, Arkarian beams. He lifts my hand and plants a tender kiss on my palm, leaving his lips to linger there while he looks into my eyes. Delicious chills sweep through me at his intimate touch and my breath stalls. To distract myself from ripping Arkarian's shirt open and running my hands over his hard abs, I ask in as steady a voice as I can manage, 'Where is this place? Are we still on Earth?'

He throws his head back and laughs, then brings his forehead down to mine with a glint of mischief in his eyes. 'If I tell you,' he whispers, 'I'll have to kill you.'

I roll my eyes.

'Come on,' he says, 'we have a lot to see in a short time.'

*Ethan.*

My heart clenches and I berate myself because for a moment I wasn't thinking of him, but enjoying myself.

Arkarian cups my face with his warm hands. 'You can't help Ethan today and probably not for another two or three days. This time away will do you good, Isabel. It will help to clear your head, gain perspective, and be the friend Ethan needs. Know that at some point, you will have to let him find his own way through his grief. He has to feel it, baby. You can't take that away, but you can be there for him when he's ready to put himself back together.'

I trust Arkarian. He loves Ethan as he would his own brother, so I have no hesitation in believing him now. But I still have to give myself permission to let go, and that's what I'm finding hardest.

We walk into a field of waist-high flowers in pastels of blues, pinks and yellows. Adjoining this is another field with vegetable crops growing in neat raised rows. A couple of young people working the crops waves at us, calling out to Arkarian by his name. We come to a paved road and walk past an orchard of orange trees, branches heavy with fruit. Houses come into view, some high in the hills, others closer to the road, contemporary homes made of bricks and timber with wide decks and glass walls.

'Where are we headed?' I ask.

'This road leads to the village center where you will find a few shops, restaurants, a school and a temple.'

'A temple?'

'It's a church that doesn't favor one religion over another,' he explains. 'It's a place where people can gather together to pray, and for special occasions, like *weddings*.'

Not sure what reaction he's looking for, except for awkwardness, I stay silent. Did he emphasize the word *weddings* specifically? Sure, one day I'm going to marry Arkarian, but not until I've lived outside Angel Falls and experienced more of life.

I end up mumbling, 'Right. Well. Yeah, that's good to know.'

He laughs, sliding his arm around my shoulders, dispelling the awkwardness with a beautiful teasing smile. I haven't seen Arkarian this carefree before and I have to admit that I like this side of him. It's as if I'm seeing all of him now.

His hand glides down my arm. Goosebumps break out everywhere his fingers skim my skin. He links his fingers with mine. 'Come on, I have some friends I want you to meet.'

'You have friends?'

His eyebrows both rise. 'Do you think I have no friends, Isabel?'

I shrug, my face heating up. 'I guess I thought you were all mine.'

He stops and tips my chin up so that I see nothing but his incredible purple eyes. 'You have me, Isabel, all of me, for all time.'

He leans down to kiss me when an excited voice rings out, 'Arkarian's home.'

'And he's brought someone with him,' another announces in a voice loud enough to startle birds from their nests.

Against my mouth, Arkarian smiles and says, 'Hold that thought.'

As if our presence has set off a silent alarm, people emerge from houses, farms, on foot and even horseback.

Watching twenty or thirty people hurrying to the town center, I ask, 'How long have you been away?'

Looking unsure, he shrugs.

A dozen or so paved streets criss-crossing over a wide road, along with a few community buildings, a couple of restaurants and the white temple with steps leading up to double front doors, make up the town center.

We reach the first street when they gather around us, coming up to hug or shake hands. I stare at them because they're so perfect, with flawless skin, vivid eyes and unusual colored hair, though Arkarian is still the most beautiful by far. He stands out amongst them. It must be because as well as being the son of the deceased immortal, Lord Lorian, his mother was a beautiful young French girl.

There are some children here too, and young teens, but not many.

One girl in particular snags my attention the moment she emerges from a store. She recognizes Arkarian and smiles to herself as she pulls her hair free from a high ponytail. Long wavy aqua-colored hair drops to her waist. Wearing low-hung jeans, a white crop top with a deep V front leaves plenty of bare golden skin. She strides down on long slender legs in black boots with a swagger I could only dream of pulling off.

People make way for her. Her confidence demands it. This is a girl used to getting her own way. She rocks up to Arkarian with a one-sided smile and a dimple some might think is cute.

'Hello, stranger.' Her voice is low and seductive, her light blue eyes spilling with need.

She wants him.

The question comes to mind, has she had him already?

Completely ignoring me, the girl leans in to kiss Arkarian's lips but he turns his face at the last moment and she kisses his cheek instead. Unfazed, and with her aqua hair draping over him, she whispers something in his ear that makes him laugh.

I hate her.

I know it's unreasonable, but I hate her so much I want to hack her hair off with shearing clippers.

An offhand gesture of touching Arkarian's shoulder turns the blood in my veins to ice.

So this is the girl I have to watch. I knew there'd be one. I just didn't think I'd find her this quickly.

She glides her long fingers around Arkarian's neck and caresses him in a sensitive spot just below his ear. The thought that this girl knows about it, and has likely done this before, sends me reeling inside. I don't care that he's persistently tugging her hand down and looking more and more annoyed. I'm going to take that girl's hand and break every finger if she doesn't stop touching him.

*Whoa*, I'm losing it, and in front of Arkarian's friends. It's just that there's something about the girl that makes me want to slap the smug smile off her face. But this is Arkarian's home, and he's looking increasingly uncomfortable. As he pulls the girl's hand away again she captures his fingers, leans around his back, and looking straight at me, blows me a kiss.

All logical thought leaves. It's as if her possessive message is stripping back my sensibilities so that all I have left is exposed raw emotion.

And my heart has had enough.

Arkarian feels me stiffen and move aggressively towards her. With lightning speed he pulls me back to his side, tucking me under his shoulder. 'Everyone,' he calls out, 'this is Isabel.'

A bearded guy with yellow eyes arches a brow. '*The* Isabel?'

I peer up at Arkarian. *The Isabel?*

He smiles down at me, his eyes locking with mine. 'Yes,' he says without shifting his gaze, and in front of everyone, eyes glowing with tell-tale flashes of his desire, he says, 'This is my Isabel.'

My breath catches in my throat.

Everyone outside the small space Arkarian and I occupy blurs out of vision. They may as well not exist. It's just Arkarian and me. And I know then, I want to be alone with Arkarian more than I've wanted anything in my life.

But the warmth these people extend to Arkarian they now give me. They invite me into their homes, and when I politely decline, they make me promise to visit before I leave. Those with children introduce me to them. Others ask a gazillion questions. How did Arkarian and I meet? What did I think of his purple eyes and blue hair? When did I realize it was true love?

A flash of a white bridge in a grey realm pitches into my head with Arkarian calling my name, but I don't get time to analyze the strange vision before a new group approaches with more welcoming hugs and questions. Meanwhile, *that* girl, now standing to the side with arms folded over her chest, stares at me like I just drowned a litter of her puppies.

Suddenly she calls out, 'She's still a child, Ark. Are you sure she's eternal? What's her bloodline? We haven't heard of any royals giving birth for eighteen years. We should collect a sample of her blood for analysis.'

Arkarian's whole body stiffens. He spins around and says in a menacing tone, '*No one* puts a needle in Isabel's veins.' Giving me an apologetic look, he grumbles under his breath and turns back to the gathered group. 'Isabel will be eighteen in thirteen months, three days, and eleven and a half hours.

She was awarded the gift of agelessness by our recently departed immortal, my father Lord Lorian, because Isabel is my *soul-mate* and he did not want me to lose her with the passing of time.'

While people gasp, I glance up at Arkarian and stare. 'Why do you know my birthday so precisely?'

He winks and his crooked smile curls my toes and makes me aware of him in a multitude of fascinating physical ways. The urge to be alone with him hits me again, but with more intensity than before. More than ever before.

Reading my mind or sensing a shift in me, he excuses us to his friends, takes my hand in his, and we walk up a green hill to a forest. Voices fade until we hear only birds and our own breathing. He lays his palms on my shoulders. 'Are you ready to see our house?'

My heart turns over. '*Our* house?'

'It doesn't have to be yet,' he says carefully. 'We don't have to live here at all. Ideally, you will finish high school and university, and work for as many years as you'd like in your chosen career. We have the time, Isabel. We have all the time we need.'

I stop him there with my hand splayed on his chest. 'My career is with the Guard. I serve the Guard. I am a Guardian and I am Named. Whatever education I do will be to enhance my abilities as that soldier.'

He folds his hand around mine and we walk deeper into the forest. 'We can make our home anywhere in the world,' he says, unable to stop smiling. It's so endearing I want to kiss him until I'm breathless. Until he's breathless. He says, 'From a remote, uninhabited island in any of five oceans to an apartment in the center of Manhattan, the choice is ours.'

'What about our hair, and our eyes? Won't we stand out?'

'Not in New York, trust me,' he chuckles. The sound pulls at my heart strings, and I realize just how much I do trust him... with everything.

'Here in the Valley, we can be ourselves, live amongst others like us when we want company, or we can keep this place as our sanctuary as we travel the world.'

My eyes burn with tears I refuse to release. I've cried so much lately because I've been sad. I'll be damned if I'll cry now because I'm happy.

But he notices anyway and abruptly stops. 'I've waited a long time for you, Isabel.' He lifts me from under my arms, raises me into the air above him and twirls me around. And I laugh with him as the breeze lifts my hair and a sense of freedom sinks into my bones.

He lowers me slowly, his eyes holding mine. 'On my life I swear I will never hurt you. I couldn't. I love you, Isabel. I live to please you.'

Tears trickle down my face, and I can't stop them. I don't even try. They're a testament to how powerful Arkarian's words are, how deeply they affect me. 'I love you too, Arkarian.' Enclosed in his arms, safe and protected from the world, is exactly where I need to be right now. 'Arkarian, where is our house?'

He lifts me again, this time scooping me up, his hands under my legs. I rest my head against his shoulder and listen to his heart beating. It strikes me how comforting the sound is, like a lullaby to my soul.

He says, 'Close your eyes, sweetheart.'

The shift is over in a blink and suddenly we're inside a foyer with double height timber ceilings and an indoor garden wall flushed with the wildflowers we'd walked through earlier. He carries me down a few steps into an open spaced living area with polished timber floors, a real fireplace in a sandstone feature wall, and floor-to-ceiling windows that frame the forest on one side, a tranquil blue lake surrounded by footpaths and benches on the other.

'This place is amazing.'

Lowering me, we walk to the window with the lake view. I can just see myself strolling around it, then sitting on one of the benches, and breathing.

'Arkarian, you meant what you said about leaving this place to travel with me, didn't you?'

'Baby, I mean every word I say to you.'

'You would leave your home for me? Leave everyone you have known here for hundreds of years, even that girl with the long legs, pale eyes and pouty lips that want to devour you?'

He laughs, then tries to sound serious, 'Wait, which one was she?'

Laughingly, I remind him of her long aqua hair and curiosity regarding my parentage.

'Ah, yes, you mean Rebecca.'

'That's her name? Rebecca? Thanks for that. I'm going to hate that name forever now.'

He laughs, but seriously, now that I'm thinking straight, I can see he doesn't feel anything for Rebecca past friendship. Somebody should tell her.

He turns me to face him. 'Isabel, my home is wherever *you* are. If you wish, we'll build a new home together. A dozen homes in a dozen different cities around the world, just you and me and our children.'

'You want to have children with me?'

'OK, so now I have officially terrified you.'

I giggle and mock-punch his arm. He captures my hand, and entwining our fingers he leans down and kisses me tenderly. My lips tingle against his. 'Arkarian, you haven't scared me. Not really. Well... maybe just a little.'

'One day,' he corrects himself. 'I meant to say, "one day" we'll have children.'

'I'd like that...'

'But...?' He frowns.

'I'm going to need to practice the making-children part.' His eyebrows shoot up and I quickly clarify, 'I don't mean I want to get pregnant.' *God, when did the temperature go up in here?* 'I mean... you have protection here, right?'

'I, uh... I do.'

'Phew.' I glance around spotting the timber staircase. 'Seriously, Arkarian, I'm going to need a lot of practice and I think we should start right away.' I point up the staircase. 'Is our bedroom up there?'

And now I've taken *him* by surprise. 'Bedroom?'

'Arkarian, I'm not sure I can be any clearer, so let me put it this way: wherever you sleep when you stay here, take me there now.'

'Am I missing something, Isabel? I thought we were going to wait before we... until you... turned eighteen.'

'I've changed my mind.' Was that why he was counting the days to my birthday? 'Huh, I get it now.'

'Get what, baby?'

'Why you figured out how long it would be before I turned eighteen.'

He lowers his forehead to mine. 'I'm counting down the days, hours and minutes until you become a full-blood eternal, for only then will I have the security of knowing that should harm come to you, your self-healing will activate and keep you safe.'

'Ohhh... Arkarian, take me to your bedroom and make love to me, and please don't make me beg.'

He swings his hands around my hips, lifts me into his arms and with glowing purple irises he asks gently, 'Are you sure this is what you want, Isabel?'

'I couldn't be surer.'

# Chapter Thirty

## Jesilla

From the clinic I run straight up to my room, bumping into Bastian on the stairs coming down. Without stopping to answer his searching look, I lock the door behind me and fall against it. Breathing heavily, I close my eyes and as trained, slow my racing heart.

Sitting at my desk with my mother's envelope in my hand, I switch my lamp on and pick up my antique, hand-crafted letter opener. In the shape of a sword, when I first saw it on the young King John's desk, I couldn't resist slipping it into my pocket. It's the only item I've lifted from the past. I use it now to sever my mother's wax seal. Taking her letter out, I lay it flat on my desk and read...

*Daughter...*

*Since you are reading this letter, my brother has finally succeeded in eliminating me from this realm. I am deeply sorry, Jesilla, for there is much I had yet to teach you, and more importantly, to explain. Now you must learn and find answers for yourself. Remember you have Marduke to guide you. He is not the monster you believe him to be. Give him a chance and you will see that. But if the unfathomable has occurred, and you have found yourself alone, here are some truths to set you on your path.*

*Your father's name was Andrej Konstantin. He was the King of Criers, a Tribunal Member for The Guard. We loved each other, and we created you from that love, never forget that. Unfortunately, Andrej preferred a broader interpretation of the word "love" to include another with whom he shared intimacies. I shall not go into detail except to explain that at the time of your conception, your father was the last immortal of an ancient royal family, and because you are of his seed and mine, you carry the gene of immortality. You will die only at the hands of another immortal.*

*Do not doubt yourself as you have the tendency to do. Do not let anyone undermine you. An immortal's powers continue to evolve after maturity. Within you is the ability to create and destroy. This is your birthright. Use it wisely.*

*Daughter, you are not alone in the task we seek, for we are part of something greater than all who live on this planet can understand. Should you fail to save the Earth, others will come, and Earth will suffer far greater consequences than what you must do for her in my absence.*

*I had hoped that opening the dark realms would persuade world leaders to hand over control of their lands to one who is superior. Humans find it difficult to agree on anything of importance, so singular control of all nations is the only answer to making the decisions Earth needs to evolve as it should. Humans allow millions to go hungry, draining Earth's resources. They allow wars to ravage their lands, displacing millions from their homes, endangering Earth's biosphere.*

*Daughter, I had hoped you could live your younger years unencumbered by the burdens and responsibilities your powers carry, but if you are reading this, that is not to be. I would do anything to change that if it were within my powers.*

*The Order is now yours to rule. Let no one steal the leadership from you on the grounds that you are too young or inexperienced or simply not ruthless enough. You are immortal. You are a superior being and most powerful. Only you can save this planet. Humans will die in vast numbers, but they brought this on themselves. Be strong and be ruthless. That is the language they understand.*

*One last thing... Remember what you did with the bird? When you are competent with this skill, restore my beloved magician to his youthful years for his loyalty is deserving of such a gift. His wisdom will serve you well.*

*Promise me, Jesilla, you will rise up and claim the leadership of the New World. And promise me you will avenge my death. But first, daughter of my heart and my blood... promise me you will instigate my plan to protect the Earth for it is the only way left and time is running out. On the other side of this letter you will find my plan explained in detail, written in ink created by Keziah, invisible to all but your eyes.*

I turn my mother's letter over and stare at the blank page. After a moment letters start appearing until her beautiful calligraphy covers the sheet. Point by point, my mother's plan unfolds for my viewing. By the time I finish reading it, I'm both in awe of her genius and staggered by her cruelty. I drop to the edge of my bed, wipe my tears and clear my vision. It's then I hear a persistent rapping at the door.

'Jesilla, open up.'

I glance at the time on my phone. 'It's late, Bastian. Go to bed.'

'You missed dinner. I brought you something.'

'I'm not hungry. Go away.'

His voice drops a few decibels. 'I'm staying here until you open your door. If I have to, I will break it down.'

I would ignore Bastian if not for his concerned voice. I still have the letter in my hand when I unlock the door. He notices everything in a heartbeat. He lowers the plate onto a small table, and lifting me in his arms, he kicks the door closed behind us.

While still holding me he reads the letter – the visible side - and sighs. Dropping it on my desk, he carries me to my bed and lies down beside me. Tenderly pushing my hair back he finds my tear-streaked face. 'It's okay to cry, Jesilla. She was your mother.'

I draw in a shuddering breath. He cradles my head with one hand, pulling me in closer with his other around my back. No one has held me like this before, like they care. He holds me while I cry for the mother I'll never see again. He murmurs soothing words. He hums comforting tunes while pulling my quilt up over us. And he keeps me snuggled in his arms until the first rays of sunlight hit my windows.

'Why are you still crying?' he whispers. 'Tell me what to do to make it better.'

'You can't,' I say between hiccups. 'There's nothing anyone can do. I am who I am. And I have to do what I have to do.'

'There must be something, Jes. Tell me. At least tell me why.'

He melts my heart and I snuggle in closer. He shifts around to make me more comfortable. Why does this boy care so much?

I draw in a shuddering breath and whisper, 'My mother died because of me. I was in a tree in her direct line of sight when her brother hurled the knife that killed her. If I hadn't been in that tree and distracted her at that crucial moment, she would still be alive today.'

# Chapter Thirty-one

## Jesilla

It's Friday evening and tonight Carter is testing Rochelle. I open my weapons cabinet inside my wardrobe and pick out my hand-sized titanium poker for later, in case she fails. The poker is easily concealed and long enough to pierce a vital organ. But I end up selecting my favorite hand-sized weapon, King John's letter opener, from my desk instead. Though smaller, it's surprisingly lethal with its double-edged, sharpened steel blade. I sheath it into a chamber inside my right boot and give myself a final glance in the mirror. Tonight I'm wearing my calf-length, slinky royal blue dress that accentuates my height though does little for my non-existent curves. I apply a light cover of makeup, emphasizing my eyes with silver liner, and fasten my straightened hair on one side with an opal clip.

With a fresh coat of dark red lip gloss, I stare at my reflection. I'm not fussing over my appearance because Bastian is waiting for me in my room. No way. Not doing that.

He's asleep on my couch. I catch my breath at how vulnerable he looks with his head on my white cushion, one hand tucked under his cheek.

He opens one eye. 'Like what you see, babe?'

The nerve.

'If you're not busy later, I can sneak back in here.' He sits up and winks.

'You wish, *babe*.' I toss a cushion at him. 'Crystal's about to knock on my door.'

That gets him to his feet. Back to business.

Rochelle greets me with her usual warm smile. Tonight, she's pulled her hair into a high ponytail, enhancing her oval eyes behind the black-framed glasses. Dressed for dinner in a pink sundress, with a short-sleeved white cardigan on top, she rocks the sweet-as-apple-pie look Bastian told me was as distant as one could get from her usual all-black boots, jeans and coats.

Bastian walks out behind me, straightening his hair with his fingers and her eyebrows rise. She looks from one of us to the other, a curious smile playing around her mouth, a question in her eyes.

I shrug. 'Dillon fell asleep on my couch while waiting for me to finish getting ready.'

She falls into step beside me as Bastian slips ahead. She notices his shirt caught up at the back and tugs it down.

I catch myself before slapping her hand. The thought of her touching Bastian triggers a release of energy that shoots up my arms like a lick of fire. The force of my own jealousy surprises me.

'Hey, do either of you know why, uh, Ethan a-and Isabel have been off school for so long?' Rochelle asks with what sounds like a tremor in her voice.

'Why do you care?' I ask, making sure to keep my tone light and adding a smile.

She shrugs. 'I don't know. They make Ancient History less boring.'

Bastian laughs, glancing at us over his shoulder. 'Are you saying your Dad's lessons are sending you to sleep in class?'

She lifts a finger to her lips. 'Don't tell him I said that. Promise you won't tell.'

'Relax, cousin, I can keep a secret.'

While Bastian and Rochelle talk about school stuff, I wonder about Ethan and Isabel. They haven't returned to school since our mission almost two weeks ago. Every morning I expect to hear an announcement that Ethan Roberts has either passed away from some undisclosed illness, or met with a tragic accident, and Isabel is too distraught to attend classes. But there's nothing so far. Isabel's absence is more of a mystery. Surely the Guard wouldn't let her anywhere near Ethan's sick bed, healer or not. But I didn't think the Guard would send two of their Named into Ancient Egypt so unprepared either.

Returning my focus to where it should be tonight, I dip into Rochelle's mind. I can't check her memories unless I sedate her. Memories are complex. They're not stored in our brains like books on a library shelf. They're encoded elements scattered throughout various areas of the brain through our neural pathways. Each memory is a reconstruction, with the stored emotion, and even the scent that accompanies it, found in other locations.

But thoughts are different. They're current. They're out in the open.

Rochelle is responding to a question Bastian asks her with a contemplative look that's even a little dreamy. There's nothing in it, but if she looks at him like that again I might rip her hair out along with her memories.

What am I thinking? She's not making a move on Bastian. As far as she knows 'Dillon' is her cousin and his mother is someone so ill she's in a Canberra hospital getting the best palliative care possible.

We hear the voices of two men talking as we approach the formal dining room entrance.

'Sounds like we have a guest for dinner,' Bastian says as the room comes into view.

Keziah is sitting in his usual seat at the head of the table looking towards the window, while Marcus Carter makes his way to the other end with his back to us.

Dad says, 'Now that you're all here, I'd like to introduce you to my old friend, Marcus Carter, a teacher at your new school.'

The three of us stop and wait. I focus on my breathing to slow it down so I can hear if Rochelle's heart accelerates suddenly. I stay alert for other changes too, like her breathing, excess perspiration, dilation of her irises, clenching of her fists, grinding teeth, or similar nervous gestures.

As he approaches his seat, Marcus turns around. 'Hello,' he says, looking straight at Rochelle. Without taking his eyes off her, he walks over with his hand extended.

Her eyes drop to his offered hand, then slowly lift, wider than usual. She blinks hard, as if thinking the action might make him disappear. But Carter's not going anywhere. Even a pregnant beast couldn't get rid of him. Rochelle licks her lips, and before closing her mouth she sucks in a huge breath, exhaling it with a shudder that passes through her whole body.

Bastian squeezes his eyes shut and, shaking his head he drops his gaze to the floor. He's disappointed. Why? It's not as if *he* has to annihilate her. Keziah looks upset too.

But I get it. Living with Rochelle these past months I too have come to... dare I say, *like* her? I find myself rooting for her, urging her to find a reason for her shocked look.

At least her heart rate is steady at sixty-four beats a minute.

If I have to eliminate Rochelle earlier than expected, well, maybe I won't like it, but I'll do it. I'd just rather do it on my terms. Not Carter's. When I'm ready. Not when Carter says so. It's not in my plans to eliminate Rochelle yet. Even if Ethan doesn't make it, I can think of a hundred other ways she could be useful.

Attempting to recover from her obvious shock, Rochelle takes Carter's offered hand, and while shaking it enthusiastically she brings out her dazzling smile. 'I know you!'

Well that's not what I expected. Everyone stares at her. Does she *want* to die?

But then she says, 'You're that teacher from Angel Falls that went missing just before we moved here.' She turns to Keziah. 'Dad, around the corner from your office there's a big color poster on the wall with a photo of this man asking for any information on his whereabouts. Only, in the photo he has more hair.' She swings her gaze back to Carter and shrugs her shoulders with a coy smile. 'Sorry, I mean no offence with my comment about your hair.'

'None taken,' he grounds out without opening his mouth.

'Oh my God, Mr Carter, everyone's been looking for you.'

Flicking me a glance, he mutters under his breath, 'Not everyone.'

Bastian rubs his chin and glances away as if he's hiding a smile. I can't be sure, but I glimpse relief in his relaxed jaw muscles now that he's not clenching them anymore. Even Keziah looks cheerier, like the world didn't end after all.

Carter says, 'A color poster, you say?'

'That's right.'

Carter leans between us, and turning in my direction he grumbles, 'Miss that, did you?'

'It's so nice to meet you, Mr Carter,' Rochelle says, her hand still held firmly by his as if he's waiting for something to happen. 'Will you be returning to school soon?'

He doesn't answer, but continues to stare at her.

She then asks, 'Would you mind telling us what happened? I'm sure it's a fascinating story. You've been gone for so long. I run a blog and I'd really love to interview you.' She gasps suddenly with her eyes widening with inspiration. 'We could publish it in parts.'

'What?' he says.

'Your story. What happened to you. I could publish chapters through my blog.'

He stares at me with his lips pressed together. 'Hmm, a photo in a school corridor.'

I give an *oops* look, but... I'm still trying to place the poster Rochelle says hangs on a wall near Keziah's office.

Keziah says, 'We should all sit down. Marcus, Dillon, girls.' He sweeps his hand over the table.

But Carter is so angry his face is turning darker every second. He's not moving, and not releasing Rochelle's hand.

'Sit down, Marcus.' I use a commanding tone that he still ignores.

How am I supposed to lead the Order when the man who was one of my mother's chief advisers doesn't obey my commands? I move round to my seat and as I go to pass him I hiss in his ear, 'I told you I contained her powers. Release her hand and sit down. *Now.* And that's an order.'

When Carter finally releases her, Bastian taps the chair next to him. 'Sit here, Crystal.'

Meanwhile Carter sits beside me but can't take his eyes, or his mind, off Rochelle. He fires question after question at her, like where she was born, where she lived before coming here, how her mother died, if she was there when it happened, what were her mother's last words.

When he finally pauses to breathe, Rochelle asks, 'Did you know our mother too?'

Not sure whether it's the question or her big sweet smile that throws him, but Carter struggles to get back on track. Things are not going as he'd planned. 'Sorry, what?' he says. 'I'm still astonished by how my impromptu trip, followed by my fall and temporary amnesia caused such concern for my well-being.'

'Everyone will just be glad that you're safe and well,' Keziah says.

Our housekeeper Roslyn brings dinner to the table. As soon as she leaves, Carter returns to asking Rochelle questions. It's not half obvious that he's drilling her. She sends me a questioning scowl a few times, a natural reaction under any circumstances. If she's acting, she's damn good at it. I stop the urge that comes over me to change the subject. This is the idea of the dinner after all.

I'm just relieved I won't be using King John's letter opener tonight.

# Chapter Thirty-two

## Ethan

I see Rochelle with my eyes closed. I see her with them open. Like now, she's leaning over me, her tears falling onto my face as she tries to heal me with the flickering electric charges pulsing from her trembling fingers.

Only, she's not really here. She's an illusion I created from a subconscious mind that knows how much I miss her, how I can't get used to her being gone, and how I never will.

When I reach up to wipe the moisture from her face, it *feels so real*, I could swear my fingertips come away with the taste of her salty tears. Then I hear one of the infectious diseases specialists remark, 'He's hallucinating again. It's all the morphine, but at this stage there's really nothing more we can do but ease his pain.'

Well... it's not as if I couldn't tell I've come to the end, though I have no idea how long I've been in this virtual glass box. At this point, with no chance of recovery, Death is welcome to open the door to my soul and take me home. Once I stopped being able to communicate anymore it got too hard, and now all I have left are my dreams.

The guys come every day - Matt, Neriah, Jimmy, Dillon, though Dillon doesn't come right in but watches through the glass walls. Arkarian and Isabel arrived a few days ago. It's so good to see them. Just knowing they're here will make my passing easier.

Working around the clock, the specialists and healers pumped my body with antibiotics, blood transfusions, and all sorts of concoctions, telling me how they would heal me. Now they avoid eye contact.

I become aware of Matt's presence as he lowers himself into the seat beside Neriah. I'm glad he's here today to care for the others. This sense of being disconnected, as if my soul has started to pull away from my body, is swelling inside, telling me what the doctor already has, that today is my last.

From the other side of my bed, Isabel's voice cuts through my dire thoughts. 'Ethan, wake up.' She takes my hand. 'Squeeze it for me, honey. Come on, Ethan, you can hear me. Open your eyes.'

It takes a minute but somehow I get the message to my hand to do what she says. She squeals with delight, making the effort worth the mountain of pain. 'He's still with us,' she says with a sniff.

When I open my eyes everything appears disjointed, as if I'm looking through a cracked mirror, my view apportioned into triangular shapes. Is this what imminent death looks like?

Sitting with his elbows on my bed, his head in his hands, Matt suddenly jerks. The whole bed moves even though it's made of alabaster. 'I should have found another way to stop the Order's plans,' he says.

Though there are others in the room no one says a word. While looking at me, he lifts his head and calls out to the room, 'I want an update. I want to hear what you're doing for him. *Now.*'

A healer confers with one of the disease specialists before quietly answering, 'His organs are leaking blood, my lord.'

'Did the antibiotics our scientists created have *any* effect?'

'Resistant, I'm afraid.'

'What of the vaccine?'

'Without it, Ethan would not have lasted so long.'

'So you're saying we've only extended his life by twelve days? Which he spent most of in agony and unable to communicate?'

'I'm afraid so, my lord.'

His voice drops. 'Is there no hope then?'

'There's nothing more we can do. He is in complete organ failure.'

'How long does he have?'

When the healer doesn't answer, Arkarian, who's standing behind Ebony, asks again, 'We need to know. It's important.'

The Healer says, 'It's difficult to assess but... not long now.'

The door opens, the room fills with bright light and everyone moves back from my bed. 'Is the boy in pain?'

Oh my God, Lord Dartemis is here?

'We are trying to control his pain,' the Healer says, 'but a precise determination is problematic when he... well, he doesn't ever complain, my lord.'

'How much longer does he have with us?' the immortal asks.

The healer sighs. 'Perhaps long enough for his friends to say their goodbyes.'

'Give me a measurement!' Dartemis bellows.

'Minutes, my lord. Perhaps five.'

His curses are so loud they ricochet off the walls.

So... I have only five minutes left. Well, it's not exactly how I expected to go out. No blaze of glory. Not that I wanted one. But not in battle either, or while on a mission to who knows where. If I had a choice, I would go out as a white-haired old man with grandchildren around me that all resemble Rochelle. On the plus side, because at a time like this looking at the plus side is all I have, at least I'll be with her soon, unless... nah, that would just suck - to die, only to discover Rochelle is still alive. God, I'd be happy for her, but, geez, I would have to ask, were we never meant to be together?

I'd forgotten Dartemis was still here until his deep voice wafts over me, 'That is all I need to hear.'

Arkarian joins him. 'My lord, should we ask him first? We've had some success communicating with blinking. One long for yes, one short for no.'

'We don't have time for games, nephew.'

'It's not a game, Father,' Matt says. 'What do you say, Shaun?'

Dad's here? I didn't know. How could I not know my father was here? Dad? *Dad?*

'Do whatever you need to keep my boy alive.'

'Believe me, Shaun, I want that too,' Matt says, 'but Arkarian is right. We should at least try to get Ethan's approval first.'

*Approval?* For what?

'There's no time, Matthew,' Dartemis says. 'Once he's gone, it will be too late.'

An alarm sounds behind my head. It's that machine that hasn't stopped beeping since they plugged me into it on my first day here. Now it's making a high-pitched piercing tone that goes on and on and... it's my heart, one of the last of my working organs has finally...

'He's in cardiac arrest,' Arkarian says, his words hurried, his voice more distressed than I've heard it before.

Matt cries out, 'Do it, Father! We can't lose him.' His voice is suddenly beside my ear. 'Hang in there, Ethan. We got your back. We got you, mate. We won't let you fall, but you have to help us. Fight to stay with us, Ethan.'

Arkarian says from my other side, 'If this is not what you want, Ethan, please forgive us. We've tried everything and now we have no choice left.'

'Leave him be, Arkarian,' Dad says. 'Let the immortal get on with it.'

Heat pours into my body from a point of contact with something burning against my forehead. It grows hot inside quickly, with the pressure building to an unbearable level. I can't take it and I scream out as my body jerks and goes into spasm, again and again, over and over, until the pressure bursts through some kind of blockage inside me and flows like honey, filling my veins and arteries, pushing through more smaller blockages and forging new growth. Previously demolished organs spring to life as my body burns and comes alive piece by piece. I hear the healers and doctors gasping and murmuring in awe.

The machine finally beeps again in a steady, strong, rhythmic sound better than before. Whatever just happened, I'm stronger for it.

'Unhook his tubes and clean him up before we wake him,' Arkarian orders.

But I'm already awake; at least I am in my mind. No matter how deep a coma you fall into, thoughts never stop. My body was broken, and now it's not. But something is different.

And I'm not sure it's something I'm going to like.

# Chapter Thirty-three

## Jesilla

After dinner Rochelle excuses herself to finish an assignment and go to bed. Before she leaves she looks at Marcus. 'It was great to meet you, Mr Carter. You're an interesting man. I hope to see you again soon.' She throws him her megawatt smile.

He rubs the spot under his nose with the back of his thumbnail. 'Thank you... *Crystal.* I'm sure we'll be meeting again now that I'm back from my... um... trip.'

She walks round to Keziah, and resting her hands on his shoulders she leans down and kisses the side of his face. 'Good night, Daddy.'

He pats her hand and gives her a sideways smile like any doting father would.

Envy claws inside, but I quickly remind myself that this isn't real affection between them. Her biological father – mine too – was nothing like the father Keziah is portraying. None in this room has experienced normal family life. Carter's brother was Marduke. Enough said. Bastian's parents were both alcoholics. His mother forgot he existed, remembering during rare bouts of dry times, while his father Peter, accepted my mother's offer of a job, a home, and a permanent cure for his alcoholism on the condition he give her all legal rights to his son. As Peter saw the arrangement, he wasn't giving Bastian a life anyway, though he did love him, and because he loved him, he agreed. As for me, well, I grew up with stalwart killing machines and a magician for role models. We're a gathering of misfits, but misfits with the power to change the world. To save it from the idiots who call themselves Presidents, Emperors, Kings and Prime Ministers. Those same idiots sit in their plush offices and watch from executive chairs as corporations make billions and ninety percent of the world barely survives.

Carter thinks I'm not strong enough to make the tough decisions. He's wrong. Since learning that I'm an immortal... well, *holy blessed mother*, I get it now. I understand the importance of my mother's plan. I will still be here when the Earth dies from mismanagement of her natural resources. From allowing its population to blow out astronomically and end up beyond its ability to provide basic needs, needs she's already struggling to deliver.

If the human race is to continue it must accept sacrifices for the greater cause. As leader of the Order it has fallen on me to make the tough choices to save the Earth.

Some will judge my mother's – I mean, *my* plan as too harsh, and in all honesty it *is* a harsh course of action, but greedy and selfish rulers brought this on us. Those in power let Earth's great habitats die. If we wait any longer to change our path, the Earth will have nothing left to give future generations.

And I'll be here to see it. I'll be walking on the devastated plains amongst masses of starving humans crying out for help, knowing I could have done something.

And now that I'm aware of what the future holds for Earth, and knowing I have the power to change it, I can't sit back and do nothing.

It sucks that my mother won't be here to experience the changes, but with the grace of all the past immortals, somehow she will see. I will make her proud. And then she will forgive me for causing her death.

As Rochelle leaves the dining room, I ask everyone to be quiet while I dip into her mind. They stop chatting immediately and I listen first to Rochelle's footsteps going up to her room. Closing my eyes to increase my concentration, I hear her pull her chair out, sit at her desk, open her textbook and read to herself. I dip into her head for her thoughts on the text. It's Ancient History. A passage on tomb paintings and the information they provide on Ancient Egyptian funerary beliefs and practices. When I'm sure she's settled into working through the topic questions, I open my eyes to the others watching me.

'We have a lot to get through tonight and this room is unsuitable for a confidential meeting. I want you all to take the lift down to Level Six.'

Carter says, 'To Lathenia's conference room?'

This man has to stop questioning everything I do. To let him know where he stands I purposefully ignore him. 'Keziah, show Pearl, Zander and Peter where to go, and organize Level Six clearance for them.'

'Wait,' Bastian says, 'why are you including Peter?'

Great. First Carter, now Bastian? I have my work cut out asserting my authority with these two. How do I go from being the Goddess's over-protected daughter to being... the Goddess herself? 'Because I said so. Now let's go.'

They fold into the conference room behind me. I sit in my mother's chair, at the head of the polished rectangular table, and run my fingers over the built in panel that operates a wall of screens connecting the room not just to the rest of the complex, but to world leaders and other identities whose significance I've yet to learn.

Keziah waits for my nod before sitting in the first chair on my left. Bastian drops into the first on my right. Carter leaves a seat vacant, taking the next along from Keziah. Zander and Pearl enter together, which is unsurprising since they share a child and an apartment on Level Three. I ask how their little girl is and Pearl says she's asleep with a sitter watching her.

The sitter is of course one of our trained soldiers. They sit beside Bastian, catch a glimpse of Carter's improved looks and gape at him.

'Damn fine improvement, mate,' Zander says, reaching out to shake Carter's hand.

Peter walks in next, hurrying to the vacant seat between Keziah and Carter. 'My apologies, Jesilla. I hope I haven't kept you waiting.' He sees Carter and jerks back. 'Marcus?' He offers his hand and the two men shake. 'Man, you recovered fast.' He whistles to the hum of surrounding laughter.

Peter's reaction is so natural, so human; it eases elevating tensions in the room. As soon as he sits, Peter's eyes go to Bastian, taking in every new mark or visible bruise on his son's body. It's as if he doesn't take a real breath until he's sure his son is OK.

'After the sizable losses we incurred against the Guard, I am now officially taking over the Order. I will make an announcement to the entire complex including our soldiers in the field over the next few days. But first, my new team of advisers is you.' I unfold my hands in their direction. 'Marcus, Zander, Pearl, and Peter.' I stare at the four, making sure they understand the importance of what I'm saying. This is entirely new for Zander and Pearl, who have been my body guards since I can remember.

'Keziah and Bastian will be my Chief Advisors and will outrank everyone but me.' Before Carter opens his mouth, I add, 'If anyone objects we'll talk in private later. I have selected those I know best and trust most. Am I clear?'

Bastian flicks a confused frown at his father. Maybe I should have told him my reasons for giving Peter so much authority before announcing my decision to everyone. But Peter isn't just Bastian's reformed father, and really, who of us doesn't deserve a second chance? In his time here Peter has gained extensive knowledge of the Order, and as an IT engineer, he keeps our complex security systems running smoothly. My mother trusted him, and his thoughts tell me he's as dedicated and loyal to me as he was to her.

Ignoring my directive to talk later, Carter complains anyway. 'Listen here, Jesilla, I was Lathenia's *Chief* Advisor.'

'Yes, because you were a double agent. But the Guard knows you were their traitor, and they're not going to let you in again.' I lift my eyebrows to emphasize the fact he's not as important as he once was. 'Marcus, Lathenia isn't here anymore. It's my team now and I say who's in it and who isn't.'

I hold my hands out again. 'You are my new team. But I want only those I can trust. If anyone wants to pull out, do it now, before we discuss the impending mission. I do not want to lock you up for knowing too much, but believe me, if I have to I will.'

Nobody moves. 'Good.' I let that sink in a moment before I make my announcement. 'The laboratory has informed me that the dragonflies are ready to launch.'

Pearl nods but her eyes narrow in confusion.

I explain, 'The disease that is going to cull the human population is ready for release. The mechanisms that are going to release the disease are the dragonflies.'

A nervous hum erupts as they talk quietly amongst each other. I listen in to their thoughts, but they're mostly wondering who knew of the plan, what the plan entails and questions about the dragonflies.

I clap my hands twice and they go silent. 'The sphere has opened a portal in time that fits our requirements perfectly.'

Pearl asks, 'What are our roles now? Will Zander and I be going on missions with you?'

'You and Zander will head up Security, oversee the mission from the Command Centre, and keep this complex safe in our absences. Do you understand?'

Sounding relieved, Pearl says, 'Affirmative.'

And Zander says, 'Yes, ma'am,' in the same manner he would answer my mother. If it weren't so important to keep a straight face, I would smile at that.

'Carter, you will operate the sphere from the control room, coordinating our time-shifts.' When he doesn't answer me immediately I stare at him. 'Is that understood?'

'Yeah, yeah, I get it.'

My stare lingers until he drops his gaze.

I turn to Bastian. 'You will be my partner on this next mission.'

He winks at me, the corner of his mouth curving into a cheeky half smile. I gnaw on the inside of my cheek not to react. Since he turned eighteen he's become too damn cute for his own good.

Keziah draws my attention back to the mission. 'Jesilla, what will I be doing if Marcus is coordinating the mission?'

A knock at the door is good timing. I'm happy to delay explaining Keziah's role.

Zander and Pearl move swiftly into defensive positions with guns drawn.

'Stand down,' I order. 'It's the lab. I asked Paul to send down a sample.'

Still, Zander signals Pearl to open the door while he keeps his gun trained on it.

But it's the lab's Senior Microbiologist, Olivia Hamilton, wearing their standard white uniform. She brings me a hand-held size container, similar to a pack of cards but in a plain cream color.

I thank her, and Pearl closes the door as she leaves.

'This is what Bastian and I will be taking with us.' Opening the lid, I show my team the seven narrow compartments, and then lift one of the dragonflies out. Passing it around, I tell them to feel the raised pattern on its back. 'That's the trigger that will discharge their wings. Once released, precisely ninety seconds later the "dragonfly" will drop its load on an unsuspecting public. Each of the seven dragonflies carries enough of the virus to infect a thousand people.'

Bastian takes the longest time studying the dragonfly. I end up taking it directly from his fingers. I set the tiny wing mechanism to the discharge position, open my hand and watch the dragonfly take to the air. 'Ladies and gentlemen, this is the delivery mechanism that will help to save the Earth.'

All but Bastian applauds. His focus remains solely on the dragonfly, his eyes following the path it takes as it rises almost to the ceiling before it circumnavigates the room. 'Where's the toxin stored?'

'In its segmented abdomen.'

'Are you sure this small thing can hold enough toxin to kill a thousand people?'

*Must you put it that way?*

He shrugs. *Just saying it like it is.*

*Are you trying to piss me off?*

He lifts his eyes to mine. 'There'll be no turning back after this.'

'There's no turning back now.'

Carter smiles, his dark eyes sparkling with enthusiasm. 'Are you putting them inside planes and flying them to different continents?'

'Not quite. We're going to release seven dragonflies at the World Economic Forum Annual Meeting where there will be three thousand government, business and society leaders attending from every country in the world.'

Eyebrows rise, heads nod and Zander whistles. They're impressed. As they should be.

'How are we going to get in?' Bastian asks. 'Security will be intense.'

'We're going to walk straight past security, past everyone.'

'How?' Bastian asks.

*Just breathe and say it.* 'Keziah is going to help with that.'

'Keziah?' Bastian peers across the table at him, and frowns.

'What virus is in these *dragonflies*?' Carter asks.

I swallow around a suddenly dry mouth. Not wanting to sound as if I'm squeaking I wait until I work moisture into my throat. It has the effect of building their anticipation. 'Smallpox.'

For a second there is only silence before they hurl questions at me. I lift my hands. 'Enough! Everyone quieten down. I'll answer all your questions but one at a time.'

Bastian gets his out first. 'How much of the world's population will be...' He stops and rubs his jaw with his hand. 'How many people will die, Jesilla?'

A hush descends as if no one has thought anyone would die from this when dying is the whole point of the exercise. OK, so no one wants to see masses of people die. We're not serial killers. Unfortunately, though, to protect the Earth's natural resources, losses have to occur. It's the only way to save the human race from starving to death on a planet that can't provide for its over-population anymore. But they know these things. They also know that historically there have always been plagues and natural disasters that reduce Earth's population to a level she can tolerate. Today, people live longer and we conquer diseases that otherwise would kill us. We want that to continue. But to have an ever-evolving quality of life, we have to do the right thing for the Earth to be able to sustain us.

I pick up the remote control in front of me, lighting the wall screen with a link to our laboratory on Level Five. It flares to life with our chief scientist Paul Withers answering my call, his team inside their bacteria-proof, glass-enclosed work stations in the background.

'My crew would like to hear the mortality figures, Paul. Can you give us the number of projected fatalities for, say... the first twelve months after the dragonflies are released?'

He glances at everyone around the table as if he's deciding whether they're strong enough to hear this, and then nods. 'What we have developed from the Ancient Egyptian Pharaoh's sample is a fast-working variation of the smallpox *hemorrhagic variole*. It's highly contagious with transmission through inhalation of microscopic droplets expressed from the nose and mouth of an infected person. To put more simply for example, when they sneeze. We have mutated the virus to bring death on as humanely as possible, meaning it will not only spread quickly but kill fast, as soon as the rash emerges.'

'Does it have the capability to spread around the world?' Bastian asks.

'We've made this strain airborne, so yes. And quickly.'

A hiss goes up around the table.

'Once the dragonflies are released as planned,' he continues, 'every person will be infected one way or another.'

'So the kill rate is one hundred percent?' Peter asks.

'I didn't say that, Peter.'

'Is there a chance this could get out of hand?'

'In what way do you mean, Peter?' I ask.

'Like kill *everyone* on the planet.'

'Not possible,' Paul explains. 'A percentage of the population will have inbuilt immunity, while another small percentage will contract the disease but not die. The large majority, though, will get sick and die quickly, but visible symptoms won't appear for three days. In that time the bodies of those infected will act as incubators, taking the disease back to their homelands before their infectious diseases centers become aware they have a problem.'

'And those figures, Paul?' I get back to the point. Time is passing too quickly now.

He brings up a graph explaining what the pretty columns mean. It drives me crazy listening to his scientific spiel. 'The bottom line, Paul?'

'Sure. Our projections show a reduction in population of eighteen percent.' He looks at me. 'Would you like to hear second year projection figures?'

'I think that will do, thank you, Paul.'

Carter whistles. 'But that's... a billion people.'

'If we don't get the timing right, Earth will not have the capability to recover. Oh no.' I freeze when I hear something I don't quite recognize. I lift my hands to quieten everyone's chattering. As they fall silent, I lean forward, tilting my head to both listen and probe at the same time. 'No, no, no!'

'What is it?' Keziah asks.

I'm half out of my seat, my eyes bulging with shock. *How did this happen? When did it start? How much has she heard?*

I whisper, 'She's listening.'

'Who?' Carter asks, hands gripping the table edge, ready to pounce.

I look at him. He was right all along. She can hear everything we're saying, for how long I don't know except for tonight. Tonight, she's paying attention, listening to all we have been saying in the conference room.

Keziah shakes my arms. 'Jesilla.'

'Rochelle.'

Bastian slaps the table with his palm. '*Jesus*, are you sure? She's been studying in her room, and even if she was listening that's...' He looks up as if he can see the floors above us through the ceiling, 'seven floors. Is she that good a Truthseer?'

In a tiny voice, I say, 'I can do it.'

Carter jumps to his feet. Rage makes his eyes bulge out of his skull. 'Are you absolutely positive the girl heard all our conversations tonight?'

'I told you, I know her. I know her thoughts, their order, how they fall. Even through seven floors of concrete and steel, she heard us.'

Keziah asks, 'What did she hear?'

'All of it.'

'That's it,' Carter says, slapping his hands and rubbing them together as if he's warming up in front of a fire.

And he's right. That's it for Rochelle. It's all over for her. Her part in torturing Ethan is over. Whether he's alive or not doesn't matter now. Before dawn comes to Angel Falls, Rochelle Thallimar will be dead and buried.

Bastian gets up. 'I'll get her. I'll lock her in the cells. She'll come easier if it's just me.'

'Not the cells,' Carter snaps, his black eyes still abnormally large. 'Take her to an interrogation room. I want fifteen minutes with her first.' He points at me. 'I warned you. You owe me at least that.'

I nod. My mind is racing. As Bastian makes for the door, I follow, calling back to the others, 'Wait here for my orders.'

Running to the lift, Bastian catches my eye. 'Don't you trust me?'

With my probe still in Rochelle's mind, I hear a voice call out to her with an urgency that brings shivers out on my arms. '*Run*,' the voice says. '*They know. They're coming for you now.*'

I swing a glance back at the conference room.

'Forget something?' Bastian asks as he holds the lift door open for me.

I get in, punching the ground floor button repeatedly until Bastian puts his hand over mine and stops me. I glance up at him and explain, 'Someone just warned her.'

'Are you serious? Who would do that? Wait, do you mean someone from here?'

'He told her to run. He told her we're coming.' The lift doors open on ground floor and as we run out, I grab his arm and swing him around. 'Was it you?'

He stops, motionless except for his lips parting and staring down at me. Then he grabs my upper arms and holds me still, his eyes glowing, but with what I'm not sure. Anger? Disappointment? Frustration? Love? He says, 'What will it take to convince you that I'm on *your* side?'

I open my mouth to answer, but he grunts, and says, 'This?'

He kisses me. His tongue in my mouth has my body reacting to his hot searching touch. I should break it off, push him back, shove him across the room, but I hang on because right now his mouth is my oxygen. His hands slide around my back, brushing my neck on their way into my hair. An unexpected shiver courses through me. He grips my head, holding me still and his cheek brushes mine as we both gasp for air. I'm losing control. Melting against him. His lips over mine, he says, '*Jesilla. Jesilla.*' He moans, searing my throat with burning kisses to my collar-bone. I fall against him in my need to get as close as I can. My hands under his shirt rove over his back. Nails claw his skin. And by the stars I enjoy every thrilling second of touching him. For the first time in my life I'm alive and I want more of this, more of Bastian's touch.

Through all the exhilarating sensations tearing through my body, reason clamors to be heard, and as hard as it is, I draw up a breath and shove Bastian back with my hands on his chest. 'Telling me that you're on *our* side would have been enough.'

His mouth opens. He wipes those sensual lips with the back of his hand and as I turn and run up the stairs to Rochelle's bedroom, he's right there with me. I open Rochelle's bedroom door with a bang.

It's empty.

We're too late.

We both hear the garage door rising at the same time.

'Oh no.' I pat my pockets and come up empty. 'Do you have your phone?'

Bastian pulls it out.

'Tell security to initiate lock down immediately.'

He calls them while we run to the entrance foyer, where six stairs lead down to the internal garage door. I hear the engine of a quadbike kick over and rev up just as the steel shutters begin to close over all the windows and external doors. Excellent. We have her now. She can't escape. Not unless she has at least one of the three roller doors open already.

When we run in Rochelle is on a quadbike with the center roller door closing down on top of her. She drops low over the handlebars, lying as flat as she can. She makes it out with the door skimming her quad's rear bumper.

'No, no, no!'

Keziah and Carter run in while I'm yelling at Bastian to organize a reversal of lock down. 'Tell Peter it's urgent and get Zander and Pearl up here now.'

I slap a hand on my chest as if I can coax my heart out of pummeling through my rib cage.

Keziah and Bastian frown when I do this. I read their concern and their questions. 'No, the Hell I'm not all right,' I yell. 'Do you know what it means if Rochelle gets away? She will throw everything we have planned into jeopardy. There is more to this project than any of you know.'

Keziah hurries to the door. 'I'll use a manual over-ride.'

'What happened, Jes-illa?' Carter spits his words out, saliva dribbling down his chin. Wiping it roughly with his shirt sleeve he folds his arms across his chest and glares at me with that accusing look that's always saying it's my fault, my mistake, my inexperience.

'Someone tipped her off,' Bastian says, pulling on a bike helmet.

The three roller doors start lifting. We squeeze under, catching sight of Rochelle's tail-lights ramming her quadbike into the entrance gate. It ricochets but holds.

'She won't get through that,' Carter says.

But there's a bend through the center that wasn't there before. She reverses and has another go, hitting it harder and at higher speed. The gate drops. She rides roughly over it, and takes off into the night.

'Son of a bitch,' Carter spits out and rushes back inside.

I'm not sure, but he could be angrier than I am.

Zander and Pearl arrive. Summing the situation up in an instant, they jump on the other quads the security and maintenance teams use to access hard-to-get-to areas of the property.

Engines roar to life. I shout over them, 'Bring her back alive! I'll need to read her.'

But Keziah, Zander, Pearl and Carter are already on their quads. The four take off to noise that's louder than an earthquake, leaving the stench of burning fuel to stink up the air. Bastian guns the quad he's on and I order him to stop.

'What? Why?' he yells.

'You're not going. That's an order.'

Sitting on his quad, Bastian watches the others leave, swearing viciously and shooting daggers from his eyes. He waits until the rumbling recedes. 'Why did you stop me?'

'They trusted you, and now they'll know you double crossed them. What do you think will happen if they catch you?'

He yanks his helmet off, and still astride his bike, legs apart, jeans taut across his thighs, he says, 'I don't care, Jesilla. It's more important that we catch Rochelle before she reaches them and tells them everything she knows.'

'Those four will bring her back.' I jerk my head at Zander and the others whose taillights we can just make out. 'It's their job, Bastian. And you know Carter will do anything for a few minutes with Rochelle.'

His nod is little more than a blink but I catch it. I also catch the tight pull of his lips, the clench of his jaw. Well, I don't like Carter either and while Rochelle *is* the enemy, I still wouldn't like to leave her in a room alone with him.

But he was right about her and I did agree. A leader has to be fair, right? True to her word?

'I had to stop you, Bastian, because...'

Bastian runs the backs of his fingers down my cheek. He's so tender, his touch steadies my heart and my lips part in a soft exhalation of air.

But is Bastian's affection for me as real as his touch implies?

How does one fake the passion of that last kiss? Or the tenderness in his touches these past months? I want to believe in him so much. *So* much. He would be the perfect partner to take forward into the new world with me. A confidant. Someone with whom I could share my concerns. Share my life.

Dare I dream that I could have a future with Bastian beside me?

But that would mean one hundred percent trust in him, and I'm not sure I'm there yet. We've known each other for so long, if anyone could get something past me, it would be him.

'You won't be going to school anymore.'

'That's cool.' Nothing in his tone reveals more than slight disappointment. He lifts himself off the quad with a shrug. 'It's not a big deal.' Pulling me into his arms, his fingers tangle in my hair. '*Jesilla, Jesilla*,' he whispers with a raw, edgy quality that caresses my soul. A tremor passes through me. He feels it and holds me like he never wants to let me go. And every moment I remain gripped in his arms the more I don't want to forget what this feels like, the more I want him in my life for ever.

Lifting his hands, he holds my face, looks into my eyes, making sure I'm looking straight into his. 'No matter what happens from here on, I want you to remember that today, right now, you are loved by me.'

At my stunned expression, his cocky sideways smile eases the tension his serious words create. 'I love you, Jesilla. And if I don't see Ethan or Matt or Angel Falls High School ever again, I wouldn't care as long as I'm with you. As long as I have you.'

'You... you really mean that? You really *love me*?'

Still holding my face, he kisses me with such tenderness it shatters the defensive shell around my heart I didn't realize was there until now. He senses my defenses falling away and wraps his arms around me. I could fill my soul to the brim with the love he's offering me right now. I want him so much.

But first... whether right or wrong, only knowing that I need to validate his words, I dip into his thoughts.

He's thinking of Rochelle, and her chances of making it to a safe house.

# Chapter Thirty-four

## Rochelle

Quadbikes roar down the mountain road behind me with a familiarity that I lack. They live here. I don't. They use these machines with a confidence that outweighs my meagre experience of a few days in the outback with Marduke some years ago.

*Arkarian! Matt! Neriah!*

Who else is a Truthseer I can trust? There's Dillon, but he's done enough tonight. He took a big risk that Jesilla might hear him. Though the way he looks at that girl can't all be pretend. For his sake, I hope he knows what he's doing.

*Arkarian, can you hear me?*

There's no reply, and a brief glance over my shoulder has me blinking rapidly. The high beam lights of four quads cause squiggly floaters to swim in my vision. I blink again but it has little effect in clearing them.

I hope Dillon is one of these four riders. The warning he shot into my head held such urgency, if not for him, I'd still be in that room they called my bedroom. And man, was he right. They came after me so fast.

God, I hope Jesilla doesn't find out it was Dillon who warned me.

Another sharp bend takes my full concentration to keep all four wheels on the road and not drift onto the rough gravel shoulder.

The quads close in on me. Their lights shimmer in my mirrors. They're making up time on the bends. I'm not going to reach safety if I don't take these bends at least as fast. There's no other way down this mountain except this road, and no way off this road until I reach the bottom. Even the fire trails up here lead back to their complex.

*Ethan...*

The kindest soul that ever lived. What I would give to see him again. To have those beautiful blue eyes gaze on me, and leave me breathless. I choke up. My vision blurs. I need to feel him holding me. Don't we deserve some time together? Some happiness?

A straight downhill stretch gives me a chance to increase my lead, but I'm going to have to gun it. From memory, the max these quads can do is a hundred and ten kilometers' an hour. I lean forward, lifting off the seat, and with my hair blowing all over my face, I take it all the way.

The road is dark without street lights, but I reach the midway mark with an increased lead. It stirs hope inside that I can do this. I can make it. I *will* make it. I *will* see Ethan again.

*It's Rochelle. I'm on a quadbike on Mountain Road with riders gaining on me fast. They're going to kill me. Can someone meet me at the bottom? I need help. I need backup. I need it now.*

No one responds but I can't give up hope. Someone will hear my thoughts. I need to be nearer, that's all. Closer to the valley, to their homes, to someone who can direct me to a safe house.

Maybe they think it's a trap. They saw me die on the day of the battle. They would have had a funeral and... my poor Ethan.

But Ethan *feels* me.

And Arkarian always hears the Named when they call him. That's the way we work. So why can't he hear me now? I have so much to tell them with all that I've learned in that house.

*If anyone can hear me, I don't know why I'm alive today, but I promise you that this* is *Rochelle. This is not a trap. The Order is coming to end my life. Does anyone* want *to help me?*

But there's only silence, and as I approach the last series of sharp bends the riders close in. Damn. *Damn*! I'll just have to take them down on my own. It wouldn't be the first time I've faced tough odds.

Their fastest quad catches up. Peering in my mirrors, it's clear this rider's physique isn't large enough to be Dillon, damn it. We could have made a run for it together.

The rider creeps up on my right hand side, so close I cop a lungful of stinking exhaust fumes. Caught in the quad's headlights, the heat from its engine lifts off in waves as he drives up alongside me, lifts his dark visor and gives me a smirking grin.

Great. It's Carter.

'Pull over, Rochelle.'

The darkest living soul on Earth.

He believes his brother is dead because of me. I would be wasting my breath trying to convince him it was the stupid curse Lorian put on me that killed his brother.

Jesilla ordered them to bring me back alive, but Carter won't blink an eye at disobeying his superior. He won't conform to her rules because she hasn't proven herself yet. Until she does, Carter will do as he pleases.

In a make-or-break attempt to escape, I enter the bend faster than I'm comfortable handling. As I take the curve, both hands gripping the wheel as I go round, Carter drops back to my right hind-quarter. He's up to something and doing a good job of blocking me from getting inside his head. So when his quad rams mine, I'm not as prepared as I should be.

The jolt is fierce. The steering wheel spins beneath my fingers and I lose control. Careering across the road, my wheels catch the rough edge and the quad flips, skidding at an angle exposing my shoulder to the road until I hit a guard rail and flip a second time. I scream and scream and scream. It's not as if I had time to pull on a helmet and protective gear before I left. On the second roll my head hits the ground. I hear the crack, and everything from my chest down goes numb.

The pain from my shoulder should knock me into a state of oblivion, but when the darkness approaches I don't reach for it. I hang on to the light. Yeah, I'm a fool, but this fool doesn't want to die. I have to see Ethan again even if it's just for one more moment, one more time. I need to tell him why I didn't run as soon as I knew, that there was more than my life at stake in that house. Jesilla plans to kill *millions* of people. Someone has to know enough details to make her stop.

Blood is pouring out of my shoulder and I'm weakening fast, so I might not get that chance after all. But now I know Dillon is on our side, I could leave it to him to expose Jesilla's plan. Death isn't something you can time neatly. It doesn't come in a box wrapped in a pretty bow. Blood bubbles out of my shoulder. Drips to the ground.

It won't be long now.

This is how it will end for me. Really end.

Carter's face comes into my line of sight when he gets down on the ground as close as he can beside me. '*Sweet Jesus*, Rochelle, I never... I... I'll get help.' But first he tilts his head, and with his power of acute hearing, he listens for my heartbeat. He will soon know how little time I have left. Suddenly, with a swift intake of breath, his eyes shoot to mine. 'Rochelle, can you hear me?'

The pain is now beyond excruciating. No one can take this. I want to close my eyes and be done with it. Go quietly into the night, rather than answer this man's senseless questioning. But if there's a chance Ethan will come before I...

'Rochelle? Rochelle!'

'Why are you talking to me?' I can't move any part of my body, speaking is excruciating, but I still want to kill this man. 'Leave me alone, Carter. Go home and gloat. I don't want your face to be the last thing I see before I die.'

He scoffs, right in my face. Does it get any lower than that? 'You're not going to die,' he says. 'Not now. Not tonight. With my luck, probably never.' A laugh of pure cynicism escapes him.

First he scoffs. Now the jerk is laughing.

But sudden movement in my neck startles me. Something is happening under my skin. I straighten my head. Moments ago I couldn't do that. Oh my God. Feeling returns to my chest giving me my first deep breath. My stomach, groin and hips tingle with pins-and-needles. What's happening to me? I don't self-heal. What is this? The tingling sensation extends down my legs to my feet. I can't resist the urge to wiggle my toes.

'Why am I healing?' I ask no one in particular as my shredded shoulder, bones, muscles, ligaments, veins and lastly skin regenerates before my own eyes.

'Told you,' is all Carter says, smirking. 'Up you get, girlie. If I have to pull you out myself, I will. You're coming back with us even if we have to chain you to my quad and drag you along the road behind us.'

I crawl out, my movements stiff but each one made with awe. Keziah, Zander and Pearl stand like soldiers in front of their quads, parked side by side to block the road. Head lights shine into my face. Still, I spot something in Zander's hand that glistens.

Cuffs. He's carrying handcuffs in one hand, a chain in the other.

Pearl has cuffs too, and she's reminding herself of the knife tucked in her left boot, the army-issue sub-machine gun in her quad and pistol in the rear waistband of her jeans.

I pick up Carter's thoughts of vengeance, his excitement at having a promised fifteen minutes alone with me. He pulls a chain from his quad, rattling it to get my attention. He wants me to see him attach it to his quad's rear. The psycho wasn't bluffing.

'You're going to need more than cuffs and chains to get me back to that house.' I say these words with more bravado than I'm feeling. I need a moment to survey the surrounding area for an escape route.

As Zander and Pearl prepare to jump me, I pull energy into my hands and hold it there, building it. When Zander gives his partner a slight nod, I unfold my fingers and let the fireworks erupt.

The distraction works long enough to smash a high kick at Carter's head, cracking his cheek bone. He drops, his head hitting the road. He groans and tries to sit up, watching me unlatch the chain from his quad and toss it into distant trees.

I turn on Keziah next. Of all of them, this one hurts most. Keziah was kind to me. He let me think he was my father, and he did a good job of being one of the nicest Dad's in the world. But this whole time he was faking.

He gets up from checking on Carter, pulling a gun on me with hands that could be steadier. 'Don't come any closer. I really don't want to hurt you, dear.'

'*Dear*?' I rip the gun from his hands and hold it out to the side. My power isn't all sparkling fireworks. 'Watch carefully, *Dad*. Next time this will be your head.' Working up my powers in an instant, I hold the metal until it sizzles and dissolves in gooey drips to the ground.

Pearl and Zander stare. Carter wobbles but gets to his feet. And it's then I hear the sound of a chopper approaching.

Hope flares.

The thought that maybe Ethan is about to arrive has me thinking – obtusely - about my hair. It began as a high ponytail. Now it's a wind-tossed, knotted jumble. I give myself a quick look over and cringe at the white shoes, short socks, short skirt and cardigan with a shredded shoulder.

'*Damn*, they got here fast,' Carter spits, holding his cheek while he stumbles onto his quad and orders the others, 'Grab the girl and get us out of here. Hurry!'

As Carter leans on the steering wheel, he watches Zander and Pearl approach me with caution, guns in one hand, cuffs and chains in the other.

Pearl says, 'Don't make me hurt you, missy.'

I roll my eyes. Didn't she see what I did with Keziah's weapon? She grins. She thinks she has me. There's no logic to some people's thinking processes. The moment she's within range I kick her hand holding the gun. The weapon goes straight up. Before catching it, I snatch Zander's from his hand, tossing both weapons into the trees.

It doesn't faze her. She pulls the knife from her boot and inches towards me.

I wait patiently so I can lay my hands on the exposed skin of her arms.

Meantime, the chopper hovers overhead, bombarding us with blinding lights, its spinning blades creating a frenzy of sound and gushing wind. I keep an eye on the chopper, flicking my focus between it and Pearl as she closes the gap between us. But Zander runs after her, yanking her backwards with his arms around her waist.

'Are you nuts?' he shouts, his voice carrying in the wind. 'She'll burn the skin off your bones.' He shoves an unusual-looking chain in her hands. 'We use this.'

It's a net, cast from a strong metal that's light and strangely malleable. One instant it's in Pearl's hands, but in the next, Zander flicks it in my direction. It spreads over me like a second skin, trapping my hands by my sides. Keziah and his magic are definitely involved in this net's creation. Pearl yanks on an attached chain and brings me to the ground. I land with a jolt on my butt.

Carter reaches for the chain. 'Give her to me,' he orders, connecting the chain to his quad's bumper for a second time.

When he jumps in to start the quad, Keziah argues with him. 'Jesilla will not like this. Let me take her back in one piece.'

'No way, old man. No one's taking this murdering she-devil from me again.'

*God*, he's going to drag me behind him, driving over the gravel edges and sharp bends. The thought alone chills me and I shudder, the slight movement making the chain tighten even further.

Somehow the crash didn't kill me, but how can I survive if there's nothing left of my skin and bones?

The chopper blows a gale as it comes down and lands on the road nearby. Three male figures, camouflaged in black from head to foot, with narrow slits for their eyes, jump out before it lands. The first two I recognize instantly - Arkarian by his distinctive purple eyes, and Matt's familiar gold ones. The third darts off into the surrounding darkness where I lose sight of him, but it's Ethan. I feel his presence with every beat of my heart.

Arkarian and Matt size up my situation in a blink. Sharing a worried glance they move quickly.

'Withdraw!' Zander orders his team.

'Not without *her*,' Carter yells. 'Cover me.'

Ignoring his broken cheek bone and bleeding skull, Carter jumps behind the wheel and starts his quad. With my gut churning, I try to turn my hands around, but it's as if the net and my skin have become one entity. The chain connecting me to the quad tightens and suddenly there's a fierce tug and I'm on the ground. I brace myself, but the quad doesn't take off. Arkarian and Matt have lifted one end, making the tires spin in the air. Carter tumbles out and crawls to the trees. They release the chain and let the quad drop to the road with a thump.

Meanwhile, Pearl, Zander and Keziah scatter around their quadbikes finding cover where they can. Pulling out their semi-automatic machine guns, they fire endless rounds. Matt takes a hit in his shoulder but doesn't flinch except for a brief annoyed glance he exchanges with Arkarian. In response, Arkarian's lips twitch and he nods. Together they whip up a shield with a thrust of gleaming gold energy from their hands.

The shield works like magic, ricocheting bullets back at the three Order members.

It's then Carter runs screaming out of the trees, knife in hand, heading straight at me. And I'm a sitting duck caught in this net unable to move.

But Ethan materializes between us. Flicking a glance over his shoulder at me, he takes in how the strange net wraps around my body from shoulders to ankles, binding my arms and making my hands useless. Clenching his fists, his beautiful eyes suddenly light up the night with an incredible burning blue glow. With only a second before Carter reaches him, Ethan spins around and slogs him in the gut. It's a hard hit. The ex-school teacher tumbles backwards holding his stomach. Ethan bears down on the man and hits him in the gut, and the face, again, again, and again. Carter drops to the ground and tries to crawl away.

But Ethan is not letting him go. He bears down on Carter, yelling, 'Get up, you piece of crap.' With his legs apart, his back ramrod straight, anger-induced energy rolls off Ethan in shimmering blue waves. I've never seen anything like it. I'm so impressed that my lips part in a soft gasp. What happened to him?

Staring down at Carter, Ethan lifts his hand to the top of his head and tugs off the balaclava. 'I won't fight you lying down.'

Carter shakes his head, cowering in the face of Ethan's rage. There's a sense of confidence, of power and fierceness in Ethan tonight. And Carter feels it too.

When he refuses to get up but starts shuffling backwards, crawling towards his quadbike, Ethan yanks him to his feet and slogs him an uppercut to the jaw, sending the man sprawling into the bushes.

Matt runs over to collect him, but after a brief search lifts his hands out and shrugs.

Carter has disappeared. Since neither the Guard nor the Order ever trusted him enough to give him his wings, he's probably running to the Order's tunnel entrance that's around here somewhere.

Ethan turns to look at me with a question in his eyes, but when our eyes meet the question disappears, and his lips part as he says my name, '*Rochelle.*'

Suddenly the air fills with a gold mist. The millions of miniscule bubbles burst when they touch solid matter, like the road, the trees, or us. Arkarian has released the shield. As it dissipates, the road winding up the mountain becomes clear and quiet but for the lingering sounds of distant fleeing quadbikes.

Then Ethan is hunkering down by my side. His hands, swift and gentle, work the clinging net off my body. When I'm free he helps me to my feet and we stand facing each other.

'*Rochelle*,' he says, eyes sparkling like the stars in our solar system, every scrap of hardness melting away.

I jump into his arms. He catches me, hoisting me higher, his hands under my thighs holding me steady. I wrap my arms around his neck and tighten my legs around his waist. I can't get close enough. His hands slide up my back and into my hair. With our faces touching, tears mingling, we cling to each other, and slowly, via some higher level of comprehension, become aware that we are finally together.

We're free. We're safe. Nothing, no one, not ever, will separate us again.

Lifting my head to see Ethan's face, my lips part with the need to kiss him, to *really* kiss him, but he has another agenda in mind first. He sets me back on my feet and methodically runs his fingertips over my skull, checking every bone of my head, down to my neck.

'Ethan...'

He lifts a finger to his lips, his eyes pleading to let him finish. I nod and he runs his gentle hands across my shoulders. He lifts the tattered edges of what's left of my cardigan, peering at me. I shrug. He continues his scrutiny, running his exploring fingers over my back, my waist, my ribs.

My body throbs where he touches. He's so intent on making sure I'm not broken that he has no idea what his hands are doing to me.

To my sanity.

I wait with something akin to sweet agony, imagining him a sculptor and my body the artwork he's bringing to life.

Staring into my eyes, he writes his name on my soul with the words, 'I thought I'd lost you.'

Oh my God, I would give him anything right now.

He tugs off his jacket, and lovingly slips it around my shoulders.

'Are you hurt?'

'I was, but somehow I'm not anymore.'

'From the chopper we saw your quad spin out of control.'

'You saw that?'

He swallows and closes his eyes tightly, as if this is how he chases away memories he never wants to relive again. 'I was sure we were too late. I thought I would find nothing left of you.'

'I don't know how but I'm not broken or in pain anymore.'

'I thought I lost you again.'

'The way my body healed itself after that crash, I don't think you can.'

He grins. 'I have something to tell you on that subject as well.'

It's finally sinking in that I'm not tonight's quadbike road kill and I lift my head back and stretch out my arms. Like an offering to the stars, I breathe in the cold night air, thanking every immortal god that ever lived that I survived.

I have survived so much. I'm truly blessed and grateful and maybe even feeling a little invincible. With my arms still outstretched, Ethan lifts me, twirling me around above him while he releases a series of whoops and howls to the stars.

Arkarian and Matt wait patiently by the chopper, their balaclavas in their hands, exchanging glances and smiles. Catching our attention Arkarian waves us over. Ethan gathers me into his arms and carries me to the chopper with a wide grin on his face.

Matt follows us in, patting Ethan's shoulder while guiding him to a seat where he can put me down between them. He helps latch my seat belt before he turns my face up to his with his thumb under my chin. 'It's good to see you, Rochelle.' With tears glistening he smiles. 'I don't know why or how we have you back with us again, but if this is a gift from the gods, I just want to say...' He glances upwards, 'thank you.' With a wink, he adds, 'I've let Neriah know and she's informed Isabel. They made me promise to tell them straight away.'

I nod. It's the most I can do right now. This sense of acceptance is new. It will take some time to get used to it.

Arkarian makes a winding up motion to the pilot. As the chopper lifts, he comes over to where I'm sitting between the boys. He kisses my cheeks and sits down opposite. His eyes study me, pausing on the glimpse of bare skin through the open jacket, and some other places where my clothes are torn and bloodied.

He finds me a blanket, and as the boys put it around my shoulders he sits opposite again and leans towards me. 'Rochelle...' he says, his voice as always gentle and all-knowing, 'when did you turn eighteen?'

Ethan tilts his head, a question in his eyes as they flit from me to Arkarian and back again.

I swallow down some lingering dried blood in my throat as I remember that day. How could I forget? No one knew. And I didn't tell anyone. 'The day of the battle.'

Arkarian smiles. 'Do you know that you have immortality in your DNA?'

'What? No. But Carter realized something when my... when I started to heal in front of him.'

He nods.

'Is that how I survived, Arkarian?'

He explains, 'When the arrow pierced your chest, your heart stopped beating. We know that positively. But you turned eighteen that day and after a minute or two, or perhaps ten...' he shrugs, 'who knows, your immortal DNA started your heart beating again.'

'Why didn't any of us hear it?' Matt asks. 'Isabel was right there.'

Ethan says, 'I was there yanking the arrow out of your ribs.'

He glances at my chest with a frown. I touch his face with my fingertips. 'I have no scars.'

He visibly relaxes, and pulling me closer he rests his chin on top of my head.

'I don't know why we didn't hear it restart,' Arkarian says. 'But I have a theory that Keziah was lurking somewhere nearby and of all of us, he was the one to hear it start again, and he got the idea to hide you from us. To ensure we didn't realize what had happened, he worked his magic on you, disguising the truth until he was able to switch your body from the crypt.'

Arkarian tries to take my hand but Ethan has them both in his and won't let go. Arkarian smiles at Ethan with great affection and understanding, and pats my knee instead. 'You are safe now, Rochelle.'

Ethan whispers, his mouth at my ear, 'You will always be safe now.'

I could collapse against his chest and sleep for days in his embrace, but I can't, not yet. 'Thank you for coming.'

Arkarian tips his head towards Matt. 'He heard you first.'

I smile at him. 'Does this mean you've forgiven me?'

'I forgave you a long time ago, I just didn't tell you. I should have. I'm sorry about that.'

'Don't be sorry, Matt. I hurt you terribly, and I'm sorry about that.'

'You did save my life.'

'Well, yeah, there is that.'

He hugs me. 'We're good now.'

I nod and turn to Arkarian. 'I have vital information you need to know.'

Arkarian flicks Matt a troubled look. 'We'll call a meeting for first light. Tonight you need to rest.'

Ethan squeezes my hands. 'I'm taking Rochelle home with me.'

I turn my face up to his. 'Wherever you make your home from now on is my home too. Ethan, I'm done with being separated from you.' I lock his smile in my heart and savor the kiss he plants on my forehead. 'But we need to make a detour first.' I turn to include both Matt and Arkarian. 'We need to gather the others. What I have to tell you can't wait until morning. You have to hear it tonight. Tomorrow will be too late.'

# Chapter Thirty-five

## Jesilla

Keziah lets me know before they get back that they don't have Rochelle.

Bastian reads my disappointment and raises an eyebrow.

'She got away,' I tell him, watching his face carefully across the conference table. But he's schooled his features into a blank screen and shut his thoughts from my probing.

'What happens now, Jesilla?' Peter asks, waiting with us.

Just then they hurry into the conference room, Zander and Pearl half carrying Carter between them. Keziah points to the nearest chair. 'Put him down there.'

'What happened?' Bastian asks, stretching up in his seat.

'We almost had her,' Zander says, catching a breath. 'Then a chopper arrived and three Guards attacked us with powers we've never seen before.'

*What's he talking about?* I mind-link Bastian. *Are you keeping something from me?*

Calmly, he looks straight into my eyes. 'All our powers surged when Lathenia and Lorian had their meeting in Athos.'

'You mean that meteor shower?'

He nods, returning his attention to Carter holding his cheek together with his hands while Keziah attends to a painful-looking head wound.

'Who beat the hell out of you?' Bastian asks.

Carter sneers with the working side of his face. 'Who do you think?'

Keziah pauses in his healing to look between the two. 'They wore disguises.'

Carter shifts his eyes to me and spits out hatred along with saliva, 'Ethan Roberts did this. And I'm going to kill him. I'll kill them both.'

'That's a bit greedy, isn't it?' Bastian points out, making me stifle a laugh.

'Given the choice, which one would you annihilate?'

Ignoring Carter, Bastian huffs softly and returns to watching the door.

He knows something.

*What's up with you?* I mind-link. But he just shakes his head.

So Ethan recovered from small pox. Remarkable. Can nothing kill that boy? On the one hand I'm glad for him, but realistically, my Order is better off with him dead. Maybe I'll let Carter have his wish, but he's going to need my help with Rochelle.

Overflowing with bitterness, Carter holds Bastian's gaze. 'So why didn't *you* go after her?'

'It was me,' I explain. 'I ordered Bastian to stay behind.'

Smashed jaw, broken cheek bone, a gash to his scalp, and in a world of pain, Carter yells, 'You did *what*? If the girl means so much to us, why stop our strongest from going after her?'

'I don't have to explain my reasons to you. It doesn't matter now. It's done.'

'It does matter because it sounds as if you play favorites with the pretty boy.'

'Back off, Carter.' I slam my palm down on the table, making it jump.

They all fall silent. It's my eyes. My burning irises let me know they're glowing. But not in the attractive way Bastian's sometimes do. Mine turn an eerie demonic red that would terrify a child.

I peer around the room, waiting until everyone is calm again. 'What matters is the Guard has Rochelle, and when they debrief her, they will know what we're planning.'

Except for Bastian, staring at the door as if he's waiting for a chance to rush for it, they glance at each other. But none of them can look me in the eyes yet, reminding me they're still glowing. I blink hard and breathe slower. 'It's imperative that this mission stays ahead of the Guard. We can't wait two more days as we'd planned. We need to be in and out before they debrief Rochelle.'

Pearl leans forward, elbows on the table. 'Tell us what to do.'

At last some enthusiasm. 'We need to be in the command center. We need this mission to go ahead now. Marcus, are you up for coordinating?'

'It's what I do best, Jesilla, and you know it.' He looks up at Keziah, still fussing with his jaw. 'Are you finished yet?'

'No, keep still. You should be on a healing bed in the clinic for this.'

'We don't have time for that,' Carter snaps. 'You're younger now; you should be able to heal faster.'

Keziah takes a deep steadying breath. He glances at me. 'I'm hurrying.'

'You're doing a great job, Keziah, but don't tire yourself out. I need your skills on this mission.'

'I understand,' he says.

While waiting for Keziah to finish up with Carter, I brief the others. 'Peter, you will assist Marcus with anything he needs to return us safely. Watch for any anomaly and let him know the instant you spot anything that might cause us a problem.'

'Affirmative,' Peter says, and turning to Carter he nods. 'I'm ready mate.'

I bite down on my lower lip before realizing what a sign of indecision that might look like. I draw in a silent deep breath and straighten my shoulders. 'Pearl, Zander, you do whatever you must to keep the command center safe from intruders. Brief our staff to be on the lookout for a possible invasion.'

'You think the Guard will attack the complex?' Bastian asks.

'I don't know, Bastian. You tell me.'

He glances back at the door again without answering and I return to the briefing. 'No one enters without Level Six access.'

Zander replies, 'Understood.'

'Bastian, you're with me.'

He nods.

'Keziah, you're coming too.'

Bastian shoves his thought into my head. *On the mission? Why?*

*Where we're going we'll need his skills. Now stop questioning my decisions.* Making my voice lighter, I say aloud, 'We need to change.' To everyone, I add, 'We can't attend a function with Kings and Presidents dressed in jeans and T-shirts.'

I get a few sniggers and a smile out of Pearl.

Keziah sighs as he withdraws his healing hands from Carter's head and sits alongside him.

*Are you OK, Kez?*

*I'm fine, Jesilla. I'm ready.*

'All right, everyone, let's go.'

Last one through the door, Bastian touches my arm. 'I have to go out for a bit.'

My stare is icy. 'I understand how you enjoy your little outings, and that my mother tolerated them above and beyond any single time I needed to escape this complex, but I'm not her, and tonight I'm in charge.'

'I'll use my wings.'

'You mean, you'll *shift*. We call it shifting here at the Order. It's not a stupid award system my uncle made up to manipulate his *special* ones. It's a power in all of our kind that can be easily released by an immortal.'

I think my little hate speech has taken him aback. It takes me aback too, but I need to be stronger than I've ever been before if I'm going take over from my mother. I have to harden up. And I have to start now.

His brows draw together in a frown. 'Right. Well. Jesilla, this won't take long, especially if I *shift*. I'll be back in no time.'

'I said *no*. You're not going out and that's my last word.'

I don't want Bastian thinking that I suspect him. The thing is I don't know for sure. There's always the possibility that I misunderstood what I heard. I want to keep Bastian close at least until I figure out his true motives. Maybe that's just me being fanciful because, well, I... I want to trust Bastian so we can be together. The truth is I don't just want Bastian, I *need* him. I'd love nothing more than to share the new world we're making with him, and with our children one day. I don't want to live the way my mother did – on her own because she couldn't trust anyone – except for that brute Marduke.

So for now Bastian goes wherever I go. When I'm sure his loyalties are with me, then I'll trust him to go and come as he pleases.

I hold his gaze and hope I'm wrong, that he wasn't the one who tipped off Rochelle. *What's going on with you? By now Rochelle would have told them about you. Your time as a double agent is over. The Guard will torture you to make you talk. We won't be wearing disguises on this mission. We'll be in our own bodies. Bastian, I don't want to lose you. And... and I don't want to do this mission without you.*

His mouth opens as if to say something, but he closes it without saying a word. His eyes search mine as if he's looking for something. But whatever it is, he keeps it to himself, hidden deep in his thoughts, far from my reach.

*Bastian, we make a great team.*

*No argument there.*

Carter notices Bastian and I lingering at the door. 'Mind sharing that secret conversation because I've had enough of you two playing games with each...'

He doesn't finish. Bastian groans under his breath and reaches for Carter, lifting him, and pinning him against the corridor wall.

Peter, Zander, Pearl and Keziah move out of the way.

Carter's feet search for the ground while he tries to shove his fingers between his throat and Bastian's hands around it. 'Are you insinuating something, Marcus, because that would be disrespectful to your superiors?'

*Bastian, put him down.*

*Just let him answer.*

*Fine. One minute, then.*

He tells Carter, 'If you don't respect your superiors, there's plenty of room in the cells below. Don't think I won't do it, and I might just forget you're there.'

Carter's eyes slide to meet mine, and he coughs, a choking sound. 'Jesilla, this is not an excuse, it's just that I'm used to seeing you as a child. But you've grown up fast, you've had to, and I apologize for being so disagreeable and over-reacting. I'm sorry.'

Bastian catches my eye. I nod and he lowers Carter to the floor, wiping his hands on the front of his jeans with a look of distaste on his face. Carter catches up to the others while Bastian falls in beside me as we continue to make our way to the command center.

'Why are we bringing Keziah?' Bastian asks. 'Tell me the truth, Jesilla. Why do we need him? Can I do it instead? He taught me the same things he taught you. Maybe between us we...'

'Where we're going, the only way you and I are going to get past security is with Keziah's magic.'

'Damn,' he mutters. 'The one thing he couldn't teach us.'

Last to walk into the command center, Bastian looks for Keziah. He finds him studying the big screens that Carter already has running on the front wall.

*But, Jes, why put Keziah at such a high risk?*

*Because I have no other choice.*

*Find another way.*

*There's no time, Bastian.*

*But, why would you risk losing the one person you can completely trust?*

He takes me by surprise with this and I swing round to confront him. 'Is Keziah really the only one I can completely trust?'

He breaks eye contact first and curses out of the corner of his mouth. 'That's not what I meant.'

'I wish I could believe you, Bastian. You have no idea how much I want to *completely trust* you.'

We walk down the ramp to the command center's main working area in silence. Here, Keziah has replaced Lathenia's sphere with the smaller, but much more advanced Atlantean sphere. It hovers above a specially designed eight-sided work station. At one of these stations I stand and watch the sphere move within its own gravity, revealing the image of an unusual and yet stunning coastal city.

Keziah shows Marcus how to operate the new sphere, which takes a few minutes, then looks over at me. 'When do we leave?'

I smile at his enthusiasm. 'Now.'

Suddenly Pearl is beside me staring up at the sphere. 'Jesilla, are you sure about this?'

I keep my eyes on her while the silence grows taut in the room and everyone looks at us. 'What exactly are you questioning, Pearl?'

'I mean no disrespect. It's just that, not long ago Zander and I were your bodyguards. We've watched over you for most of your life. We were there when you took your first steps, picking you up when you fell. It's like one day we're taking care of you and the next...' She swallows and takes a deep breath. 'Well, now you're going to cull a billion people from the world's future population and I need to know, will my daughter be safe?'

'I promise you, Pearl, the Earth will be a better world for your daughter to enjoy and raise her family.'

I look at each member of my team. 'It's time you realized that my mother is gone, and I have taken her place. Undoubtedly, she would have done things differently to me, but how long do you think it will take the Guard to catch up and make their move to block us? Right now, Rochelle is telling them all she knows about our plan. They will panic. And they will pull out anything they can to stop us.'

# Chapter Thirty-six

## Ethan

In Arkarian's meeting room in his mountain chambers it's midnight but nobody cares. The girls, my Dad and Jimmy are already here when we arrive. They greet us with a barrage of hugs, kisses, cheering and questions, but above all they greet Rochelle with love and acceptance. Unmistakable in their eyes, it's also in their relieved expressions. They get to start again with her. And that's all Rochelle ever wanted.

I'm so proud of them that tears fill my eyes. For a guy, I've cried more than my fair share this year. I've shed every type of tear generated out of every emotion the human body is capable of producing. But tonight my tears come from joy. My heart is freaking jumping with it.

OK, so some of what I'm feeling is because I get to take Rochelle home after this. I get to hold her in my arms until long past the sun comes up. It's a school day tomorrow, but I don't give a damn. We're taking the day off. Yep, we might even take the whole week.

Rochelle is having no luck holding back her tears either. She gave up trying the moment she stepped through the door. She's relishing her welcome home, as she should. As she deserves.

With King Richard about to arrive, it's only Dillon who isn't here. He isn't answering Arkarian's calls either and Arkarian is looking increasingly worried.

King Richard materializes carrying two bottles of Champagne which he immediately offloads to Matt. 'Put them somewhere cold for they will unfortunately have to wait.' He then looks straight across the room at Rochelle and smiles. The room falls silent. 'Welcome home, Rochelle.'

Rochelle returns the smile. 'Thank you, sire.'

'The bells are ringing all over Athens to herald your return.'

'You're joking, my lord.'

Today, in black leather pants, a cream sweater with a black sports blazer, and sporting a closely cropped beard, he opens his arms. 'I joke not, my lady. Now come here.'

He meets her halfway, closing his arms around her in a bear hug. 'This is a grand day in Athens,' he says. 'Lord Dartemis set all the church bells in motion with a sprinkle of magic. Nothing will stop them ringing for the next forty days.'

Everyone stares at him.

Matt says, 'But, sire, didn't my father understand how that would attract attention?'

'I suppose he did, Matthew,' he shrugs. 'They have already reported the curious phenomenon on CNN.'

Everyone laughs and finally King Richard releases Rochelle. And like magnets not meant to be apart she returns, seeking my hand, entwining our fingers together. My heart, so recently decimated by loss, now beats with the power of eternal love. My soul-mate is back in my arms.

We sit around the conference table with King Richard at the head, Arkarian and Matt on either side. When we're all quiet Richard glances at me and asks, 'Ethan, since you became an immortal, have you felt your powers strengthen or change?'

'I have, my lord.'

He raises an eyebrow and waits for more.

'Both strengthen and change, sire.'

'Right.' Clearly, he expects more, but I'm not at ease with my newfound powers yet. 'Well... excellent news.'

In the seat beside me, Rochelle squeezes my hand. She understands. I bring our joined hands to my lap and fold my other hand over them, silently vowing that no one will come between us again.

Isabel sits on Rochelle's other side, next to Arkarian, while Neriah, with Richard's brush as always in her hand, sits across the table between Matt and Jimmy. Dad sits opposite me, while the seat on my right remains notably vacant.

And while looking at that chair my instinct tells me something is wrong. 'Is Dillon in trouble?'

Arkarian answers, 'It's time you all learned some things about Dillon.'

That gets everyone's instant attention.

'The day Dillon defected from the Order of Chaos he came to me with the idea of working as a double agent.'

Rochelle stiffens. *I should have known. It all makes sense now.*

*I'm not sure who you're talking to in that beautiful mind of yours*, I forge my first mind-link with her, *but I hope you mean me.*

Her eyes fly to mine with her lips parted in a soft gasp. *Would this be one of those strengthened powers our king mentioned now that you're IMMORTAL?*

I nod and she winks.

My mind whirls with possibilities of what that wink could mean. If no one would notice, I'd sweep her out of here to somewhere more private. Matt clears his throat and covers a grin with his hand over his mouth.

*It's why Dillon didn't stay as long as I did in the debriefing unit*, she forges. *I always wondered about that. I just thought the Guard trusted Dillon more than...*

I kiss her forehead softly. She stops wondering and smiles to herself.

Arkarian says, 'After the battle, I wanted to pull him out and I called him via our usual communication methods.' He points to his head to indicate mind-linking, and it finally hits me what Dillon's other power is.

*What?*

I try to recall some of the things I thought about while in his company, but it's impossible to remember *every*thing.

Matt and Neriah glance at each other before breaking out in uncomfortable laughter. But it's Isabel's reaction that has our attention.

'Dillon is a Truthseer? Oh my God, tell me it's not true. Ark, are you sure?'

'Yes, but...' He strokes her hair, his mouth twitching with amusement. 'It's all right, Isabel.'

She drops her head and bangs it repeatedly on the table surface, making everyone cringe.

Arkarian pulls her up by her shoulders. 'Hey, hey, don't do that. It's OK.'

She shakes her head. 'It's not OK. You have no idea what I've thought about while in Dillon's presence.'

Arkarian lifts her face with his two hands. 'Tell us. It's probably not as bad as you think.'

She glances around the table, her face darkening with each new set of eyes she encounters. 'He joked all the time and didn't seem to take anything seriously.'

'Still doesn't,' Matt mutters, grinning. 'So you didn't trust him.' He shrugs. 'Big deal.'

Isabel says, 'I would plot to get rid of him. I'd make terrible excuses. To think that all those times he could hear what I was thinking. I can't look at him again.'

Arkarian tries to soothe her. 'Dillon understood to keep out of his friends' heads.'

Everyone scoffs at that, even Dad. Even King Richard.

Arkarian checks that Isabel is OK before returning to his explanation about Dillon. 'A few days after the battle Dillon was preparing to leave, but when he next made contact he said he couldn't pull out yet. They were hiding someone in their clinic.'

I ask, 'He didn't tell you they had Rochelle?'

'He didn't know until later the identity of that person in isolation. When he discovered it was Rochelle, other factors had come into play, complicating everything.'

*Dillon knew?* 'Like what?'

'Lathenia's daughter Jesilla had taken control of the Order. She made it clear she intended to finish what her mother had planned, and avenge her mother's and Marduke's deaths. She also controlled Rochelle's memories and powers, and Dillon didn't want to jeopardize them. The Order had become organized again, and Dillon was our only eyes in there.'

'Why didn't he tell me once school started?' The tension coils into anger, catapulting me to my feet. Suddenly waves of blue energy pulse from my fingertips like laser beams. They shoot across the room forcing Dad and Jimmy to duck for cover. Arkarian appears behind me and, laying his hands on my shoulders he pushes calming energy into me until it stops.

I sit and apologize to everyone but especially to Dad and Jimmy. It still bugs me that Dillon knew Rochelle was alive. 'How could he keep that from me?' But everyone is still staring. 'What is it?'

Rochelle strokes my face with her warm hand. *Your eyes*, she forges. Her voice in my head while we maintain eye contact is such an intimate connection that my body reacts with the need to hold her, to pull her onto my lap and kiss her until we're both senseless.

I manage to say, *What about my eyes?*

She smiles. *They're glowing. Bright blue and, hmm... so stunning, if we were alone right now...*

*Not helping.*

*Sorry, baby. Let's try this...* She cups both sides of my face with her palms. *Breathe. Don't think. Just breathe.* The burning eases, though now everyone is staring at Rochelle's hands as they flicker with colored electric charges, like lightning streaking under her skin. But they're clearly harmless. She taught herself to control her power, something she once feared she would never be able to do.

*I knew you could.*

King Richard starts clapping. 'Well done!' And everyone joins in to Rochelle's beaming smile.

'We must continue,' Arkarian's voice has everyone settle down quickly.

But I still need answers. 'Why did Dillon tell us he had cousins who were sisters?'

'It wasn't Dillon's story. He had to play along with it. Dillon walked on a tightrope in that house. Even now, he still needs Jesilla to trust him. When he came to me with the information that Rochelle still lived, we discussed bringing you in on it, Ethan, but your reactions to Crystal had to be natural. Jesilla's revenge involved torturing your emotions. My only consolation was that it gave us time to figure out how to extract Rochelle with her memories and powers unscathed.'

I glance at Matt. He knows what I'm going to ask before I voice my question and raises both hands in the air. 'I didn't know. I swear.'

'There was too much at stake,' Arkarian says, 'to involve anyone else.'

Dad says, 'If Jesilla is anything like her mother, she wouldn't hesitate to kill Dillon for double crossing her.'

'Dillon convinced me to leave him undercover,' Arkarian says. 'He assured me that he was safe, that he knew what he was doing, and that he would be in the complex should something go wrong.'

Rochelle sits back in her seat and sighs. 'Like tonight when he warned me. He put his own life in danger to protect me,' she says, and I can see the clogs of guilt churning in her worried eyes. 'After dinner I went up to my room and suddenly his voice crashed into my head, telling me to run, that my life was in danger.'

'He chose to stay to protect you,' Arkarian confirms, 'but also to keep the world safe from the plans of a deceased Goddess.'

Dillon deserves a medal. When I see him next I'll make him one myself. I'll tattoo it to his chest so everyone will see what a freaking hero he is.

Matt asks, 'Why wasn't Dillon on the road chasing Rochelle down the mountain? We could have pulled them both out together.'

'That's one of my immediate concerns for him,' Arkarian says. 'And also that he hasn't contacted me yet. If Jesilla suspects Dillon is double-crossing her, she won't let him out of her sight.'

Stunned at the dire situation Dillon is now in, we fall silent until Rochelle says, 'Jesilla doesn't miss a beat. She would have heard Dillon warning me. He's is in real danger.'

Arkarian glances at King Richard, who pushes out from the table. 'I'll organize his extraction immediately.'

'That house is a fortress,' Rochelle warns. 'You trip a sensor, they'll lock it down. And, my lord, you'll have to move fast. Jesilla will bring it forward. It wouldn't surprise me if they leave tonight, taking Dillon with her.'

Matt frowns at Rochelle. 'What are you talking about?'

'The mission,' she says. 'The first key point of her mother's plan to change the world. It's where she gets to wipe out millions of people.'

# Chapter Thirty-seven

## Ethan

'Go ahead and explain, Rochelle,' Arkarian says after King Richard leaves to organize Dillon's extraction from the enemy's complex. 'Tell us how the Order is planning to eliminate millions of people.'

She speaks quickly and clearly, explaining how seven, high-tech mechanical 'dragonflies' will distribute a fast-acting variation of the small-pox virus to a gathering of more than three thousand government and business leaders from around the world. 'This mission was set for two or three days' time, but after my escape Jesilla will make this happen earlier. Probably tonight. Unfortunately, I didn't hear the mission's details, so I can't tell you where they'll be going, or when, only that it's the first mission of its kind. To my way of thinking, that could only mean...'

'The future,' Neriah announces, unconsciously strangling her brush's bristles.

'How do you know that?' Rochelle asks her.

'With every practice session a future date draws me towards it. It's like the brush knows when a portal is opening and pulls me to it.'

Arkarian says, 'It's more likely your own instincts picking up on the opening portal than the brush. Once you learn to trust your own instincts you won't need the brush to open a portal, just your mind.'

Neriah shrugs. 'Anyway, it doesn't matter how Jesilla pretties it up with thoughts of saving the planet, what she's planning is mass murder. Instead, she should use her energies to look into providing housing, food and clean drinking water to Earth's growing population.'

Matt agrees. 'We have to stop her before she pulls this off. Anything could go wrong. What if future scientists can't eradicate this particular small pox variation fast enough, or they fail to make enough vaccines before it spreads beyond their ability to control it? Humanity would be screwed.'

Dad's fingers play a tattoo on the table top. Arkarian notices. 'What are you thinking, Shaun?'

'While King Richard is at the complex extracting Dillon,' he says, 'he should shut down the laboratory, but not destroy it until our own scientists examine what else they're producing there.'

'Good point. I'll let him know.'

Jimmy says, 'How do we extract Dillon if Jesilla has already taken him on her mission?'

'There's only one way,' Rochelle says. 'We have to send a team after them. Find him, and return him here.'

'Oh boy, I hate to do this,' Jimmy says, 'but how do we follow them into the future? The sphere has stopped spinning altogether. Sir Syford can't get the super computer functioning after the last mission failure.'

'We have Neriah,' Arkarian says.

Hope has Rochelle leaning towards her. 'So you can open a portal?'

Neriah says, '*Almost*.'

'Oh.' She sits back. 'Well, *almost* isn't going cut it. We need to go after them now, before the portal closes behind them.' Rochelle lowers her gaze. She wants to say more but stops herself.

'What's the problem?' Isabel asks, and purposefully glances around the table. 'There are some clever people in this room.' Her gaze lands on Jimmy, who salutes her with a tap to his forehead.

'Isabel's right,' Jimmy says. 'We might be able to help you figure this out.'

'Well...'

'Maybe you could show them,' Matt suggests.

Dad and Jimmy move their chairs to the side as Neriah steps into the space between them. We watch as first Neriah takes a few moments to center herself, then begins painting the air with her brush. 'I'm being pulled to this place,' she says. 'It feels like it's where I should be. I don't know why, I just know it's right.'

'Sounds like how my instinct works,' I say.

She looks at me and nods.

Images appear of a spacious hotel foyer furnished sparingly in gold lounges and glass tables on dark red carpet. Guests in formal wear, long gowns and black suits, stand around chatting and sipping drinks as others stand in line, gradually making their way towards a set of double entrance doors. I suspect the hall is where the event is taking place. There are armed security agents in uniforms and dark suits making their presence known, and soldiers wearing United Nations insignias.

Neriah moves deeper by 'painting' over the portal, straight through the middle, or at an angle to forge a new direction.

Everyone leans one way or another as Neriah widens the portal and we 'walk' up to a pair of U.N. soldiers packing smooth silver handguns in their belts with automatic machine guns hanging over their shoulders of a type none of us has seen before. They stand on guard at the entrance to the event-room where the next couple at the front of the line steps up. One soldier runs a handheld device over the couple from head to foot. It crackles like a Geiger counter and is probably a bomb detector. It forms a life-size hologram beside them that clears when the security guards allow them entrance.

As the door opens we catch a glimpse inside before it closes and Neriah brings us back to the foyer, when suddenly Rochelle jumps to her feet. 'Neriah, stop. Look who's on the gold lounge against the auditorium wall.'

'Where?' Neriah asks.

We all peer into the portal to help locate the person Rochelle is trying to point out. It takes too long and Rochelle grows agitated. She goes up to the portal and points, but still no one can see it. She then glances at me. 'Can I have a pointer?'

I produce one with my mind that appears in her hand. She smiles her thanks and uses it to point out a very small gold spot.

Neriah paints over the spot with her brush, bringing the area into larger focus. And now everyone sees what has Rochelle's heart racing, but how she picked them out is just as astonishing and she gets some serious stares.

She shrugs. 'It's Dillon,' she says, returning to her seat. 'He's there already. The girl in the middle in the black dress is Jesilla, and the man on the right –'

'That's Mr Quinn,' Isabel says.

'Yeah,' Rochelle confirms. 'He pretended to be my father when in fact he's really Keziah, the Magician.'

This stuns everyone.

Arkarian and Matt scrutinize Keziah's image. They glance at each other and Matt shakes his head. 'That's impossible.'

'Dillon informed us that Jesilla had renewed Keziah's health,' Arkarian says, 'but I can't imagine taking more than a thousand years off a man's physical age.'

Matt rubs his eyes. 'It's a complete transformation.'

'Lathenia's daughter did this?' Dad asks. 'How?'

'I'm sorry, Shaun, but I have no idea.' She gives Arkarian a beseeching look.

He nods. 'Yes, now we know where Dillon is, we need to hurry.' He turns to Neriah. 'Thank you for that display. Now can you explain what's happens when you try to step through the portal?'

'Sure.' She turns, raises her hand and tries to put it through, but as soon as she touches the space it sizzles and sparks white light, tossing her arm backwards.

'I've tried everything.'

'Maybe it has nothing to do with the portal,' Matt muses. 'When we travelled into the past we had the supercomputer working in conjunction with the advanced technology of the spinning sphere. But here, now, you have your own power and only what you can glean from the machinery in Arkarian's workroom.'

'You need a boost, Neriah,' Jimmy says.

Arkarian explains, 'The atmospheric conditions created by the octagonal shape of my workroom are conductors that enhance Neriah's natural gifts, her affinity with electricity, for instance, and anything magnetic, like the lightning bolt weapon from the treasury. Neriah reaches into the surrounding technology to enhance her powers, but without the sphere my workstation is not enough.'

'Can we make a booster?' Isabel asks.

Jimmy shakes his head. 'The machines are wrecked beyond repair.'

With his elbows on the table, Matt's eyes suddenly light up. 'Neriah, remember the day we had the first meeting after the battle?'

Isabel scoffs, 'The morning you disappeared, and Neriah and I were out of our minds with worry?'

'Yeah... ah... sorry about that. I went down into the ancient city,' he explains to the rest of us, 'to check if the Prophecy had changed. While down there I saw something that could work as a power conductor.'

Arkarian frowns but stays quiet.

Matt pushes back from the table, taking the brush from Neriah's hand. 'How do we close this portal?'

'Reverse the brush strokes, but, Matt -'

He starts reversing her brush strokes but nothing happens and he looks at her puzzled.

She takes the brush back, rolling her eyes. 'It only works for me.' She moves the brush in reverse strokes over the portal. 'You were saying?'

'Behind the safe there's an area about a meter square in an octagonal shape that radiates power like you wouldn't believe.'

'That's the foundation stone,' Jimmy says. 'It's the power source the early immortals used to build the city. It powers all the technology hidden within the walls. The Ancient Egyptians and the Mayan pyramids have these stones too, hidden beneath their pyramid floors. If exposed to the atmosphere it will become unstable and over time will lose its power. Without its power, the ancient city will crumble. The entire mountain will come down.'

Arkarian says, 'It's what Marduke and his wren were looking for when they stripped the city on battle day.'

'They didn't find it,' Matt says. '*I* did. And now we can use its power to save lives.'

'But without the city...' Arkarian's eyes glaze over as he glances around, 'this will all be gone.'

Nobody knows what to say. Isabel sighs, and with her heart clearly melting she turns to him. 'Arkarian, you have a home. It's beautiful, and I would very much like to live there with you when I finish high school. Or if this mountain falls. Whichever comes first.'

There's only silence, and Matt rolling his eyes as Arkarian reaches for Isabel's face and kisses her.

'Let's take this to a vote,' Matt calls out. 'Raise your hand if you agree to use the Foundation stone to save the lives of millions of innocent people.' He looks at each of us. 'Keep your hand down if you believe we should *not* use the Foundation Stone.'

If Arkarian's mountain should fall every one of us will feel the loss for some time, but especially Arkarian. I spare him a sympathetic glance. It would be the end of an era without his secret mountain chambers.

Change is difficult, but it always works out for the best, we just can't see it through the clouded emotions of loss.

Hanging on to that thought, I raise my hand to join all the others.

# Chapter Thirty-eight

## Ethan

Now that we know how to boost Neriah's powers we need to get moving and make this portal happen. The Order has already jumped. Who knows how long it will take them to do their damage and get out. With no time to waste, everyone is on edge as Matt and Arkarian sit huddled together in private communication.

Rochelle raps her fingers on the table. Matt gives her an irritated glance. They're selecting the team, the two of us who have the best chance of succeeding in this one of a kind mission. It's the first time the Guard will be jumping into the future, and by all the anxious glances at this table, everyone wants in.

But time is ticking, and King Richard's last update let us know he had to call in reinforcements, including a team of demolition experts and the kind of soldiers trained in breaching complex structures.

Finally, Arkarian and Matt turn their attention back to us.

Arkarian says, 'Lord Dartemis asked me to remind you that the Order must be stopped, that this is the mission that must break them.' He pauses, his violet eyes darkening. Under the table Rochelle squeezes my hand. 'Your orders are to use whatever means necessary.'

'Well then,' Dad says into the momentary silence, 'Who are you sending?'

Matt gets to his feet and looks at each of us in a way that makes me think he's still making up his mind. 'My instinct is to give Ethan and Rochelle a night off.'

Around the table, Jimmy, Isabel, Neriah and especially my father, vocalize how much they agree.

And yeah, I can't wait to spend time with Rochelle, to hold her close while forgetting everything going on around us. But this mission is too important to narrow the field if Matt needs my skills to succeed.

'If you don't send me, you'll be making a mistake,' Rochelle says, her lowered voice silencing even the slightest murmur. She glances at me with sorrowful eyes. *I'm sorry, baby.* Returning to Matt and Arkarian, she says, 'There'll be time for Ethan and me. If we get this right tonight, there'll be time for everybody.' She takes a shaky breath. 'I've been sitting here thinking, what reason could Jesilla have to take Keziah with them, and the only thing that makes sense is that she needs him to work magic so she and Dillon can slip past all the security without being seen.'

'He's going to wrap them in a glamour of invisibility,' Arkarian says, exchanging a troubled glance with Matt.

Matt swears under his breath.

'They'll be able to walk into any room at that function,' Dad says, 'without being noticed.'

'You have to send me,' Rochelle says, 'because I know those three better than anyone else here and I can identify them from their thoughts.'

'Matt, Arkarian, you have to pick me too,' I tell them, 'because I can create the illusion that we're invisible. I can get us into any room at that forum as assuredly as Keziah.'

No one looks happy, least of all Dad. In his attempt to protect me he comes up with half a dozen reasons that make me unsuitable for this mission. Only, they don't make enough sense to take seriously and now he's wasting precious time.

I catch his eye and say softly, 'Give it up, Dad.'

Matt leans towards me, elbows on the table, his voice low. 'I can create an invisibility screen too.'

I hold his golden stare. 'If you send Rochelle on this mission, I'm going with her.'

Rochelle squeezes my hand.

Matt sits back grumbling, 'I thought you'd say that.'

# Chapter Thirty-nine

## Jesilla

We're standing in the foyer outside the Diamond Globe Ballroom. It's the last function of the three-day forum and except for a few late-arriving guests; the three thousand attending the forum's closing ball are inside, mingling in their extravagant ball gowns and impeccable black suits. What I hadn't counted on were the attendees bringing partners, adding at least another two thousand guests and planting this virus into more varied communities than I had considered.

Dressed in a black suit so as not to stand out, Keziah could pass for any one of the male dignitaries here tonight. If someone asks why he's not inside with the rest, he need simply explain he's getting some air.

In the red-carpeted foyer, he sinks into a comfortable chair, one of two near the ballroom's entrance doors. He's close enough to maintain his magic on us when Bastian and I go inside to release the dragonflies, but not too close that someone might find his presence suspicious.

So far all is going well, with no indication the Guard is here. It's doubtful they've found a way to the future yet, but they're surprisingly resourceful, and I'd be a fool to ignore the possibility no matter how miniscule. At least for now we're on our own, and I'm close to completing the first vital step of my mother's profound plan for Earth's future. Wherever she is, she will be proud of me and I will have come part way in making up for causing her death.

Euphoria is already simmering inside, but I can't risk losing focus for even a second. There'll be time to celebrate when we return home. It's then I'll show Bastian what I really feel for him, inviting him to spend his life with me, and sharing everything.

The seven dragonflies will infect thousands tonight, and spread like the plague it is before anyone realizes what contagion they're dealing with. Scientists, in their attempts to create an antidote will search for Patient Zero. But that will be impossible to locate since there will be thousands of them scattered around the world, in a vast range of communities.

My mother created an ingenious plan. *I won't let you down, Mother. I made you a promise and I'm here doing what it takes.*

She would have made a legendary global leader with her confidence, poise and brilliant mind. She would have changed the world.

Now it will be me. And why not? Why shouldn't I be the most powerful being in the world? By the stars, who will there be to stop me? My weak uncle? A few immortal members of the Named? They will all be broken by the time I finish with them.

Keziah can tell my mind has drifted. He touches my hand. *Are you ready, my girl?*

*Kez, I'm more than ready.*

He laughs lightly. *Then we should get started. Bastian, are you ready?*

Standing beside me, Bastian has the look of someone who's preoccupied. He sees me watching him and his nostrils flare with a sharp intake of breath.

Damn, he looks good tonight. At six feet three, in a black wool *Zegna* tuxedo that enhances his stature, along with those magnetic green eyes, he's breathtaking. He notices me checking him out and raises his eyebrows. *Do I pass your inspection, sweetheart?*

I smirk at his cheek and watch as his eyes rove over my strapless black dress with lace shawl that drops all the way down to my heels, stilettos high and elegant. *You, on the other hand, are stunning this evening, Miss Quinn.*

I'm not expecting his compliment, and my mouth falls open. I swear that every man and woman in this foyer can hear my heart thumping.

*What's wrong with you two?* Keziah asks. *Jesilla, Bastian, are we doing this?*

I swallow and bring my thoughts back to where they should be. *We're ready, Kez.*

Bastian nods, glances around, and in a blink and a heartbeat Keziah makes the two of us invisible, even to each other.

*Showtime*, Bastian says, but the altered state gives me an odd sense of isolation.

When I don't answer, his voice in my head becomes more considerate. *Just stick to the plan and remember though you can't see me I'm beside you all the way.*

*Thank you, Bastian. Do you have the package?*

He pats his coat pocket twice, which I hear rather than see. And with that reassurance he finds my shoulder, runs his fingers along the lace fabric at the back of my dress. His intention is to link our hands together, except, as his fingers graze the bumps and ridges of my shawl he inadvertently catches his cuff link and freezes. I feel the heat of his gaze on my face as he says into my mind, *Damn, that was my cuff link.*

*Don't panic. I'll fix this.*

*Give me a second, Jesilla. It's down the center of your back. I'll do it.*

*Fine, but stop and find your focus first.*

He draws in a deep breath but it's as if he has butter fingers. My shawl slips completely off my shoulder. Luckily I catch it before it hits the ground. Bastian must have gone for it too, because when we come up our heads crash.

*Aw, hell. Jesilla, are you OK?*

*I will be if you don't move. Now leave this to me, Bastian, and that's an order.*

Cautiously, I track my fingers to the spot and unhook the cuff link. Unfortunately, it drops to the floor, where it automatically becomes visible, catching the eye of a security guard. She swoops down and collects it right in front of us. I hold my breath as she looks around at the few other couples in the foyer, deciding it must have been the young Prince in full Arabic dress that dropped it. She strides over, politely offers it to the Prince, who, along with his female companion, appears surprised. The Prince checks his sleeves. I don't hear the exchange with all the blood pumping between my ears, but I see the prince shake his head.

*What now?* Bastian asks. *Should we abort? Find another time, another event?*

*Forget that! We're here now. We're rolling. There's no point putting this off only to have to start all over again.*

*You're right,* Bastian says. *Besides, we don't know how long Keziah can hold this invisibility glamour.*

A frisson of something resembling fear races up my spine and a sudden urge to hurry grips me. *Come on. Let's go. What are we waiting for?*

We catch up to the Prince and his female companion standing at the ballroom entrance where U.N. security personnel check one, then the other for explosives. The flashing handheld device flickers as the guard runs it over the pair from head to foot, bringing up a red and blue digitized image of the pair with all metal and plastic highlighted.

Another guard checks the hologram. 'Clear,' he says, dismissing their image and waving them through.

*Get ready to move,* Bastian says. *I'll get us inside but you have to trust me. Can you do that, Jesilla? Can you trust me?*

Can I trust him? Is this Bastian telling me that I *can*? That I *should*? I want to trust him so much so I can ask him to be my equal in leading the Order.

Cleared to enter, the prince and his partner begin moving through the open door. Bastian lifts my hands chest high and holds them still. *Now, Jesilla. Let yourself go. Tell me you trust me. You have to tell me to believe it. Tell me, Jesilla!*

*I do, Bastian. I do trust you.*

He lifts my hands above my head and spins me around so we're facing the same direction. He pulls me backwards, molding me into his concaved chest. His right arm swings over my stomach to clutch my hip as his left crosses my chest, his fingers gripping my lower arm, fusing us together.

He twirls us one way, ducking under the woman's silk-covered elbow. He spins us around so we're back-to-back with the prince without touching him. He moves like a professional dancer, keeping us as close to each other as two layers of skin while shadowing the Arabian couple.

And then we're in the ballroom with the gold doors closing behind us.

Bastian brings us to a stop with my back against a darkened auditorium wall. He peels himself off me with gentle movements to stand by my side, his breathing even, heart steady, touching only my hand.

While I get my breath back, I study the hall. There are three types of uniformed security personnel making their presence known patrolling the ballroom, while plain-clothed security guards mingle among the guests. But Bastian and I don't attract any attention. We're still invisible. Nobody can see us.

*Kez, you're a legend.*

From the entrance foyer, he replies, *Thank you, my dear.*

Exhaling in relief, euphoria bubbles up inside me again and I smile. It doesn't matter because no one can see it. And with that in mind, I move round to face Bastian, wrapping my fingers around his arms. Hearing no objection in his thoughts, and feeling no tension in his muscles, I slide my hands along his arms, moving them up over his shoulders to the back of his neck.

Then I tug his head down and kiss him.

# Chapter Forty

## Ethan

With no time to spare, we leave Isabel, Jimmy and Dad behind, while the rest of us go down the lift and make our way through the cold dark spaces of what's left of the ancient underground city of Veridian. The upper half is mostly dry with rocks strewn across paths and walls in fragments everywhere we tread. From what I can see of the lower levels there are spasmodic pockets of water left here and there after the flood.

I keep Rochelle's hand held tightly in mine in case I wake up and this is all a dream and she's not really here. Not with me. Not... *alive*.

She stops in the middle of a narrow path, waving at Arkarian to keep going. Once we're alone she traces her knuckles down my cheek. 'I'm not a dream, baby. Look in my eyes. Hear my voice. Feel my touch. When we get back from this mission, I'll show you how alive I am. We'll go away for a few days, get a cabin on a secluded beach up north, and it will just be you and me.'

I put my arms around her and hold her close, breathing in the scent of her hair and her skin. 'I missed you so much.'

She cups my face in her hands. 'I don't know why, but something amazing happened to us. Call it what you want. A fluke. A lucky break. A twist of fate. I'm comfortable calling it a miracle. Or a gift. However it happened, for whatever reasons, we have a new shot at living this life together.'

'A second chance.'

She smiles. It's radiant. She switches to a private link, and hearing her voice inside my head while looking into her eyes is the next closest thing to standing together with our souls entwined. *Ethan, I promise to love you every day until the Earth stops spinning and the sun drops from the sky.*

I kiss her forehead and simply hold her. She says, *Are you OK?*

*I'm more than OK. I have you back.*

*We should catch up with the others then.*

*Pity, but yep, we should go.*

Matt, Neriah and Arkarian stand before a wall of boulders the size of cars tossed on top of each other haphazardly.

Studying it and shaking his head, Arkarian says, 'It will take too long to move this.'

Neriah comes to stand beside Rochelle. She asks softly, 'Are you guys all right?'

'We're good. Thanks for asking,' Rochelle says with a tender smile for me.

'What's with the wall?' I ask.

'It wasn't there the last time Matt came down, and now it's blocking our path.'

'Is there another way?'

Matt shifts his eyes sideways to me. 'Well, there is a shortcut.' He points back the way we came. 'But it's...'

'What, Matt?' I ask. 'Dangerous?'

Rochelle says, 'Make a decision, Matt. We need to hurry.'

'Follow me.' Taking Neriah's hand, Matt heads back to where a path lies buried under shattered rock and smashed machinery. We clear the path as we go along. For the most part it's not too bad and I wonder what Matt seemed so worried about.

With Rochelle's hand still in mine, we follow Matt down a set of hand-carved stairs. I recognize where we are, and let Rochelle know it won't be far now. We're almost on the city floor. Only, there's been a landslide and a cave in. Matt uses his hands to shift a few boulders aside that are too heavy for the rest of us. Rochelle and I watch in mutual amazement. It's as if he's playing with marbles. Even Neriah and Arkarian look surprised and impressed.

When Matt clears the path, we follow him around a corner where one side is a high rock wall, the other a drop so deep that when Neriah tosses a stone over the side we don't hear it reach the bottom for so long we're about to give up when there's a faint splash.

Neriah gasps. 'Moments like these make me grateful for my ability to shift into a bird.'

'Show off,' Rochelle says, and the girls grin at each other.

'I'll go first,' Matt volunteers. 'I'll make sure the ledge is strong enough to hold our weight.'

'Be careful,' Neriah says, pressing her palms together. 'Remember, you can shift too.'

He smiles at her with more tolerance than I thought I would ever see in Matt. 'I'm not going to forget that,' he says, lightly jogging around the narrow path and making it look easy. When he returns he hurries us along. 'It's strong enough. We're almost there. Neriah, you go next.'

When it's Rochelle's turn, I tell Matt I'm going with her.

But he stops me with his hand on my chest. 'It won't hold you both.'

I lose sight of her when she steps around the corner and my heart leaps into my throat.

'She's fine,' Matt says. 'Trust me.'

I glance at Arkarian behind me, and he nods.

Matt makes me wait a few more seconds before finally letting me go.

The ledge is narrow. I marvel at how smoothly the girls did it. My feet bump into each other. The ledge isn't wide enough to put them side by side. I move carefully, butterflies the size of bats flying around in my gut, but once I turn the corner and see Rochelle encouraging me with a stunning smile, I forget my awkward feet. Without those oversized black-framed glasses Rochelle's eyes are as exquisite as I remember. I will never tire of looking at her.

This close to the Foundation Stone has a strange effect on the air. As I try to figure out what it is, everyone's hair lifts. Arkarian's slips out of its band and frames his head like a Smurf. It's a pity Isabel can't see the blue halo. She would laugh her head off.

Cackling, Matt runs his fingers through it. Arkarian stands there quietly amused. 'How long?' he asks.

Matt assures us the effect will pass in a few minutes. It's just as our hair returns to normal that I hear the sound of an idling truck motor. Only, it's not a truck. We round a high silver wall and the Foundation Stone is in front of us, a gold beam of raw energy, zinging with purple and white streaks of electricity, rising from an octagon-shaped base of about a meter in diameter. It pulsates all the way up to the ceiling high above us.

Matt has the four of us wait while he checks the stone's radiation and electromagnetic levels. When he returns, satisfied they're safe enough, he brings us to within one meter of the stone. From here the pulsating beam warms our faces. The thought of stepping into it makes my mouth go dry.

*We'll be all right. Won't we?* Rochelle checks with me privately.

*Well, yeah. Matt checked it. Arkarian's not stopping us.*

She glances up at me, her lips twisting with doubt. I get it. There's colossal power in that beam and we're finally together.

*"Trust is what the Guard is all about,"* she recites from our early training sessions. *"Faith in what doesn't always make sense."*

But our doubts reduce substantially when Neriah begins to paint. Her brush strokes flow through the beam with new-found confidence. Just as Matt thought, being this close to the ancient city's energy source is fueling her power.

I glance down into Rochelle's heart-shaped face and her emerald eyes stare up at me with a pleading look. She tilts her head to the side. 'Will you kiss me, Ethan? I need you to kiss me.'

I swallow, moisten my lips, and in my thoughts I let her know, *This is the last time you ever have to ask.* I wrap my arms around her and tighten my hold.

Lifting onto her toes, she clings to me and a tremor runs through her. It breaks me up. My heart swells for her, and I kiss her thoroughly, deeply, the kind of kiss that would last into perpetuity.

My instincts are compelling me to run, take her to the coast and don't look back. We could begin our new life together where nobody knows us, and nothing can tear us apart again. I start to contemplate the idea seriously. After all, it's my instinct.

But then Matt clears his throat and says, 'It's ready, guys.'

Neriah has created a portal that is so real we can smell the scent of perfume and champagne, hear the sounds of clinking glasses and shoes treading lightly on a carpeted floor. We see crystal chandeliers, walls painted red, gold lounges and people dressed in elegant, formal long dresses and black suits.

The portal Neriah created back in Arkarian's meeting room and this one, don't compare. Here, it's like there's nothing between us, nothing to stop us, even while the golden energy swirls around it like a curtain of fire.

Neriah says, 'I'll be watching you both and keeping the portal open the entire time you're away. When you move, I will do my best to follow so that when you're ready to depart you'll only have to turn and step back into present time.' She takes a breath and her eyes darken with her deep, genuine sincerity. She kisses the air on either side of our faces. 'May the speed of the universe be in your legs and its spirit be your guide, and keep you safe.'

Arkarian steps into her place and puts one hand on my shoulder, his other on Rochelle's. 'I'm proud of you both,' he says. 'I want you to know that.'

Rochelle inhales a deep breath. Hearing this means a lot to her. It means a lot to me too.

'A final word of caution,' he says. 'You must not *die* in the future.' He takes a quick breath. I'm not used to Arkarian being so unsure of himself, or nervous. He's my mentor. I always thought of him as the guy who knows everything. 'There will be no Grey World to catch your soul. We think your body would simply disintegrate, while your spirit floats aimlessly in a void possibly for eternity, or until the realms of Earth and the Underworld catch up in time. We don't know. So you must both return through the portal.' He grins. 'Or Isabel will make my life not worth living.'

His joke cracks a smile out of us, easing the tension, slowing my racing heart but not by much. Even Matt smiles grudgingly as he comes and stands in front of us. 'The same rules for travelling in the past apply to the future,' he explains. 'Don't take anything from this time period with you, and don't bring anything back. And don't get side-tracked by the things you see. There will be differences that will catch your attention. Don't let them. Don't even look.'

'Matt,' Rochelle says, 'we need to go.'

'I know.' He runs a hand through his hair, but doesn't move out of our way.

I grip his shoulder. 'Mate, we're going to be fine. This is what we do.' He nods, but his eyes are saying something else. 'Unless there's something you're not telling us?'

'There's so much that we don't know about this time period, about the world and what you're going to be entering into.'

'We understand that, Matt,' Rochelle says. 'We'll be careful.'

His eyes flicker to me and I nod.

'We'll be watching you closely through the portal.' He points to Arkarian and Neriah behind him. 'And like Neriah said, she'll match your movements with her brush strokes. In that way we should be able to move where you move, and make a quick extraction. That's the plan. But four or five thousand strangers could throw our plans into disarray, so try not to split up because here's the thing... we can only follow one of you.'

'Stay with Rochelle.'

‘Hey, no!’ Rochelle counters. ‘No special treatment.’ She turns to me. ‘Ethan, please...’

How can I resist her eyes begging me to understand? The part that sucks most is that I do understand. I remember how hard she struggled with getting us to accept her as an equal member of our team.

Arkarian says, ‘Leave that decision to us.’

I trust Arkarian, have done so since I was four years old, why wouldn’t I trust him now? I nod. Rochelle squeezes my hand and gives me a small smile. But there’s still something else they need to tell us. It’s in Matt’s eyes, only he’s hesitating to spit it out.

It occurs to me, the one thing no one has mentioned yet. ‘So...’ I flick my thumb at the portal, ‘how far?’

He exchanges a look with Arkarian. I brace myself. He says, ‘Fifty-two years.’

‘*Whoa.*’

Rochelle stares, her mouth falling open.

‘You have to remain focused at all times on this mission,’ Matt reinforces, but he’s really trying to distract us from the thought of jumping five decades into the future. ‘Come back to us. That’s an order.’

Neriah slips under Matt’s arm, ‘I have one last thing to give you,’ she says. ‘Close your eyes.’

We do as she says. A few seconds later she tells us to open them again. But I already know, and I flick some remaining knowledge dust off the shoulders of the black formal suit I’m now dressed in, and Rochelle’s spectacular white gown.

Neriah smiles at her handiwork and we start to step into the portal when rumbling vibrations become louder and the mountain rocks with a grinding tremor. It shakes the walls and causes a collapse somewhere in the city’s northern section. Debris blasts out of open spaces, filtering down broken stairwells and rearranged tracks. We hold still while the force of the explosion ebbs and flows around us. Finally the ground settles.

It's the first sign the portal is already affecting the Foundation Stone.

'Let's go, Ethan,' Rochelle's voice is urgent, 'before a bigger tremor snuffs this portal out.'

I glance at each of them. 'Is that possible?'

Matt says, 'Not going to happen, mate.'

'Not if we can help it,' Arkarian clarifies.

Clutching Rochelle's hand we step into the portal together, into an unknown era, more than half a century from now.

# Chapter Forty-one

## Jesilla

Releasing me slowly, Bastian ensures I have my footing before he lifts his mouth off mine and asks, *What was that for?*

He sounds annoyed. It takes me aback and I don't know how to answer him. I shrug instead, forgetting he can't see me.

*Seriously, Jes, why did you kiss me... like that?*

*I don't know. I just wanted to.*

*That's it?*

*What do you want me to say?*

*Oh, I don't know, maybe that you love me too. When I bared my soul to you I thought you felt the same way.*

*Bastian, I'm still trying to trust you.*

*Right, so after all this time and all the missions we've worked together, you're still trying to trust me?* He steps around me. Cold air replaces his body and I shiver though the room is warm.

*Bastian, wait...*

*We should get back to work.* His icy thoughts in my head chill me to my core. I try to pull my hand out of his, but he grips it tighter. *Not when we're invisible to each other.*

I've stuffed up. I do love him. I do trust him. He's right. All the things we've done together for the Order, he had plenty of opportunities to break my trust, but he never did. And I have no proof the voice warning Rochelle earlier was his. Tonight, he took me by surprise, as I did him when I kissed him.

Damn the stars and all the dead immortals; is it my curse to be alone for all time?

*Look at this place*, he says.

I gather my bearings and look around, the moment gone, beyond my reach, at least for now.

The ballroom glitters with chandeliers and jewels catching the lights. But this is more than a ballroom; it's also a concert hall with a stage down the front and giant screens dominating both side walls, lit with changing images of Earth's landscapes. It would be easy to immerse myself in watching the changes fifty-two years have made, but I drag my eyes to the center dance floor where couples sway and swirl and shimmy to a band I don't recognize playing upbeat music I've never heard before.

To our left are stairs, wide enough to fit a dozen people standing side by side. They curve dramatically upwards to an overhanging gallery packed with table and chair settings for hundreds of guests, with many standing at the railing overlooking the dance floor. Behind the dance floor, tucked under the overhang, a large service area has wait staff in white one-piece uniforms rushing backwards and forwards serving alcohol and bringing out food.

*We should find a toilet*, I forge.

*Are you kidding? Why didn't you go before we jumped?*

*That's not what I mean, genius.* I tap the box of dragonflies in his inside coat pocket.

*Ahh*, he says, our nerves turning to soft laughter.

Tugging on his hand, I lead the way around the dance floor's outside edge, making sure not to bump into the crowds watching from the sides. In the busy service area we find a door with the image of a little girl and boy on the front.

The unisex toilet is deceptively huge inside with rows and rows of frosted glass cubicles. Still, with so many, it's not until we walk past the eighth row that we find one with a green light.

The frosty glass door slides open automatically, locking itself after us with a soft click. Our invisibility flickers twice and disappears.

Bastian's stare shows his concern.

'It's probably just too many walls between us for Keziah to keep the glamour working. It will activate again once we're back in the ballroom.'

'I hope you're right and it's not –'

'It's *not.*' Switching to a mind-link before someone overhears our raised voices, I reassure him, *Keziah is the strongest he's ever been. He'll be okay.*

*I agree that's he strong, but he just healed Carter and the time shift -*

*Don't say that, Bastian. Keziah can handle it.*

He stares into my eyes but I can't read what he's thinking before he blinks and pulls out the container. One by one we set the dragonflies to flight mode, testing the wings before returning them to their individual slots.

Once we release them in the ballroom they will fly for ninety seconds before they discharge their toxic load. Our scientists have done an amazing job, giving the dragonflies time to spread out across the room and Bastian and I time to clear out.

All the wings work except for the last one. Bastian tries again, but the tiny wings refuse to move and the dragonfly slips from Bastian's hand, dropping to the cement tiles.

'Damn,' he says, swooping down and collecting it.

I hold my hand out as he's about to shove it in his pocket. 'Let me try.'

'Go for it.'

I take my time with the wing mechanism and it kicks over into flight mode.

'Well, what do you know?' he says.

I return the dragonfly with my suspicions aroused, working fast to clear the doubts from my face before Bastian sees them.

So what just happened? Did Bastian tamper with one of the dragonflies?

'All it needed was a girl's touch.' He flashes me one of his crooked smiles that's so adorable it's hard not to smile back. I resist for as long as I can, but when he pushes his hands out in front of me, wiggling his fingers, and saying, 'Look at them. They're monsters,' I buckle under the pressure and roll my eyes. On close inspection, they really are big hands with long fingers. They might cause him some grief with the tiny mechanism.

It's a relief to give him the benefit of the doubt.

But if he does something else, I won't let him off so easily. There's a thin line between love and deception, and deceiving someone you purport to love is crossing that line in a way you can't come back from whether you're lovers, work mates, or friends. No matter how much it would hurt, that would be something I couldn't ignore.

I promised my mother I would do whatever it takes. I hope it doesn't come down to a choice between Bastian and the mission. It would break my heart to lose him.

As we exit the cubicle, Bastian links, *With no sign of the Guard yet we could be out of here in a few minutes.*

*I'm hoping for the same thing, and yet somehow they always find us.*

*C'mon, you love the challenge the Guard brings to our missions.*

I give him a sharp look, noticing with growing concern that we're still visible. *You reckon?*

*Admit it. Without Ethan and the others lifting the stakes, you'd feel as if something were missing. The thrill of winning is the part that gives you a sense of accomplishment.*

Who doesn't need acknowledgement for what they do? My mother hardly ever praised me. It was not her way. She thought it would make me weak. Still, I smirk at him all the same. *You're full of crap.*

His sideways glance comes with another cocky crooked grin. He knows me too well. It makes me vulnerable. I'm starting to realize Bastian is my weakness. But that's only because I let him in.

Back in the main auditorium, Bastian whispers, 'Did you see that?'

'See what?'

He shows me his hand where one moment it's visible, the next it's not. The same happens with my limbs. Fortunately the lighting here at the back of the dance floor is low and the crowds pay more attention to dancing, chatting and drinking, than us.

*Keziah's screen is failing*, Bastian says into my thoughts.

*Don't say that. Let's move closer to the doors. We can release the dragonflies from there if we have to.*

*Good idea. I'll lead us straight through the dance floor. It'll be quicker.*

He takes me in his arms, pulling me against his chest so there's not even a speck of space between us. I allow myself a moment to enjoy the sensation of being close to him. As he weaves us expertly around the dancing couples, I imagine us dancing for real with no one else in the room.

'Breathe,' Bastian whispers so close to my ear his lips cause shivers to break out over my arms. I feel the goose bumps rather than see them because we're invisible again and this time it seems to be holding.

*Jesilla, we should take Keziah home before he's too weak for the shift*, Bastian says. *I can get us out fast. Do you trust me?*

I do trust Bastian, with all my heart, but... Because I have feelings for him, I'm not sure it's the smart decision. I let him lead and he weaves us expertly towards the dance floor edge. He doesn't let go of me, and before long we're standing a footstep from the gold door waiting for someone to open it for our opportunity to leave and take Keziah home.

But...

I tug his hand and make him stop.

I can't see him but I can tell his eyes are on me. I listen to his heart. It's beating fast, but so is mine. As a couple enters, Bastian pulls me in close to his chest and twirls me around, pinning my back to the wall with his body shielding me. At first I think he's protecting me from the couple who just entered since, even though we're as close to the exit doors as we can get, we're suddenly visible again.

I'm so worried about Keziah that I'm not thinking straight, and doubts hit hard. I try reaching him. *Kez, what's happening? Can you hear me? Speak to me!*

He doesn't respond. I need to make sure he's all right. But there's something else I need to do first. Looking up into Bastian's eyes, I forge the link, *Tell me it's not true.*

His heartbeat accelerates so fast that without conscious thought I put my hand on his chest, willing it to slow down.

*Tell you what, Jesilla? What are you asking?*

*Tell me that you weren't leading me out of the ballroom before we released the dragonflies. Tell me you weren't trying to sabotage this mission.*

His racing heart skips a beat and everything becomes clear. 'Oh wow, it *was* you. You warned Rochelle. You told her to run. You've been trying to sabotage this mission from the beginning, dropping the cufflink, pretending the dragonfly didn't work. What else, Bastian? What else have you done?'

Inhaling a deep breath and closing his eyes, it's as if time comes to a grinding halt.

As he turns around he steps to the side so that we both have our backs against the wall, and with unmistakable recognition, he nods at someone. With a sinking feeling in the pit of my stomach, I shift my gaze to the person he's acknowledging. It's the couple who just walked in. Two people who don't belong here, not in this place and not in this time.

'Well, well, Ethan, Rochelle, you came.' My thoughts spin. *Why these two? Haven't they been through enough?*

The thought snakes into my head that they're the two who know me best, who have the knowledge and, at least with Rochelle, the immortal capability to kill me.

While I half expected the Guard to follow, I didn't think they could actually make it work. I was sure they didn't have the sphere that could open a portal to the future. My mother swam to the bottom of the ocean to find it on that day Atlantis fell. There was only one.

So how did they do it?

*What does it matter, Jesilla? They're here now. It's all over.*

How is Bastian in my head without my knowing? More to the point, how long has he been able to do that? *Holy immortals.* I yank my hand out of his and step away from him. 'You played me. From when? The beginning?'

His beautiful long lashes quiver as they come down, and when he opens his eyes they glisten and burn. 'It's over, Jesilla.'

*So it's true. Even though I knew, just for a second I hoped...* I take another step sideways as Ethan, in an immaculate black suit, and Rochelle, in a white, figure-hugging evening dress, move closer. 'Stop right there.' I hold out my hand. 'It's not over as long as I have these.' With my other hand slipping under my shawl, I pull out the container with the seven pulsating dragonflies.

Bastian smacks his top inside coat pocket and curses.

I laugh bitterly. 'Did you think I was going to leave them with you now they're activated? But that would mean I trust you. I was a fool to fall for your charming games and cocky smiles, but as you see, I don't trust you with the things that matter.'

Keeping my eyes on Bastian and feeling increasingly sick to my stomach, I ask the other two, 'What did you do to Keziah?'

Rochelle holds a mobile phone out that I recognize as Keziah's. The image on the front has me choking back a sob. I can't help it and couldn't have stopped it. It's the shock of seeing him old again, his skin with a greyish tint, his hair peppered black and white and falling out in clumps, his face wrinkled, shoulders stooped.

'You knew this could happen,' Rochelle accuses.

Tears hit my eyes and I shake my head to dispel them. Turning to Bastian, I plead with him, 'We have to help him. Please. Bastian, do something. Help me to help Keziah.'

Bastian has that tormented look he sometimes gets. He's not going to help me.

It's Ethan who says, 'Hand over the dragonflies and we'll take you straight to Keziah. You can do your rejuvenating thing and return him to his youth in time to save his life.'

'And if I don't, are you just going to let him die?'

'We'll take him home and make him comfortable,' Rochelle says. 'But none of us can do for him what you can.'

'We need your decision, Jesilla,' Ethan says. The way his eyes appear slightly glazed, he's using one of his powers, which is probably what's keeping security away. 'I don't know how long the magician has left, but I wouldn't take too long if I were you.'

I clutch the box to my chest, tracking my finger along the sides until I find the release mechanism that will set the dragonflies free. *I can do this. I can at least do this one thing for my mother. After all, it was my fault she died.*

Blocking everyone from hearing my thoughts, including Bastian now that I know how clever he really is, I reach out to the *only* one I can trust, *Keziah, can you hear me? I'm so sorry. I never meant for this to happen. Kez... I'm in a difficult position and I need you to find the strength to do one more thing for me. I need you to make me invisible and to hold the glamour for as long as you can.*

*Jesilla, you must know that I care for you as if you were my own child. Many times I wished that you were. But if I do what you ask I will probably not have the strength to make it home.*

*Kez, you believed in me when no one else did. Marcus and Marduke thought me a spoilt little girl incapable of making hard calls. Even my mother didn't believe in me, you know that. I'm sorry you have to carry the burden of the hardest call of all, but I can't fail at what my mother left for me to do. Do you understand, Keziah? Will you help me?*

Tears pour down my face. I can't swat them, so I leave them and let the three Guards frowning at me wonder what I'm thinking.

*If you order me to do this,* Keziah says, his whispery thoughts weak and pitiful, *I will do my best.*

I take a deep breath. *Keziah, I order you to make me invisible. I order you to do it now, and to hold it until your last breath.*

# Chapter Forty-two

## Ethan

She's up to something. It's in her eyes. Not the tears, they could be for any reason. She could be playing us to gain our sympathy, especially Dillon's. His eyes are glassy, his stare intense. There's something between those two that's as thick as blood.

It's how her eyes shift from one of us to another without connecting long enough to get an idea what's really going on inside her head. And as hard as I try to read her thoughts, she has a block up as strong as a titanium skullcap. Maybe it's because I'm new at Truthseeing, so I check with Rochelle, *Can you get into her head?*

*Not yet, but she's talking to someone.*

*Dillon, can you?*

He gives a slight negative shake without taking his eyes off her.

*Do you know what she's doing?*

*I don't know, mate, we had no idea you were coming. She didn't plan for this. She's going off script. But Rochelle's right, she's talking to someone.*

*Like who?*

*It has to be Keziah,* he says. *He's not letting me in, and no one else from the complex came with us.*

*Rochelle, you saw Keziah out there, could he be a threat in his condition?*

*He's so weak he's only just hanging on.*

Dillon huffs. *That man will do anything for Jesilla. He'll dig deep for her.*

In a heartbeat, Jesilla vanishes. I know she hasn't gone anywhere when she tosses the dragonfly container into the air. It becomes visible as soon as it leaves her hand. The dragonflies escape, circling above us as if gathering their bearings before scattering in different directions.

Suddenly Rochelle screams, *Ethan!* And again from further away, *She's taking me to the roof!*

Still invisible, Jesilla drags Rochelle to the stairs going up to a mezzanine level. They run into people, but Jesilla ploughs through them, tripping them over and sending a few screaming over the balustrade.

Soldiers come from everywhere packing serious artillery. The glamour I created to keep us incognito fails as alarms sound throughout the auditorium, and chaos spreads.

I take off after Rochelle, but Dillon grabs me from behind and swings me around like a ragdoll. Face to face, his hands are steel clamps on my shoulders. With tortured eyes he says, 'Rochelle will have to take care of herself for ninety seconds because that's all the time we have to collect the seven dragonflies before they release their toxic load.'

'What? *What?*' I could smash Dillon for giving me a reason to let Rochelle slip through my fingers. 'Do you know what you're asking of me?'

His voice is hollow. 'Yeah, mate, I do.'

'So how do we fix this? And for God's sake, hurry!'

Two military guards chase after Rochelle. They can't see Jesilla, who remains invisible. When she reaches the mezzanine level Rochelle's visible body lifts off the ground in what resembles a flying leap for the exit. It causes confusion and people around her stare. The guards check each other in disbelief and shake their heads.

Soldiers move through the crowd, no longer concerned with keeping their cover. They check IDs, search for weapons, for explosives, for anything suspicious. Paramedics take care of the injured while plain-clothes security guards gather up presidents, queens and other dignitaries, rushing them into safe rooms with announcements made in numerous languages pleading for calm.

'We know she's taking her to the roof,' Dillon says. 'Let's get these toxic bugs back in their box and go after her. At least the guards haven't connected us to this chaos yet.'

Collecting the container, Dillon stands still, eyes narrowed, searching the dragonflies, studying their movements. He points to the walls on either side of the main auditorium where screens flash bright colors of the Earth's changing landscapes.

*It's the light*, he forges.

I see what he means. These mechanical bugs may not be real but whoever designed them instilled so many characteristics of the true dragonfly breed they're behaving as real ones would. It's ironic that their perfection is also their flaw.

We separate, shifting from one dragonfly to the next, meeting back at the foot of the stairs where we secure each one in their tiny compartments.

'How many did you catch?' Dillon asks as I slot my last one in and quickly count them.

'Three. You?'

His eyes meet mine. 'Same, but that makes only six.' His shoulders sag as his eyes continue to sweep the room with renewed urgency.

'Wait. You found three, right?'

'That's what I said.'

I count the dragonflies again; this time noticing one of them has a pinched wing. It's a slight fault I can hardly make out. 'I count seven, Dillon. Check for yourself, but I'm not waiting any longer. I'm going to find Rochelle.'

He shifts a second later, meeting me at the roof's exit door. Though unlocked, something is keeping it from opening. With green eyes blazing, Dillon rams it with his shoulder. The two military cops who charged after Rochelle are lying face down and motionless, pools of blood spreading beneath them.

He drops to the ground, checking for a pulse at their necks, then lifts his eyes to mine and shakes his head.

'How did she do it?' I ask.

He rolls them over, carefully, one at a time, but my focus shifts to my surroundings. It's dark on the roof. A cold night has fallen. Clouds obscure the stars, while the city lights are too dim to make much difference. Isabel's gift would come in handy. My vision adjusts to the darkness and I jump on a metal box. I don't see Rochelle or Jesilla anywhere yet, but I blink hard at what I *am* seeing. Chunks of ice appear like white tips across the bay. What happened to this city? Where did the sky scrapers go?

Behind me Dillon says something about the dead bodies, how blood is seeping from their facial orifices, but I tune out. I'm struggling to drag my eyes away from how close the deep-looking ocean is to the building we're standing on, and the chunks of ice slapping at its sides. The famous landmarks are gone. I tilt my head to the side to better examine a structure sticking out of the water at an odd angle. 'Oh my God, is that...?'

But Dillon isn't listening. He's bent over one of the cops, opening the man's jacket. '*Whoa!* Ethan, where's your head, mate? Come look at this man's chest. This is what we're up against.'

A massive amount of blood soaks the man's shirt. Dillon rips the shirt open. I swallow down bile not to gag. The man's chest has caved-in. Fragments of his ribs are all over his torso like matchstick splinters. Muscles lie flattened against the back of his ribcage while the man's heart has imploded and collapsed in on itself.

'What weapon does the Order have that can do this?'

Dillon covers the man's chest as best he can and looks up. 'That's no weapon, bro. That was Jesilla's fist.'

*Ethan, northeast corner. Hurry, I need you.*

Dillon falls in beside me as I take off, leaping over air conditioning units, exhaust vents, a section of domed glass roofing and anything else separating me from Rochelle.

'Where are we going?' Dillon asks.

'Northeast corner.'

I stop suddenly. Even though my instinct is telling me I'm already too late, I refuse to believe it. There's a weak fluttering at the back of my neck like a wispy moth flapping its papery wings against my skin. *We're close.* I raise my hand to let Dillon know that from here in we tread carefully. *Whatever Jesilla says, we have to stay calm.*

*Got it.*

Then I see Rochelle. *Holy freaking hell.*

Dillon swears under his breath. *Not going to be easy, dude.*

*What isn't?*

*Staying calm.*

He speaks first, his voice pleading, 'Jesilla, what are you doing?'

'Don't you speak to me, you vile traitor.'

'Please don't do this. Don't go down a path you're not going to be able to come back from.'

'Shut your mouth.' He takes a tentative step closer, but she yells, 'Stay back. Stay back or I'll jump right now.'

In bare feet, and with creepy, red glowing eyes, Jesilla is balancing on a round pipe circling the building's outside edge. There are no supports, only a drop of at least a hundred meters into the murky depths of a dark Pacific Ocean swirling with ice. I couldn't care less if Jesilla was balancing on this pipe alone and threatening to off herself, but she has my girl with her, locked in a tight, awkward grip, holding her back against her own chest by an arm I now know is stronger than steel.

Rochelle's white dress is drenched in blood. I follow the trail to a neck wound that Jesilla is holding with two fingers.

*God*, what has she done?

'My work here is finished,' Jesilla says, looking at me. 'I'm ready to go home. All that's left is to exact revenge that's long overdue. Then my mother can finally rest.' She glares at me with her eerie eyes. 'You ruined my mother's life by killing the man she trusted and cared for.'

'You mean Marduke?'

'Don't ask me why, but she loved him, even after you turned the man into a despicable, disgusting beast.'

'The Grey World changed his appearance.'

'After you stuck a knife in him while in the past.'

'A *curse* killed Marduke after he tried to kill me. Rochelle was an innocent bystander.'

Rochelle moans and squirms, which causes Jesilla to tighten her hold. 'Move and you die quicker. Understand?'

Rochelle's nod is slight but satisfies Jesilla, who returns her attention to me. 'Marduke never meant to kill *you*.'

'What?'

'Marduke had your arrows and your bow.'

*God, she's right.* The bow and arrow set Matt had only just given me from the Treasury of Weapons. It had special powers to hit where you meant, not necessarily where you aimed.

I glance at Dillon. 'Marduke wanted to kill Rochelle? Not me?'

'Duh!' Jesilla mocks. 'Marduke knew Lorian had applied the curse. He knew he would die, but die avenged knowing you would suffer as he did when your father sliced half his face off, losing the love of the woman he adored.'

*Aneliese.*

With half-opened eyes, Rochelle tries to forge a mind-link. She needs to tell me something, but she's weak with blood loss and I can't hear her. Jesilla notices. She makes her hands glow red and shoves them into Rochelle's chest.

Rochelle screams.

'*Stop. Please stop*,' I plead. 'Don't hurt her anymore.'

'Don't hurt her anymore?' she mocks. 'Your *soul*-mate will be dead before she hits the water. There's nothing you can do to save her now. I've pierced her carotid artery. The only thing stopping her from bleeding out is the pressure from my fingertips. When we drop into the harbor, I'll swim away and she will die before you rescue her. You see, Rochelle's body won't heal itself because she's my sister and we're both immortals. The puncture to her artery is a lethal injury.'

*My God, no!*

'And I made sure she's lost plenty of blood already so that she'll die quickly once I let go. If you try to stop me I'll lift my fingers and she dies here. Now. So it's either on the roof or in the water.'

I draw in a deep breath to keep my mind from racing and being useless. 'Jesilla, if Rochelle dies tonight, I promise that I will hunt you down, even if it takes all of my life. I will kill you slowly, and you will die an excruciating death screaming for mercy.'

*Dude,* Dillon links, *I thought you were going to keep calm.*

*Plan B.*

'You're forgetting that immortals can't be killed by human hands,' Jesilla says.

'News flash – I can, and I will kill you.'

She frowns. 'My uncle made you an immortal? Is that how he saved your life?' She waits for me to confirm it. I nod. 'Well, he can't do that for everyone who contracts smallpox.'

'You won't be around to see what he does.'

'You think you have all the answers, don't you?'

'No, Jesilla, I would never claim to know everything, but if you release Rochelle we can at least talk this out.'

'Oh, Ethan,' she mocks, 'do you think you'll recover from losing Rochelle twice?'

Her question sucks the air out of my lungs and for a few seconds I can't breathe. A shuddering tremor works it's way through me. I look into her eyes but she's staring at Dillon in an unguarded moment that sees tears fall down her cheeks. She flicks her head to dispel them and catches my eye. She raises her eyebrows, waiting for my answer, and I tell her the truth, 'No, Jesilla, I would not recover.'

'It wasn't supposed to end like this.'

'It doesn't have to end at all.'

'You don't understand. I don't have a choice anymore.'

Dillon rolls his head and groans. 'C'mon on, Jes, you don't want to hurt Rochelle. You protected her from Carter.'

She glances over her shoulder at the icy dark water lapping at the building's foundations, and then locks her gaze to Dillon's. 'I really did love you,' she says in a whispered breath that sounds too much like good bye.

'Don't jump,' I shout. *Dillon, you know this girl. Tell me how to stop her. What can I do? What do I say?*

'Do you seriously think Mr Double-cross can help you? He's the one person you can *never* trust. You should remember that.' The malice Jesilla has for Dillon darkens her red eyes to an even more eerie color. 'And now that I'm finished -'

'But you're not finished,' Dillon says, his calm façade slipping. With his fists clenched, he says, 'Not if you call this being finished.' He pulls the box of dragonflies out from his trouser pocket and holds it up so that even in this strange, altered city light, she can still see the seven fluttering bugs inside.

Her eyes widen. 'Y-you caught them?'

Dillon smiles, but there's no joy in it. 'Ethan caught three. I caught three.'

'That still leaves one.' Hope sparks in her eyes, for a moment slowing their wild frightened look. 'That's enough to do damage when those infected people return to their homes on different continents. It will just take longer to achieve the desired outcome.'

'I don't think so. You see, that last one had a faulty wing and didn't leave the box when you threw them out. It was stuck in the container the whole time.'

Her shoulders drop. Her face crumbles. 'Then I have truly failed her, in life and in death. And now I have nothing.'

'There's always something to live for,' I tell her. 'There's your sister.'

'Yeah, right, Ethan. Rochelle would never forgive me after what I've done.'

'You don't know that. Give her a chance to find out.'

She yells, 'There's no point! There's nothing left for me. I killed the most loyal person in my life. I felt his spirit leave his body when he finally gave out. Keziah was the only one who was always honest with me.' She shifts her burning gaze to Dillon. 'While the boy I loved only pretended to love me while he served my enemy's cause.' She inhales deeply and a tremor runs through her body. 'The only thing left for me is to avenge my mother, take away the one person her enemy loves most.'

*Ethan,* Rochelle forges a weak whispery link, *whatever happens next; however this ends, remember I love you forever, and I will find you, baby. I promise.*

*Rochelle, no!*

Dillon hisses into my head, *Be ready, bro.* His eyes are telling me to trust whatever Rochelle's planning. But I *love* her. I don't want her to sacrifice her life again. It wouldn't be fair and I couldn't live with that.

But I believe in her, so I prepare myself for anything, giving Dillon the slightest nod.

Jesilla notices. Her eyes shift between us. She thinks we're planning to take her down and sneers, 'Not a chance.' She releases Rochelle's neck, allowing Rochelle's blood to sputter out in weak beats.

*No!*

But Rochelle is waiting for this moment. She feels Jesilla's hold loosen and spins around so now the sisters are staring at each other. Jesilla's body suddenly jerks, her demonic-looking eyes opening into a wide surprised stare. Rochelle squirms and works an arm free. She reaches for me. But Jesilla finds an inner strength and propels them both off the building.

Dillon is fast. But I have more to lose. I have *everything* to lose, and I reach them first. Catching the pair around their hips, I stop them falling, but I'm on a bad lean and losing my balance fast. Inching my hands higher I try to improve my hold. I dig my fingers where I can, clawing my way to their waists, only, Rochelle's blood everywhere is a hindrance and my hands start slipping.

'Dillon, I can't hold them any longer.'

'I'm here.' He secures a foothold near the edge and reaches for us, but even his long arms aren't enough. We're tottering on the outside of the building, standing on a circular pipe. 'I can't reach you. Dammit!'

Putting everything I have into holding the girls, I dig deep inside, so deep that my arms and legs grow hot, my eyes burn, and my body trembles as if with fever. But suddenly I'm feeling power surging into my limbs and muscles, legs and hands. Understanding that it's now or never, I tighten my arms around the girls, bend my knees, arch my back and toss the girls back onto the roof.

Dillon catches them, easing them to the ground. He sees me hanging on to the circular pipe, but I'm pulling myself up and scrambling to Rochelle before he finishes pulling Jesilla away.

I search for Rochelle's wound, only there's so much blood on her skin, her neck, her hair, her dress, my hands are as slippery as soap. I keep going, closing my eyes and relying on my senses. I finally find the tear in her skin, follow it through to the artery and push two fingers down so she doesn't lose another drop of her precious blood.

I open my eyes and to my surprise Rochelle is looking up at me. She smiles. It's feeble and my heart breaks to see her tears as she passes out.

Her pulse beneath my fingers assures me she's still alive. I pray and plead and beg that it's not too late.

Dillon is on the ground gently rocking Jesilla in his arms, only she's not moving and her eyes are wide and staring up at the night sky.

'What happened?'

He lifts his arm to show me her blood-soaked chest and an open wound to her heart.

'Did you...?'

'Not me,' he says, and laying Jesilla's body tenderly on the concrete floor he lowers his hand over her eyes, closing them for the last time. 'I wouldn't be able to stop her heart. Only another immortal could do that.'

We both look at Rochelle, unconscious, her hands clenched tight.

Dillon unfolds the fingers of her right hand. But there's nothing there. He opens her left hand. A miniature silver sword about ten centimeters long clatters to the ground. 'It's Jesilla's letter opener,' he says. 'The one she nicked from King John's desk on one of our missions.' He looks at me. 'This is what she used to stab Rochelle. I didn't think she would really do it, you know. Hurt Rochelle.'

We give each other a long look and watch it unfold in our minds as first Jesilla stabs Rochelle, dropping the letter opener, Rochelle scurrying to collect it while mortally injured, and waiting for her chance, she hides it in her palm.

Jesilla's body shudders, and before our eyes she breaks apart, morphing into microscopic pinpricks of energy, hundreds of them, changing from silver to white to gold to silver again.

Ensuring I keep firm pressure on Rochelle's wound, I watch with awed fascination as the masses of particles rise up, gaining momentum on their way to the stars.

I lower my gaze to the icy city I don't recognize anymore, and call out to Neriah to bring us home.

# Chapter Forty-three

## Ethan

Isabel is waiting for us. 'Over here,' she calls out. 'Listen to my voice.'

'There she is.' Dillon points to a square of gold light off the ground at about waist height. I have to twist to see it as nothing will move my hand off Rochelle's artery until Isabel says I can.

'I'll carry her,' Dillon says, 'while you maintain pressure.'

'Good idea.'

'Ready?'

'Yep.'

'On my count of three.'

'Go, Dillon.'

'One. Two...'

The portal is no bigger than the size of a window, not even a meter wide. Neriah paints the edges furiously to no effect. Rumbling noise is the only warning before dust and small rocks fly through it. We have to lean back to avoid them and angle Rochelle's body not to cop a hit.

'What's going on?' Dillon asks.

I recall the tremor when Rochelle and I were stepping into the portal. 'Neriah, how bad is it now?'

She moves into view and shakes her head. 'The mountain's coming down.'

'*What*?' Dillon stares at me. 'What's she talking about?'

'Now is not the time,' Isabel says. 'Better to let Arkarian explain later.'

Neriah wipes her forehead with the back of her wrist and sighs. 'I'm so sorry, but that's all there is. You're going to have to squeeze through. And you'd better hurry.' Neriah's anxious voice does nothing to calm the sense of desperation my instinct keeps shoveling at me. She makes hurrying motions with her hand. 'Come on, guys.'

'The portal's too small,' I explain. 'Somehow you have to enlarge it.'

'I'm sorry, Ethan, but keeping the portal open has drained the Foundation Stone. It has no energy left to boost my powers. This is why the mountain is coming down around us.'

'So this is it?' I motion to the square-shaped window between us.

Neriah's face collapses. Her eyes say she has nothing left.

'The portal's closing?' Dillon tries to understand. 'But Rochelle is injured. They have to make the portal bigger so we can carry her through it without your hand coming off her neck.'

I glance at Dillon and say quietly, 'We won't fit and I'm not letting Rochelle go. But if you lay her down, you could make it. Go home, Dillon. You deserve it.'

'Don't talk rubbish, buddy. I'm not leaving you here without help. What are you going to do? Call Emergency with Keziah's antique phone?'

'Someone will come up here eventually. Those two soldiers will be missed.'

'Rochelle has a lethal wound made by an immortal. Without immediate healing it will kill her.'

'I *know* that,' I ground out, adding softly, 'And she's too weak to self...' My words fade away as I look at Rochelle's pale face, all color drained and yet still the most beautiful creature I've ever seen. This is the girl who carries my heart in her hand, and my soul in her heart. I can't live without her. There's no way in Heaven, Earth or Hell I'll walk away from her now.

'Ethan, listen to me,' Dillon says. 'I'm on your side, bro, but you have to face facts to make the best moves.'

'And what would that be? The best move?'

He shrugs. 'I have no idea, mate. What does your gut say?'

I shake my head and he doesn't ask again.

'What's going on?' Isabel calls through the portal. 'Why aren't you all here yet? And why is Neriah sobbing? What did you say to her?'

Another tremor hits the ancient city and Isabel drops to the ground with dust and debris falling around her. The rumbling intensifies and a cracked wall behind her gives way.

'Isabel, run!' Neriah shouts.

A deep echoing rumble and ground tremors rock the mountain. Isabel comes back to the portal, her hair stuck to her face, skin covered in dirt. 'Ethan, Dillon, pass Rochelle to us, and then you two quickly follow.'

Dillon's eyes lower to Rochelle, still unconscious after her effort with the letter opener, and he shakes his head. He's right, if Rochelle were going to self-heal it would have kicked in by now. She has a fatal wound made by her immortal sister. When she runs out of blood and her heart stops, she will die, and while her body will morph into star-like molecules, we have no idea what would happen to her soul.

Isabel catches on. 'Oh, God, what's wrong with her?'

'She has a punctured carotid artery,' Dillon explains, looking down at her in his arms. 'Jesilla drained most of her blood. She lost more when Jesilla tried to throw her over the side of a building. It's a miracle she has any blood left to keep her heart beating, but this is Rochelle. And she's hanging on...' He jerks his head at me. 'For him. No doubt.'

Isabel shifts her eyes to mine with a mountain of sorrow in tears ready to fall. 'I'm so sorry,' she says softly. And in the same sorrowful voice she relays the situation to Neriah, whose mouth opens in a soundless gasp.

Arkarian's voice carries from a distance, 'Girls, what's taking so long? We can't hold this track open much longer.'

Rochelle stirs and calls my name. Opening her eyes she looks up and sees Dillon holding her. 'You're not...'

He grins. 'No, I'm not the great and wondrous Ethan Roberts.'

I roll my eyes. 'I'm here, baby. I'm right here.'

She grabs my shirt in her fist. 'You and Dillon have to save yourselves. Don't stay behind because of me. *Please...*'

I squeeze her hand and look into her eyes. 'Save your breath. No matter what you say, I'm not leaving you.'

'Me neither, kid,' Dillon says, winking at her.

Isabel is at the portal again, only this time she's climbing through it and muttering under her breath, 'Sorry, my love. If I don't make it back, I hope you can forgive me and I'll see you in fifty-two years.'

'*Damn it*, Isabel, what are you doing?' I ask.

Neriah tries to grab her, but Isabel has one leg and her upper body already on the roof with us. She hops a little to pull her other leg through the portal and shrug Neriah off.

'Lay her down flat,' Isabel orders.

Never before have I been so relieved, so terrified and overwhelmed with pride at the same time.

She sees everything I'm feeling in my eyes, and says, 'I haven't saved her yet.'

Meanwhile Neriah's hissing at us. 'Hurry, Isabel. I promised Arkarian I wouldn't let you jump.'

Isabel rolls her eyes. 'It's scary how well he knows me.'

'Can you heal her?' Dillon asks, sitting beside Rochelle now while my hand, saturated in her blood, still maintains pressure on her punctured artery.

Isabel doesn't reply but closes her eyes to assess Rochelle's injury. Her hands begin to glow with her healing power as she works on Rochelle for a few minutes in silence. I hear sirens rushing through the streets below, but Isabel pays no attention to her surroundings, to anything but healing Rochelle. When she opens her eyes she's looking straight at me. 'Remove your hand now, Ethan.'

'Are you sure?'

'I've repaired the artery, but I need to build Rochelle's blood volume so she can walk out of here with us. Her own body will do the rest.'

Rochelle tries to sit up. 'Not yet.' Gently, Isabel pushes her back down.

It's a nervous wait. Neriah doesn't stop calling for updates. 'Seriously, Isabel, can't you finish healing Rochelle in *this* time? At least *one* of you has to come through this portal now. I'm serious. It's about to close and I won't be able to open it again.'

Color returns into Rochelle's skin and Isabel and I help her to her feet. She sways but turns to Isabel and hugs her, whispering her thanks, then turns to me and wraps herself around me.

Neriah sees us through what's left of the portal and screams at the top of her lungs 'Thank God and all the immortals that ever walked the Earth! Now, I want the biggest, tallest, largest butt to come through first.'

'That would be you,' I tell Dillon, patting his back.

As he stands before the portal, I meet his gaze. 'Just in case, you know, I don't see you again for a while... thanks for sticking around and, well, for everything you did for Rochelle.'

He curves one half of his mouth into a smile. 'My pleasure.' Glancing at Rochelle, still clinging to my chest, her legs wrapped around my waist, he catches her eye and winks.

When he's through the portal, Neriah yells, 'Isabel, you're next.'

She stubbornly refuses. 'No. Ethan's the next biggest.'

Rochelle extracts herself and stands beside me. 'You have to go.' I'm shaking my head already, but she says, 'The sooner you return home, the sooner Isabel and I can follow you.'

As much as I want to argue, I can't with that logic. I kiss her mouth briefly but with enough depth to suck out her soul. Turning to the portal I try to ignore the fact that it's shrinking before my eyes, the edges burning with raw and powerful energy. Knowing that the two most precious people in my life have to squeeze through after me, I don't stop to think how

I'm going to approach this. I inhale a deep breath, lift my hands over my head and like an arrow shot from its bow, I aim for the bullseye.

My shoulders graze the sides, burning them, but I push on, making my body spin. My hips slither through and I land on a rock base. Rolling to soften the fall, I scramble back to the portal, dismissing the chaos around me of walls exploding, the ground vibrating and cracking open. I look through the portal that's far too small for anyone to get through and I glance at Neriah. 'Can you widen it?'

But the tears in her eyes are saying no. *Ethan, at the rate this portal is shrinking, only one of them will make it through before it closes.*

*And you're positive?*

She nods.

*How positive?*

*A hundred percent.*

*God, no.*

I turn to Rochelle and Isabel, standing on the other side deciding who's going next. 'Stop everything,' I tell them. 'You have to come through together.'

'What?' Isabel asks. 'How are we supposed to do that?'

But Rochelle is looking into my eyes. *It's going to disappear, isn't it?*

*Yep.*

'Isabel, you heard Ethan, we're doing this together.'

'OK, but how?'

'I don't know, but let's think like a pair of contortionists trying to be one entity. We can do this.'

Nodding, Isabel bends forward from the waist, turning sideways to face Rochelle as she does the same. Though they face each other, their heads are at opposite ends of their torsos. They wind their arms around each other, keeping their body lines as straight and as close as they can while standing on their feet.'

'Hurry up!' Neriah calls.

Lifting one foot at a time towards the portal, I grasp Rochelle's ankles and pull her towards me while Neriah calls out directions. Rochelle's legs and thighs follow, along with the top of Isabel's head. Only, that's where they get stuck. The scent of Isabel's hair and Rochelle's blood-soaked dress burning make me sick to my stomach.

'Keep pulling,' Rochelle cries out, switching to a mind-link, *You mustn't stop or Isabel will disengage to ensure I come home. She's already trying to release me. I don't know how long I can hold on to her.*

I have no intention of losing either of these girls today and I yell out in my thoughts to Arkarian that Isabel is in trouble.

He materializes beside me, covered in dirt. 'Where is she?' But he figures the situation out in a glance, his eyes widening at the small size of the portal. He doesn't say a word. He wraps his arms around Rochelle's hips and nods at me.

We pull together.

It's not enough and we keep trying, straining to find more power to draw into our hands. The smell of burning flesh warns us that we don't have much longer before we'll have to let them go. We can't risk the portal closing on them. What if it burnt them through?

Neriah groans, cursing and swearing at the brush still in her hand. Her efforts at stopping the portal from shrinking further go nowhere. She turns haunted eyes on me and in the instant we connect I hear her thoughts. I know what she's about to do.

'*No, don't!*'

But she still does, tossing the brush in a high arc. It hits what's left of a bridge on a higher level and tumbles down a gaping split in the ancient city's floor.

'What now, princess?' I can't help the sarcasm. She's only just learned how to use the thing.

Licking her lips, she takes a deep breath and closes her eyes. Her hands go quiet by her sides. Arkarian nudges me. I turn and see the portal's circumference grow a few centimeters. It's just enough. And we pull the girls out.

Arkarian goes to Isabel, who is clearly the most affected by the closing portal. He carries her to a quieter area and we follow, worried. But she's back on her feet in no time. 'I healed myself.' She looks at Rochelle. 'Are you OK?'

'Yeah, I'm good,' Rochelle answers.

'Come on then,' Arkarian says. 'We need to move.'

Dad and Jimmy are working hard at keeping a path clear of small rocks dropping over them like hail. When Dad sees us coming, his face turns more radiant than the sun. He wraps his arms around both Rochelle and me, and squeezes hard.

'Dad, let go. Dad!'

'I was so worried. I thought I lost you both.'

Arkarian taps Dad's shoulder. 'There'll be time to catch up when we're out of here, Shaun.'

'Of course,' Dad says, and at Arkarian's instructions we climb a rock wall entwined with mangled machinery jutting out at odd angles we find useful as foot holds. Up on the next level we collect Dillon and keep moving. With so many collapsed walls, the ancient city resembles an empty cavern. When there's not enough supports left to hold up the outside walls, this mountain will collapse. But somehow we find enough steps and walls and broken paths to keep rising.

Another tremor moves through the empty city, followed by a shockwave that knocks us off our feet. The ground beneath us opens up with cracks quickly turning into fissures. One splits the ground like a fork. I wrap my arms around Rochelle's waist and hold her tight. Whatever happens, at least we'll be together.

When the shockwave passes, Arkarian, Isabel and Dillon are out of sight. Dad and Jimmy take charge, calling their names, scrambling to the fissure's edge on their hands and knees, looking down into the fissure through a heavy screen of dust.

'Are either of you injured?' Dad comes over to check us out.

'I'm fine, Dad.'

'I'm OK too,' Rochelle says. 'Who's missing? Can we help?'

He doesn't answer, our attention taken by Jimmy waving us over to the edge of a steep drop.

Isabel and Arkarian are attempting to scale a sheer rock wall inside the fissure. Dad hurries over to help while Rochelle and I follow, finding Dillon on the way, shoving rocks off his legs.

Luckily, he too is uninjured.

With the rope tied around his waist, Jimmy abseils down the sheer wall to where Isabel and Arkarian are hanging on by their fingertips. On his way a few rocks come free and tumble down, making faint splashes. My eyes meet Rochelle's troubled ones. I gently stroke her tangled hair, leaning in to kiss the top of her head. She looks so worried, and after all she's been through, I try to allay her fears, 'Jimmy won't let anything happen to Isabel.'

'He's sworn to protect her,' she says.

'Yep, and remember, Arkarian has his wings. He's just not using them until Isabel is safe, but if she falls, he'll catch her.'

She rests her head on my shoulder, completely worn out. Even though it's not much, this time out will give her a small rest. Help her body to finish healing. Not that she's complaining.

Not a single word.

Thinking ahead to when Rochelle and I can spend some quiet time together gives me a second wind. I point over my shoulder. 'Hop on.'

'Oh, Ethan, no, please save your energy. I'm OK.' But her eyes are saying she's tempted.

'One time offer.' I tilt my head to the side and smile.

She grins and climbs aboard.

When we start moving again, Arkarian says, 'Matt is at the entrance to my chambers. With half the mountain above him, his power is the only force stopping it from collapsing on us and on himself.'

When we finally reach Matt, he's standing in the center of an arch of solid rock, Arkarian's chambers nothing more than empty caves around us. The sunlight filtering in behind Matt gives him a golden aura while his hands holding the ceiling up throb with his power. They release blue light that extends over the underside of the ceiling like flames licking at a rock wall.

But the struggle to keep holding the mountain up shows in the deep creases of his forehead, around his glowing eyes, and in the tense muscles of his neck and shoulders. It's a reminder that immortals are also human.

Neriah stops us some steps away with tears running down her face. 'Tell us what to do.'

He motions with his head to the exit. 'Just go. Run. Tell everyone to stay back from the entrance.'

'Hang on,' Dillon says, 'you look like you could use a hand.' Drawing on his own powers, one of which is clearly strength, he lifts his hands to the arch and joins his power with Matt's.

We jog out between them in single file. And when Jimmy, the last in line, clears the exit, Dillon and Matt share a glance and run out simultaneously. When they reach us we all turn and watch.

It's our last look at what used to be the invisible door to Arkarian's secret chambers. Ironically, it's Arkarian who hears the first rumble, but once it builds, roaring up through the ancient city known to us as Veridian, no one in Angel Falls misses the terrifying sound. It gathers velocity rapidly as the now hollow ancient city collapses, section after section, sinking into the Earth, until, with one final thrust the mountain crashes down and the aftershock blows its dust all over the valley of Angel Falls.

# Chapter Forty-four

## Ethan

The devastating earthquake that struck Angel Falls destroyed many of our landmarks, roads, buildings, and houses near the epicenter. The focus and hardest hit area was Arkarian's mountain. Landslides and a collapsed bridge saw Angel Falls isolated for six days. Declared a disaster zone, the Australian Army delivered food and medical supplies by helicopter drop. On the seventh day the army drove in with bulldozers and trucks stacked with building supplies, beginning the massive clean-up and repairs.

Angel Falls High School was on their priority list.

Once school reopened, we decided to leave Rochelle's name as Crystal Quinn. It would have been too complicated to explain her resurrection.

It's December, and Angel Falls is in full summer bloom, the best it can be considering Arkarian's mountain is now nothing more than a hill with a stream running through it. Grass has grown over it, ducks have moved in, and families come with their children to picnic. If only they could know what lies beneath, the battles fought, the history the Guardians of Time saved, and recently the future they protected.

There isn't a sign, a plaque, or anything. But we who know will never forget.

With high school over for the year and on our summer break, Arkarian is hosting a dinner party at his place in 'The Valley', as we've come to know it recently. He wants us to celebrate how well the year turned out after all, or at least the last six months since the day of the battle.

Everyone is here. By everyone I mean all of us who are Named – Arkarian, Dad, Jimmy, Neriah, Matt, Isabel, Rochelle, myself and Dillon, who has officially left his secret double life behind. Even the name 'Bastian' that Lathenia gave him when she first brought him to live with her is now history.

The royal Tribunal Members are here too, continuing to let us further into their world. As always dressed in their finest – ball gowns, golden slippers, floor-length cloaks, silken hair in fancy styles, including Lady Arabella, who has forgiven Matt now that her daughter is back where she belongs, safe and well and never far from my arms. It's lucky that Arabella approves of me. I'm just glad she finally admitted to being Rochelle's birth mother. Though some of us, including Rochelle, had already figured it out. Arabella's over-reactions to the events of the last six months, especially how distraught she was when she thought she'd lost Rochelle, just one of the clues.

The immortal that Arabella believed was her true love would not identify as a male, instead choosing to lead the Guard with the impartiality of having no specific gender. Lord Lorian's rejection hurt her deeply.

And when the royal, King Andrej Konstantin, laid on his charm, she fell for him without knowing he was already in a relationship with their enemy, the Goddess Lathenia. When Arabella learned she was pregnant Lathenia had already stripped King Andrej of his title, powers and memories, announcing to all that the king had died tragically in battle. In her grief, Arabella felt it best to give her child away and pretend it didn't happen. But fate didn't want her to forget, and she couldn't anyway. When her baby was due, Arabella had found an infertile couple she felt drawn to. The man's name was Gerard Thallimar and he resembled Andrej strongly. Years passed before she confronted Lathenia, who admitted the man she'd given her baby to was in fact the child's father, King Andrej.

There are others here tonight too; a dozen of Arkarian's friends from the Valley, including a girl named Rebecca. Tall, with long hair the color of the ocean, and light eyes that contrast her golden skin, Rebecca hasn't taken her eyes off Dillon since arriving. Like now, she watches him move around the open living area where he pours himself a drink from Arkarian's alcohol cabinet, then walks across the room to the glass fireplace in the wall and sits beside me. She tries to get his attention, smiling when their eyes meet, but it's as if she's a ghost he can see straight through.

Losing Jesilla hit Dillon hard. Staring, mesmerized by the yellow flames of Arkarian's living room fire, he says, 'I loved her, you know. She loved me too. I saw it in her eyes. I read it in her thoughts. I was sure that without Lathenia she'd see things differently. But once I found out she blamed herself for her mother's death, I knew she'd find it too hard to break away on her own.'

That Dillon is doing so well is a testament to his strength, and I don't mean his physical powers but inside where it counts more but hurts most. He lived with the enemy. And yet he had no problem processing the way in which Lord Dartemis closed down their headquarters.

Dartemis himself replied to King Richard's call for backup that night, bringing with him a fleet of helicopters packed with two-hundred of the Guard's specially-trained fighting forces. Those soldiers swept down into Lathenia's property, infiltrating her complex, evacuating all personnel, confiscating machinery, computers, closing research labs and taking over guardianship of the Atlantean Sphere. By sunrise the following morning it was all over. The Guard had blocked the tunnels and sealed the lower six levels so no one could use the complex again.

And with the help of Rochelle's special gift of testing loyalties, in those following weeks Dartemis was able to rehabilitate and rehouse those of the Order deemed not a threat. Dillon's father Peter Sinclair was one of those. Dillon had vouched for him, and father and son now live in a house together near the town center. Only Dillon has decided to take off for the summer. Where he's going is something even he doesn't know yet.

Other members of the Order Dartemis had rehoused included the security guards Zander and Pearl. Dillon heard they chose an overseas posting to a small village in Spain, content to lead a quiet life raising their family.

It was not such a favorable outcome for Marcus Carter, though. Rochelle found this ex-teacher's traitorous soul so stained with hatred that Dartemis couldn't risk housing the ex-teacher amongst the general populace. Instead, Dartemis stripped Carter of his powers and most of his memories, sentencing him to an uncharted island in the cold Arctic Circle under twenty-four hour guard for the rest of his days.

With more than thirty guests, when dinner is ready to serve, Arkarian sends us out to his deck overlooking the blue lake at one end, a forest at the other. A long table made from fallen timbers with chairs for every guest stretches across the center. But the sun is setting; painting the sky shades of yellow, pink and crimson, while at the other end the sun's rays set the trees ablaze in rust and gold.

It's simply too spectacular to ignore, especially when, without notice or fanfare, Lord Dartemis appears in a whirl of shimmering gold light, stepping out of the forest with his assistant Janah, and his two pet lions walking beside him.

Matt and Neriah head down the deck stairs to greet him. Neriah calls over her two dogs. On seeing the lions, they change into their snow leopard form and join the lions in a game. While Neriah plays with the unusual pack, Matt shares a few words with his father. The three walk up onto the deck a few minutes later while Janah takes the pack into the village to greet others who live here.

On the deck Dartemis comes directly to Rochelle and me, standing at the timber rail. 'Have I commended you both yet for your bravery on your last mission?'

We both try to hide our grins. He has to know this is at least the third time in as many months.

'Thank you, my lord,' Rochelle says with a sweet smile. 'I believe you may have mentioned it previously.'

'Always worth repeating when well deserved.' He unfurls his hand towards the table. 'Come, I want you both to sit beside me.' We follow him to the deck's forest end where Dartemis sits at the table's head. 'Everyone, find your places and let us begin this celebratory banquet.'

Everyone moves. Matt and Neriah sit opposite Rochelle and me, while Arkarian and Isabel sit next to them. Dad sits next to Rochelle with Jimmy next along. The mouth-watering aromas from Arkarian's kitchen have been teasing us for hours already, making our stomachs growl non-stop, but none as vigorously as Dillon's gut. It's so loud I'd hear his gurgles sitting at the opposite end of a crowded school bus. He gets a sheepish grin on his face when his stomach growls again.

It takes a while for our laughter to settle, but less for Dillon. He finally notices the girl from the Valley sitting opposite him. He frowns at her, like he hasn't seen her following him around all afternoon. She stretches her hand across the table. 'Hi, I'm Rebecca. I don't believe we've met.'

He glances at the girl's hand too long without taking it. Instead, he nods and in a soft voice says, 'Dillon. Dillon Sinclair.'

The royals fill the seats towards the center, making soft chatter with the invited guests from the Valley.

When everyone is seated, Arkarian claps his hands loudly twice and a steady stream of uniformed waiters brings the first course of food out on silver trays. Other waiters serve chilled spring water and plenty of wine from the Valley's own vineyard, served in crystal glasses.

Over a banquet of seven courses we talk and laugh and share our future plans. Those of us who are either eternal or immortal, which is most of us now, talk of building our houses here in this sublime hidden valley, completely off the grid. We'll have a safe place to be together, somewhere to return to when we need to rejuvenate or simply want some peace and quiet. We talk about travelling together when we have all finished high school, as long as there are no more threats to history, or to the future. A flicker of something resembling doubt appears in the exchange Isabel has with her brother at the mention of our future plans, but it's gone quickly and I leave it alone for now.

'We would return in a heartbeat, Father,' Matt assures Lord Dartemis. The rest of us who are *Named* nods in agreement.

As waiters return to collect the last of our empty plates, Lord Dartemis thanks Arkarian for preparing this magnificent meal and for his generous hospitality. He then pushes back from the table and rises to his full height of well over seven feet, where he leads us all in a minute's silence to honor the Guard members who lost their lives in battles this year and others from past centuries. He remains still even after the minute ends, indicating he has something important yet to say. Everyone waits with a quiet sense of anticipation. He then looks at Dillon and says, 'Rise, young man.'

Unsure if Dartemis means him, Dillon looks to his right, then left.

Isabel slaps his knee under the table. 'Get up, Dill, he means you.'

'Are you sure?' he whispers, slowly getting to his feet.

Coming straight to the point, Dartemis says, 'For your service to the Guard, for your bravery under duress, for your suffering and for what you were willing to sacrifice, I offer you the gift of agelessness. And because you have already turned eighteen, this will mean that from today you will not grow older.'

While the entire table goes nuts cheering, hooting and stamping their feet, Dillon's mouth falls open and a frown forms. Dillon's eyes flicker to Rebecca as the word *eternal* passes from one end of the table to the other. 'My lord, I... I don't know what to say.'

'Well that's a first,' Matt says to erupting laughter. 'Are you sure you're not sick? Isabel, feel his head. Heal him quickly so we can head inside for a nightcap.'

'Ha ha,' Dillon says. 'But I'm serious. Do I accept and watch those around me grow old and sick and eventually die?'

When no one answers because only Dillon can make this decision, his eyes flicker over Rebecca again, but so briefly I doubt anyone noticed. 'My lord, thank you for your incredible offer but... I don't want to wake up one day and find I'm all alone.'

Arkarian lowers his palm on Dillon's shoulder. 'If you were to become an eternal you could live here in the Valley with others who don't age and you would never be alone. Your fellow Named will begin constructing their houses here next year. You would be welcome to build one of your own.'

'Are you kidding me? I could have my own house here?' He looks around, his eyes taking in the forest and the lake, lit now by green, blue and red lights dancing in the sky, more commonly known as the Aurora Australis or the Southern Lights.

Dillon inhales a deep breath, his eyes returning to roam over Matt, Isabel, Rochelle, myself, Arkarian and Neriah, and he smiles at Lord Dartemis. 'I accept, my lord. I totally accept your offer.'

'Since we have an abundance of witnesses here,' Lord Dartemis says, 'and before you change your mind,' he adds to some soft laughter, 'let us do this now.'

The immortal's announcement brings out loud cheering. 'Come, young man, stand before me.'

Sitting silently, friends from the Valley alongside the royal Tribunal Members and the Named, watch as Lord Dartemis lowers his hand to Dillon's head where it immediately begins to glow. 'Dillon Sinclair, I anoint you with the special gift of agelessness for bravery and selfless service to the Guard.'

The golden glow flows over Dillon's body all the way from his head to his toes. When it's over, everyone goes up to congratulate him. Dillon glances at the still-glowing skin of his arms.

Arkarian ruffles his hair. 'Don't worry; it will fade during the next twenty-four hours.'

'Nah, I wasn't worried,' he says.

After a while, Lord Dartemis leaves. It starts a flurry of departures with first Arkarian's friends from the Valley, and then the royals, also known as eternals.

Then it's just us sitting at the table - Matt, Neriah, Arkarian, Isabel, Dad, Jimmy, Dillon, Rochelle and me. The nine who are Named, without Marcus but with Dillon. We're all a little tipsy and nicely mellowed out, so when Arkarian offers coffee with a serious tone in his voice, we quickly agree and watch as Isabel pops up to help, looking very comfortable at Arkarian's place.

She brings out two dozen cupcakes she made herself. They're so good I end up eating more than I should after that huge banquet. Looking at the empty platter, I think we all have.

Not long after Arkarian suggests we head inside where we sit in deeply-cushioned lounge chairs and soak in the warmth of a freshly-stoked fire. Matt hunts around in Arkarian's alcohol cabinet and hauls out a bottle of brandy, pouring us each a small glass.

A sense of peace unlike anything I've felt before sinks into me, a state of tranquility I'm happy to see reflected in the faces of my friends.

Meanwhile, curled up and sleeping on my lap, Rochelle stirs and reaches up to caress the side of my face with her warm gentle fingers. 'I love you forever,' she whispers.

Everyone hears her drowsy declaration and exchange smiles mixed with soft laughter.

Arkarian taps my shoulder and says, 'I think I speak for everyone when I say, we're very happy for you both.'

Getting to his feet, Arkarian glances at Isabel. She nods, losing all her light-heartedness in a heartbeat. Arkarian draws a deep breath as if gathering his strength to deliver bad news. A knot forms in my gut. Unconsciously, I tighten my arms around Rochelle. She stirs, her eyes opening, and seeing Arkarian on his feet, she straightens up, tugging down her black skirt. 'What's going on?'

I shrug, the knot in my gut growing at an astronomical pace.

'Some months ago Isabel experienced a vision,' Arkarian says. Everyone's eyes dart to her, but she's looking down at her tapping feet and Arkarian continues, 'Lord Dartemis and some of the royals have been working with Isabel trying to decipher what it means. Isabel's vision predicts a significant event in the Earth's future, but specific details are sketchy and without solid dates or identifying places, no one outside of the Guard will take it seriously.'

Everyone has questions, but Arkarian holds his hands up. 'Isabel's vision speaks of a new threat to the world.'

The room goes silent. My heart races. Rochelle's too. We glance at each other. She leans into me.

'This threat is more dangerous than anything the Goddess and her daughter caused this world.'

He sits and in the quiet moment he takes Isabel's hand and squeezes it. She looks across at me. There's fear in her eyes, and this is so unlike Isabel that I brace for the worst. She says, 'I saw a city that at first seemed to be in the throes of a celebration. I thought it was New Year's Eve. A million people or more filled the streets, lined the shores and hung out of balconies waving a flag I didn't recognize but seemed to be a combination of the flags of different nations.'

Dillon leans forward, sliding his elbows to his knees. Dad flicks me a look wondering how much I know. I shake my head.

'I was in a hotel suite high off the ground,' she says, 'and Arkarian was there. You all were, but only Arkarian spoke to me. He told me it was a protest that every city around the world was holding at the same time. Then I heard drone-like sounds coming from the sky but they weren't drones and they made my skin crawl.'

'What made the drone sounds?' Dillon asks.

'The vision didn't show me, only that these things came in massive numbers and attacked the city.'

'What city?' Rochelle asks. 'We have to warn them.'

Isabel gives a big shrug. 'A major Australian city but I can't confirm which one.'

Neriah asks, 'Can you describe it?'

'I wasn't allowed on the balcony, so no, I can't.'

'You mentioned people lined the shores?'

'There were yachts. I saw the tops of their sails. I smelled the ocean, tasted salt in the air. I heard the chatter from the roads below. And... when they attacked it was full scale. People screamed as buildings crashed to the ground.'

She hauls in a deep breath. Clearly, the vision still affects her and I know my partner well enough to tell that she's leaving something out.

Matt smiles at his sister. 'Thanks, Isabel, I'll take it from here.' He turns to us. 'We know there is going to be an attack from the sky on a major Australian city situated near a coastline. It's not a lot to go on but over time Isabel might receive more visions, hopefully enough to identify which city it is.'

Jimmy asks, 'So what do we do? How do we prepare?'

'Firstly, we need more information before we alert authorities.'

Closing my eyes, my heart sinks as I recall those few glimpses I caught during my last mission to the future. As I'd stood on that roof, the things I saw that confused me then make sense now. I clear my throat. Everyone turns to me as they realize I have something to add. 'I saw this city with my own eyes when Rochelle and I travelled to the future.'

Arkarian says, 'Tell us everything you know, Ethan.'

'The city is Sydney.'

Gasps of horror and questions hurtle at me. Arkarian quietens everyone. 'Go on, Ethan.'

'I can't tell you what year Isabel's vision will play out, but I know for certain that within the next fifty-two years, Sydney will be completely destroyed with every famous landmark ending up on the ocean floor. I saw the wings of the Sydney Opera House submerged at odd angles. The top two meters of one of the Harbour Bridge's brick pylons was the only structure remaining above water from the old city.'

I pause at the sight of their stunned faces. 'But there's hope,' I tell them. 'Within this fifty-two year time frame, not only will something destroy Sydney, but the people will rebuild it. And the new city looks like something out of a science fiction movie. The architecture, the construction materials... they haven't been invented yet.'

Dillon shakes his head. 'I'm sorry, guys, I was on that roof too and I didn't even look.'

'You're forgiven,' I say, 'since you were busy saving Rochelle's life.'

Dad catches my eye. 'Ethan, we'll put you together with an innovative architectural design team and have this city you recall drawn up digitally. Then we'll consult with the best engineers and construction experts the world has; see if we can narrow down how many years it will take to build a city such as the one you describe.'

Arkarian says, 'When we figure out what year this attack will occur we will alert the authorities.'

'What this means,' Matt says, 'is that by the time this event occurs, we will need to be ready. The safest place to do that is here in this valley. This is where you will come to prepare. Plans are already under way for the construction of a new training facility. And the royals have begun their search across the globe for others like us, others that, for one reason or another, were born with powers beyond what society considers normal. They don't know it yet, but they will be brought here and trained by you in the skills you're each best at.'

I glance at the others as they stare at Matt. It's a lot to absorb. And yet there's one thing I saw that I haven't told them yet. I recall the image of Sydney Harbour swirling with chunks of ice, something unheard of, even in the thick of winter.

Matt asks, 'Is there something else, Ethan?'

We've had a lot to absorb tonight; so maybe this news could wait a few days. 'No. Nothing.'

'All right, then, everyone, listen,' Matt says. 'Whatever the future holds, we will get through it. Together we make a strong force. And as I see it,' he slides back into the lounge chair, linking Neriah's hand with his, 'we recently eliminated a great threat to Earth. We saved the lives of millions of people; some that are not even born yet. But the immortals assigned these powers to us and lengthened our lives to continue to protect the Earth and humanity. We don't get to retire at eighteen.'

Dillon tops up everyone's brandy while Matt nods at him and then stands, tugging Neriah up alongside him. 'Let us hope that our future activities will always bring peace to the Earth, keep our loved ones safe and our friendships close together. Let that be our code from this day forward.'

He lifts his brandy. 'To our future. And to our renewed roles to protect Earth.'

Arkarian raises his glass and touches it to Matt's. 'To our renewed roles. And to humanity.'

The rest of us do the same before settling back into our lounge chairs. After a few minutes Dad and Jimmy say their goodbyes and head home to their loved ones, Dad to my mother and Jimmy to Isabel and Matt's mother.

As soon as they use their wings and shift, I take Rochelle's glass and set it down on the low table beside mine. Dillon proposes another toast, and when Rochelle hears it she pinches the inside of my wrist. Once she has my attention, her voice in my head says, *Want to go upstairs? They'll probably be making toasts until dawn.*

Making sure to block every other Truthseer from overhearing, and hoping it works since I'm still mastering this skill even after months of trying, I reply, *Your room? Or mine?*

Giving me a cheeky sideways glance from under thick dark lashes that always sends my pulse fluttering, she says, *But your room* is *mine, and I can think of a whole lot more interesting things we could be doing than making toasts until dawn.*

*Until dawn, you say?*

*Definitely, and then some.*

*Baby, I love the way you think.*

With a round of quick good nights, I sweep Rochelle into my arms and carry her upstairs. I only just restrain myself from kicking in the first bedroom door I find until Rochelle says, 'Uh, this is Arkarian and Isabel's.'

'Right. Thanks for that.'

She's still giggling when I stand outside the next one. She nods, and her teasing smile has me tripping over the rug on the inside, but I manage to find my balance and shut the door with my heel.

We roll onto the bed, Rochelle's laughter ringing like Christmas bells in my ears. 'I love you forever,' she says.

'I love you forever more.'

She tickles me in the ribs. 'Not a chance. I died for you.'

I never thought I'd laugh at *that*, but here we are. 'You got me there.'

We don't talk much after that.

Sometime after dawn, Rochelle falls asleep with her head on my chest, my fingers stroking her hair and the warm skin of her back. Who knows what lies ahead for us? What adventures are yet to come? What new threat will we face from the skies?

I don't know the answers. But I'm an integral part of a powerful group of people whose purpose is to protect and take care of our world.

And with Rochelle by my side - in an uncertain future there's nothing more I need.

Nothing more I want.

# Acknowledgements

This book was two years in the making and twelve years in the planning. I originally intended to write the fourth book immediately after the release of The Key in 2004, but that was the same year I was diagnosed with Myelofibrosis (bone marrow cancer) and I had to take time off to have a stem-cell, bone marrow transplant. My bone marrow had turned to scar tissue and I had very little time left to live, but I thank God every day that my sister was a perfect match and her stem cells have gone on to thrive.

I am so grateful to be a writer. I enjoy every moment I work on bringing new stories to life, and I'm especially pleased to finally give you the conclusion I'd always wanted for The Guardians of Time Series.

Now I want to thank some very special people in my life, my three children who have grown up and become exceptionally helpful with my writing. Thank you, Amanda and Danielle for your editing and re-editing expertise, and Chris for your male perspective, and your understanding of the fantasy genre. Thanks also, Danielle, for the cover that I love. The support and encouragement the three of you gave me helped keep me positive throughout the making of this project, all the way to the release date.

Special thanks go to my sister Therese for her overwhelming belief in me and in this book. I love you dearly, sister. I always will. And also special thanks to my sister-in-law Mary for her editing and proofreading skills. Nothing was too hard for you to tackle, and your dedication to detail was inspiring. Thank you both so very much.

I want to also mention that I have two outstanding and extremely handsome brothers who mean the world to me.

And most importantly, I thank *YOU*, my readers. Your love of this series has been the biggest inspiration of all. Thank you for loving my characters, and for giving me a reason to bring them to life again.

## Contact Details

E: marianne.curley7@gmail.com
W: https://mariannecurley7.com/
Fb: https://www.facebook.com/MarianneCurleyAuthor/
Fb: https://www.facebook.com/marianne.curley.75

## Books by Marianne Curley

Old Magic

The Guardians of Time Series
The Named
The Dark
The Key
The Shadow

The Avena Series
Hidden
Broken
Fearless

Made in the USA
San Bernardino, CA
19 March 2018